Dedicated to Mr. Keith Owens
who never got to read my first book.
Rest in peace.

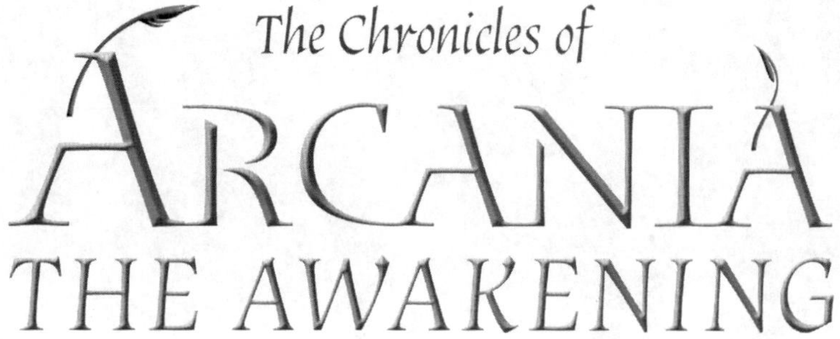

ANNIE SCHNELLENBERGER

www.mascotbooks.com

The Chronicles of Arcania: The Awakening

For more information, please contact:
Mascot Books
620 Herndon Parkway, Suite 320
Herndon, VA 20170
info@mascotbooks.com

Library of Congress Control Number: 2018912404

CPSIA Code: PREFRE0319A
ISBN-13: 978-1-64307-192-3

Printed in Canada

PROLOGUE

The front door of a small English house swung wide open, and a tall pale man stepped forward. A young man and his wife were sitting at the breakfast table by the bay window with their young daughter. "Give me what I came for," he growled, taking several steps towards them. The man whose house he had invaded stepped forward. "It's not yours to take," he said. "Please leave my house and family in peace."

"I can't do that, and you know the reason why."

"Leave," the man shouted.

"I won't until I get what I want. Give it to me or I shall hurt your family."

The woman cowered in the corner, clutching her small child. "Please," she said. "Just leave. We don't have what you are looking for, we never did."

"Liars!" the man slammed his fists down on an end table, breaking it into pieces.

"She speaks the truth," the other man said. "We don't have what he is after."

"Don't try to play games with me. You know what you have stolen. Now we want it back. It's ours."

"I'm telling you I don't have it. I never did."

"Please, can't you just leave us," the woman cried clutching her child even closer to her. "We speak the truth. I'm sure he will understand."

"He understands nothing when people steal from him. Give it

to me, give it to me now!" He punched the light blue wall, making the plaster crack under the strength of his fist.

"Okay, okay, I'll get it for you," the young said. He opened a drawer and started to pull something out. Within a flash he threw something on the tall man that made him scream. A faint smoke came off of him, and burns started to form on his pale skin.

The young man then turned to his wife. "More will be coming," he said. "Take her upstairs."

His wife looked at him. She nodded then made her way around the other man, holding tightly to her daughter. Two more guys came through the door just as she was going upstairs. She put her daughter in the hallway closet. "Stay here," her mother said. "And keep quiet. I've got to go help Daddy." She kissed her daughter then headed downstairs.

The little girl couldn't see, but she could hear the commotion from downstairs. Little did she know that her parents were being slaughtered. She closed her eyes as a piercing scream filled the air...

Twelve Years Later...

CHAPTER ONE
SEEING RED

I stared through the crowd as cars honked, people passed, and music filled the air, trying to understand what I was seeing. If I was really seeing it. The sun was shining, and it was a beautiful summer day to be out and about in New Orleans, Louisiana. I concentrated on what I was doing. Staring through the crowd, concentrating on a group of people across the street.

I could barely hear my friend Maggie talking to me.

"Addie," she said.

I didn't answer.

"Hello, Addie, are you with me?"

For all it was worth, I would not break my concentration.

"For the love of God, ADDIE!!!"

I shook my head, breaking my concentration to look at her. "What?" I asked, looking for a good reason for pulling me out of my haze.

"Oh, she talks," Maggie said.

"Funny," I said.

"Are you okay? You looked really focused on something."

"Yeah, I'm fine."

"Are you sure? 'Cause I mean you were like really into it."

"I'm fine." Other than my head killing me, I was super.

"Do you want to tell me what you were looking at?" she asked.

I shook my head. I didn't want to tell her what I was staring at because I didn't know what it was. Actually, it really wasn't anything. Just a haze. A faint haze that I see everything when I get into one of these trances.

My friends know I get into these staring moods. I don't know why I do it, I just do. Sometimes I think it's my mind trying to get me to see things that nobody else is supposed to see. Crazy, right? I never see anything, I just see the faint haze then get a headache after that.

But that changed today.

I shielded my eyes from the sun as we stood by the Sanger Theater on Canal Street waiting for Max and Ava, who told us they would be here. I searched through the many tourist crowds, trying to catch sight of Max's tan skin or Ava's red hair, but I didn't see any of that. "What time did we say that we'd meet up?" Maggie asked.

"Four-thirty," I said. "Long enough for us to eat then head on our way."

"What time is it now?"

I checked my watch. "Four-fifteen," I said. "Where are they?"

"Maybe they decided to go to Café Du Monde."

"I doubt it. They wouldn't go by themselves, not without us. Plus, we are not allowed after all."

"Please, since when has that ever stopped them?"

"True."

I tapped my foot on the concrete walkway, scanning the crowd every few minutes for them. Suddenly something caught my eye. A tall guy with fair...no...pale skin, white blond hair, and dressed in Victorian-style clothing was standing in the middle of a crowd of people. He was just standing there, coolly, calmly staring at me. I returned his gaze. He didn't move. I didn't know whether to keep staring or run. His eyes bore into me. As if they were looking directly into my soul.

Maggie must have taken notice of this because she said, "Um, what are you staring at again?" I didn't answer. It wasn't the guy staring at me that was freaking me out, it was the color of his eyes. They were a deep, deep red. Like the color of blood. Those eyes. I've seen them before. They struck an unknown fear in me that I suddenly had no control over. I wanted to move. I wanted to hide. I didn't know why, but something was telling me that we needed to get out of there. It wasn't safe.

"We need to move," I said.

"What?" Maggie asked.

"I said we need to move like now."

"Why?"

"Trust me, you'll thank me later." I grabbed her arm, but when I tried to move she stopped me.

"Wait, Addie," she said. I looked at her then glanced back up at the guy who...wasn't there anymore. I couldn't believe it. He was there. Yes he was there. He had to be. Either that or I had seriously lost it.

"Addie," Maggie said.

"Nothing," I said, knowing what her question was going to be. "It was nothing."

"Are you sure? 'Cause I have never seen you that freaked before." I looked back to where the guy was standing, and there was still nothing. A shakiness came over me as fear left my body, now powered by something else: curiosity.

I turned back to Maggie, who was really looking spooked. "Sorry," I said smiling.

"Do you want to tell me what the hell is going on with you?" she asked.

I sucked in a breath. "I thought I saw a dangerous guy across the street," I said. "Crazy, right?"

"Not really, since New Orleans has been under the influence of a lot of crime lately. What did he look like?"

"He was tall, dressed in an old T-shirt, and jeans. He was scary looking, so I just kind of jumped to conclusions that he was dangerous." I was not going to tell her what I really saw, then she'd think I was crazy.

"It's okay, it happens. At least you didn't go over there and confront him, now that would have been embarrassing."

"Yeah, no joke." I ran my fingers through my long blonde ponytail, looking around again for the pale-looking guy. I didn't see him anywhere.

"You still looked pretty freaked," Maggie said. "Maybe you've been in the sun too long. It's hotter than normal today as well. You might need to drink some water to rehydrate."

"No, it's not that," I reassured her.

"Well either way it's probably best if we get out of the sun anyway. Too much can be a bad thing."

"Or Ava and Max better hurry their asses up so we can start this stupid football game that he agreed on."

"Don't blame him. Blame Tyrone and Andrew for getting him into it."

"And the rest of the football team as well."

"Is he going to try out again this year for it?"

"I don't know. I think he wants to play baseball next year too."

"And track. Man he wants to do it all, doesn't he?"

"He sure does."

"How's living with your aunt and uncle still going?" I closed my eyes for a bit and tried to imagine that she did not ask that question.

A long time ago my parents were killed in a home invasion. I was only three at the time. After that, I was sent to live with my aunt and uncle, who were so reluctant to take me in. More my aunt than my uncle. Things had been great till last year, when my aunt decided that I couldn't do anything that I wanted to do.

I couldn't go out on Saturday nights, I had to come straight home after school, I had to dress properly and not like a slut, which yeah, I understand that one and it's not like I would, but still. She wanted to control my whole life. Right down to the people I hung out with. She approved of Maggie, Max, and Ava because we had been friends for so long, but anytime someone new wanted to hang out with us she had to approve first.

It's so frustrating that I had to run everything I wanted to do by her so she could approve before I do it. I was surprised she let me go out today. "As long as you don't go near the French Quarter I'll let you go," she said before I left. "Just be back before it gets to dark." It just felt like it wasn't my life anymore.

I open my eyes. "Why did you have to ask that?" I said.

"I just wanted to know how things were going," Maggie said. "I haven't heard you complain, so I guessed that things were okay."

"They are for now. Until she locks me in my room for another night like I'm freaking Cinderella or something."

"At least you don't have to clean up after her, or have evil stepsisters who hate you, or have to take care of an evil cat who hates you just as much as the stepsisters."

I looked at Maggie and laughed. "You always know how to cheer me up."

"That's what I'm here for," she said, smiling.

About twenty feet from us I saw a tall, slightly muscular guy with tan skin and curly hair. "Max," I called. "Over here." He smiled then jogged his way over to us, carrying his so-called "lucky football."

"What up, chicks?" he said, stopping by us still smiling.

Maggie rolled her eyes. "Please, do you have to call us that?" she asked. "You know it's an insult to women."

"Hey, there are lots of girls who love it when I call them a chick," Max argued.

He got Maggie there. Pretty much all of the girls at our school thought that he was a god. I could argue with them there. He was attractive, but he was like a brother to me.

Maggie gave him an annoyed look. "Regardless, I think that calling a girl 'chick' is a sexist comment, and it shouldn't even be said anymore. You're basically comparing us to farm animals."

"Yeah, cute little farm animals." A cute smile appeared across his face that made most girls melt. Maggie looked even more annoyed with him. "Fine," he said, knowing he'd lost. "I'll stop calling you two chicks."

"Great."

"But now other girls..."

"Aww, here we go."

I laughed. They had such a cute love-hate relationship, which didn't make me sick at all. "Where's Ava?" Maggie asked.

"She's going to meet us there," Max said. "Which by the way we better get going, some of the boys want to warm up before we start. I am one of them."

"Then let's go." We started to make our way to our school. To get into shape for next year, Max and some of the football guys decided that they wanted to play a little touch football to see who's the best. Some kind of man thing, I guess.

"Why do we have to go all the way to the school for this?" Maggie asked as we passed more tourists.

"Because all of the parks close at a certain hour, or are not open, or charge to get in," Max said, using his quick reflexes to move out of the way for a girl on a cell phone. She turned back to look at him, a smile appearing on her face.

"You know we'll be breaking like three school rules, right?" Maggie asked. "Not to mention one of the teachers or coaches could be there. I know it's Sunday, but they have been known to go there, including Miss Miller."

"Would you relax, Mags," Max said, turning to look at her. "It's all going to be okay. That's why we are leaving so late. Jackson told me that the only person there right now is the janitor, and he will be leaving soon. Perfect for our little game."

Maggie rolled her eyes.

Aromas from the nearby restaurants and markets filled the air, including something else that almost made me want to puke. It smelled sweet but not like chocolate or ice cream. It smelled more like...well, I didn't know what it could possibly smell like; it was just to overwhelming. I started to cough.

"Addie, you okay?" Maggie asked.

"Yeah..." I said in between coughs. "Do you guys smell that?"

"Smell what?" Maggie asked.

"That scent. It smells like fermenting fruit mixed with cough syrup."

Maggie and Max sniffed the air. "I don't smell anything like that," Maggie said.

"All I can smell is whatever's cooking at Palace Café," Max said.

I looked around to see what it could possibly be. If it's someone's perfume then it's very lingering. Also they must not have had a nose if they were wearing something that smelly. "Never mind," I said. "Forget about it, it must be someone's perfume."

"Already forgotten," Max said. "Come on, let's go."

"We've still got an hour to kill," Maggie said, looking at her watch.

As we walked I wiped my forehead. The summer heat was starting to take a toll on me. I should have worn shorts instead of capris. Maggie didn't look like she was hot in her boho sundress. Her dark brown bob was pushed back with a hair band so you could see her purple crystal earrings.

Still the sun was beating down on us. I kind of wanted to go get under one of the palm trees, but that would mean going out in the middle of traffic, and no one wants to be in Canal Street traffic. We crossed over to Magazine Street then made our way to our school's district. Next to a high-class restaurant stood two tall boys both with short dark hair. "Van, Vince," Max called. Both of the boys stopped to look.

"Hey," Van said, walking up to us. "'Bout time you got here, bro." He and Max did that whole fist pounding thing guys do.

"Well, well, well," Vince said, coming to stand by his twin brother. "Don't you look good today, Addie."

"What are you talking about?" I asked.

Vince looked me up and down, staring at me. I was starting to feel uncomfortable. I'd known Van and Vince since we were in middle school, and they meant no harm, but regardless I didn't like people staring at me. Vince should've known that. "He's talking about what you are wearing," Van said.

"Yeah, um, I've never seen you in a halter top before," Vince said, rubbing the back of his neck with his hand.

I glanced down at my teal halter top. "Oh," I said, feeling my cheeks turning red.

"You look good," Vince said. "Like really good. Hot even."

"You're just making this more uncomfortable for her, aren't

you, Vince?" Maggie said.

"I can't help it if I think she looks good. It's a compliment."

"And thanks for the compliment, but can we go now? I thought we needed to be there soon?"

"Yes, we do. Jackson texted me, he said there is no one there now," Van said, looking at us. "The janitor left."

"Awesome," Max said. "Let's go." We started heading down Magazine Street. Like on Canal it was full of people shopping, dining, and drinking. Even on a lazy Sunday afternoon people were still out and about.

"Oh, I hope you guys don't mind, but we ordered some food from a place not too far from here," Van said as we passed a small bar and grill. I could smell the spicy scent of fresh seafood and jambalaya as we passed. "All we need to do is go pick it up."

"Great, I'm starved," Max said.

"You guys didn't have to do that," Maggie said.

"Well, we figured that you guys would be hungry," Vince said.

"So we decided to order some food," Van said.

My stomach growled at the mention of food. "Good," I said. "I'm starving." We arrived at a new little restaurant called Crawl and Brawl and picked up the food. Van and Vince had ordered burgers for them and Max, fish boxes for me and Ava, and a garden salad for Maggie. We all helped pay then started walking down the street.

We reached our school forty-five minutes later. It was starting to get a little dark. We rounded our way behind the school to the sports fields, where three boys were already there. Van whistled to the guys, who looked up.

"What up, guys," a skinny but built black boy said, coming towards us.

"What up?" Van said.

“Nothin’ much, just ready to play some football.”

“That’s what I’m talking about, man,” Vince said, bumping fists with the guys.

“You sure the place is empty, Jackson?” Max asked.

“Yeah, I’m sure. I’ve been here with Andrew and Tyrone, scoping it out for at least an hour. The janitor came then left. Place has been clean ever since.”

“Okay, let’s get to playin,’” Van said.

“First let’s eat,” Max said. “I’m hungry.” We went over to where Andrew and Tyrone sat on the wooden bleachers facing the practice field.

I set the bag I had on the bleachers and greeted the three boys. “Addie,” Andrew said.

“Yeah,” I said, looking at him. He was staring at me like Vince was doing a while ago. I rolled my eyes. They’re acting like they were seeing me for the first time.

“I know, right,” Vince said to Andrew. “She looks great, doesn’t she?”

“Tell me about it.”

“Oh calm your hormones,” Maggie said. “Sheesh, a girl wears a halter top and suddenly it’s rutting season.”

“You look good too, Maggie,” Andrew said. “I wish that dress was a little shorter...”

“Please, I do not want to hear it,” Maggie said, holding her hand up. She climbed into the bleachers, taking the box with her salad. I joined her, and we all ate. By dark the boys started playing their little game. A few senior guys who I did not know joined them, and I started to feel like I was really watching a football game.

“Hey, guys,” I heard someone squeal.

I turned to see Ava running towards us.

"Hey," Maggie and I said, hugging her. Her fiery red hair swung over her shoulders when she hugged us.

"I'm so late," she said. "I couldn't get away from my mom. Ugh, she can be so overprotective sometimes."

"I know how that goes," I said, thinking of my aunt.

"You're here now, that's all that matters," Maggie said. Ava sat next to us, and Maggie handed her a box. As the boys played I couldn't help but get the feeling that someone was watching us. I inconspicuously looked around the fields but couldn't see anything. As it started to get darker, the feeling started to grow. The air felt cold, colder than normal. I turned to Maggie and Ava, who didn't seem to notice.

I turned my attention back to the boys, who were oblivious to anything strange going on. The hairs on the back of my neck stood up. I took a few deep breaths, but it was no help in calming the suspenseful feeling in the pit of my stomach. I turned around, looking out towards the dark street, almost hoping to see someone behind me to prove that I wasn't completely crazy.

Nothing.

I turned back and noticed something out past the fields close to the school.

A pair of big glowing red eyes.

Fear filled me once again. I started to panic and shake. I tried to calm myself, but it wasn't working. The fish that I had eaten a while ago threatened to come up, but I kept it down.

I felt Maggie's hand on my arm. "Are you okay?" she asked. I didn't answer. I couldn't answer. I was so stricken with fear it had paralyzed my ability to speak.

"Is she okay?" I heard Ava's sweet voice ask. I turned to her, saying nothing.

I looked back towards the school, and those damn eyes were still there.

"Max," Maggie called. "Something is wrong with Addie."

The boys stopped and ran towards me. "Addie, are you okay?" he asked.

"I'm..." I tried to say, "...fine."

Van and Vince turned as a wind blew then started talking to each other. Suddenly we heard a loud crash that sounded like it was coming from the school. Then another, then another, then nothing.

"What the hell was that?" Jackson asked.

"No idea," Andrew said.

Then we heard what sounded like a scream. Where and what it came from we didn't know. It was neither animal nor human.

"Okay," Tyrone said. "I think we need to, like, I don't know, get the hell outta here!"

"He's right," Van said. "We need to go now. It's almost ten, and crazy things happen at night here in New Orleans."

"Let's go," Max said.

Everyone got their things then started to go their separate ways.

"You guys can ride with me," Jackson said. "I've got room.

"Okay," Ava said. "Thanks."

"No problem." We all piled into Jackson's car with Max up front and us girls in the back. Van and Vince decided to ride with Andrew and Tyrone.

Jackson started his car, shifted gears, and drove though the school's parking lot then onto the road. Once settled in the back seat I started to feel better, but I still felt like we weren't out of danger. I turned around to see if I could see anything at the school. There was nothing. I turned back around and looked straight ahead. Suddenly I saw a flash of red in Jackson's rearview mirror.

I quickly turned around and saw a dark figure standing in the road with a pair of red glowing eyes staring at me.

CHAPTER TWO
JUST ANOTHER MURDER

I woke up the next morning to the sound of my alarm clock blaring in my ear. I had fallen asleep on my desk and woke up with paper and sticky notes attached to my face. After I hit the alarm's snooze button, I tore off the paper. I got home about ten-thirty last night, which did not sit well with my aunt and uncle at all. But they were too tired to do anything, so for now I guess I was off the hook.

I didn't dare tell them about the eyes or feeling like someone was watching me. That would just put them over the edge. I should have known better than to stay out that late with school the next morning. Yes it was a half day, but still. Who cared though, right? My summer vacation started tomorrow, so why worry about being late for school?

I looked at the clock. Only seven-twenty. I probably would be late. I sighed then stretched. I thought back to how and why I had ended up at my desk. I remembered coming home, facing them, then taking a shower, but I thought I had gone to sleep. I didn't give it too much more thought as I started to get ready for school. I lazily took my pajamas off then picked out some clothes for school.

My aunt was always nagging about how I should start laying my clothes out before school, so that way I didn't have to spend time picking them out. It's not like I had a lot to choose from. I had jeans like any normal teenager, T-shirts, a few dress blouses and skirts, but no dresses. My fashion sense was easy and simple. To my aunt it's a nightmare. Like I really cared about her opinion, though.

She would have loved for me to come down wearing a nice skirt and heels, but that was never going to happen. I was comfortable in my T-shirt and jeans. I changed into a gray T-shirt and jeans. As I bent over to grab my converse, my head started to hurt and the room felt like it was spinning. That faint haze started to appear, so I just rode out the pain until it stopped. But it didn't. I finally sat on my bed waiting, then as quickly as it came it left.

I took in a huge breath, trying to remember what I was doing.

"Addie," I heard my aunt call. "Come eat breakfast.

Hearing her voice snapped me back into reality. I didn't really have much of an appetite now after that. I stood up very carefully, combed my hair, pulled the curly mess back in a ponytail, then brushed my teeth. I gathered my backpack then looked at my desk. There were still pieces of paper lying on it from where I was sleeping.

As I looked closer it looked like something was on it. I walked over to them, but before I could get a really good look, my aunt called me once again. I sighed then headed down stairs.

My aunt was placing a bowl down on the table in front of my uncle, who was reading the newspaper. "They found another one," he whispered to my aunt so I wouldn't hear. I stopped. "Dead."

"Really?" she said. "I just can't believe that. Things are getting worse and out of control."

I waited by the archway into the kitchen, listening. "Things are getting more complicated nowadays, Wanda. You know that."

"You're right, you're right. I just don't see why...oh good morning, Addie." I jumped at the sound of my name.

"Um...morning," I said. I walked over to the kitchen counter and sat down.

"Do you want anything to eat?" she asked.

"No I'm good, I'll eat later."

She didn't answer. She looked like she had something on her mind. She put her hands down on the counter and looked at me. I looked up at her. "What?" I asked.

"Don't speak to me in that tone," she said. I rolled my eyes. "We need to talk about last night."

"Why?" I asked. "I came home late, not too late, but..."

"You still came home late, and you didn't tell us that you were going to be late."

"It's not my fault. I didn't know the boys' little game was going to take that long."

"You could have called," my uncle said in a flat tone.

"Yes, you could have," my aunt added.

I scoffed. "Well sorry," I dragged out how I said sorry. "You know it just didn't occur to me at the time with the game going on, having fun, and the..." I stopped before I said something I would regret later.

"The what...Addie?" my aunt asked. I looked at her. Too scared to say anything. She had those kind of eyes that just bury into you, trying to find the truth. I guess being a lawyer made her like that.

Still I held my ground.

"Nothing," I said. "I just got caught up in the hype, that's all."

My aunt didn't say anything. She just stared at me with those piercing gray eyes.

"Look can I go now?" I asked, irritated. "I'm going to be late for school and it's the last day."

My aunt looked at me. "Fine," she said. "Go."

"Finally," I said. I grabbed my things then headed for the door.

"But this isn't over," I heard my aunt say.

I stopped in my tracks. "What?" I asked, turning around.

"This isn't over." She crossed her arms. "You still need to pay for missing curfew and not telling us that you were going to be late. That is something that I just can't let go of."

"But, Aunt Wanda, I..."

"No 'buts,' Addie. You know the rules."

"Come on, that's totally unfair."

"You break the rules, you get punished. That's how it goes."

"I make one little mistake, and you want to punish me for it?" I said, my voice rising with anger.

"Wanda, don't be too tough on her," my uncle said. My aunt looked at him. "It was just one time. And I'm sure this will never happen again. Am I right, Addie?"

"Yes, he is so right. It will never happen again. I promise."

"Maybe we should let this one slide."

"We can't, Jeff," my aunt said. "She broke the rules, she needs to understand the consequences."

"Wanda..."

"Jeff, I don't want to hear it." She held up a hand to him. "My mind is made up."

My uncle turned to me. "I'm sorry, kiddo, I tried." My uncle and I had never really been close, but I knew I can always count on him to get me out of situations. And I knew that he cared about me, unlike his unbearable wife.

My aunt looked at me.

"To and from school today," she said, pointing to the door then at the floor where she stood. "Nowhere else." I nodded. "I will tell you what your punishment is when you get home, understand?"

"Yes, ma'am," I said.

"Oh wait."

"Yes?" I asked. What now?

"Here, don't forget to take your vitamin." She handed me a small pill bottle.

"Gee thanks," I said sarcastically.

"Good, now off you go, I don't want you to be late."

I started for the door once again. I headed out the door and onto the front porch.

God, I wanted to scream. Why? Why should I be punished just because I forgot to call or came home later? It wasn't my fault. Some creepy-ass thing with glowing red eyes was stalking me last night, so of course I forgot. I was scared half to death. But of course I couldn't tell them that because then I really would be locked away for the rest of my life like a princess in a castle.

"It's not fair," I said to myself.

I stepped off the steps of my house and onto the sidewalk of Seventh Street in the Garden District. Nice houses (also called mansions) built in the Antebellum-style with wrought iron fences and manicured lawns make up the fine community Everyone here was so nice with good jobs and never minded lending a helping hand. It made me sick sometimes. The overall day-to-day of this place was just so redundant. Everyone did the same thing every day.

Wake up. Go to work or school. Come home. Go to bed. Then do it all over again in the morning.

It could be pretty boring around here. If Ava and Maggie didn't live in the same area, then I would have gone crazy a long time ago. I waited for Maggie and Ava in our usual spot, a lamppost just before you reach the end of Seventh Street. After a few minutes of waiting, I saw Maggie walking fast towards me. "Slow down, or you're going to pull something." I joked.

"Ha, ha, very funny," she said, huffing a bit. "Come on, we are going to be late."

"I thought we needed to wait for Ava?"

"She's coming, but she'll be late. She texted me and told me to go ahead. I thought she texted you too."

"Ugh, I forgot my phone."

"It's the last day, you won't need it. Come on." We started making our way for St. Charles Avenue. "Have you calmed down from yesterday?" Maggie asked.

"Yeah I'm fine," I said. "I'm just never going to Canal Street again."

"Sorry. I shouldn't have dragged you along."

"It's okay, you needed to do some shopping before we met the boys, and I needed to get out of the house. We had to walk farther, but we got to meet up with Max. It all worked out." We both got quiet as we exited the Garden District and walked onto St. Charles Avenue.

"By the way, I'm so grounded for coming home late yesterday," I said to Maggie.

"Really?" she asked. "I'm sorry."

"Don't worry about it. My aunt will get over it soon."

"How bad is it?"

"I really don't know. My aunt told me that I know better to break the rules because I know the consequences or something like that. She told me that she'd tell me what my punishment is when I get home today."

"Yikes. Aren't you nervous or scared?"

"What? Of my aunt? Please. She's the last person I'm scared of. I just can't stand her."

"You two used to get along when we were younger."

"Yeah, but that was before, when I needed her for things because she was all I had next to my uncle. I'm not saying I don't still need her, but I'm sixteen. I can make a few of my own decisions, right?"

"I'm not answering that."

"Why?"

"Because it's controversial."

"Controversial?"

"I mean, yeah, I believe that teenagers should have a say in what they can and can't do before they are the age of eighteen. But how many teens do you know make the right choices?"

I didn't answer.

"Exactly. So yeah, I guess on one hand it's okay for a parent or guardian to let their teen make a few of their own decisions in their life. But there is also nothing wrong with them wanting to step in and help them make the right ones. Do you get what I'm saying?"

"Kind of," I admitted.

Maggie started to smile. "You're hopeless," she said, trying not to laugh.

"No, no I get it really. Honestly."

"Sure you do. Let's get to school." We started walking faster.

As we approached our school's campus I heard a series of loud noises coming from behind the building. "What's that?" Maggie asked.

"I don't know," I said, looking around.

Just then Max came running up to us his face in disarray. "Max what's going on?" Maggie asked.

"It's the janitor," Max said, barely winded. "He was killed last night."

Both of our mouths dropped. "He...he...he," Maggie stammered, "was killed last night?"

"Yeah, around ten is what I heard the coroner say."

"Ten," I said. "That's around the time we left, wasn't it?"

"Yep, and when we heard those strange noises." Max stopped

talking, searching for words. "I guess that was him getting killed."

"That can't be. Those...or that scream, or whatever we heard wasn't a human scream," I said. "That's...just...not possible."

"If you don't believe me come see for yourself." Max led us towards the back of the school. Three police cars and an ambulance were parked in the sports field parking lot. Several students were standing around, trying to get a glimpse of what was going on. I squeezed through the crowd, watching a paramedic pushing a gurney with a body bag on it.

I started to remember the pair of red eyes from yesterday. We were standing right about where those eyes were. I wondered if those eyes had anything to do with the janitor's murder. Fear started to fill me again, and I started to shake. "Oh my gosh," I heard Ava say next to me. "What happened?"

"Mr. Dex was killed last night," a junior boy said.

Ava looked at him. I knew she was thinking the same thing. We were all here last night around the time he was. We heard the noises, no matter how strange they sounded. We could have helped him.

"Okay, move along, students, come on," Mrs. La Rowe, our math teacher, said, shuffling students out of the way. "There is nothing to see here, move along. Let the police do their job."

We were ushered out of the parking lot and back in the school. Already at eight in the morning the school was alive with what was going on. I walked into homeroom ignoring the chitchat from the halls. Mr. Delay, our homeroom teacher, walked with a tired look on his face. "Okay, that's enough, everyone," he said. "Settle down now."

"I can't wait to get out of here," Max said from behind me after we took our seats. "That murder has just got me all freaked out now."

"Me too," Ava said from the seat next to me. "And to think we were here last night. We could have gotten killed as well."

"It's okay, guys," Maggie said. "We are safe, everything is going to be fine."

"Mr. Delay looks kind of rough," I said. "I mean rougher than he normally looks."

"He should be," Jackson said, jumping in the conversation. "That was his cousin that was killed."

"Mr. Dex was his cousin?" Ava asked.

"Yep, afraid so."

Ava's eyes teared up. Vince and Van came to sit with us. "Listen," Jackson said. He looked around to make sure no one was in earshot then said, "Don't, I repeat, don't tell anyone that we were all here last night and about the noises. We don't want to call attention to ourselves."

"But we have to say something," Ava said. "Anything..."

"We can't, Ava," Van said. "Then the police will be all over our asses wanting to know what we were doing here."

"Van is right," Jackson said. "We can't say anything."

"Don't you think that we owe something to Mr. Dex's family? To Mr. Delay? What we heard...we could have helped him."

"And got ourselves killed in the process," Max said.

Ava held back tears. "So you guys are just going to act like nothing happened? Like we didn't hear anything last night? It could help catch Mr. Dex's killer."

"No," Jackson said, more irritated now. "If we say something, then we are involved, straightforward. Got it?"

"Yeah."

"Good."

"It's still wrong."

"Let the police handle it. This is just another murder to them."

"Yeah, another murder and counting," Max said. "Just another day in New Orleans."

"Please," Van said, "you've got as good a chance of getting murdered in New York, Chicago, Houston, or any other large city as you do New Orleans. It's just a fault of big cites."

"So true," Vince said. "Ain't nothing you can do about it."

"How did he die anyway?" Max asked.

"Pff, why do you want to know, Max?" I asked.

"Just curious. Does anyone know?"

"I heard the coroner say something about that he lost a lot of blood from some bite wounds in his neck."

"Bite wounds?" I asked.

"Yeah," Jackson said.

"What, like from an animal or something?"

"That's what I heard."

"What's a wild animal doing in New Orleans?" Max asked. "We are far away from any woods or country."

"Could an animal have escaped from the zoo?" Ava asked.

"We would have all heard about it," Maggie said. "Still, an animal, that is just really strange."

"I saw the bites right before they put him in the body bag. It was two perfect circles right on the side of his neck. I don't know what kind of animal has a bite radius like that."

"Circles?" Vince asked. "Really?"

Jackson shook his head. "He also had claw marks on his arms, deep ones too. It didn't look good at all. Poor man."

After being quiet for a few minutes, Ava, Maggie, Jackson, and Max started talking. I listened and put my two cents in every now and then, but Van and Vince didn't join in the conversation. They were talking amongst themselves. I saw the way Vince was grimacing. I could tell whatever they were talking about wasn't a good thing. Still why would he be making that face?

After homeroom, we went to our next class.

School was only a half day today, but we still had to go to our regular classes like we would on a normal school day. It sucked, but at least we got out after one.

I sat at my desk and waited for my friends. "I wonder if you can still see the police from here?" a boy asked another as they walked up to the window.

"I don't know," the other one said, joining him. "I think they have already left."

"That's quite enough, you two," Mrs. La Rowe said, walking up to the boys. "Have a seat right now." Both boys exchanged scared glances then sat down. I laughed to myself. Jackasses. My friends came and sat down then Mrs. La Rowe took attendance. "Rivera."

"Here," Max said.

"Roper."

"Here," a boy in back said.

"Chappell."

"Here," Ava said.

"François."

"Here," I said, reluctant to raise my hand.

After she called the rest of the names, Mrs. La Rowe looked at all of us. "I know that this morning's events have been tragic," she said. "But I want you all to understand that this is a very, very serious situation, and I want each and every one of you to take it seriously."

I understood the situation completely, but Mrs. La Rowe's words were going up in smoke. Nobody was really listening. Many of them were just staring at the ceiling or the floor.

"Don't act like this is part of some show or that it's cool or whatever you teenagers are into this day and age," Mrs. La Rowe continued. "This is a serious matter, and I will not have anyone treat it as such. Understand?"

The class nodded.

"Good, you may now talk quietly amongst yourselves. And I do mean quietly."

I turned around to face Max, Ava, and Maggie. "What was all that about?" I asked them.

"I think some kids in her homeroom class were making a mess out of what happened," Max said. "I think they were like calling themselves the CSI team and all this other stuff."

"That's awful," Ava said.

"Very," Maggie put in. "What kind of person does that?"

"Cruel people," Max said.

"Well Van and Vince are right. The police will catch the person responsible, and this will all be over soon. Then Mr. Dex's family can have some peace."

I turned back around in my chair, lost in my own thoughts. At some point I thought back to what Jackson said about the bites and possible claw marks on Mr. Dex's body. There was no possible way that a wild animal could have made them unless one escaped from the Audubon Zoo, which was most unlikely. And the biggest animal that could possibly be in the city is the occasional raccoon. It just didn't make any sense. Not to me. Then again, I was just one person.

But something inside, something deep, deep inside me was telling me that this is not just another New Orleans murder.

CHAPTER THREE
QUESTIONS

After we left Mrs. La Rowe's class, we had a little break. The cafeteria didn't fix breakfast since we were getting out half day, so by the time we left for break I was starving. Max, Ava, Maggie, and I sat outside at one of the round picnic tables enjoying the sun. Soon my stomach started to growl. "What was that?" Max asked.

"My stomach," I said, placing my hand on it. "I didn't eat breakfast."

"And why not?" Ava asked.

"Because I was fighting with my aunt and I ruined my appetite."

"Are you hungry? I've got an energy bar in my bag," Max said.

"Sure, if you don't mind."

"I don't, here." He reached into his backpack and pulled out the bar. I tore the paper off and started eating it like it was going out of style. "Whoa," Max said. "You really are hungry."

"I told you," I said as I swallowed the last bite. "The one day the café doesn't serve breakfast, and I skip it."

"Don't forget to take your vitamin," Maggie said. I stared at her. "What? Your aunt told me to remind you. Sometimes you forget."

"Ugh, I hate taking that thing. It's nasty and leaves a bad taste in my mouth."

"But it's for your health," Ava said. "I take a multi-vitamin every day."

"I bet yours is better tasting than mine."

I got up and went over to the vending machine to get a bottle of water. I put the money in, pressed the button for the water, then sat back and waited. When it came out of the machine I opened my pill bottle and took out my vitamin. I popped it in my mouth then drank the water behind it. I was already starting to taste the bitterness of the white pill. I gagged a bit then went back over to my friends.

"There, I took it," I said to Maggie.

"Good," Maggie said.

"I wish this day would end already," Max said, stretching his arms. "I want to go home and relax and not have to worry about coming back here for three months."

"I hear ya," I said. "I want my vacation to start already."

"It will be over soon," Ava said. "Just a few more hours to go."

"Ugh," I sighed.

The bell rang for our next class to start. We got up from our table. When we started walking towards the door, I noticed something across the street at a nearby business. I tried to focus on it, but my mind wouldn't let me. Instead my head started to hurt, and I felt dizzy like I did this morning. I then put my fingers to my temples and started rubbing them. It wasn't helping. I closed my eyes then opened them again.

A faint haze had clouded my vision again.

I squinted my eyes shut, trying to ignore the pain, but it was no use.

"Addie, are you okay?" I heard Ava ask. I didn't answer. I just lowered my head. After what seemed like forever, it stopped. I opened my eyes again and the haze was gone.

"Dude, you okay?" Max asked.

I looked at them. "I'm fine," I said.

"Are you sure? 'Cause it didn't look that way to us," Ava said.

Maggie just stared at me.

"I told you guys I'm fine, really I am."

"Well, it just looked like you were in a lot of pain," Max said.

"I had a bit of a headache, but I'm fine now." I tried to reassure them.

"That looked worse than a headache," Ava said. "That looked like a migraine."

I rolled my eyes and was starting to get very pissed. "It's nothing," I said. "It was probably a side effect of not eating. I just downed that bar, it's going to take a while for my body to digest it, right?"

Ava sighed. "Okay," she said. "If you say you're okay then I guess you're okay."

"Thank you, now can we go? Two more hours left of school, and then we are done." We started walking through the doors. I turned back to look across the street to see if I could find what I thought I saw. I didn't see anything, but that didn't mean that there wasn't something there.

When the final bell rang, I was one of the first ones out of the door. "Summer is here!" a student said, running down the hall. I laughed then walked to my locker. My books had all been turned in, but my locker was still a mess. I started to shove the old homework assignment sheets, class notes, and various other things in a garbage can that someone left.

"You still haven't cleaned your locker out?" Ava asked, standing next to me.

I shot her a look. "No," I said. "I kind of forgot about it."

"How can you forget to clean your locker out at the end of the school year?"

"By being too lazy to do it or so focused on summer vacation that it just slips your mind."

"Speaking of summer vacation, this weekend is the first weekend of summer. We need to do something."

"Like what?"

"I don't know. Go out, eat somewhere, throw a party."

"Yeah and where are we going to throw a party at?"

"I'm just making suggestions. But seriously we need to do something."

"The only thing I'm planning on doing this summer is sleep, eat, and sleep."

Ava giggled. "Yeah, that sounds like you," she said.

"Can't argue with that," I said.

"We'll think of something awesome to do, don't worry." Ava was one of those people who was always looking for something to do or somewhere to go, even if it's nowhere. She's always active, always helpful, and just an overall great person. It's hard to live up to someone like that, not that I was trying, I just admired her so much. Sometimes she could get annoying, hell, all my friends could, but I wouldn't trade my friendship with them for anything.

I'd even die for them, believe it or not.

I finished cleaning out my locker. "Okay, locker," I said, holding its door. "This year has been great, but you know what they say, 'live long and...'" I slammed the door, "...screw it."

"Um, no one says that," Ava said.

"I do. Come on, let's go find Max and Maggie." We started to walk down the hall. Max was at his locker cleaning it out too.

"You didn't clean yours out either?" Ava asked.

"Yes I did," Max said. "Two months ago when we had spring break. Now it's summer break, so it's getting cleaned again."

"I'm going to have to teach you and Addie a little something about locker hygiene."

"So we can clean our lockers out every month? No thank you."

"Hey, a clean locker is a happy locker."

"Now no one says that," I said. Ava smirked at me then started laughing. "Where's Maggie?" I asked Max.

"Beats me," he said. "I thought she was with you two."

"Nope. I haven't seen her since our last class," Ava said.

"I'll go find her. I want to enjoy our walk home together before I go back to Alcatraz." I turned and started walking down another hallway. I turned the corner and saw Maggie talking with Van and Vince. They looked like they were in a real deep conversation, but I couldn't make out any words. Maggie looked kind of upset.

Her expression was tight as she spoke to them. Van was arguing with her as far as I could tell. Vince was just standing there, his face tight and strained like Maggie's. I wonder what the hell was going on. I started to walk over to them very slowly. "Addie," Vince said. "Hey."

"Hey," I said in a curious tone. "What are you guys talking about?"

"Oh, you know, just the events of today," Vince said. Van elbowed his brother then shook his head. Vince grimaced then turned to me.

"We were just discussing the War of Avengers game," Maggie said. "We were trying to figure out who's better, Altori or Orion."

"Orion clearly," Van said. "He's got the weapon of Eons, triclix armor, and all of the Galenites at his side."

"Yes, but Altori has the centum pearl, which controls Centium City and as you should know lies within the main Capitol. With that and the people of the city at her side, she is unstoppable and can defeat the Toritons."

Van looked taken aback.

"So you three were in a heated discussion over a stupid video game?" I asked.

"Yes, I guess we were," Van said.

"It's a very good game," Vince said. "And we take it very seriously."

"I can tell."

"It's a fun game, Addie," Maggie said. "You should try and play it one day."

"And cross over to the dark side of Geek Nation? No thanks, oh, no offense."

"None taken," Vince said.

"Well, Addie, I believe we should get going," Maggie said, turning to me. She still looked like there was something on her mind. She looked tense and a bit off. I guess the discussion really got to her, maybe.

"Yeah, let's go." I said.

"Bye, girls," Vince said. "See you around."

"You too," Maggie said. She linked her arm in mine, and we walked down the hall.

"So is War of Avengers really that good?" I asked.

"Yes it is," Maggie said. "It's very fun, full of adventure, action, and romance. You really should try to play it one day."

"Sure, one day." Like in a million years.

We joined Max and Ava then started walking towards the door. All around us students were rejoicing that it was the last day of school. I could feel the excitement rise within me at just looking at how happy they were. I started to smile. Then I remembered what my aunt had in store for me at home, and my smile faded. "Hey, guys," I said. They turned to me. "Let's take our time going home."

"Why?" Max asked.

"Because her aunt wants to punish her for coming home late

last night," Maggie said.

"What? No way," Ava said.

"It's true. She is a dictator after all."

"I thought you said that you weren't scared of your aunt?" Maggie said.

"I'm not, but I know her and I know that she is going to make me regret coming home late. I want to enjoy the freedom I have of her right now before it's taken away."

"Then she's just going to get more upset because you're not home on time after school," Maggie put in. I didn't think of it that way. "We can take our time but not too much. Right, guys?" Ava and Max agreed.

"Fine," I said, rolling my eyes. "Let's go." We walked through the door and onto the campus. We walked down St. Charles Avenue back towards the Garden District.

After coming to Seventh Street, Max turned to us. "I'm sorry, I gotta leave you guys here," he said.

"Why?" Ava asked.

"I promised the guys I'd go the park with them and throw the football around a bit. You guys can come if you want." Max paused then looked at me. "Sorry, Addie."

"It's okay," I said, feeling a little bummed out.

"I can't," Ava said. "I've got some baking to do for the summer bake sale that's coming up soon. I'm going to try some new recipes."

"I can't either," Maggie said. "I've got to somehow prove to Van and Vince that Altori is much better than Orion."

"Have fun anyway," I said.

"I'll try. See ya." He walked off.

Ava, Maggie, and I started to walk down the sidewalk towards my house. "Well there it is," I said, looking at the white house with its tall columns, shutter windows, and black wrought iron fencing. I almost didn't want to go in.

"You'll be fine, Addie," Maggie said.

I shook my head. "I doubt it."

"She might have cooled down after you left," Ava said.

I looked at them dumbfounded. "I still doubt it," I said.

"Just go in there and tell her how very sorry you are and that it will never happen again," Maggie said. "Swallow your pride for once."

I sighed. "Okay, I'll try," I said. "But I can't guarantee anything."

"Text us later if you can," Ava said.

"I will." They left and I was alone. I took in a breath then exhaled. "Let's do this," I said. I unlatched the gate then walked down the cobblestone path up the stairs to the glass door, fished my key from my bag, and opened it. The smell of fresh magnolias hit me as soon as I walked in. I didn't see any sign of my aunt or uncle, so I started to slowly make my way to the stairs.

"Hold it," I heard my aunt say.

I was just about to put my foot on the first step. *Damn it,* I thought. *So close.* I slowly turned around to face my aunt, who had her arms crossed, looking mad as hell. She looked the same as this morning. Still dressed in her light gray suit, her brown hair pulled tightly back in a bun, and her face just as cold as ever.

"Hey," I said in a fake singsong voice.

"How was your last day of school?" she asked, seeing right through my facade.

"Great," I said, my voice rising in my singsong voice. "It was great. Other than dragging on forever. I thought you had to work today?"

"Court doesn't start for another hour."

"Well then you might want to start getting ready. I know you wouldn't want to be late..."

"That's enough, Addie," she said, cutting me off. "You're not getting off that easy." I froze. "I still remembered what we talked about." She stepped towards me. "And I still intend on punishing you."

"Come on, that's not fair. I said I was sorry, isn't that enough?"

"You live in my house, and what I say goes. If I say you need to be punished, then you do."

"For one little mistake? That is completely unfair." My voice started to rise.

"No, it is not. You break the rules..."

"You get punished, I know, I heard that speech this morning."

"When we took you in, we decided to do what was best for you. That means punishment if the rules are broken as well. Like any normal household."

"This sucks. Why can't you just forgive me? You're so unfair."

"I can afford to be unfair."

I balled my fists up, trying to control my anger.

"Your punishment will be to clean the house, and you are not allowed to go anywhere with your friends for two weeks."

"Two weeks? But it's summer vacation. This is my chance to have freedom before school starts back in the fall."

"Oh please, Addie. It's just for two weeks. If you keep fighting me on this I'll make it a whole month."

I bit my bottom lip then surrendered.

"Fine," I said. "I'll start cleaning the house."

"Good," my aunt said, walking over to the living room table. She picked up her purse and keys then headed for the door. "I expect this house to be clean from top to bottom when I get back," she said, turning to me.

"Aye, aye, captain," I said sarcastically, saluting to her.

"Don't be a smart mouth. Keep this door locked. I should be home later." She walked out the door.

A few hours later, I was on my hands and knees scrubbing the bathroom floor. My back hurt from being on the floor and so did my knees. My hands felt sweaty and hot inside the rubber gloves, even with the air conditioning on I was still covered in sweat. My bangs fell in my eyes, so I pushed them back behind my ears. Now I really was feeling like Cinderella.

I started to hum that song that she sang in the movie when she was cleaning then stopped because I couldn't remember how it went. Then I started to hum "Whistle While You Work." It was starting to make the cleaning better. Not bad for a song from Cinderella. *Wait, that's from Snow White not Cinderella,* I thought. *What am I thinking? Like I care.* I had more important things to worry about than fight over Disney songs.

After the last corner had been scrubbed, I threw the brush in the bucket of soapy water next to me and sighed. "Finally," I said, taking the gloves off. "Done." Next I went to my room to pick up my dirty clothes. I gathered them up then put them in the hamper. I straightened up the things on my dresser, made my bed, organized my closet, and even removed a dirt speck from my sea foam green walls.

By late evening I was exhausted.

I cleaned my room, my aunt and uncle's room, all the bathrooms, the hallways, the living room, and my aunt's home office. Basically the whole house. So she couldn't come home and bitch and gripe that I didn't do anything. I fell flat on my bed, exhaling extremely loudly because I was done. I stared at the ceiling, letting my mind wander. I closed my eyes for just a few minutes.

I woke up suddenly, shaking from a dream I had.

I tried to replay the dream in my head, but I just couldn't. All I could remember was a boy, in the darkness, surrounded by shadows.

My hand instantly went to my forehead, trying to sooth my aching head in any way. I felt dizzy, weak, and was out of breath for some reason. Once again I tried to relay the dream in my head, but the more I tried the more it faded into my memory.

I looked outside my bedroom window. Dusk had fallen, sending a creepy vibe through my room and my body. Shadows started growing on my walls, making my unlit room darker. The only things stopping them from getting any bigger were wall hangings, shelves, and posters. I jumped off my bed, wanting to get the hell out of my room. It didn't feel safe for some reason, or maybe it was just me. I went into the hall and took a breath. *This is stupid,* I thought. *I'm sixteen years old, afraid of the dark. How stupid can I be?*

The hallway felt better, though. Warmer even. I felt safe standing in it.

My stomach started to growl, making me realize that I hadn't eaten lunch. I started to walk down the stairs when I heard the front door slam. Panic rose in me. I paused at the middle of the staircase. My aunt came bustling in, hair a mess and mad as hell. I breathed a sigh of relief and watched as she threw her keys and purse down on the side table next to the wall then walked into the kitchen.

She didn't even see me.

"Hi, hon," I heard the voice of my uncle say. I didn't even know he was home. "How was court?"

"Terrible," my aunt said. "Just outrageous. You know they are going to let him walk after what he's done? It's horrible."

"I know, but it's their decision. What can we do about it?"

"I have no idea, but Jeff, this, this is just crazy. I'm telling you things just aren't what they used to be back when we were with them."

What?

"Things have changed," my uncle said. "Some for the best, some for the worse, I will say that. Besides, you know the reason why we got out was because things were falling apart and because of Addie."

At the bottom of the stairs hidden from view I clapped my hand over my mouth so I wouldn't make a sound. *What were they talking about? What or who did they work for at one point? And why did it involve me?* I pressed my ear to the wall, trying to listen better.

I could hear my aunt sigh. "I just wish things were better," she said. "I just wish they hadn't gotten so out of control."

"You know why things turned out the way they did," my uncle said. "You know the reason."

"He didn't mean to do it, and you know that, Jeff. They all know it, or else they wouldn't be risking everything to protect his daughter. He screwed up, he wasn't thinking, it's that simple."

What's the reason? Who screwed up? My dad? Those questions whirled around in my head. And more importantly what were they hiding from me?

CHAPTER FOUR
LATE-NIGHT PLANS

A few days later, I sat outside in the backyard reading a book, enjoying the day. I was trying to avoid my aunt and uncle at any cost. I had no idea what they were talking about the other day, and it didn't really look like they wanted to let me know anything about it either. All I knew was that it was about me, or at least had something to do with me. That much I gathered. So for that obvious reason I should know.

I tried my best not to think about it, because the more I thought about it, the more I wanted to ask them about it. So it was best if I just try and ignore them as best as I could. It's not that hard. I just stayed to myself, which they knew I did a lot. I was grounded, so it's not like I could go anywhere. I stayed in my room, or outside, and I hardly ran into them. I'd let them think that I was mad at them for grounding me, which, for the record, I was still pretty pissed about.

Whatever they didn't know wouldn't hurt them. I guess they thought that same way with me. If they didn't know that I overheard them, more power to me. Two can play this game and keep secrets. Well, three if you want to get technical about it.

I sat outside at a stone table with a good book, just enjoying the morning before it got too hot. Next to me my phone beeped. I put the book across my lap and picked up the phone. There was a text from Ava. "Hey, how's your punishment going?"

I texted her back. "Okay so far. I'm not talking to them, though."

"Why?"

"Cause I don't want to."

"You have to eventually; they are your aunt and uncle after all." I couldn't tell her the real reason, no matter how bad I wanted to. It's no use bringing my friends into something that was more of a family thing. It's not their battle to fight, as far as I was concerned. It wouldn't be fair to them, so I kept my mouth shut.

After a few minutes, I texted Ava back. "Please, they don't care."

"They do, and you know it," she texted back.

"I know they don't, if they did they would ask me if I'm okay and we'd talk, trust me on this, they don't." It's a harsh truth, but it's the truth. If they really did care about me they would be asking me if everything was all right, and then if it wasn't we'd talk about it. We'd work things out and everything would turn out just peachy.

But that wasn't how it worked in my life. Not in this house, not in this town.

Ava and I texted back a few times when I noticed a shadow on the grass. I quickly turned around and saw my aunt standing there with her arms folded, looking down at me. "Oh...dammit," I said when I realized it was her. "Don't scare me like that, would ya?"

"What are you doing out here?" she asked in a cold voice.

"Trying to get some fresh air before it becomes too hot to breathe. Why? Is 'not enjoying the outdoors' in your punishment as well?"

"No."

My phone beeped.

"But texting your friends is."

"No, you said I couldn't see them, you said nothing about texting them."

"And I thought that you would be good and not text any of them. Clearly I was wrong."

"Then you should have mentioned it beforehand if you didn't trust me that much."

My aunt sighed. "I thought I could," she said.

We both got quiet. *Tell me what you and Uncle Jeff were talking about the other day,* I wanted to ask, but I knew better. If I did I would just be met with resistance.

"Let me make myself clear this time," my aunt said. "No seeing, texting, Instagraming, Snapchatting...or whatever it is that you kids do now these days...with your friends for the remainder of your punishment."

"What?!" I almost screamed. "You can't just add on to my punishment after you've already told me what it will be."

"Yes I can. I am your aunt and your legal guardian. I can do whatever I want."

"This is so unfair. First you punish me for something that was out of my control. Then you tell me what that punishment is, next after I do what I'm told you completely change it. What is it going to take for you to just get off my damn back with it?"

"Until I think that you have learned your lesson, which you have clearly not."

"You're unbelievable. I can't take this anymore." I picked up my book along with my phone and started back to the house. I walked up the porch steps and went inside, trying as fast as I could to get away from my aunt. But I could hear her footsteps behind me.

"Where do you think you are going, young lady?" she asked before I could reach the steps.

"What does it look like I'm doing?" I said, biting back. "Getting the hell away from you."

"Don't cuss at me. Addie, look at me, look at me now!" I was just about to place my foot on the top step when she started to yell.

I slowly turned around to face her. "What?" I asked. "Haven't you yelled at me enough today?"

"I have hardly done any of that," she said. "Meanwhile it's you that keeps yelling at me."

"Because you are not listening to me."

"Addie, don't fight me on this please..."

"No, you don't fight with me about this, and listen. I don't care that you're my legal guardian, and that this is your home, and that I have to obey your rules. What you've set here is wrong and completely unfair. You can't just decide what you want to do with me because of all of that."

"That's called parenting, Addie. It's what I..."

"You're not my parent! You're not my mom! I don't have to listen to you!"

"Yes you do, young lady, for legal reasons. Until you are eighteen, you are in your uncle's and my care."

I was starting to get really, really angry. More angry than I had ever been before. Tears were even coming to my eyes, and I started to shake. I couldn't take much more of this. I could feel my face getting red as I tried to find the right words to say. "I'm over this," I said. "I'm going to my room."

"No, you're not," she argued. "You are going to stay right here and..."

"Why? So you can yell and punish me some more? For the last time you're not my parent, you don't tell me what to do." My voice was starting to crack. "You couldn't be a parent anyway," I whimpered. "A parent listens to their child, not scolds them for every little single thing they do wrong. They treat them right, they are there for them no matter what. You are never there for me! All you do is tell me what I am doing wrong! You never ask if I'm okay and if you do...I know you don't mean it." Tears streamed down my cheeks as I let the past four years come off my chest.

My aunt just stood there, stone cold as usual.

"I know I'm not your kid," I said. "But I wish for once you would just treat me like I was." I sucked in a breath. "Sometimes... sometimes I wish that when my parents died, I wish that I would have died with them so that I wouldn't have had to come here and live with you."

I stood there a few minutes, going over what I just said. *Was I too harsh?* I thought. *No, of course not. This is how I really feel, this is what she needs to know.* I waited for a response from her, but by the look on her face it didn't look like I was going to be getting it anytime soon. Without uttering another word I ran up to my room and slammed the door.

After what seemed like forever, I woke up from a long, long nap. I look at my wall clock, which read seven-fifteen. Tearstains were on my sea foam green pillow along with a bit of drool. I must have been out. Part of me wanted to stay in my room, but the other part of me wanted to go see where my aunt and uncle were. That, and I was starting to get hungry.

I got out of bed then started down the stairs.

"You don't get it, Jeff," I heard my aunt say from the living room. "She's just not listening to me."

I sat on the middle step where they couldn't see me and listened. It seemed like they'd been doing a lot of this lately. I watched as my aunt paced back and forth with her hands on her hips, her face in disarray. My uncle was on the couch, looking calm as ever. "I tell her to do something, she does the opposite," my aunt continued. "I just don't know what else to do with her."

"She's a teen, Wanda," my uncle said. "Teens do things like this. They don't listen, they don't obey, you give them too many rules, they bend and break them. It's perfectly normal behavior."

"Yes, I know. I just didn't think that she would be this stubborn and hard to handle."

"You pushed her. That's why she's acting like this."

"What are you saying?"

"I heard you two a few hours ago, and she is right. You don't listen to her, and frankly I need to be around more as well."

"No, it's fine, I know how hard you work. I just wish she would understand why I'm doing this. Why I'm protecting her." She walked over to the window. "Maybe I do need to be a bit more sensitive," she finally said. "Maybe I need to try to give her a little rein."

"That sounds like a great idea," my uncle said very cheerfully.

"Ugh, but how do I do that? You know I was never good at the sensitive, mushy gushy stuff, and I'm still not."

"Just try. I know you can do it. You did when she was a baby."

"Yeah, but that was easy. She was little and she didn't have an attitude. I'd tell her to do something, and she'd do it with no questions asked. How things have changed."

Part of me wanted to gag at her reminiscing about when I was younger, then another part of me was grateful for what she did. It made me feel that somewhere deep inside her heart she did care. Still I want to see her try and change her methods of punishing me and be more sensitive towards my feelings and opinions. I didn't think that she could do it. She didn't have a sensitive bone in her body.

We'll see how far this goes.

The next day, I peeked my head into the kitchen, where my aunt was making breakfast. My uncle was already sitting at the table, reading the paper as usual. I strode into the kitchen, feeling out the situation. We didn't see each other after my breakdown yesterday, so I wanted to see how she would react to me today.

I bounced into the kitchen with my long high ponytail flipping all around me.

"Good morning," I said in a fake singsong voice as I sat at the counter.

"Good morning," Uncle Jeff said. "Someone is in a good mood today."

"Why wouldn't I be? I mean, it's such a beautiful day. Don't you think so, Aunt Wanda?"

"Hm?" she asked as she poured something into a bowl over by the stove.

"I asked if you thought today is a beautiful day?"

"Well...um...yes, I guess it is a beautiful day." I could tell by the look on her face that she was having a hard time with this. My aunt cooked some pancakes and started to pass plates to us. "Um, Addie," she said, barely looking at me.

I put a few pancakes on my plate and looked up at her. "Yes?" I asked as non-sarcastically as I could.

"I've been thinking," she started. "Maybe I have been a little too hard on you lately." I blinked my eyes a few times, not believing what I was hearing. "I've thought about our conversation yesterday, and I guess I really haven't been paying attention to what you want and what you are trying to tell me."

I couldn't believe she was actually listening to me. She was staring at me like a deer in headlights, so I wasn't even sure if she could hear me. But now I knew she really was listening.

"Well, in other words," she said. "I've decided to lift your punishment. I did get a little carried away. It was wrong to be so harsh and I'm...sorry."

This was too good. My stone-cold aunt actually admitted that she was wrong and was apologizing. Someone call the Nola 38 action news. This was just too good.

"But I want you to understand why I did what I did," she continued.

I nodded. "Okay."

"I did what I did because...I thought it was best for you. I was only trying to protect you."

Protect me from what? I wanted to ask.

"I went overboard."

"It's okay, I forgive you." *Kind of,* I thought.

"But I don't want you to ever feel like we will never listen to you. Your uncle and I always will. We may not be your parents, but we are here for you. I promise that." She grabbed my uncle's hand, who gently squeezed it in return.

"I understand," I said. "And I'm sorry too for, you know...blowing up at you."

"Apology accepted. Now that we have cleared this up, why don't you go have fun with your friends today."

"Really? I can?"

"Yes you can. Just be careful and don't go near the French Quarter. That's still a rule."

"Yeah, sure, I promise, just thank you, thank you so much." I ran up and hugged her and did something I hadn't done since I was eight. I kissed her on the cheek. She smiled, which made me do the same. "I've gotta go call them and tell them we can hang out today." I ran up to my room to text them.

I opened a group message and selected them. *Guess wht? Punishment over, we can all hang out. Txt me if you can.*

I ran back downstairs, ate my breakfast, then waited anxiously by the phone. Within a few minutes it started to beep.

Sure I'm game, Max answered. I smiled.

Me 2, Maggie texted.

Oh that's wonderful. Count me in 2, Ava replied.

Excitement rose inside of me. "Where are you all planning on going?" my aunt asked.

"I'm not sure," I said. "I guess the park."

"Okay, just be careful."

"I will, promise." I went upstairs, brushed my teeth, then headed out the door. I texted Ava and Maggie to meet me by the end of Seventh Street then from there we'd go get Max. After we all met up, we decided to go to Audubon Park. Max wanted to go to City Park, but I wasn't walking all over New Orleans. About thirty minutes later, we walked through the entrance to Audubon Park.

A gardener was by the park sign attending to the flowers in the colorful flowerbed around it. The park was in abundance with park life. Some girls around our age were stretched out on beach towels trying to get tans. A few young men were throwing a football back and forth, women with strollers walked by with their babies as they slept inside them, safe from the heat.

And all around the park huge old oak trees stood, providing shade for anyone who might need it.

My friends and I found a shady spot under one of them and sat down. “This is nice,” Max said, putting his arms behind his back on the ground, supporting himself. “It’s not too hot just yet, and this tree makes it even better.”

“Why can’t it always be like this?” Ava asked.

“Because we are in the South,” Maggie said. “It’s supposed to be hot.”

“Yeah, but this is also Louisiana,” I said. “Wait about five minutes, the weather will change.” We all giggled a bit at the sound of the common Louisiana joke.

“So how did you get out of your punishment, Addie?” Maggie asked.

I froze. I didn’t want to tell them.

“I don’t know,” I said. “My aunt just decided that I had learned my lesson and let me off the hook.”

“What did you have to do exactly?” Ava asked.

“Clean the house and I couldn’t hang out with you guys, which I did by the way. So I guess with that in mind she figured I was good to go and here we are.” I gestured to the park.

“Well it’s a good thing,” Max said. “It is a beautiful day, even if it’s hot.”

We relaxed under the tree, just talking and enjoying our first week of summer vacation. As we sat there a faint breeze started to blow. I started a coughing fit as a familiar aroma filled the air. *No way,* I thought. *How?* It was the same as the one I smelled when we were on Canal Street. I started looking around, but I couldn’t find the source of it.

“Addie, what’s wrong?” Ava asked.

I turned to her. “Oh nothing. I just though I smelled some perfume.”

“I wore some today,” Maggie said. “It could be that.”

"It must be." I didn't want to tell them that I was smelling weird things again.

"We need to do something this weekend," Ava suddenly said.

"We've been through this, like what?" I asked.

Ava thought for a moment then perked up. "You know where I have always wanted to go but my parents won't let me?"

"Where?" Maggie asked.

A smirky smile that was so unlike Ava appeared on her face. "Bourbon Street," she finally said.

"Bourbon Street?!" Maggie exclaimed.

"Yeah."

"You want to go to Bourbon Street?" Max asked.

Ava nodded.

"Seriously?" I asked. "Why?"

"I don't know, I just do. I feel like we need to do something exciting this weekend since it's the first weekend of our summer vacation. We need to do something crazy and cool."

I looked back and forth between Max and Maggie. This was so unlike Ava. "Are you sure, Ava?" Max asked. "Bourbon is not really a place for teenagers. It's dirty, smelly, there's a lot of drunks, and crime."

"Not to mention we are under age," I said, dragging out the "under age" part.

"I just want to go, and I don't want to wait until I'm twenty-one. Come on, guys, it will be fun."

We all looked at each other, trying to process just what Ava had said. Her words seemed to be hanging out in the air as we all pondered what to say next. "I don't think we will even be allowed over there," Maggie said. "If someone figures out that we are teenagers I'm sure they will send us back home."

"Well then we'll just have to make ourselves look older," Ava said. "That's what makeup is for, right?"

"I don't know," Max said. "It sounds pretty risky, not to mention we'll be in so much trouble if we get caught."

"I'm all for sneaking out in the middle of the night if that's what we have to do," I said. The thought of it made my body twitch with excitement. "But going to Bourbon, that's a different story."

"Come on, guys. Don't you want to have fun this summer?"

We all looked at each other. "We'll go down there, have some fun, then come back before we are missed, simple," Ava said. "We don't have to go to any clubs or drink."

"There are a few dance clubs down there," Maggie said. "We could go for just a while."

"Seriously?" Max said. "You're considering it?"

"We can go there at night then come back," Ava said.

"Addie, what do you think about all of this?"

I let his question sink in. Part of me wanted to go out and have a little fun, but another part wanted to stay home and not risk it.

"I'm for it," Maggie said. "As long as we stay together and don't stay out too late."

"I am too," Ava said. "Of course I am."

I knew Max didn't want to go, so I was technically the deciding one. "I'm in," I finally said. "It'll be fun."

"Whoo," Ava said, clasping her hands together. "It's a plan then. Max, sorry but I think you've been outnumbered."

"Ugh," Max sighed. "We need more boys in this group."

"Looks like we are going to Bourbon Street," Maggie said. And a bad feeling inside of my stomach started to form.

CHAPTER FIVE
NIGHTMARE ON BOURBON STREET

When Saturday came, I asked my aunt and uncle if I could go over to Ava's for a sleepover. They said yes, and I started to pack my stuff. A few hours later, I was walking to Ava's house on the other side of Seventh Street close to Eighth Street. I walked up the white marble steps to the front door and knocked. Ava answered immediately.

"Hey," she said. "Ready for a great night?"

"You bet," I said, still feeling a bit uneasy about it, but I pushed the feelings aside.

I saw Maggie walking down the stairs, her face expressionless. "Hey, Mags," I said to her. "Ready for tonight?"

"As ready as I'll ever be," she replied.

"It's going to be fun," Ava squealed. We started walking up the stairs. "My mom and dad are going out later, and Avery is at a sleepover as well, so we should be able to pull this off." We all walked into Ava's room.

I set my stuff down on the floor then we all sat on Ava's bed. "So what's the plan?" Maggie asked.

"This," Ava said, getting a little closer to us. "My mom and dad are going to leave around six and won't be back until later. When they leave, we start getting ready. I've pulled together enough makeup for all of us to use and a few fashion magazines to go by."

She pointed to the pile of magazines on her desk. "Damn," I said. "That's a lot."

"Where's all the makeup?" Maggie asked.

"Over there," Ava said, pointing to her dresser. Three big bags were filled to the brim with all kinds of makeup, including fingernail polish. I looked at Maggie. She in turn looked at me, taking a deep breath.

"Jeez, what did you do? Rob a fashion show?" Maggie teased.

Ava just smiled. "I found a few makeup tricks in those magazines that can help us look a bit older. But not too old."

"How are we going to dress?" Maggie asked. "I doubt our normal clothes would get us anywhere on that street."

"I have a few things that you two can borrow. We are going to dress cool but not like a slut or anything."

"Good, I don't want some sleazy old drunk to think I'm a hooker or something," Maggie said.

I agreed.

"Well that seems to be it. All we have to do is wait for my parents to leave, and then we can get ready."

A few hours later, we heard Mrs. Chappell's voice as she came into her daughter's room. "Hey girls," she said, smiling.

"Hey, Mrs. Chappell," Maggie and I both said.

She nodded to us. "Your father and I are leaving now, and we won't be back until late."

"Okay," Ava said, smiling, not showing the slightest hint of our plans for tonight.

"You girls have fun, don't stay up too late, though."

"We won't. We are just going to read a few magazines and do our makeup. Typical girl stuff."

Mrs. Chappell smiled. "Okay then, I'll see you later." Blowing a kiss to her daughter, Mrs. Chappell left. We all ran to Ava's bedroom window and watched them pull out of the driveway and down the street, their car disappearing in the night.

Ava breathed a sigh of relief. "That went well," she said. "I was afraid that she was going to suspect something with all of those magazines and makeup."

"You covered that up good," Maggie said. "Too good."

Very, I thought.

"Okay, well now let's get down to business. Let's figure out what we are going to wear then do our makeup. I'll text Max and tell him that we are getting ready. This is so exciting," Ava squealed. I was starting to pick up on her excitement. I didn't want to feel that way, but I couldn't help it. It was starting to take over my body. There's just something about sneaking out of the house knowing you'll get caught and going to have the time of your life.

It just felt like such a rush.

Ava, Maggie, and I walked over to Ava's closet and started pulling out clothes. After what seemed like forever, we narrowed it down to what we thought would be appropriate to wear, something that was cool but not trashy.

Finally after what seemed like forever, Ava found something for herself. She paired a red three-quarter-sleeve V-neck shirt with a tight black skirt leftover from last Halloween when she was some kind of witch. She tucked the shirt into the skirt then paired it with some ebony black stockings.

"Well," she said, turning to Maggie and me. "How do I look?"

"Awesome," I said. "The skirt is not too short either, and the shirt is not that low cut. It's perfect. Eye catching but not anything trashy." And it was. The skirt only came up about an inch past her knee, and the shirt was cut low but not low enough to see her chest.

"Good, that's what I wanted. Now it's time for you two."

I went through Ava's clothes and mine, trying to find something cool but not trashy. I finally settled on a pair of skinny jeans, a sky blue halter top, and to top it all off I put a long gold, layered necklace on along with some gold bangles and rings.

"How do I look?" I asked, striking a pose.

"Like you always do," Ava said. "Just a little more blinged out."

"What is up with you and halter tops?" Maggie asked.

"Nothing," I said. "I just thought it looked good."

"Well it does. You look great, you really do. By the time we fix your hair and makeup you won't look like yourself anymore."

I gulped at the sound of that.

"Okay, Mags," Ava said, turning to her. "Now it's your turn."

"Great," Maggie said.

While Ava and Maggie tried to match clothes, I glanced out the window. Night had completely fallen, and the moon was casting shadows on the front lawn. An eerie feeling started to creep inside of me. I shook a little then turned back to my friends.

"Ta da," Ava said, gesturing to Maggie. "What do you think, Addie?"

I looked at Maggie, who was now wearing a short strapless dress with a cropped jacket, and stockings like Ava. "Whoa," I said. "That looks so good on you, Maggie."

"Thanks, I hate it," she said.

"Why?" Ava pouted.

"Because this is not really my style. The length is good but...I don't know. Strapless, really?"

"You've got a jacket, it's fine. You look good, and that's what matters. Okay, let's do hair and makeup then head out." Ava pulled out the magazines and walked over to her vanity. "Who's first?" Maggie and I both looked at each other. "Addie," Ava said. I rolled my eyes then walked over and sat down in the chair. Ava opened one of the magazines. "I found a look in here that I think will suit you perfectly," Ava said. "It's strictly for blondes."

Thirty minutes later, I opened my eyes to my new face.

I slightly jumped when I saw my refection in the mirror. Ava had contoured my face, brought out my cheekbones, covered the circles under my eyes, put mascara on them, and even did that smokey eye look that I never thought I would be able to pull off. My lips were painted a mocha color, and it seemed to just pull the whole look together. "Wow," I said. "Is that me?"

"Yes, it's you," Ava said, almost laughing. "See what a bit of difference a little makeup can do."

"It makes you look older too," Maggie said. "As in like eighteen or nineteen."

"Now for hair," Ava said. She pulled out her curling iron and went to work. A few minutes later, my hair was curlier than ever. She made it look longer and thicker with just a simple curling iron.

"Now that is amazing," I said. Ava smiled.

"You need to start acting more like a girl, Addie," she joked. Maggie took my spot, and I waited on the bed. Something outside caught my eye.

A pair of red glowing eyes were staring at me.

I felt panic rise in my chest. *No,* I thought. *Not here.* I quickly ran over to the window. "Addie," Maggie said. I looked outside and saw a human-type figure was standing right on Ava's front lawn by the big willow tree. I gripped the white windowsill as panic and fear set in once again.

"Addie, what's wrong?" Maggie asked. I blinked my eyes a few times then finally spoke.

"There's...there's," I stuttered. I couldn't hold it back anymore. I had to tell them. "There's this figure outside with..." I trailed off when suddenly there was nothing there anymore.

"A figure?" Ava asked. "What figure?"

"Nothing," I said, stepping away from the window. "Just seeing things again. Must be the mascara."

"Sure it is," Maggie said. Ava went back to Maggie's hair and makeup. She had chosen to go darker with Maggie's lips and eyes. She filled in her eyebrows like she did mine. The whole look went well with her fair skin.

"Great job, Ava," I said, looking at Maggie, who really didn't look like herself. "You look great, Maggie."

"Thanks," she said, twisting her newly curled hair. "I don't feel like myself, but I guess that's okay."

"It's okay to try and be someone else every now and then," Ava said, sitting at her vanity. She did her own hair and makeup with a tiny help from Maggie. Ava chose a dark red lipstick to go with her look, which really made her look older. After she was finished, we took a look at ourselves in the mirror. "I think we look great," Ava said. "Hot even."

"Let's not go that far," Maggie said.

I laughed. I put a pair of tan wedges on, Ava put on some black ankle boots, and Maggie put on some black high heels. "Okay, I think we are ready," Ava said. "Let's go." We walked down the stairs and out of the house.

We met Max at the corner of St. Charles Avenue a few minutes later. "Wow," he said, staring at us. "You girls look amazing. Van and Vince would be so jealous of me right now."

"Yeah right," I said.

"I'm serious. You guys really do look good. I'll have to be watching you. Make sure that no one steals you away."

"That'll be the day," Maggie said.

We started to walk down St. Charles Avenue. From there we crossed over to Canal Street and went right on into Bourbon. The city street was already alive with people socializing, drinking, and partying.

"Wow," I said, turning my head this way and that, trying to take it all in. Bar, restaurant, and dance club signs were glowing, illuminating the street, making it look like a light show.

"This is so cool," Max said. "My cousin painted me a different picture of it."

"He was probably farther down," Ava said. "That's where the craziness really happens."

"Really? 'Cause it looks like there's some craziness already happening here," Maggie said, inconspicuously pointing to some women who were drunk off their asses, stumbling into the street and bumping into people.

"Farther down is worst, so I've heard. That's why I said we should just stick to the upper part. It's better."

A mixture of jazz, blues, and pop music filled the street as we started to venture just a bit farther down. People were dancing and still drinking. Some were dining in the restaurants. The street looked bigger at night for some reason. "I didn't realize how big Bourbon Street is," I said. "It's huge and long."

"Tell me about it," Maggie said. "If I had known this then I would have worn better shoes."

In a restaurant on the side of the street we were on, a couple was eating. I could see them in the big restaurant window. I stopped a minute to watch them, thinking about my aunt and uncle. *Maybe*

I should tell them to go out one night, I thought. *In payment for my bad behavior.* Through the music and crowd I heard something. I focused my hearing on it again. It sounded like a growl. Then right where I was looking at the couple the eyes appeared.

I quickly turned around but saw nothing.

Not in the streets, not across it, nowhere. All I could see where happy normal people, just enjoying another great night on Bourbon Street, New Orleans.

I caught up to my friends, who were looking at this club. "Hey," I said, glancing at the club. "Club De La Roux," I said, reading the neon sign. "Do you guys want to go in?"

"Can we?" Max asked. "It's not a strip club, is it? My parents would kill me if they found out I went to a strip club."

"It's not," Maggie said. "If it was then we'd be seeing half naked women strolling around."

"You guys, it's a dance club, look." Ava pointed to the sign and right underneath it that read *dance club.*

"Alright then," Max said. "Let's go, it's an eighteen and older club." Max started to walk inside the club. Lights illuminated from every aspect of the club. A mix of pop, hip-hop, and dance was playing. People were out on the huge floor dancing wildly. Gyrating and twerking all around each other. Close to the ceiling was a balcony that held a DJ.

My friends and I watched for a few minutes before we walked up to the bouncer. He took one look at us then let us enter the dance floor.

"We got in!" Ava yelled over the music, the blue lights making her red hair look mystical.

"Great," I said. "Let's go dance!"

"Ya'll go," Max said. "I'm not much of a dancer."

"Come on, Max," Ava said. "We came here to have fun, now let's go have it."

"Okay, I can't win with you guys anyway."

"No you can't." I grabbed his hand along with Ava's, who grabbed Maggie's, then we made our way through the thick crowd. I started dancing as best as I could close to my friends, who looked like they could dance as well as I could. And by that, I mean we couldn't. Still we jumped up and down, swung our limbs, and just tried to make it look we knew what we were doing.

At least the club DJ was playing a good selection of music. From Jessie J, to Maroon 5, even Justin Bieber. My favorite song came on, and I started to dance even more. I tilted my head, moved my hips. I let the beat of the music take me away. It pulsated through my body like blood. Suddenly I wasn't even aware of my surroundings, just that I was dancing.

I somehow got away from my friends, but I didn't care. In that moment I didn't care about the world around me. I jumped up and down, threw my arms up into the air, and spun around, letting my hair flow all around me. It was energetic. I felt alive. I felt someone grab me from behind, and I turned around. A tall dark-haired guy stood there smiling at me.

"Want to dance?" he asked.

I looked him over, and without even thinking I said, "Yes." His smile got bigger.

I held onto his back as we danced together. A few times he spun me around. We laughed as we danced. It was fun. When the beat slowed down just a bit, he put his hands on my hips. I froze. The reality hit me. This guy had to be at least in his twenties. At least twenty-five, whereas I was merely sixteen. He's way too old for me. And I didn't want to end up on the six o'clock news as another horny teenager getting in trouble with an older guy. No matter how hot.

"I'm sorry," I said to him.

"What's wrong?" he asked.

"I think we need to stop now."

"Why? It'll pick back up. That DJ hardly ever plays any slow songs."

"It's not that, I just...I just think we need to stop. I need to find my friends." I tried to pull away, but he held me closer.

"Don't go," he said with his face inches from mine. My heart was beating so fast I could barely breathe. Fear started to rise in me, and I found myself wanting Van and Vince with me right now. *Max, Ava, Maggie,* I called in my head. *Help!*

I tried to wiggle free from his grip. "Look, I really need to go," I said. "It's getting late, and I need to find my friends."

"Oh really," he said. "What's the rush? Gotta work in the morning?"

"No, I don't work. I'm still in school."

"So you're what, sixteen?"

"Yes."

"Oh jail bait, wonderful. I guess you should be getting along then. Don't wanna miss curfew, little baby."

"I'm not a baby, and I don't have a curfew," I snapped.

"Okay, sorry, don't need to get all bitchy all of sudden." The more he talked, the angrier I got. "Go," he said in a light tone. "Find your friends."

"Thank you." I pushed him back just a bit. Before I could get a good foot in front of me, I felt him grab my arm and hold me steady.

"Hurry home, Addie, little girls like you shouldn't be out in a place like this when the demons come," he whispered in my ear. My voice caught in my throat. I didn't know what to say. He said it so low I didn't even think he said it, but he had.

I turned around to see no one standing behind me.

I looked around the club. No one saw what happened or even cared. They just continued to dance the night away. I pulled my phone out and saw that it was close to eleven. We needed to get home like now. I started looking for my friends. Suddenly my vision blurred, and my head throbbed in pain. I saw five big guys coming towards me. They got closer and closer until they were close enough to touch me.

All five looked at me hungrily, their red eyes burrowing into me as they pounced.

"AHHHHH!!!!!" I screamed.

Just about everyone in the club stopped to look at me. Apparently I had my eyes closed. I looked around but didn't see the five guys or their red eyes. I felt my face get hot with embarrassment then pushed my way through the crowd to find my friends. I found them sitting at the bar. "We have to go," I told them.

"What?" Ava asked, turning in her barstool. "What are you talking about? We just got here."

"No we didn't. We've been here for almost two hours. It's time to go."

"Addie, are you okay?" Maggie asked. "You look pale."

"How can you tell with all of these lights in here?"

"Believe me, I can."

I needed to convince them. We had to get out of here. I turned around when I felt someone's eyes on my back. The guy I was dancing with before was staring right at me. His words played back in my head and ran chills down my spine. Tears filled my eyes. "You guys," I wailed. "We've got to get out of here like now please."

"Addie, calm down," Maggie said. "What's wrong? Did something happen?"

"No it's just...we need to get out of here like now, our lives might even depend on it."

"What are you talking about...? Wait was that you who screamed a while ago?" Max asked. I didn't answer. "Okay guys," Max said, taking a breath. "You've seen Bourbon Street, now let's go." We hurried out of the club. We started walking down the street. I was ahead of everyone. My shoes clicked as my pace quickened.

What did he mean by "when the demons come?" It didn't make any sense.

On the rooftops I swore that I could hear something. It sounded like someone jumping. I glanced up just for a second. "Um, Addie," I heard Max say.

"What?" I asked, irritated.

"Are you sure that we are going the right way?"

"Of course I'm sure. In fact we should be on Canal Street right about..." I stopped when I didn't see Canal Street. "Where the hell is Canal Street?" I asked.

"We went the wrong way," Ava said. "This is downtown Bourbon."

"The bad part," Maggie put in.

"Okay, then we will just go back," I said. There was hardly anyone on this street. When we turned around two guys approached us. "Ah," we all said.

"Where are you kids heading this late in the night, huh?" one asked as he sauntered over to us.

"No...nowhere," I said. "We are just trying to get home. We've had enough fun for the night." My friends nodded.

"I'm sure you have," the man said. "But I think you guys can stay around for a little more fun."

From behind us another man hissed, showing two rows of sharp teeth. We jumped then cowered back. "Leave us alone,"

Max said. "Now!"

"Tough kid, he's mine," the first man who spoke to us said.

"No, he's not," Ava said. "Just let us go please." The man looked at Ava as three more men approached us. I started to shake. We had all been pushed together in a huddle. They had us surrounded, and there was no way we could escape. To make matters worse, no one was passing by. That means no one saw us or the men. As the lights shown on their faces, I noticed something that made me completely terrified.

They all had red eyes.

"Get them," the man yelled.

Four out of the five started to come after us. I heard Ava scream as one picked her up. "Ava!" I yelled. But one was coming for me. He bared the same sharp rows of teeth as the others. He ran towards me, and I dodged him. He ran into the nearby wall, making a huge crack in it. I didn't see Max, Ava, or Maggie, but I could hear Ava screaming. Suddenly there was a bright light and all the men screamed.

"Damn it, they found us," one said. "Come on, let's go, they'll be here soon." They left.

I ran over to Max and Maggie. "Are you two okay?" I asked.

"Yeah," they both said.

"But where's Ava?" Max asked. We looked around and found her lying on the corner of the street.

"Ava!" I yelled, running over to her. I rolled her over on her side. She had holes in her neck and blood everywhere. "It's okay, it's okay," I said, stroking her hair as she started to shake. I heard voices and thought it was the men coming back.

"Hey," someone said. "Are you all right?"

"Call an ambulance!" I yelled. "My friend is hurt!"

The guy nodded then pulled out a cell phone.

I turned back to Ava. “It’s okay,” I said, tears filling my eyes. “You are going to be okay. The ambulance is going to get here, they are going to take you to the hospital, and you are going to be okay.”

She coughed and spit up blood. I put my hand over hers. It was a cold as ice. Ava started to roll her head over to the side. “Hey, wait,” I said. “Look at me, Ava, look at me,” but she wouldn’t. I could see past the makeup that she was getting paler and paler, and her hands were growing colder. Soon she closed her eyes and breathed her last breath. In the distance I could hear the ambulance approaching, but they would be too late.

CHAPTER SIX
A LOVE LOST

Sirens filled the air around us from the police cars and the two ambulances. I sat in the back of one of them getting myself checked over while Max and Maggie talked to the police, and while poor Ava lay dead on the ground just a few feet away. Crime scene investigators were everywhere, taking pictures, looking for evidence, and talking to eyewitnesses. Just like they do on TV. But this was far from play. This was reality.

A reality that I never thought I would be in.

Through hazy eyes I took it all in, trying to somehow convince myself that it all wasn't real and that it was just a bad dream. I wasn't doing a very good job of it. I couldn't, knowing what I had just witnessed.

After the paramedics finished examining me, a woman dressed in a police uniform approached me. Her sandy blonde hair was pulled tightly back into a ponytail. She looked like the type of cop who didn't take any shit from anyone. Criminals and regular people. I felt intimidated just looking at her.

"Excuse me," she said. "Are you Addie?"

"Yes I am," I said, barely looking at her.

"My name is Officer Demouchet, I'm from the New Orleans Police Department. I need to ask you a couple of questions about what happened."

Do you have too? I asked in my head. "Okay." I nodded.

"These men that attacked you, have you ever seen them before?"

"No, why would I?"

"Just a routine question." She smiled then wrote something down. "Did these men say anything to you? Like if they were going to rob you or hurt you?"

Tough kid, he's mine. I thought about what the main guy said when Max stood up to him. But I didn't know if I should tell her that. "One of them did say something to my friend Max." I decided that it could be useful.

"What did he say?" Officer Demouchet asked.

"He said 'tough kid, he's mine' when Max stood up to him. And before that, he asked us 'Where are you kids heading this late in the night, huh?'"

She started writing again. "How many were there?" she asked.

"Six," I said, relaying them in my head. "Two approached us first. A third came from behind us, then three others came later just before the attack."

"Can you remember what they looked like?"

I couldn't really remember what they looked like. I tried my hardest. "They were dressed normally," I said. "Just casual. You know, jeans, T-shirt, sneakers. Nothing out of the ordinary."

"Can you remember any facial details?"

I thought back to the men. "The first man who approached us was older. He had to be at least in his forties. The others were younger. Twenties and maybe thirties if I had to guess." I was surprised at how much I could remember. *They also had red eyes and rows of sharp teeth,* I wanted to say, but I knew I couldn't.

"I don't know what hair color or skin color they were," I told her before she asked. "It was too dark, and there were too many."

"That's okay," she said. "My partner talked to your friends. I'll see if they know anything." I shook my head, wanting her to leave so I could rest my eyes, and my aching body. "I'll let you rest now. Thanks for all your help. If you remember anything else, please give me a call." She handed me a card.

"Okay," I said. "I will." No I wouldn't.

She gave a small smile then walked off. Out of the corner of my eye I saw a man and woman running to me.

"Addie."

I looked up and saw my aunt and uncle coming towards me.

"Aunt Wanda, Uncle Jeff," I said, whining for them. *Oh I'm in deep shit now*, I thought. There was no way they were going to let me off the hook for this. I was never going to see the light of day again, and for once I didn't blame them. It was stupid sneaking off in the night with them gone, not knowing where we were. What were we thinking?

As they came to me I prepared for the fallout.

"Aunt Wanda, I'm so, so, so sorry," I sobbed, tears running down my cheeks. "I didn't mean...we didn't...we didn't want this to happen...please..." My aunt put her arms around me and held me to her. I did the same thing and let all of my anger and frustration out.

"It's okay, it's okay," she said. "We're here now."

I buried my head into her chest. When I calmed down a bit I looked over her shoulder and saw two paramedics and a coroner go past us, pushing a gurney with a body bag on it. I knew who was in that bag, and it only made me get upset again looking at it. I started sobbing louder again. I could feel people staring at me. My aunt held me tighter, so did my uncle.

"Addie," my aunt said, looking at me. "Tell us what happened."

I didn't even know where to begin, so I began where I thought was a necessary start. I began with our plans a few days ago. I told her Ava wanted to do the Bourbon Street, how she convinced us, which didn't take that much to do. I told her about us sneaking out, coming here, going to the dance club, trying to leave, my mistake of leading them the wrong way, then the men attacking us.

"We didn't know this was going to happen," I wailed. "We were trying to be careful. I guess we weren't careful enough."

"Sweetie, it's not your fault," my aunt said, petting my hair. "It's not, believe me."

I gulped then looked at her. "It feels like it, though. We should have talked her out of it. Wait...how did you know I was here?"

They looked back and forth between each other. "A friend told us," Uncle Jeff said. "He works down here. He said that there was an accident on Bourbon and when he went to check it out he saw you kids here."

"Oh," I said. Good for him then.

I looked around at the scene of the crime. A skinny girl with the CSI walked over to where Ava's body had been and took a sample of the blood. I saw her look up to the rooftops almost like she was looking or waiting for someone. I could even sense a presence that I couldn't see but I could feel. There was someone else here watching, waiting, I was sure of it.

Later, we were all sitting down at Ava's house with her parents and sister, who had come home from her sleepover when she found out what happened. Max and his mom, my aunt and uncle, and Maggie's aunt, who was staying with her while her parents are out of town. Mr. Chappell paced the living room floor, face red and eyes puffy from crying. Mrs. Chappell was on the couch holding Avery, who had her head buried in her mom's chest.

Her screams were still ringing in my ear from when she arrived at the scene and saw her older sister in a body bag. I glanced over at Max and his mom, who were sitting on another couch. Miss

Rivera did not look happy, but she had her hand on her son's leg, reassuring him. Maggie sat on the love seat with her aunt, whose face was as cold as stone. No wonder Maggie couldn't stand her sometimes. And she complained about my attitude towards *my* aunt.

After a few moments, Mr. Chappell spoke. "How...?" he started. "Why...did this happen? Why?" He started to cry then he stopped. "Why would you kids do something so dangerous and reckless in the first place?" His voice rose with anger.

"Richard," his wife said. "It's not their fault. These things happen..."

"Don't start with that. This is not one of those situations. This could have been prevented. Just what in the world were you kids thinking?"

"We weren't, I guess," Max said. "None of us were."

"You should have protected my daughter," Mr. Chappell said, looking straight at Max. "You should have..."

"I'm going to stop you right there, Mr. Chappell," Miss Rivera said in a calm voice. "I know how hard this is for you, believe me, I know, but I don't think shouting and pointing the blame on these kids is going to solve anything."

Mr. Chappell's face relaxed a bit.

"It was reckless on their part," she said. "Especially without consulting us about it, but don't you think that this is just as bad for them as it is for you?"

Mr. Chappell thought for a moment. "I guess you are right," he said. "I'm so sorry, kids." We nodded. In a way I think we deserved it. Me more than anyone. If I had just gone the other way then Ava...

"Why did you guys go?" Avery asked.

Max, Maggie, and I looked at each other. "It was Ava's idea," Maggie said. "Believe it or not. She wanted to go so bad so she convinced us that we would just go down there, dance a bit, have a good time, then come back before you guys got home." Maggie paused. "Guess we weren't quick enough." Tears filled her eyes.

Mrs. Chappell started to cry along with Avery.

Soon everyone was in tears. I tried to stay strong, but I finally broke. I sat there with my aunt and uncle as I cried my eyes out once again, praying that the night would finally just end.

When I got home I went straight for my room then walked into my bathroom. I flipped the light on and looked at my face in the mirror. The mascara had run down my face, my eyeliner was smudged, and I looked like a raccoon. My hair was still in loose waves around my shoulders, but it was a little frizzed. I rested my hands on the bathroom counter, taking slow deep breaths trying to soothe myself.

I needed to wash up and get ready for bed, but I didn't want to ruin what Ava had done to my face. The last piece of work that she had done. I grabbed the soap, hesitantly splashed some water over it, and started washing my face. After that, I combed my hair, changed into my pajamas, and crawled into bed. I curled myself up into a ball, hugging my pillow tightly.

I couldn't go to sleep. Thoughts and images of what happened kept playing around in my head like a never-ending orchestra. I tossed and I turned. Finally, sleepiness came over me, and I was able to fall asleep.

A week later, we had Ava's funeral. It was a dreary day to celebrate the end of a life. A good life, a wonderful life to a wonderful person. I walked with Max and Maggie as we made our way inside the cemetery. A few of our classmates had gathered in a small group, some crying, others just standing around. We joined them and the service began.

"We are gathered here today to honor this young girl," the priest began. "A young girl who was taken from us too soon and that she may rest in peace..."

I blocked out there. I didn't want to hear what he had to say. He didn't even know Ava, not like the rest of us. Who was he to say anything about her when Max, Maggie, and I have known her since kindergarten?

"Would any of her friends like to say a few words?" the priest asked. I looked around.

"I would," Max said. The priest moved out of his way. Max stood in front of the casket and looked around at the people.

"I just wanted to say on Ava's behalf that she was one of the best friends I could ever ask for," he said. "She was always there when I needed her...no matter what." His voice stuttered and broke with every word. "She was always very special to me. That night when we were attacked I would have done anything to help her, I guess I just wasn't strong enough to save her." Tears came to my eyes.

What Max said next shocked everyone and almost brought me to my knees. "I loved her," he said. "More than anyone could ever know. More than a friend, more than anything...and now she'll never know. That's all I have to say." He came and stood by us.

Tears streamed down my face along with Maggie's and Avery's. Maggie hugged Max. I looked at him. I never knew he felt that way about Ava. I saw the signs, but I thought they were just good friends. I wondered if she felt the same way too. Now we'd never know. Maggie and I said a few words as best as we could then we said goodbye to our best friend.

When the service was over Van and Vince came up to me.

"Hey," Vince said. His eyes were red.

"Hey," I said in a weak voice.

"How are you holding up?"

"Okay, I guess," I lied. "What about you?"

"I'll be fine, we'll both be fine." He looked at Van, who looked mad as hell. His face was tense and he just stared at nothing. I felt so bad for him. For all of us. "Ava was a good friend," Vince said. "With a good family and great friends and an even greater life. We'll all miss her."

"Yes we will. It's just that night, I can't help but think if I had done something different..."

"Hey..." he wrapped me up in his strong arms, and I started to cry right into his black suit. "You can't think like that, Addie," he whispered. "What happened, happened. I'm sorry, but you can't change that. It's not your fault." He pulled away but kept his hands on my arms.

"These things happen?" I asked, finishing for him.

"Unfortunately, yes they do, and it's not right, and it's not fair, but what can we do about it?" I sniffled.

"Just pray that the cops find those sons of bitches who did that to her and make them pay," Van said suddenly. "They will and you know it."

I looked back and forth between both of them. "You're right," I said to them. "You're both right."

All three of us hugged.

They left and I went to find Maggie and Max. I saw Maggie

talking with a few girls from our school. They left when I approached her. "You okay?" I asked.

"I'm fine." She wiped a tear away. "I don't think Max is, though." She pointed to where he stood by Ava's freshly dug grave. He looked so poor and pitiful, sad too, like a lost puppy. I knew that he had been knocked down by all of this, we all had, but I bet he was taking it the worst.

"Let's go over there," I said to Maggie. She nodded and we went over by Max.

He stared down at the grave, a blank expression on his face. Maggie stood by his right side, and I stood on his left. A single tear ran down his face. He quickly wiped it away. "Max," I said in a low gentle voice. "You okay?"

He looked at me and gave a small smile. "I will be," he said, his voice still shaking. "I guess I will be." My heart hurt for him. I couldn't imagine having feelings for someone and never being able to tell them how I really felt.

I put my hand on Max's shoulder. He looked at me. "I think..." I started. I took in a breath, trying not to cry. "I know she would have felt the same about you."

Tears started to run down Max's face, but he didn't try to wipe them away. "Thanks," he said. I hugged him. After that, I knelt down in front of Ava's head stone. Two angels had been carved by her name. I've never been much of a religious type, but I hoped that she was with them. She was too good of a person not to be.

My vision went past the headstone and farther back towards the cemetery, where I saw what I swore had to be the guy I was dancing with at the club the other night. I looked harder, and yes it was him. Standing far away in the background where no one could see him. No one but me, that is. I bet anything I own that he had something to do with her death. I didn't know how, but I just had a creeping feeling about it.

What he said to me was not a normal thing to say, and he didn't look like the kind of guy who spoke that way for no apparent reason. He was dead serious when he whispered that in my ear. I shook at the thought of it. I glared at him, and he did the same back. I didn't see a pair of red eyes on him, and that made me feel better. Still something was just...*off* about him.

Besides, who comes to a cemetery where a funeral is being held and just stands in the background like a creeper?

"What is it, Addie?" Maggie asked.

I decided to come clean. They needed to know. "See that guy over there?" I said, pointing across the cemetery to where he was standing.

"Yeah," she and Max said. "What about him?" Max asked.

"The night we went to Bourbon I danced with him at the club. After a while, he wouldn't let me go. I finally got away from him, but he said something to me after."

"What did he say?" Maggie asked.

I turned to look at them. "He said, 'Hurry home, Addie, little girls like you shouldn't be out in a place like this when the demons come.'"

"What?!" Max said.

"He said that to you?" Maggie asked.

"Yeah he did," I said. "Right when I went to walk off. Then he just disappeared."

"What do you think it means?" Max asked.

I scoffed. "Nothing, Max," I said. "It can't mean anything, right?"

"Addie, it has to. I mean, he says that then minutes later Ava ends up dead. It's like he knew something was going to happen."

"Maybe."

"He's watching us," Maggie said.

I turned to look back at him. "Yes he is," I said. "Come on. Let's go." I got up from the grave and started to walk off. As the wind blew I thought I heard what sounded like a whisper in it. I turned around, but there was no one there. Just Ava's silent grave.

"Goodbye, Ava," I whispered. "I'm sorry."

CHAPTER SEVEN
MOVING ON

News had spread all over Louisiana about Ava's death. I couldn't turn on the TV without seeing something about it. "Teen Girl Killed on Bourbon Street: No Leads on the Killer," read a newspaper article. "Terror in the Streets—Sixteen-year-old girl killed on Bourbon Street. Killer not yet found." The articles were spread out in front of me on the kitchen counter. They hardly even mentioned Ava's name. One had all of us in it, even a picture of Bourbon that night.

It was a terrible night in New Orleans on Bourbon Street the Saturday night before last as a sixteen-year-old-girl was murdered right in the streets, I read.

Local teen Ava Chappell was out with her friends Max Rivera, Maggie Gill, and Addie François that night when they were approached by two men. The men teased and taunted them, even threatened them. The four teens tried to get the men to leave them alone, which only made things worse. "One even hissed at us," Max Rivera recounted in a police interview. Four more men approached then attacked.

Addie, Max, and Maggie were able to get away, but Ava was not so lucky. Her throat had been slashed and she had been stabbed. By the time an ambulance arrived it was too late. People from a nearby bar heard the commotion but didn't react, which is questionable as far as the New Orleans police are concerned.

So far the police have no leads.

"We are doing everything we can to find these men," Chief Officer Demouchet said. "We are working around the clock to keep our streets safe."

For anyone who goes out anywhere in New Orleans, remember to be safe.

When I finished the article I slammed it down on the counter. I couldn't believe there were people who heard what was going on but they didn't even think to help us. I just couldn't believe that. *Southern hospitality,* I thought. *Yeah right.* I read more articles that went a little more detailed about what happened that night, and even a parenting one criticizing our parents about letting us go. Like it was their fault.

I saw my aunt come into the room. "Please stop reading that," she said. "It's not good for you."

I looked up at her from the article I was reading. "I can't," I said with tears in my eyes. "I...I...I have to see if there is any news on catching her killers." My aunt looked at me with a sympathetic look. One that I didn't see too often. My aunt and uncle, Ava's parents, Max's mom, and Maggie's parents all got together and decided that we should not be punished for what we planned. They figured what had happened was enough of a lesson for us.

I was glad, because I couldn't take it if they decided to punish us. Ava's death was punishment enough.

I flipped through more articles, but none had anything that I hadn't read already. I pushed them aside then went into the living room and sat on the couch. I turned on the TV and saw the news on. The newscasters were talking about what happened on Bourbon and were comparing it to what has happened in recent years and months.

They talked about old cases, how some were still open and how some were similar. It was all too much for me and I started to cry. I heard my aunt walk over to me. She sat down on the couch and hugged me as I sobbed. "It's okay, Addie, it's okay," she soothed. I cried even louder. I did that for a while then finally calmed down.

"That's why you don't need to watch this," my aunt said, turning the TV off. "Or read any of the articles. It's not healthy for you."

"I know," I said, still sobbing a bit. "I'm sorry, it's just, I have to see if there's a break in the case. It'll be in the newspaper, right?"

"You let me worry about that. I can find out if there is any change anywhere."

"How?" I looked down.

"I have my sources," was all she said.

More secrets, I thought.

More and more. I doubted my uncle really had a friend who saw us on Bourbon that night. If he did, why didn't he tell him where we were in the first place? And if they were friends, how come I'd never met him? Something just wasn't adding up, and it hadn't for a while. I couldn't take it. I felt like I was going to explode, but I didn't want to take it out on my aunt. We were getting along okay despite what's been going on, and I didn't want to ruin it. Besides, she might start going all hard-ass dictator again.

I pulled back from my aunt.

"What's wrong?" she asked.

"Nothing," I said, blinking tears out of my eyes. "I just have to go."

"Go? Go where?"

"I don't know." I could feel my anger rising, but I kept it under control. I got up from the couch and started walking towards the door. "I'm sorry," I said, turning back to my aunt. "This, this is all too much. I need to go. I need to get out of the house and just go... clear my head or something."

"Addie," she said, stepping towards me.

"I'm sorry." My voice broke. "I just...I just have to go." I opened the door and ran out of the house. I ran down Seventh Street towards Ava's house. In the huge bay window I could see her parents and sister. They were sitting at the family table, still upset over Ava. Mrs. Chappell hugged Avery as she started to cry. Soon they were all hugging each other and crying. It was a heartbreaking sight.

Tears rolled down my face.

I brushed them away then started back down the street. I went down St. Charles Avenue. From there I went to Magazine Street, then on to Canal. It was as busy as ever. I guess even with the news of six murderers loose on the streets, it wasn't stopping people from shopping and enjoying their days. *New Orleans' pride.*

I walked through the crowds of people, passed the theaters, restaurants, and boutiques, then turned around and walked back again. I needed to clear my head. I probably looked like a crazy person doing that over and over again, but I didn't care. I felt pent up and mad as hell. I stopped and looked at the people around me. If someone was in trouble right now would they help the person in need? Or would they just let them suffer?

I didn't know why it bothered me so much that no one helped us. Maybe because it should. Maybe because if a normal person thought that someone was in trouble the humane thing to do would be to help, right? Also if someone did think that something fishy was going on, it might have saved us all and Ava wouldn't be dead.

I tried not to think that way. I tried clearing my head once again by walking up and down Canal Street. I stopped when I heard a whisper. It wasn't a whisper from any of the people passing by. Just a sound, but I knew it was there. Maybe it was only meant for me to hear. I started following the sound of the whisper. I followed the whisper down an alleyway in between Canal and Magazine Street.

I walked down the alleyway, only to let it lead me to a dead end.

Still I could hear it, but only a little. As I focused my hearing it was starting to become clearer. It was starting to sound more like a human voice in a way. Just not as clear. What could make a sound like that but still sound human? A ghost? Maybe. Or worse, a demon. *No, it's not possible,* I thought. *Those don't exist.*

Suddenly, I heard footsteps behind me. I froze where I stood. I could hear the footsteps getting closer and closer. I didn't hear a voice, which made me even more scared. I balled my fists, ready for a fight. I turned around and... "Ahhhh," I said.

"Ahhhh," Max and Maggie said, jumping.

"Ugh, what the hell, you two? You scared me to death." I was very surprised to see them. We hadn't spoken since Ava's funeral almost two weeks ago. It felt weird seeing them in front of me. It's like I was seeing them for the first time.

"Sorry," Maggie said. "We didn't mean to."

"Next time say something before you sneak up on someone like that. You almost gave me a heart attack."

"Sorry," Max said. "We really didn't mean to scare you."

"Plus we were saying something. We were calling you."

"Really?" I didn't hear them. "I had no idea."

"You seemed really focused on something," Max said. "What was it?"

Yeah, like I was going to tell them that I was hearing voices. They were really going to think I was crazy. "Nothing," I said. "I thought I heard something and it led me to here."

"What did it sound like?" Maggie asked.

"I thought I heard someone say my name. Turns out it was nothing."

"It could have been that guy from the club the other night," Max said. "You know, the one that you danced with?"

"Yes I know, Max, thank you for reminding me," I said sharply. I didn't know why I was being so harsh. I just felt so irritated all of a sudden. Must have been getting close to that time of the month, or maybe it was just me.

Max looked like a kicked puppy after I said that. "Sorry," he said in a low voice.

"It's okay. I'm just in a very bad mood. Forgive me."

"You don't have to apologize," Maggie said. "We've both been in moods today." I just noticed their red eyes. They also look like they hadn't slept in a while.

"You guys can't sleep either?" I asked.

"Nope," Max said. "Not since that night."

"It's hard," Maggie said. "I close my eyes, and all I see is Ava lying there in the street covered in blood..."

"I do too," I said, cutting her off. "I've been reading the newspapers, trying to find out if the police have any leads. That just makes me even more upset."

"You shouldn't do that. That's not good."

"So my aunt tells me."

"Do you guys want to go somewhere else?" Max asked. "This place gives me the creeps." I looked around at the small alleyway. It did have that creep vibe to it. Graffiti had been spray-painted on the walls, at least the ones not covered with mold, mildew, and what looked like rust stains. Trash was piled up in the corners. It also smelled really bad.

"Yeah," I said. "Let's go somewhere else.

We walked out of the alleyway and down the street.

An hour later, we were in Audubon Park sitting at a picnic table. Today wasn't as hot as it had been lately. With rain showers almost every day it was just enough to cool it off. Ava would love weather like this. *No,* I said in my head. *Don't think about her.* When I thought about her it only made me think of that night and the pure terror I felt. Then the sadness and the loss of losing Ava. I could tell by the look on Maggie and Max's faces that they were feeling the same thing.

"What are you guys thinking about?" Max asked, breaking the silence.

"What do you think?" Maggie asked in a low voice.

Max sighed. "Yeah, it's all I think about too."

I looked at both of them. This was too much. I got out of the house to break out of my somber mood, not jump right back into it. I wanted to do something. I needed to do something to take my mind off of things, but what?

"Do you guys want to go walk around the park?" Maggie asked. "Or swimming? Or biking? Or something?"

"Not really," Max said.

I wanted to, but then again, I didn't. It felt wrong knowing that Ava wasn't here to enjoy it with us. It felt weird to try and move on knowing that she's gone. Yes, we were supposed to, but still it just didn't feel right. It felt, horrible. Around us people played, laughed, and lived. It made me sick. *How dare you?* I said in my head. *How dare you all go on about your lives when someone else's is gone?*

It wasn't my right to ridicule them. It's not fair.

I looked down at the table, lost in thought. "You know I've been thinking," Max said, rubbing his fingers together.

"Oh no, that's never good," I said, trying to joke. No one laughed, which didn't make a bit of difference to me. I really wasn't trying to be funny.

"I've been thinking about what you said about the guy at the club," Max said, continuing the conversation.

"What about him?" I asked.

"I was thinking that maybe you should go to the police about it."

"Why?" Something in me stirred.

"Because don't you think it's a little weird that he was there the night she was killed after him telling you about demons?"

"Well...yeah I think it's a bit strange but...it's New Orleans, Max. It's a city, there are a lot of strange people here."

"Yeah, but you think that..."

"I try not to think about it, okay," I snapped. "Anyway you shouldn't either. Maggie is right. We need to get up and go do something instead of sitting on our asses all day moping."

"Okay, then what do you want to do?" Max asked, his tone a bit hard.

"I don't know." I felt myself shrinking down a bit.

Max took in a breath then looked at me. "I wanted to tell you what I thought that guy might have meant," he said gently.

"Oh yeah," I challenged. "Like you know."

"Actually I think I do."

Both Maggie and I leaned closer to him. "What?" Maggie asked. "What did he mean?"

"It's just a theory," Max said. "My brother said that, a few years back, New Orleans had trouble with gangs. There are some still around, but they are just not as bad. Anyway, with that in mind, I'm thinking that the guy could have been trying to warn you about a gang coming."

"Gangs?" I asked. "That's your theory?"

"Yes it is."

Maggie and I exchanged glances.

"Look, you don't have to believe me, I mean, after all it's just a theory, but it makes sense."

"Okay then, why would he warn me if there was a gang in the area? If he's with them then why would he do it? Out of the kindness of his heart? I doubt it. Oh and the most creepy factor of them all, how did he know my name?"

"Now that was a bit strange, I know, but the other thing makes sense, right?"

"In your world apparently."

"Come on, Addie," Maggie said. "He does have a point, in a way. Gangs appear out of nowhere all the time. Those people that we ran into that night could have been them, and maybe their gang name is Demon."

I didn't want to believe them, but they did have a good point. I just didn't want to accept the fact that Ava could have possibly been killed by freaking gang bangers. It was too much to bear. Her being killed was one thing. Her being killed by a gang was another. It hurt more somehow.

"I still think that you need to go to the police about it," Max said. "If this is gang-related activity, then they need to be informed."

I knew in my heart that they did. But I just couldn't let them know. Telling them what happened before would mean reliving it, and I just didn't know if I could do that.

"Don't do it for you," Max said. "Do it for Ava."

His love sickness has gotten the better of him, I thought. But he was right. "Okay," I said. "I will go to the police station and tell them what else happened."

"Great," Max said, smiling just a bit. "Now we just try and move on, right?"

"Right," Maggie said. "If that's possible."

"It has to be. What choice do we have?" I nodded.

I went home later with a promise that I would go to the police station as soon as I could. *I'll do it tomorrow,* I thought. *Tomorrow is another day.* I walked through the door feeling heavy as hell. The mood in the house had changed big time from frigid and tense to somber and gray. My aunt and uncle were in the kitchen talking as usual. This time I decided not to eavesdrop on their conversation. I was too tried to do that.

I started to walk up the stairs.

"Addie," I heard my aunt call.

I turned around to look at her. "Yes?" I asked.

"Are you okay?"

I shrugged a bit. "I don't know. I guess so." There was a pause. "I'm sorry I ran out," I wailed. "That was stupid. I shouldn't have done that."

"It's okay," she said. "I knew how upset you were. I just wished that you would have stayed to talk about it."

"I'm sorry I couldn't. I talked to Max and Maggie, though."

"How are they?"

"About as good as I am." She looked at me with a sympathetic look. "Um, I'm going to go to bed now," I said. Max, Maggie, and I ended up walking around the park, eating, and just trying to take our minds off of things. It worked a little. We didn't realize what time it was until it was something past five.

"Okay," my aunt said. "Do you want anything to eat before you go to sleep?"

"No thank you, I'll just eat in the morning." Without another word I walked up to my room and fell flat on my bed.

Moving on. That was the name of the game for us now.

I didn't want to move on. I didn't want to move on, then again I didn't want to remember what happened either. Moving on, I guess, is a way of letting go. If I let go I'd forget what happened, then again if I let go I'd forget Ava. I felt confused, weakened, and restless over it. I rolled over so that I was on my back. I stared into the ceiling, thinking about what I was going to say to the police tomorrow.

I didn't want to go, but I made a promise to my friends, and I kept my promises to my friends. I shut my eyes and fell asleep soon after.

CHAPTER EIGHT
TALL DARK SAVIOR

When the next day came around, I gathered myself up and headed down the stairs. I had been going over in my head what to say to the police about the guy in the club. I should tell the truth, but I was afraid to do that. I also got to thinking, if this guy really was working or knows the gang that was responsible for Ava's death, wouldn't Maggie, Max, and I be targets since we got away?

It made sense because we saw the crime. We were witnesses, and we could turn them in, so they had every right to come after us. And lately I'd been feeling like someone was watching me.

I felt like the more I told the worse off I'd be.

But Max was right, I needed to do this for Ava, not me. I was still alive and well. Poor Ava was six feet in the ground. I guess I'd just have to take the chance and hope that this feeling of being stalked was just me being paranoid.

One more thing I needed to get past was telling my aunt and uncle about it. That was the big conversation I was dreading. They would want to know more about the guy. What happened when I was with him, what we talked about, did anyone see us, blah, blah, blah. Not to mention I may be tempted to tell them what he said to me.

Guess I'll do it and get it over with, I thought. *For Ava.*

I slowly walked down the stairs, barely picking up my feet. I didn't see my aunt or uncle. I found a note on the counter written in my aunt's handwriting:

Gone to work for the day. Both of us will be home late.
Stay in the house.

— ***Wanda***

Great! Well going to the police station was out until they got back, which was going to be late. I crumpled the note up and threw it away. Granted, yes I could go to the police station right now, tell them about the guy then, be back before they even knew I was gone. But I didn't feel like lying to them. After everything that had happened, I didn't think it was right.

After all, lying was what got us all into trouble in the first place.

I walked into the living room and sat on the couch, planning out my next move. I could go to the law office where my aunt worked and tell her about me going to the station, but I didn't want to interrupt her, especially if she was in court. She's been working her ass off on a big case, and I didn't want her to get distracted. I could go to the government office where Uncle Jeff worked, but with something like this I'd rather get my aunt's permission.

I was stuck.

I didn't have to go today, but I just wanted to get it over with. Rip the bandage off and be done with it.

I fell back on the couch, closing my eyes.

I woke up a few hours later. I checked my phone and saw that it was just a little past two. I felt more tired and weakened. Feeling a bit hungry, I decided to fix something to eat. After I made myself a sandwich, I noticed a newspaper lying on the kitchen table. Shockingly there was a story about our misadventure on Bourbon.

The police still had no leads on who could have murdered Ava. In fact, according to the article, seemed like they were giving up.

I put my sandwich down after taking a few bites when I read that part. *No,* I thought. *They can't just give up. They can't, it's not right.*

They need another lead, a voice seemed to say in my head. *Something that will give them an edge.*

Like what I knew, what I could tell them.

Feeling an adrenaline rush, I finished my sandwich then went upstairs. I grabbed my worn-out blue jean shoulder bag along with my phone then headed out the door, locking it behind me. I had to tell the police about the guy. I didn't want them to give up, if that was true or not. I couldn't let them. I would deal with my aunt and uncle later. Right now I had to do this. For Ava.

I walked out of the Garden District and headed towards the French Quarter. I walked down St. Charles Avenue and passed Lee Circle. From there I took a cab down the rest of the Avenue. A few minutes later, I was on Canal. I got out of the cab then walked a little ways down Canal and headed down Royal Street. I stopped and looked around. I was standing right in the legendary French Quarter.

"Wow," I said, taking it all in.

To some people who don't live in Louisiana, the French Quarter was just another part of the city, but that's not the case. The French Quarter had so much history. Famous chefs had restaurants here, movies were filmed here, then there's its rich history in culture. Granted, yes it could be dangerous, I've found that out pretty quick. Despite that, I was glad to be able to see it in the daylight. I could now see what I missed when I went to Bourbon Street. Like Canal and Magazine there were people everywhere walking and shopping.

Horse-drawn carriages shared the same roads as the cars, bringing back that vintage feeling and making you think that just for one second you were back in time when this city became famous. I walked down the sidewalk, taking in the various shops, smells, sounds, and overall culture of this small part of New Orleans.

I passed the Hotel Montelone. Halfway down the street I pulled out the card that Officer Demouchet gave me. After figuring out where the police station was, I started for it. I walked on to Conti Street and found myself face to face with the police station. I walked up the stairs, put my hand on the door, and froze. My adrenaline was starting to wear off, and I wasn't feeling so sure of myself.

A panic started to rise in me for some reason and I felt like I was being watched.

I quickly turned around, making a passerby jump. When he looked at me funny I gave him a look back then turned back to the door. *Come on, Addie, do it,* I told myself in my head. *Stop standing around like an idiot and get a grip, you need to do this.*

I took in a breath then walked into the police station.

Policemen and women were hard at work taking phone calls and dealing with criminals. I was really starting to feel like this was a bad idea, even more so when a very creepy looking guy was staring at me. He was sitting on a bench next to an office. From what I could tell he was handcuffed. He had reddish brown hair, fair skin, and was dressed in black. He wouldn't take his eyes off of me no matter what.

I looked at him. He had to be about my age, or maybe even just a year or two older. He also looked to be half Asian. I stared him straight in the eyes as if to say stop looking at me. They weren't red, so I was glad, but they weren't a normal color either. They were cold black. I jumped when I heard someone yell, then turned my attention back to the guy.

He was still looking at me, and I had enough.

"Excuse me," someone said. I jumped and noticed a woman standing in front of me. "I'm sorry, I didn't mean to scare you," she said, smiling.

"It's okay," I said. I briefly turned back to the boy then looked back at the woman.

"May I help you?" she asked.

"Yes, I was looking for Officer Demouchet," I said.

"Which one?" she asked.

"Which one?" I asked, confused.

The woman gave me a smile. "There are two Demouchet's here, they are husband and wife."

"Oh, um, Mrs....Officer Demouchet then please. I need to speak with her. She's handing the Bourbon Street case, right?"

"Yes she is. I'll lead you to her, follow me." I followed the woman to another office across the station towards the back. I could see Officer Demouchet sitting at a desk talking on the phone. She was scribbling very fast on a note pad.

"Rae," the woman said, knocking on the door.

Officer Demouchet looked up from her desk. "Hold on," she said to the phone. "Yes?"

"She needs to talk to you."

"Okay...hey, I'll call you back...yeah, yeah, I know, bye..." She hung up sounding so cold and stern. Officer Demouchet looked at us. "Okay so, now what's going on?" she asked.

"Um, I needed to talk to you," I said, a little unsure. She looked like she wasn't in a very good mood. "About the Bourbon Street case."

"Well then have a seat. Mary, thank you." The other woman, Mary, smiled then walked out of the room, shutting the door. I sat in a chair that was in front of her desk, looking around the small room. I could see the rest of the station through the windows. I tried to speak, but I felt my throat go dry. I felt like they could all hear what I had to say.

"Relax, Addie," Officer Demouchet said. "No one can hear you in here, I promise. If you want to I can close the blinds."

"No, that's okay." I tried to relax. "I'll take your word for it."

Officer Demouchet straightened in her chair then leaned forward. Placing her hands on the desk in front of her, folding them as well. "So," she said, "what have you come to tell me?"

"It's about that night." I took in a breath. "I really don't think it's anything, but my friends have convinced me otherwise."

"It could be. No little detail is too small when handling a case. Just so you know."

I nodded, feeling a bit relieved but not very much. I started to talk. "The night on Bourbon Street. At the club we were all previously at...well...what happened, I was dancing with a guy."

Officer Demouchet stared right at me as I spoke.

"I danced with him for quite a while." My voice started to break. "When I turned to leave he wouldn't let me go. Finally, I did, but he said something to me before I left, something disturbing."

"What did he say?" she asked.

I gulped, remembering his chilling words rolling off the tone of his voice.

"He said, 'Hurry home, Addie, little girls like you shouldn't be out in a place like this when the demons come.'"

Officer Demouchet looked unfazed by the words I said. I was sure in her years as a cop she'd heard worse. "I see," she said.

"I knew it was just something stupid that he said," I told her. "It probably means nothing, right?"

"Not necessarily. Tell me, this guy, how was he acting?"

I darted my eyes back and forth from wall to wall. Trying to process her odd question. "Um..." I started. "Tall, kind of tan, short black teased hair. That's all I can remember. I really couldn't see, the lights in the club where a dark blue."

"Did you know him by any chance?"

"No, not in the slightest. I've never met or seen him in my life."

"What club was this at?"

"Club De La Roux, I think."

Officer Demouchet got quiet for a moment, lost in her own thoughts I guess. She was also muttering to herself very low. So low that I couldn't hear. I spaced out too, and then it hit me. The dizziness, the headache, the tiredness, but they were also accompanied by some other feelings. Nausea, weakness, body pain. I felt like I was dying.

Officer Demouchet didn't seem to notice. I tried to stay calm, but I was fighting a losing battle.

"Addie, are you okay?" Officer Demouchet asked.

"Yeah," I said, almost hunched over. "I...just...this. Talking about that night makes me a little...uneasy."

"I understand." Officer Demouchet looked out her office window towards the rest of the station. Mainly towards one particular person. The half-Asian guy I saw when I first came in. He was looking our way, not taking his eyes off of us for one second. I thought I saw them flash a color of some sort for a minute.

"Excuse me," Officer Demouchet said. "I need to take care of something." She got up from her desk and walked out of the office. I saw her walk over to the boy and say something to him. A few minutes later, I was starting to feel better. I had calmed down a lot. Then I started to focus again. Officer Demouchet walked back in her office, shutting the blinds before she sat down.

"Sorry about that," she said. "That guy out there doesn't know when to stop staring at people."

"I guess he thinks that he's going to see something if he doesn't look away," I said.

"You're so right. Well I'm going to look into what you have told me today."

"Do you really think that he could be connected to the crime?"

"He could. I'm more worried about how he knows your name, and you swear you don't know him."

"I really don't."

"And I believe you. If and when I find him I'll question him about what you have told me. He could know something." I nodded then looked down at the floor. "Addie," Officer Demouchet said, "I don't want you to worry about a thing. We are going to catch these guys no matter what."

"That's what all cops say," I said, scoffing. "I've seen the shows."

"And they don't depict half of what we go through. Those cops are just actors in front of a camera portraying what they think they know. I do know for a fact that my team and I will stop at nothing to find these guys. That I can promise you."

I nodded. "Okay." A tear ran down my face. "Please do, for Ava."

"We all will." I got up when she did, and she gave me a hug, which I was not expecting, but I took it anyway. After leaving her office, I started for the door of the station. The guy was still sitting on his bench, but he wasn't looking at everyone who was passing by, or me.

In fact his eyes looked bloodshot. I didn't notice before but they also had bags under them. I noticed a few other things too. His skin wasn't just fair, it was clear of any pimples, bumps, or blemishes. It was flawless and strange. Without another glance I walked out of the police station and into the pouring rain.

I didn't even notice that it had started raining.

It wasn't just raining, though. It was storming. I couldn't even see the street in front of me. Or the cars, or the people, or really anything. And here I was without a jacket or rain boots. Pulling out my phone I checked to see what time it was. It was passed five o'clock. I tried to call my aunt to tell her where I was, but the call wouldn't go through. I then tried to call my uncle, and it did the same thing.

"Damn," I said as the rain fell harder. I started to try and make my way down one of the sidewalks. I didn't know where I was going, but I tried my best to get back home. I stayed out of the road, even if I could possibly cross, but there was no guarantee that a car could see me even with the lights on or the help of windshield wipers.

I walked down a block, or at least I thought it was a block, then made my way to another sidewalk. I ignored signs, figuring I could find my way back on my own. I walked down another sideway, passing some shops, then found myself at the St. Louis Cathedral. I walked down another street, passing more shops, and ended up in Jackson Square.

Panic started to rise in me as I walked this way and that.

I pulled out my phone to check the time. It was now past six o'clock. The rain was getting heavier and the sky was growing darker. A feeling of dread started to gather inside of me. The dreaded feeling: I shouldn't have done this. I sat down on a corner of a sidewalk under an overhang, planning my next move. I felt cold, I felt hungry, I felt weak, and I felt scared. I just wanted to go home.

A half-hour or so passed, and the rain was still coming down hard.

I finally got off my ass and started another way. Through the rain I could see a few buildings that looked the same. In between them was a small alleyway. I started towards them. I didn't know where it would lead, but I had to do something. I walked into the alleyway. It was small but not as small as I thought it was.

Cold rain pounded my skin like needles. It got colder with every drop. I brushed the water from my face and kept walking through the alleyway. About halfway through it I heard a hiss from behind me. I froze. The hair on the back of my neck stood up. I couldn't feel the rain or the cold anymore. All I could feel was fear. I recognized the hiss.

I heard it not too long ago.

I slowly started to turn around.

A tall figure stood at the entrance to the alleyway. I couldn't make out any facial features, but I could tell it was a guy, he was at least five-foot-something. He stepped closer to me. I backed up. In what little light was coming from some signs I could see his face. He was Caucasian from what I could tell. He wore an old jacket, had dark wet hair, and red eyes.

A scream stopped in my throat.

He sauntered towards me. An animalistic growl came from his throat as he closed the gap between us. I couldn't move. I could only watch in horror as he was just inches from my face. He looked at me and smiled. Showing a set of perfectly sharp teeth. He then made a noise that didn't sound like a growl, or a hiss, but something in between.

Then, he roared like a jungle cat.

I screamed and started to run. I turned around to see if he was behind me then ran into something. I looked up and it was him.

"Ahhh," I said.

"You shouldn't run," he said in a chilling voice. "You're surrounded." As if on cue three more had jumped from the building rooftop. I jumped and turned around.

These were not the guys who had cornered my friends and me on Bourbon that night. But they were still just as terrifying. I tried to run, but one caught me. I fought hard against them, but I was no match for them. They were strong, too strong.

"Where do you think you're going?" the one that was holding me said. I could feel his cold breath on my neck.

"Let me go," I said, fighting back tears. "Please."

"I don't think we can do that," one said from in front of me. "His orders."

"Whose orders?" I asked.

"Like you don't know."

I don't, I thought. And I was kind of glad of that. They were going to kill me whether I knew or not so why beat around the bush.

I stared at all of them. Two more showed up after that. "Well boys," the first one who approached me said as two more showed up. "Look what we have here." As they approached one of the guys started to get really excited. He was acting crazy. His head was twisting and turning, He was salivating, shaking, he just looked like a mess. I cowered back, trying to seem small.

"So," one said. "Who gets her first, boss?"

"None," the first guy said. "His orders. He wants her unscathed and unharmed. But if she resists then he said do whatever it takes to bring her in." He looked my way. "Even break her if we have to."

Tears filled my eyes and I broke away from my captor. I ran for my life only to trip and fall. They took advantage of this and picked me up then pinned me to the wall. I whined, screamed, kicked, anything I could do to get away again, but this time it wasn't happening. The first guy had me. "Now, now," he said. "Did you really think you were going to get away that easy?"

I started to sob.

"Now there's no need for that." He started stroking my cheek. "A pretty little thing like you shouldn't cry. Don't worry, all of this will be over soon. Once he gets you." Without thinking I bit his finger. "Ooowww," he said. "Why you little bitch. You'll pay for that." He raised his hand, and I braced for what was about to happen.

Suddenly, there was a loud clap of thunder.

A figured dressed in all black jumped down from the rooftop.

He landed crouching down on his feet, holding two big curved swords in his hands. He wore a knee-length Gothic-style trench coat, tight black pants, and black boots. A hood covered his head. In an instant he took it off, revealing his face. Black hair fell over his right eye and touched the tip of his nose. The rest stayed behind his ear.

He looked up, and the guys around me hissed.

"You," one said. He started for the guy. The guy in black stood up, slung his swords, and gutted the guy running towards him in an instant. Another came and he struck him down too. The second one didn't go so easy, though. After he had been struck down, he still tried to fight. The guy in black, kneeling, again stabbed a sword into his chest. He was done after that.

The guy in black looked towards the others. A wicked smile appeared across his face. He then raised his hand up in the air and motioned with his fingers for them to come at him.

One by one they all started coming for him. He struck them all down like nothing I'd ever seen before. I've seen people on TV do martial arts before and have even watched Max do his fair share of those moves as well, but this guy was something different.

He was better. So much better.

The way he moved was impossible. He flipped, attacked, dodged, counter attacked like it was nothing. Like it was second nature to him, and the rain wasn't slowing him down one bit. After he cut down every single one, he turned to the first guy and me. In seconds I was wrapped up into the first guy's arms with a knife to my throat. "Ahhh," I said.

The guy in black stepped towards us, out of breath but still willing to fight.

"You're next," he said, picking up a sword he had dropped.

"You can't kill me," the guy said.

"Well I can't let you live now, can I?" the guy in black said, coming a bit closer. I tried to place his heavily accented voice.

I stared at him, wanting him to do something. "Please help me," I begged. He stared at me.

My captor threw me down on the ground. "Take her," he said. "She's not worth getting my ass killed, no matter what anyone says."

"You go," the guy in black said. "But I will find you, mark my words."

With a growl my captor left, disappearing in the shadows.

I sat up and looked at the guy in black. He looked down at me with dark eyes. I started to feel a bit scared. Not as scared as I had been earlier but scared enough to be cautious. I mean, this guy just murdered seven guys in cold blood, for all I knew he's some kind of psycho. He looked at me then walked over by one of the bodies, got something from it, then started down the alleyway.

"Wait!" I called.

He stopped.

"Who are you?"

He stood as still as a statue. Slowly he turned his head to look at me. Through his hair I could see his piercing eyes. "Your savior," he said. My breath caught in my throat. He smiled that wicked smile, and then he was off, leaving me awestruck. Hanging onto his every word.

CHAPTER NINE
HIDE AND SEEK

After my encounter with the guy in black, the rain started to let up, and I was able to finally find my way home. I took a streetcar back to the Garden District and raced down Seventh Street to the comfort and safety of my home. I glanced over my shoulder to see if anyone was following me. I didn't know if one of those guys would come back for me or not. I kept feeling like someone was watching me, but every time I turned around I didn't see anyone.

I fumbled for my keys in my purse as I walked up the steps. My hand shook as I stuck the key in the lock. I looked around one more time, just to make sure that no one was watching. On the other side of the street I could see a dark figure watching me. *Oh no, not again,* I thought. I turned the key in the lock then pushed the door open.

I slammed the door as soon as I got in then sunk down to the floor.

"Addie," I heard my aunt from the kitchen.

I looked up as she made her way over to me, her heels clicking on the floor as she walked. "Are you okay?" she asked. Pure concern was written on her face, something that I rarely saw. With tears in my eyes I jumped up and hugged her. I sobbed into her shoulder, and she wrapped her arms around me. "It's okay, sweetie," she said. "Everything is going to be okay." She didn't even know what happened, and yet she was still consoling me.

My sobs got a little quieter, but I was trembling.

"I'm sorry," I said. "For sneaking out, but...but...it was important."

She pulled away from me, her arms still on my shoulders. "I came home and you were gone," she whined with tears in her eyes. "I thought that someone had taken you. I thought they..."

"I went to the police station. I remembered something else from that night, and I had to tell someone about it."

"Oh, well why didn't you let me or your uncle go with you?"

"I'm sorry, I wasn't thinking straight. All I was thinking about was Ava and how this might help catch her killers. I'm sorry really, I didn't mean to scare you."

She hugged me again. "The important thing is that you're safe," she said. I heard a ruckus coming from the stairs. I looked behind my aunt to see my uncle running down them as fast as he could. "Is that her?" he asked. "Addie?"

"Yes it's her, Jeff," my aunt said, wiping tears away from her eyes and looking at him. "And she is okay. Everything is okay." I hugged them.

I didn't have much of an appetite, so I went straight upstairs to my room. I walked into the bathroom and drew myself a well-deserved hot bath. I soaked in the tub, relaying the events of the night in my mind. I thought of the guy dressed in black. His dark eyes, his wicked smile, the way he moved when he killed those men.

I couldn't stop thinking about him. The thought of him took over my whole body. His image filled my mind, taking it over along with my core. Like a white hot obsession, something that I couldn't let go of. The more I thought of him, the more something tried to convince me that it was a dream. Until I looked at all the bruises those men put on me, then I knew that it wasn't.

There I was at twelve o'clock, still thinking of him. Still wrapped up in the wonder of him and where he could have possibly come from. *Maybe he's some kind of ninja,* I thought. *He was dressed in black after all.* And it would explain the huge swords, though the more I thought about them, the more I recalled them looking a bit wicked. Like what cosplayers would use, but those were real.

Maybe he's some serious cosplayer that takes things just a little too far.

No, that can't be right either. Why would someone do something like that and even be good at it? Unless they have done it before, but more importantly, why did he save me? Sleep was finally starting to catch up with me. I rolled over in bed and shut my eyes. His words echoing in my mind one more time.

"Your savior."

Morning finally rolled around and I was exhausted.

The sun was shining right on my face, forcing me to get up. I sat up in bed then looked at the clock. It was something past eleven. I tried to stretch but stopped on account of the shooting pain throughout my arms, legs, and back. I tried to remember what I did to make my body hurt this much then I remembered last night and the men who attacked me.

I started to tremble then relaxed when I thought of the guy in black who saved me.

I started to stare off into space, thinking of him. *This is stupid,* I told myself in my head. *Obsessing over a guy who doesn't even know my name, and I don't know his.* I pushed the covers off of me then stretched, ignoring my body's aches and pain, then went downstairs. I saw boxes scattered at the very bottom of the stairs.

Stepping over them, I peeked into the kitchen and saw my aunt packing plates into another box with two already sitting on the table. I walked up to the kitchen counter, very perplexed at the sight. "Um, Aunt Wanda," I said hesitantly. "What are you doing?"

"Packing," she said with her back to me as she taped a box.

"Why? Are you going to store them somewhere?"

"No," she said, putting the final touches on the box she had. "We are moving."

"Moving?"

"Yes moving. Out of the city today, as soon as we can. Out of the state if possible."

"But why? New Orleans is our home, why would you want to move...?"

"Because we have to, Addie," she snapped. "We just have to."

"Why?" I crossed my arms, switching my tone over to my I-want-to-know-something-right-now voice. I thought back to the conversations she and my uncle had in the past. Up until now I've brushed them off thinking they were nothing. But in that moment they were coming back to me. I always had a suspicion that they were hiding something from me. This proved it. It had to. Why else would we be moving?

But had they always had this planned? It seemed so spur of the moment. It didn't make any sense. As much as I hated to ruin the good relationship my aunt and I had been having lately, I needed answers and I needed them now.

"Why do we have to move?" I asked, irritated. "Why now? What's going on?"

"There is nothing going on," my aunt said, clearly lying. "We just have to move. I got a better job offer and..."

"Oh cut the crap," I yelled. "I know it's not true."

"Young lady, don't you..."

"Don't you what? 'Take that tone with me?' Yeah, you've used that one before. I know something is up, I have for a while now. I don't know what it is, but I want to know."

My aunt sighed then looked at me. "I can't..." she said, taking a breath. "I can't tell you."

I was speechless. So my suspicions had been right. There was something going on. My heart sank. I was really hoping that there was nothing and that I was just being paranoid. Guess not. I stared at my aunt. Trying to keep up my not-scared façade. "Tell me, please," I said. "Please."

"Addie, can't you just accept that what your uncle and I are trying to do right now is protect you?" she asked. "Isn't that enough? That we are trying to do what's best for you to keep you safe...like we couldn't last night."

"Last night?"

"Yeah."

My heart sank once again. "You know about last night?" I asked.

"Yes," she said. "All of it. That's why your uncle and I have decided that we need to get out of New Orleans. It's not as safe as we thought it was."

So the guys who attacked me do have something to do with why we were leaving. Why? I still had questions, and things that just didn't make any sense. *Can this have something to do with my father?* a voice asked. I looked at my aunt, who looked like she was about to pass out. All of this. They were doing all of this to protect me, but from what?

"Where's Uncle Jeff?" I asked.

"Clearing up some things at work," my aunt said. "Now Addie, please go pack whatever is necessary. We leave as soon as he gets back."

Taking her word, I ran up the stairs. First I changed then I pulled out a suitcase along with my duffel bag. I started shoving clothes and anything else I needed into them without really thinking. I walked over to my desk and started putting the contents of it in my bag. I was gathering everything when I noticed a picture that I had drawn not too long ago. I looked at it closely this time, taking in what I had drawn.

It was a boy dressed in black wielding huge swords.

That's him, I thought. *That's so him. It has to be*. Why did I draw him? I didn't even know him then. What does this mean?

I heard the doorbell ring from downstairs and my aunt's voice. "Yes," I heard her say as the door opened.

"Hi, ma'am," came a man's voice. "We are here to disinfect your house for pests."

"I didn't call pest control."

"Are you sure?"

"Yeah, I'm sure."

I slowly walked out of my room and crept over to the stair railing.

I saw two men dressed in pest control outfits. One was short and stocky while the other was tall with muscles that I could see through his shirt. A panicky feeling welled up inside of me as one of the men started to speak in a gruff voice.

"We got a call about a house that needed to be sprayed for pests," the short one said. "And it came from this area."

"Well then you must be mistaken," my aunt said. "Because I haven't called anyone. Why don't you try the house down the street. Maybe they are the ones with the problem, good day." My aunt tried to shut the door, but one of the men stopped her. I jumped.

"Ma'am, I'm sorry, but I think this is the right house," the short one said. "It has to be."

"And I am telling you this for the last time," my aunt was very irritated now, "you have the wrong house. Look, I am in the process of moving. I can't deal with this right now."

"We can't let you leave, ma'am," the tall one said.

My aunt stopped. After a few seconds of quiet, she turned around very quickly. She looked up at me. "Addie, run!" she yelled. But I couldn't. I stood right there, wanting to know what was going on. In an instant the men shed their uniforms and had stripped down to clothing made of leather, fur, and bones.

The tall one grabbed her and held a knife to her neck.

"You did all you could to protect her," he said. "Better than anyone would have ever thought."

"But you can't stop this," the short one said. "You can't stop the inevitable. Her fate is sealed. It always has been."

"Please don't do this," my aunt begged with tears in her eyes. "Please don't."

"I'm afraid we can't," the tall one said. "His orders."

"Since the others failed we have to proceed," the short one said

"You've done well. Not it's time to end this." They looked up at me with dark, scary faces. Then with one quick movement the tall one slit my aunt's throat. She fell to the floor, splattering blood everywhere. Anger welled inside of me, along with every other emotion in the world. Finally, I screamed. Finally, I reacted. Then finally I started to run, which I should have done a long time ago.

I ran into my room, slamming my door shut and locking it. Like that was going to help, but what other choice did I have?

I could hear their footsteps as they came up the stairs. "Addie!" one of them said, banging on the door. "Open up, I know you're in there." I darted my eyes around the room as I shook uncontrollably, thinking. I had to do something. I needed to get out of the house and now. There was nowhere to run. I could go out the window and face a twenty-foot drop or hide in here and face them finding me.

Either way I'd lose. I'd either get seriously hurt falling from the window or killed if they found me.

Suddenly I heard the door crack.

Screaming, I turned around and saw that one of them had an axe and was hacking his way through. At a last-minute attempt to keep myself safe, I pushed my desk towards the door. I piled it high with anything solid in my room. Then I went into the bathroom. I shut the door then pushed a cabinet in front of it.

There, I thought. *That should hold them for a little while.*

I could still hear them hacking away. I needed to find another way out. I searched the bathroom. There was nothing here. I looked under the counter and remembered something. I knelt down underneath it and opened the small door leading to a small tunnel, which leads to a closet in the hallway.

When I would play hide and seek with my friends years ago, I always hid in my bathroom because I discovered the secret door it had. It made for a great escape then, and it was going to make a great one now. I slipped through the door then closed it behind me, hoping the men wouldn't find it. I crept my way through the tunnel and ended up at the other door to the closet.

I opened that door and found myself in the closet. After closing the other door, I pressed my ear to the closet door to try and hear the men. There was silence. I carefully opened the closet door and saw the men enter my room. I got out of the closet then ran down the stairs. I tried to go out the front door, but every time I tried to even get near it something pushed me back.

"What the hell?" I said.

I tried three times before I gave up and tried the back door but with no luck. I could hear the men stirring upstairs, forcing me to give up and head for safety. I ran to the only safe place I knew in the house. My aunt and uncle's bedroom. I ran in the room and shut the door quietly behind me. I locked it as well then pushed the dresser in front of it for good measure.

Exhausted, I sunk down into the plush carpet and thought about what happened. My aunt was dead. I saw them slit her throat. They were after me for reasons I had no idea why. It wasn't fair, it didn't make any sense. Completely out of it, I leaned against the wall and shut my eyes for just a few minutes.

I woke up later with my heart pounding in my ears. I was hoping that what I went through was just a dream, but when I found myself in my aunt and uncle's room I was brought back to reality. I hadn't heard anything in a while. Of course I had been asleep, but maybe they gave up and left while I was out. I sat up, still shaking.

Bump.

I jumped at the sound of something outside the door.

I hurried into my uncle's closet and sat quietly as they pounded down the door and the dresser. I could hear them going through the room, probably tearing it apart. I heard my aunt's closet door open. I froze. My uncle's was on the other side of the room. I could hear them walk right next to the door, but they never came in.

"She's not here either," one said.

"Maybe she escaped," I heard the other one say.

"There's no way. We have blocks all around this place."

"Maybe she can get past them. She is John's daughter after all," one huffed. "Let's go check again," the one that huffed said. "I don't have time to chase this damn girl all over New Orleans." After a few minutes, I heard them leave.

When I deemed it was safe I ran out of the room.

I started down the stairs, looking back, making sure they weren't behind me. I got down the stairs and almost stepped on my dead aunt's body. I gasped silently, looking at her cold, still body. Tears welled up in my eyes. I bent down and touched her head, not grossed out in any way at touching her. "I'm sorry," I whispered. "You did what you could." I closed her eyes.

I felt something grab my arm.

"Ah ha," the short man said. "Got ya."

I started hitting his arm, which wasn't fazing him at all. "Let me go!" I screamed. "Let me go now!"

"Oh you're a feisty little thing, aren't you? Just like your father, but you look like your mother. Your beautiful mother."

"You'll die like them too," the tall one said.

I stared at him in horror.

"Not yet," the short one said. "Not until after he sees her. Remember, he's the one who wants her, and boy he is going to make her pay."

I whined as the man's grip got tighter around my arm. "For what?" I asked. "I've done nothing wrong."

"Like you don't know," the man said. I didn't realize it before, but he had an accent. They both did.

"I don't," I said. "Can you let me go now?"

"Ha, like it was going to be that easy. Oh no. You're coming with us. You've got a party waiting for you where you're going." Both of them started laughing maniacally. A chill ran down my spine. With all of my might I kicked the guy right below the belt. He grimaced in pain, and I made a break for it.

I was almost to the door when I felt something wrap around my legs.

I fell to the floor. A sharp pain running through my left arm. I turned to see that a rope was tied around my legs. The tall man started for me. I tried to crawl away, but he grabbed my legs and started pulling me towards him. I dug my fingernails into the granite floor, making my fingers bleed trying to escape, but it was no use. I had been caught.

The man flipped me over on my back and pulled me close to him. "Our leader wants you alive," he said. "But I could care less about that. You're not worth keeping alive. Your family wasn't, so why should you be?" The musty scent that was coming from his breath was making me sick. His teeth weren't helping either.

"I'm going to end you like I ended your parents a long time ago." He raised a huge curved sword at me.

"Dreg, don't," I heard the short man say.

I closed my eyes.

Suddenly Dreg grunted, and his grip loosened on me. I opened my eyes, looking right into an arrowhead that had been shot into his chest. He turned around. I looked around him and saw a young guy, maybe a few years older than me, holding a bow with his aim in Dreg's direction. He wasn't the one I saw last night, but he was dressed in black.

He was a bit more built than my savior, and he had Hispanic features, like short black hair and tan skin.

"You," Dreg said to him.

"Yes," the guy said. "It's me." He shot another arrow into Dreg, who roared like an injured lion on an African plain. Dreg dropped me and then headed for him. The guy dodged Dreg, rolling like a gymnast to the other side of the room, loading his bow. He shot another arrow into Dreg, who was still coming for him.

Another arrow hit Dreg, but it didn't come from the guy.

I glanced up and saw a young man dressed in a black cassock holding a crossbow in Dreg's direction. He looked to be older than the other one. If I had to guess, maybe in his early twenties. "Give up," he said in an accent. "It's over."

Dreg growled and headed for him.

Suddenly a girl came out of nowhere and slung a machete at him. She was dressed in an old ruffled off-white Victorian-style dress with a brown corset vest and knee-high black boots. The dress came to her ankles. A section had been cut in the front from her knees down. Her long wavy dark brown hair swung in every direction she turned.

Dreg came at her, and the two guys shot him with arrows.

"Enough of this," the second guy on the stairs said, jumping down from them, landing gracefully on his feet. He pushed his black hair back away from his eyes. "Let's finish him."

They all cornered Dreg.

He fought them tooth and nail, but they could not bring him down.

From the stairs I saw a girl with short reddish-brown hair throw something at Dreg. After it hit him, he started convulsing. Finally, he fell to the ground, I presumed dead. The other came at me now, pulling me by my hair. "And where do you think you are going?" a familiar voice said. I turned around from my position on the floor and saw my savior from last night standing in the doorway bathed in the evening sunlight.

"You," the man said. "Get out of my way."

"How about no," my savior said, holding his swords.

"You...little...ahhhhh." The man started for him. My savior

dodged him then, when the man turned back around, he ran his sword right through him. He fell to the ground too close to me. I glanced back and forth from Dreg and his accomplice and was happy that they had been vanquished. Then I looked up and stared at the five killers standing in my house.

CHAPTER TEN
THE REGULATORS

I stared at the five people in my house.

They all stared back at me. *What am I supposed to do now?* I asked myself. *They won't turn on me, will they?* My savior in black didn't and he was here, so maybe they wouldn't either. The Hispanic one with the bow looked up at the stairs where the girl with the reddish-brown hair was still standing.

"Nice save, Day," he said, smiling at her. "As always."

"Just doing my job," the girl—Day—said, walking down the steps. She was dressed like a 1950s pilot with some weird gadget on her wrist and old goggles around her neck. She tilted her small, foxlike face, scanning her eyes over Dreg's body.

The older guy who was dressed in a black sleeveless cassock with the crossbow turned to the girl in the Victorian-style dress. "I'm going to have a look around," he said. "Make sure there's no more."

"You're the boss," she said. "We'll keep an eye out in case any come back."

He nodded then started searching the house.

The Hispanic one walked over to Dreg's lifeless body. "I can't believe it took so much to bring him down," he said. "They are getting stronger and stronger."

"Then we'll train harder and harder to take them down," Day said, stopping in the middle of the room. "That's all we can do."

I stood up and slowly started to make my way into the kitchen away from them.

I heard a grunt behind me and turned around to see my savior darting his eyes from me then to his accomplices. They all looked at me. "Oh sorry," Hispanic guy said. "We forgot that you were here."

"I don't see how," I snapped a bit, not meaning to. "With all the commotion and everything."

He gave me a strange look.

The girl in the Victorian-style dress suddenly walked up to me.

"Hi," she said in a singsong voice, holding out her hand. "I'm Genevieve."

I looked at her. Was she kidding? Wanting to shake my hand and formerly meet me after what's happened? Yes, granted, they saved my life, but still. I had no idea what the hell was going on here, my aunt was dead, and two guys came after me. I'm more worried about putting those pieces together than meeting anyone right now.

I look from her hand to her, trying to say with my face that I didn't want to shake her hand. She's a brunette not a blonde, she should get that. Finally, after a few seconds, she got my drift and lowered her hand with a slightly sad look on her face.

The guy in the cassock walked back in the room. "The house is clean," he said. "Nothing here."

"Great," the Hispanic guy said.

The guy in the cassock then looked at me. "Are you okay?" His face and tone both stone cold. I didn't know how to react.

"I'm...okay," I said in a shaky voice.

He nodded then turned to his friends. "We need to get what we need from here and go," he said, turning to the others, ignoring me. "So gather what you need for your reports and then let's go." They all started to move.

"Who the hell are you people?" I asked, almost screaming.

They all turned to look at me once again. "Like you don't know," the guy in the cassock said, walking around looking.

"No I don't," I snapped. I folded my arms to make sure they knew I meant business. "So would someone like to enlighten me on what's going on? Because I have no idea." They all looked back and forth between each other.

"Oh come on," I said, irritated. "Can't you just tell me?" I pointed to the bodies of the dead men. "I think I have a right to know."

Cassock guy sighed, looking down at the now bloodstained floor. "Fine, if you must know." He cleared his throat like he was getting ready to give a lecture. "That's Jules Batiste." He pointed to the Hispanic guy with the bow who smiled. "That's Genevieve Radcliff." Genevieve smiled and waved at me. "That's Dayton Devereaux." He pointed to Day, who was standing by the bottom step with her arms folded. "Behind you is Rohl Sivan." I turned to look at Rohl.

Finally, my savior had a name.

"And I'm Jax Whittington." Jax pointed to himself. "That's all you need to know."

"Good to know. So would you mind explaining what happened here?"

"I told you, our names are all you need to know, nothing else. It's a risk telling you our names in the first place."

"You can't expect me to just want to know your names and not what happened here."

Jules looked at Jax. "Jax."

"Don't start, Jules. She knows too much already."

"So what's a little more?"

"Too much for her and for us."

Jules and Jax stared each other down until Jules finally looked away. He turned to me. "We're called Regulators," he said.

"Jules!" Jax said, almost yelling.

"She's got to know," Jules said. "After what we did here, I think she needs to know."

"That's why we wipe people's memories after we've saved them if and only if they see us," Dayton said. "That's what this is for." She flashed some kind of device at him. Jules rolled his eyes.

"You were going to wipe my memory?" I asked.

"Yeah," Jules said hesitantly. "Sorry."

"Well there goes my thank you for saving me."

"It would be for your own good," Jax said. "No one can know we exist."

"Then I guess I'll be the only one, because you are not wiping my memory with that thingy of yours." I gestured to the wicked device Dayton was holding that looked like it had been forged from an old radio or something.

"We're not going to wipe your memory," Jules said. "Right, Jax?"

Jax looked at me. "No," he said. "I guess not." Relief filled me. "Because we need some answers out of you," he said, walking over to Dreg's partner's body. "Do you know why these two attacked you?"

I sucked in any fearlessness I had left in me and answered him. "No, I do not."

"You sure?"

"Do I look like I'm lying?"

"Watch your mouth."

"Watch your mouth? Are you kidding me? Uh, news flash, buddy, you are in my house, so I think I can talk to you however I want."

"Did you talk to her like that?" He pointed to my aunt's body.

My fearlessness stuck in my throat. I felt like I was losing my confidence. "Sometimes," I admitted. "I never meant to, though."

"I'm sure you didn't," Jax said, not believing me.

"Why does it matter if these two were after me or not?" I asked. "What do they have to do with anything?"

"Oh believe me, they have a lot to do with a lot of things," Jules said. I gave a small nod.

"They work for a bad guy that we are looking for," Jax said. "We are just wondering why they would be after you."

"Yeah I'd like to know that too," I said.

The room got quiet as they started to look around. "So this guy you are all after...what has he done?" I dared to ask.

"A lot of terrible things," Jules answered me. "Horrible, in fact."

"Don't tell her, Jules," Jax said. "It's nothing for her to know about."

"You don't speak for me. I would like to know, actually, since these men broke into my house, killed my aunt, and ruined my day. Like I said before, I have a right to know."

"She's right, Jax," Rohl said, coming to stand in the middle of the room where I had a good view of him. "She has a right. Plus we know this guy and what he does. We know that he wouldn't send his goons after someone random. He must have a reason for going after her."

"That I can't think of," I said, "or know. I don't know who you people are talking about or what you are or what you do. All I do know is someone in here better give me a straight freaking answer or someone is going to pay."

"Ha, nice threat. You almost sound like you mean it," Jax said.

"I did," I said, looking him straight in the face. "Don't think I didn't for one second. I just need answers, that's all. Then you guys can go back to what you're doing, and I'll go back to my life."

"And you won't tell anyone what we tell you?" Jax asked. "Not a single soul."

"I won't, believe me, I won't. I swear."

"Fine, but you're not going to like it, hell, you may not even believe it."

"Try me."

Jax walked over to the kitchen window and closed the blinds. "I'll start with what Jules said earlier," he said. "We are called Regulators, or Regs for short. We regulate the supernatural population in New Orleans, actually Louisiana but mainly here in New Orleans. We are their police. If they do something wrong they have to answer to us.

"We are after a guy who has done some horrible things." Jax scoffed. "Actually," he said. "Horrible doesn't even explain the half of what he's done. Anyway, he's wanted where we are originally from."

"And that would be?" I asked.

"It's not important, not now anyways," Jax said.

"So you guys dress weird and hunt the supernatural."

"We don't hunt them," Genevieve said. "We just watch out for them. Keep an eye on them, and if they do something wrong, then they pay the price whether big or small."

I nodded, looking back and forth between all of them. Then I started to laugh. "You guys have got to be kidding me," I said. "Supernatural? Really? You guys really go after the supernatural. Wow, that is just hilarious now, tell me who you guys really are."

"I'm not joking," Jax said, his voice growing dark.

I stood there and thought for a minute.

They couldn't be supernatural police. That's impossible. The supernatural didn't even exist. All the lore about it, they were just stories, fantasies, something to tell around campfires or when the lights go out. It wasn't real, it couldn't be real. It just wasn't possible. Was it? I thought about those guys from last night. They all had huge animal-like teeth, like an animal from supernatural folklore would have. They moved too perfectly to be anything human. I replayed their inhuman growls and hisses in my head, shivering as I did so.

So it could be true. It really all could be.

"No, that's not right," I said, trying hard not to believe him. "The supernatural is not real."

"Oh yes it is," Jax said. "Far too real."

"Just to be clear, we are talking about witches, werewolves, vampires, and ghosts and...demons," Jules said.

"Yeah. So all of that, all of that is real?"

"Yes, I'm afraid so," Jax said.

"And if you want proof," Dayton said. "Then we can get you proof. Though I don't think you'll need much"

"That just...no, it can't be real, there is no possible freaking way that it's real. All of those things are meant for fairy tales, TV shows, movies, and...and crappy romance novels...and it just can't be real." My voice broke, and I felt like I was going to puke.

I knew they were right, why would they lie? I just didn't want to believe it.

"Yes, it's all real," Jax said. "Sorry, but yes it's true, now if you'll excuse us we need to do our job and get out of here then report our findings to our supervisors." Jax went to step past me when we all heard something coming from the back of the house. We all froze and the Regs held up their weapons.

"Stay sharp," Jax called, holding his crossbow close to his face. "Dayton, get one of your tasers ready."

"I can't," Dayton said.

"Why not?"

"Only one, sorry, this was just a test run, remember?"

"Damn it, I forgot." They focused on the back of the house as a strange noise came from it.

"Stay behind me," Rohl said, gently nudging me behind him.

"Okay," I said. I got behind him. He readied his swords, and I peeked over his shoulder. The noise was getting louder. I realized it was a type of hiss. Finally, a man appeared. He stopped when he saw the Regs with their weapons at the ready.

"Stop," Jax said.

"Give me the girl," the man hissed.

I cowered closer to my savior.

The man flashed sharp teeth like the ones from the men the other night. He started for Jax, who shot him with an arrow. It barely slowed him down. Next Genevieve swung a machete, just missing him by inches. Jules fought with him just using his bare hands. He was strong, maybe too strong for all of them. Still Jules didn't give up, then Jax came in.

They held the man down while Genevieve walked over to him, swinging her machete.

"Who sent you?" Jax asked as the man struggled while he held him down.

"Go to hell," the man hissed. He looked towards me. "I want her," he said. "I want her bad."

Rohl stepped close to me, blocking my view. "You don't need to see this," he whispered.

"See what?" I asked. They were just talking to him.

"You'll see."

Genevieve was still slinging her machete. She cocked her head to the side, looking at the man. She smiled, her red parted lips revealing beautiful white teeth. "I'll ask then," she said. "Who sent you?"

"Like I'd answer to you," the man hissed.

Genevieve looked at Jax and Jules then crouched down in front of the man. She did so that her dress went up her thigh a bit and her breasts peaked just a bit over the tight corset she was wearing. "It's okay," she said in a seductive voice. "There's no harm that is going to come to you. Just tell us who sent you and we'll let you go."

"Yeah right," the man scoffed. "I've heard that before. You Regulators can play your little games all you want, but I'm not falling for them."

"Oh so you're a smart one then, I could tell that the minute I saw you. So you know better than to lie to us, right?"

"I guess."

"Good, 'cause I can make sure that if you tell us exactly what we want to know then we'll let you go. All you have to do is cooperate and it will be done."

"I'm still not telling."

Genevieve's eyes suddenly went dark. "Then you're of no use to us," she said. After that, she used her machete to cut off the man's head. Blood sprung from his decapitated body like oil from an oil rig, and I felt like I was going to be sick.

"Told you shouldn't watch," Rohl said. Jax and Jules let go of the man then Jax huffed.

"Well we know where he came from," Jules said. "Actually we know whom he came from."

"I thought you said the house was secure, Jax?" Dayton asked.

"Yes it was," Jax said. "He must have slipped in."

"Let's go before anymore unwanted guests show up," Genevieve said. They all started to move.

"Wait," I asked. "What about me?"

Jax took a step towards me. "You'll have to stay here," he said. "You can't come with us."

What?! "And be left alone to deal with something like that coming back?" I pointed to the headless man. "Really?"

"She's right, Jax," Rohl said. "She can't stay here, it's too dangerous."

"She can't come with us," Jax argued. "She just can't." Rohl then whispered something into Jax's ear that I couldn't hear. After a few moments of that, Jax sighed. "Okay," he said. "I guess we have no choice but to take you with us."

"With you where?" I asked.

"You'll see."

"Jax, aren't you forgetting something?" Genevieve said.

"What?" he asked. She pointed to all of the bodies in the room. "Oh yeah, almost forgot," he said. He raised his arm where a weird device was on it.

"Hold on, I got it, Jax," Dayton said. She lifted her left arm and pressed a button on it. Something shot out of the device and scanned each and every body. Making them disappear out of thin air.

Soon the house was clean and there was no sign of the murders.

"Leave evidence of a struggle," I heard Jules whisper to Dayton. "Make it look like it was a kidnapping, not a murder. The police should be able to take it from there."

"Got it," Dayton said, pressing a button on the device. It shot out a blue light. In seconds all the signs of a struggle were there, just no blood or bodies.

"Wow," I said. "Where did you get that thing?"

"Dayton made it," Jules said. "She makes all of our electronic devices, so we are always one step ahead of everyone else. She's our own personal geek."

"Thanks Jules," Dayton said. "I'm touched."

"Any time." He winked at her.

I rolled my eyes. I guess they could have fun too.

We all started to leave the house. "Wait," I said. They all turned back to look at me.

"What now?" Jax asked, annoyed.

"I'm sorry, but is it alright if I get something from my room?"

Jax didn't answer right away. I asked him since he looked like he's the one in charge here. Why couldn't it be one of the others? "Yeah fine," he said. "But be quick about it."

"Okay." I ran as fast as I could up the stairs. Everything that I had packed was now all over the place. I knew I couldn't bring everything with me, so I chose the one thing every teenager needed. My phone and the charger.

I found it in my bag of clothes, not damaged at all.

I grabbed it, holding it to my chest. I took a breath then looked around the room. All of my posters had been taken down and ripped into shreds. My shelves had been smashed, my desk broken in two, it looked like hurricane Katrina came through my room. Tears welled in my eyes, but I blinked them back.

I couldn't show weakness, not yet. Not with the Regulators around.

I didn't think I would be coming back here, but I couldn't exactly pack anything. As I was about to leave I heard someone come up behind me. *Not again!* I wailed in my head. I braced myself for a fight. I turned around and saw Rohl standing behind me. "Hey," he said. "Are you okay?"

I searched my brain for words. "Yeah," I said breathlessly. "Yeah I'm fine just...looking at my wonderful room."

He gave a small smile, looking at the floor. It wasn't his wicked smile from the other night. I guess he only did that when he's killing. "Yeah, I can see why you're a little spaced out right now," he said.

I nodded, not knowing what to say. "Um...thanks for last night with the guys trying to attack me."

"Just doing my job..." He stopped short. A strange look came across his face. He ran his fingers through his parted black hair.

"I'm Addie," I said a little too excitedly. "I know I didn't introduce myself earlier."

Rohl smiled. "Nice name," he said.

"Thanks." There was an awkward silence

"Anyway we talked Jax into letting you bring a few things with you, like clothes. I think you might have to stay with us for a while."

"Really? And is he okay with that?"

"Not really, but he'll get over it."

"So I can pack a bag? Because I really need a few more things here."

"Sure, just hurry, Jax doesn't like to wait a long time."

"Right." I found a messenger bag and started shoving what wasn't torn into it. I grabbed my toothbrush, toothpaste, and deodorant out of the bathroom then walked back into the room with Rohl. "Okay," I said. "I think I've got everything...oh." I walked over to where my broken desk was and looked for the picture I drew.

I found it not torn but in okay condition. I grabbed a notebook and carefully placed it inside then put it in the bag. "Now I'm ready."

"Great, let's go," Rohl said. We walked down the stairs.

"So are we ready to go?" Jax asked in an annoyed voice.

"Yes I am," I snapped back. "Let's go." We walked out of the house and down the street.

We started down St. Charles Avenue. "So where are we going?" I asked, trying to keep up with them.

"The French Quarter," Jax answered. "It's where we stay."

"Good to know. So what happens after this? Like what do you guys do after you've...done your job or whatever?"

"You know, for someone who just witnessed a horrible thing you ask too many questions," Jax said.

I scoffed.

"Oh give her a break, Jax," Genevieve said. "She's probably just trying to deal with it in her own way. Leave her alone."

"Thanks," I said, looking at Genevieve. I regretted now being so rude to her. She looked like a really nice person.

"What happens now is that we go back to our headquarters and report what we have done and seen to our supervisor," Jules said, answering me. "Also get you settled in. You're going to be staying with us for a while."

"Great," I said.

"The Safe Haven is not so bad," Genevieve said.

"Safe Haven?" I questioned.

"It's where we Regs stay, sleep, train, relax, live really," she said. "It's our home."

"Once you become a full Regulator you live there," Jules said. "It's a great place."

"Plus it's warded against anything evil," Genevieve said. "Nothing can get in."

"That's why it's called the Safe Haven I bet," I said.

"Yep, you're so right," Genevieve said.

"Okay enough with the tell-all," Jax said. "She doesn't need to know all of that."

"I think I do if I'm going to be staying with you guys for a while."

"Until someone comes to claim you, hopefully."

"Seriously? I'm not a dog, I..." midsentence I just realized something. "Oh no," I said.

"What?" Jax asked.

"My uncle. He's at work, or so I think he is. Today we were

supposed to move and..." I closed my eyes, holding back tears. "He's going to freak when he finds that my aunt and I aren't home. We have to do something."

"Like what?" Jax asked. "What would you like us to do?"

"Find him. We have to tell him."

"She's right, Jax," Genevieve said. "We have to."

Jax groaned. "Okay," he said. "Fine, let's go find your uncle."

"Do you know where he works?" Jules asked.

"Yeah I do. Come on." We started back down St. Charles Avenue again.

Night had fallen pretty quickly by the time we made it to St. Joseph Street. Then the rain started. The sky grew darker and soon night had fallen. We had been waiting for an hour for my uncle to come out of the building. "Maybe he's not in there," Jules said, standing next to me at the edge of the parking lot. "Are you sure he worked today?"

"Yes I'm sure," I said. "I know he did."

"I don't see any fresh tire marks from any cars," Dayton said, looking out at the parking lot. "No one has been here all day."

I looked at the building. "He worked today, I know it." But something didn't feel right. I walked up to the front doors and peeked inside. The building was completely empty then a sign on the door caught my eye. "Closed due to construction," it read. According to the date it had been put up last week.

So my uncle hadn't been at work? Why? And what had he been doing all this time?

The Regs caught up to me. "What's going on?" Jax asked.

"It's closed," I said. "And it has been since last week."

"What?" Jules said, looking into the windows.

"Addie, have you ever actually been here?" Rohl asked.

I thought for a moment. "No," I said. "Now that you mention it. I've never actually been in this building."

"Why do you ask?" Genevieve said.

Rohl kept looking at something inside the building. "This building doesn't look like anyone has worked in it for years," he said. "I can tell by the condition it's in."

"What? That's impossible. My uncle has worked for this company ever since I was little."

"Then what does he do?" Rohl asked.

I couldn't answer because I didn't know.

"Do you guys smell that?" Dayton asked. As the wind blew I caught a scent of something. It smelled like rust.

"It's coming from the back of the building," I said. "Come on." I started towards the back.

"Addie, wait," I heard Jules call. I followed the smell, which led me to the back of another building.

At the back of that building lay something on the ground.

I couldn't make out what it was through the rain, so I inched closer. As I got closer I saw hair, arms, legs, and realized it was a body. My heart started pounding in my chest. I finally saw the whole body, and my heart once again sank to my stomach when I realized who it was. There in the cold lay my uncle with a bloody chest and his throat ripped out.

CHAPTER ELEVEN
SAFE AND SOUND

My world had been completely crushed.

I could feel every emotion leave my body as my brain tried to process what I was seeing. Finally, after I came to, I realized what was going on. My uncle was lying dead on the ground behind a company that I thought he worked at with his throat ripped out. A scream rose in me, finally I let it out.

My legs gave out from under me, but I didn't hit the ground. Instead I felt someone holding me up.

"Addie." It was Rohl. "Addie."

I could feel his strong arms around me as I felt myself trying to collapse, but he wasn't letting me. Instead he pulled me closer to his chest where I felt safe, but I was still a wreck. I wrapped my hands and arms around his body, trying to stay up as well. Heavy rain pelted us, showing no sign of letting up. Thunder boomed, lightning struck, but there we stood, not moving an inch.

Suddenly we heard a growl.

I jumped, still in Rohl's arms. "What was that?" Jules asked.

Everyone started to look around. I could hear things above us moving. "Look up!" Genevieve yelled. "The top of the buildings."

I looked up along with everyone else and saw them. Dozens of humanoid creatures with glowing red eyes. I gasped and I felt Rohl's arms slip from around me. I could hear metal clashing as the Regs took out their weapons. "Wait, there are too many," I said. "How are you all going to fight them?"

"One at a time," Rohl said, smiling wickedly. "That's all we can do."

"Rohl, she's right," Genevieve said. "We can't defeat them. We are way outnumbered."

"We got to get back to Safe Haven," Jax said. "We got to get Addie to safety. We don't have time for them. They will just slow us down." He looked at Rohl as everyone holstered their weapons.

"Rohl," Jax's voice boomed over the pouring rain. "Let's go. Now is not the time to fight." I looked at Rohl, who had a pained look on his face. After a few seconds, he holstered his weapons.

"Okay," Jax said. "Let's move..." The things started jumping down from the buildings. "Now!"

We started running back towards the parking lot. I could hear the creatures as they ran behind us. The Regulators were so much faster than me. I was the last one running behind in the group, bringing up the rear and the closest to our pursuers. I could practically feel the things on my heels. Soon I felt something grab my shirt. "Ahhh," I said. Rohl came and killed the thing with his big wicked sword.

"Come on," he said, grabbing me by the arm. "You stay by me."

I nodded and tried my best to keep up with him. He held onto my arm, making it easier for me to keep up. We ran all the way to Danneel Park, and they were still on our tails. I heard the sound of my shirt tearing and felt something graze my back. "Ahhh," I screamed. One of them had caught up to us. I could see it now in the park lights.

It was human-looking but far from, it was green up close with lizard-like features.

Rohl let go of my arm then turned to face the thing. "Get down!" I heard Jules say as he loaded his bow. Rohl grabbed my arm again, and we took off. I could hear Jules firing arrows and the creatures screaming as we ran through the park onto Danneel Street, where finally the things began to give up.

The Regs were showing no sign of slowing down, but I couldn't take it. Between the events of the day and probably just running three miles or more, I was tired. I couldn't do it. I collapsed right on the sidewalk next to a building, totally exhausted. "Addie," I heard Rohl say. I ignored him. I breathed in and out, trying to catch my breath, but ended up dry heaving instead.

Please do not throw up, I said to myself. *Not in front of them.*

I could feel someone kneeling beside me. I brushed my soaking wet hair back and saw that it was Rohl. His hair was falling into his eyes, and he reminded me of when I saw him just yesterday. How my life had changed so much since then. "Addie," he said softly.

"How can my uncle not work there?" I blurted out. "How? I used to watch him go to work every day, for years...how? How?" I started sob uncontrollably.

"Maybe there is a logical explanation for all of this," he said. "But the fact of the matter is until we figure this out, we need to get you to a safe place. And unfortunately that place is in the French Quarter, miles from here. We need to keep moving."

I sobbed and sobbed. Trying to get myself under control.

"Those things could come back any time," Rohl continued. "They won't stop until they find you, so please try to pull yourself together. Be strong and be brave."

His tone was reassuring, but he was also annoying me as well. Even though with every word I was drowning in his accent. I was glad he was the one saying this and not Jax. "What if they do find me?" I asked. "What if they come for me at the Safe Haven? What if they go after my friends Max and Maggie next? Oh God, no, they can't. We lost Ava a few weeks ago. I can't lose them too. What am I going to do? What am I going to do?" My voice rose with every sentence I said.

Rohl grabbed the sides of my arms and kept me from standing up. "It's okay, it's okay," he said, soothing me. I cried again. I felt like I was never going to stop.

"There is no place safer than the Safe Haven," Rohl said. "I promise you that. And we..." he turned to look at the other Regs, "are not going to let anything happen to you. Okay, this is what we do. We save people from the supernatural. We are trained for this. As long as you are with us you are safe. Do you understand?"

I took a breath and nodded. "Yeah," I said weakly. "Yeah, I do."

"Okay, then let's get you outta here." He helped me up. "Want me to carry you?" he asked. "It's a long way back."

"Shall I call a taxi or a carriage for the lady?" Jax joked and with his accent it made it worse. I glared at him.

"Stop it, Jax," Genevieve said. "And they are called streetcars here in New Orleans, not taxies." That was twice Genevieve had said something to Jax for picking on me. I thought I could be friends with her.

"Here," Jules said, removing his bow from around his back. "Hop on my back. I can give you a ride."

"Really? A piggyback ride?" Dayton asked.

"So? My little sister loves them." He smiled.

"I guess I could, but I'm not sure," I said. "I don't want you to have to carry me all the way there. I might be too heavy."

"Please, it's no problem. I lift weights like this all the time." I hesitantly walked over to him. Yes, I was tired, but I didn't want to make him carry me so far. Finally, I climbed on his back, wrapping my arms around his strong neck. "Oh please, you're not heavy," he said. "Wow, you're light, like really light."

"Good, then it won't be tough on you," I said.

I felt him laugh a bit. We started making our way down Danneel Street. I rested my head against the back of Jules' head and closed my eyes for just a moment.

"Hey Addie, wake up," someone said. I jumped at the sound of a guy's voice. "We are here," Jules said. I was still on his back, standing in the middle of a dark courtyard. I could just make out a fountain, wrought iron benches, and old-fashioned lampposts like you see in old movies.

I jumped down from Jules' back and looked around the small courtyard. We walked down a cobblestone path that led to a tree arbor. The trees made it feel like I was in a cave. I felt trapped, and I started to feel panicky.

"Calm down," Dayton said next to me. "This is just the entrance to the Safe Haven."

"Okay," I said. "I'll calm down."

She rolled her eyes then walked off.

Ahead of us Jax, Genevieve, Rohl, and Jules were walking down what looked like a cobblestone path to a set of rock stairs that led to a huge castle door. "Whoa," I said, looking at the masterpiece of a castle in front of me. I could see turrets sticking out from atop the castle even in the dark.

Where are we? I thought. There was no place like this in New Orleans. Not even in the French Quarter.

I walked up the stairs with the Regs and waited under the overhang as Jax started to open the huge wooden door. I saw Jax pull out a crystal and wave it over the door. Symbols suddenly started to appear on the door. I could hear locks unlocking behind it, and soon it opened right before my eyes.

"The Safe Haven is guarded by various symbols that keep certain supernaturals away from it and keep us safe," Rohl whispered in my ear. "It's designed so ordinary people like you can't see it."

"But I can see it," I said, turning to him. "So why can I see it?"

"That's something we need to figure out."

"Indeed," Jax said, putting the crystal away. "And I know just the person who would love to do that."

I followed the Regs into the huge castle. We walked into the entrance hall, where two sets of staircases were attached to a high mezzanine. I could see open corridors under the mezzanine and on top of it. The castle itself was lit by candle and very low light, making it hard to see. The walls were made of brown stone just like the outside of the castle.

I expected a musty rocky smell, but it actually smelled quite clean.

My eyes were starting to adjust, and I could see a man standing atop the mezzanine. As the Regs and I made our way into the entrance hall a bit further, he started walking down the staircase on my right side. "There you are," he said in a semi stern accented voice. "I was beginning to get worried. I thought I would have had to call the realm and send a search party for you all."

"Sorry, Gaspar," Jax said. "We meant to hurry."

"I thought that's what you were doing in the first place," Gaspar said, still not sounding very angry, but I could tell he was a bit displeased. "Do you have any idea what time it is? Honestly, I thought that something terrible...oh my," he said when he finally noticed me. He was now standing in front of all of us in the light and I could make out his features.

He a tall man, about six feet at the most with grayish white hair, and a kind face with soft pale blue eyes. He looked to be in his early fifties. "And um..." Gaspar said, clearing his throat. "Who have we here?"

"This is Addie..." Jax said, turning to me.

"François," I said. "Adalyn, but everyone calls me Addie."

"And you...you...were saved by them?" He pointed to the Regs.

"Yes, sir. They saved my life many times today."

"More times than we had to in fact," Jax said. I glared at him.

"Orfeous' men came after her," Rohl said. "We saved her just in the nick of time."

"But my aunt and uncle," I said, trying to hold back tears. "Couldn't be saved."

"We figured she needed to stay here for a while," Jules said. "If that's possible."

"Well of course it is," Gaspar said, his mood suddenly changing from somber to happy. I started to wonder if he was faking or joking like Jax seemed to do. "This is a Safe Haven after all. She's more than welcome."

"Look, if you think that it's wrong for me to stay here because I'm not like one of you, then..." I said, getting angry.

"Oh no, no, you misunderstood me," Gaspar said, smiling. "I meant yes, it's okay if you stay here for a while until we get this sorted out. We are Regulators after all, this is what we do."

I breathed a sigh of relief.

"I'm so sorry about your aunt and uncle, though," Gaspar said. "Really I am."

"Thank you," I said, once again fighting back tears.

"Well now, you should get settled in for the night. I'll let the girls show you where you'll be staying and..."

"Oh, are the children back?" I heard a high-pitched voice say.

I turned to see a plump woman with curled orange hair coming our way, dressed in an old raggy dress and an apron. She stopped when she saw all of us. "Oh, they are back," she said, sounding like she was about to cry. "Oh, I thought something terrible had happened to them with all this chaos going around and..." She saw me and paused.

"Addie," I heard her say.

I opened my mouth to say something but was cut off.

"They are fine, Mildred," Gaspar said. "All of them. They are home now safe and sound."

"That's wonderful." She walked up to them.

"Hello, Mildred," Genevieve said, hugging the woman. "We are fine, as Gaspar said."

Mildred hugged each and every one of them, then when she got to me she stopped. "And who is this lovely little thing here?" she asked.

That was weird, I thought. *I could've sworn she said my name.*

"This is Addie François, Mildred," Gaspar said. "She was rescued by them from some of Orfeous' men."

"Oh, you poor thing. I bet that must have been scary."

Lady, you don't know the half of it, I thought. I kind of liked Mildred, but she came across as an over-motherly type figure who cared a little too much and was very over protective. Somehow in some way I felt comforted by this.

She cupped my face with both of her hands. "You look a little pale," she said. "And a bit weak. Would you like me to fix some tea for you?"

"Oh no, ma'am, I'm fine," I said. She took her hands away. "I couldn't impose with it being so late after all."

"It's fine, Addie," Gaspar said. "You are going to be staying with us for a while. Whatever you need we will provide."

Wow, overbearing much? I thought.

"I could sure use a good meal right about now," Jules said. "How about you guys?" The rest except me agreed.

"Oh, I'll go fix something now," Mildred said, heading for one of the halls.

"Mildred, not now," Gaspar said. "It's too late. They will just have to wait until morning for breakfast."

"But that's too far away," Jules said. "I need to eat. I'm a growing boy."

"You're five-foot-seven and nineteen, Jax," Dayton said. "You've stopped growing."

"Oh whatever," Jules said. Mildred smiled and gave him a light pat on his arm. I watched them. They all looked like family. If I didn't know any better I would think they would be.

"I expect full reports of today by the end of tomorrow from each one of you," Gaspar said to the Regs. "No later."

"Yes, sir," Jax said. "Will do."

Genevieve and Dayton turned to me. "Come on, we'll show you the way to the rooms," Genevieve said. I nodded and followed her and Dayton down a corridor.

Halfway through the castle and two flights of stairs later, we finally made it to the corridor housing all the rooms. "Here we are," Genevieve said in a girly singsong voice. I rolled my eyes as I walked down the corridor with her and Dayton. "So my room is down the hall on the left, Dayton's is adjacent to mine, and yours can be...well any one you want."

I looked down the hall.

"Are all the rooms the same?" I asked.

"Yes and no. They can be whatever a person wants them to be as long as they think hard about it," Genevieve said.

"Hm?" I asked.

"They can change," Dayton put it simply. "Whatever you want them to be they will be. It's magic."

"They are charmed that way," Genevieve said.

"Magic? Charmed? What does all that mean? Who does all that?"

"Witches," Genevieve said. "When this place was first built a group of witches were hired by the Regulators to seal the place from any supernaturals and charmed the bedrooms so that they change into whatever anyone wants them to be."

"Why?"

"So the Regulators who stay here can feel at home no matter what. It's our way of expressing ourselves."

I nodded. "What is this place used for exactly?"

"Resituate for Regulators both in training and on the job," Genevieve said as if she was quoting a book. "We live and train here while we wait for any sign of any supernaturals breaking the laws or worse."

"It's also used as a learning facility as well," Dayton said. "We have many young Regs in training that pass by and live here just to get the feel of the job before they fully start doing it."

I nodded, starting to get the picture a bit.

Genevieve opened a door next to me and stepped inside. I did the same. The room looked like a room in a castle from a fairy tale. High ceilings, four-poster bed fit for a queen, furniture, big windows, and even a door to a balcony.

"Wow," I said, never seeing anything so beautiful in my life. "And why would you want to change something like this?"

"To fit my style," Genevieve said. "I'm not really into the whole princess stuff, despite living in a castle." Genevieve, as girly as she acted, didn't come over to me as the princess type either. Though this would make me want to stand on the balcony almost hoping I would meet prince charming. Almost.

"So go ahead," Genevieve said. "Imagine whatever type of room you would love to have. It can be anything from a place on the beach to a cozy cabin in the mountains."

I gave a small smile then closed my eyes.

I imagined mint green walls, a polished hard wood floor, huge white French-style doors, a comfortable bed with bluish-green covers, clothes everywhere, a desk, and a dresser with a mirror on it. I opened my eyes and was standing right in my un-ruined room. It was as I had left it before those men trashed it. Even the pictures of my aunt, uncle, and me from our vacation a few years ago were in a picture frame on the wall.

My posters, my desk, dresser; everything was just like it had been. Even the dent in the wall behind the door where I kicked it during a temper tantrum.

It was all there. It was so perfect, so real, then again it was so unreal.

"This isn't real," I said. "This isn't real."

"Calm down," I heard Genevieve said. "It's all real, Addie. It's all very real, that's the power of magic."

I looked around the room one last time then back at the girls.

"We'll leave you to get settled," Genevieve said with her hand on the door. "I bet you're tired from today."

"Yeah, I bet you guys are too," I said.

"Goodnight then. We'll see you in the morning." I told them goodnight and was then left alone in my new/old room in the Safe Haven. After I took a very, very long bath (which was included when I thought of the room), I changed into some clothes that I brought and got into bed. Even the shadows on the walls from trees that had been outside my original room were there. I really did feel like I was back home.

I relayed the events of the day back in my head.

Fear plagued me once again. I fought it back along with tears and reminded myself that I was safe. Nothing was going to hurt me, not in this huge-ass castle that people were not even supposed to see. That made me feel a little better. Then I thought of Rohl and how he saved me yet again. He was so concerned about me. He even made sure I didn't fall behind when we ran from those reptilian things.

I was safe and sound here for now. When morning comes I wasn't so sure.

CHAPTER TWELVE
HOW THINGS CAME TO BE

Knock, knock, knock.

That's funny. Who's knocking on my door at this time of the morning? "Addie," I heard Mildred say from the other side of the door. "Wake up, sleepy head, you'll sleep your life away." I groaned then opened my eyes. *Wait where am I?* I wondered. Then I recalled the events from yesterday. Oh that's right. I sat up in bed, feeling worse than I did yesterday.

I looked at the clock and saw that it was a little past lunch time. No wonder Mildred woke me up. I wondered how the others slept. Poor Jules was hungry, I hope he got to eat. I got out of bed then walked over to my door. I opened it and saw a bright-eyed Mildred standing there, her orange hair pulled back and apron stained.

"Hello, dear," she said. "Oh, I hope I didn't wake you."

"No you didn't," I said, forcing a smile. "I was about to get up anyway."

"Good, I didn't want you to sleep through lunch too. It will be ready soon. I just wanted to let you know."

"Okay, thank you. I'll be down in a bit."

"Alrighty then, I'll be seeing you." She smiled then left. I peeked down the hall and saw the other doors closed. I figured Dayton and Genevieve would be up by now. The boys as well. I changed into some clothes I brought then walked out of the room. I walked down the corridor and through the way Genevieve and Dayton showed me yesterday.

I needed to find the dining hall, if they had one.

I walked down a hallway then down one of the flights of stairs. Then down another hallway then down another flight of stairs. *Damn,* I thought. *How big is this freaking castle?* A long time ago my friends and I used to joke about going to England and touring the castles. Now I was actually kind of living it.

Though I bet the castles there were a lot easier to navigate than the Safe Haven.

I finally made it to the entrance hall from last night. But from there I was lost. I was just about to give up hope when I saw Gaspar coming from one of the halls. "Hey, Gaspar," I said.

"Ah, Addie," he said, looking up from his book. "Glad to see you out and about. How was your first night here? I trust the girls told you how the rooms work."

"Yes they did, and I had a very restful night. I just wish it could have lasted longer."

"Yes indeed. Did you need my help with something?"

"Yeah, I was wondering where the dining room is? This place is so big."

"It's through that archway right over there." He pointed behind me. I turned to look at it. "Just go down that hallway, and it'll lead you straight to both the kitchen and the dining area," Gaspar said.

"Okay," I said. "Thank you."

"You're welcome, oh, and the others are in the study cleaning their weapons, which is up the stairs through the middle archway if you need them. They'll be there for a while. And if there is anything else you need please just ask."

"I'm sure I will."

He smiled then walked away. I turned to look back at the archway leading to the dining room, then I looked up towards the mezzanine at the archway leading to the study. I wanted to go see if lunch was ready, but then again, I wanted to go see how the others were. Suddenly my stomach growled. "Okay," I said. "Dining hall it is." I started for the hallway.

The hallway felt creepy and unwelcoming. It wasn't very well lit, so that was making it worse. I wondered how old this castle was, because it seriously needed some lighting updated. I found my way to the kitchen finally, where I saw Mildred cooking in the spacious room. She was cutting away at vegetables, not even noticing I was there.

"Oh Addie," she said when she saw me. "You startled me."

"Sorry," I said.

"That's all right, dear. Lunch will be ready in just a bit. Why don't you go and have a seat in the dining room." She gestured to a huge wooden door. I nodded and walked over to it. I pushed it open and found Jax, Jules, Genevieve, Dayton, and two men I didn't know sitting at a huge oak table.

They were all talking away and didn't even know I was there.

Now they really did look like a family.

"Hey, Addie," Jules said from his spot at the end of the table. Everyone turned to look at me.

"Oh good, you're awake," Genevieve said. "How did you sleep?"

"Great," I said. "I slept great actually."

"That's because you felt like you were in your room," Dayton said with a bit of edge to her voice. *And for the fact that I was practically almost killed yesterday too. It can really make a person feel tired,* I wanted to say but held my tongue. With her around it would be best. I felt like I didn't want to trust her or any one of them really.

"Well don't just stand there," Jules said. "Have a seat. Mildred will be serving us soon."

I nodded then took a seat at the far end of the table next to Rohl. There was a man at the other end of the table who wouldn't stop looking at me. I looked him straight in the eye then directed my gaze somewhere else. Rohl was looking at me too, so that made me feel a little better.

"Addie, this is Emile and Butch," Genevieve said, gesturing to the two men sitting on the other side of the table. "They sort of live here as well."

"Butch is our training instructor," Jules said. "And Emile comes and goes from here. He works for the police department and notifies us if anything strange goes on."

"Hi, it's nice to meet you," I said.

"Nice to meet you too," Emile said, tipping his glass to me with a smile. He had to be in his forties at least, with dark hair, bit of a beard, and a kind face. Butch on the other hand was the one who kept looking at me. He looked similar to Emile, but his face looked darker and it was scratched in a few places.

"I'm sorry, but have we meet?" he asked me over everyone else.

Everyone paused.

"No," I said. "I don't think so."

"You look strangely familiar to me, that's all." He stared at me, making me feel uncomfortable.

"Oh now here we go," Rohl said. "She hasn't been here five minutes, and you've already made her uncomfortable." Rohl then turned to me. "I'm sorry, he's got a thing for the young ones," he said. "And blondes."

"That's a damn lie, and you know it," Butch howled.

Rohl laughed. "Just a joke, man, chill out."

"Oh I'll chill out all right, Sivan, when I see you doing three hundred pushups when it's time to train again."

Sivan? Why did that name sound familiar?

"You're on old man," Rohl said, slamming his hand on the table and smiling.

I huffed. They really did act like a family.

"Where's Nils and Gaspar?" Jax asked.

"Nils doesn't eat, remember," Dayton said. "And Gaspar is probably investigating where Orfeous might strike next."

"Um, that's our job, remember?" Jules said.

"He knows that, but I think he wants us to rest today since we were out so late last night," Genevieve said.

"Sorry," I said, knowing that I was the reason they stayed out so late.

"Oh don't be, it's what we do," Jules said. I felt a little better at him saying that.

"All right, dears," Mildred said, coming in with a serving tray filled with food. "Lunch is served." She put all of the plates of food on the table. I gasped when I saw what was on them. Chicken and dumplings, greens, potato salad, black-eyed peas, house salad, fried chicken, and apple pie. It was a regular Southern meal.

"Wow," I said. "Jules, now I see why you were upset about missing dinner last night."

"Amen, sister," Jules said as he filled his plate. "Mildred's cooking is the best. Just wait until dinner tonight."

"And I'm fixing it up right now as we speak," Mildred said, smiling. "Now Addie, you don't be shy now. Go ahead, there is plenty to go around."

I was a little nervous at taking anything despite how hungry I was. These people were taking me in for I didn't know how long. They were already giving me so much without asking anything in return. I just felt weird about eating their food. "Come on, Addie,"

Genevieve said. "Before the boys take it all."

I grabbed a plate and started to fix what I wanted. I got some chicken and dumplings, house salad, black-eyed peas, and apple pie. I stabbed my fork into the chicken and dumplings and took a bite. It tasted so good. Better than anything I'd had, either that or I was just really hungry.

"Good, hn?" Jules asked with his mouth full.

"Jules," Genevieve said. "Don't talk with your mouth full, it's rude."

"Sorry," he said after swallowing.

I finished my main course then went on to the apple pie, which tasted even better than it looked. "Oh my God," I said. "This is good."

"That's nothing," Jules said. "Wait till you taste her blackberry cobbler. It's amazing. I mean, if you like blackberries."

"I don't, but I'll be willing to try some."

"It is really good," Rohl said, eating his pie. "Reminds me of home."

"You're not originally from Louisiana? I mean I figured you weren't because of the accent, but you seem to know New Orleans well."

Rohl smiled. "You're right. I'm not originally from here, but I do have a few family ties here, though it's not many."

"Where are you from then?"

Across the table Jax cleared his throat. "I think that's enough questions for right now," he said.

I glared at him. What was this guy's problem with me?

"If you are all finished, we need to start cleaning our weapons. A new case could arrive at any time, and with Orfeous still around we might want to be prepared." He excused himself then walked out of the room. Soon the others followed him after they thanked Mildred as she walked in to gather the plates.

"What is his problem with me?" I asked

"Don't mind Jax," Emile said, helping Mildred clean the table. "He doesn't like it when non-Regulators stay here at the Safe Haven, even when they really need it."

"I wish he'd just get over it."

"I do too. Don't worry, you're not the only one. He gives me the cold shoulder as well." He walked into the kitchen. I wanted to know more about them, these Regulators. And I wanted to know it now. If I was going to be staying here then I needed to know who these people were. It's only fair, right?

I got up from the table. I decided to go and find the study and possibly the Regs.

I walked up the stairs to the mezzanine and went through the archway in the middle, which led me to a flight of stairs leading to a big room. Bookshelves made up the majority of the walls from the very bottom to the top of the glass ceiling. Statues of various animal-like creatures were placed in random stops. Glass cases with weapons of all kinds also stood in different places all over the room.

Skeletons of animals, beings, and sea creatures hung from the ceiling on wires. They looked big and scary. One had a huge hump while another one looked like some kind of sea horse, and the biggest one of all took up most of the ceiling and had a huge mouth.

The further I got, the more I saw.

This is more like a museum than a study, I thought.

I turned and saw a bronze statue of a man dressed in what the Regs wear, holding a weapon in his hand striking down some creature. I looked at it more closely. Captivated by it.

"Finding your way around the castle now," someone said. I jumped and saw Rohl standing behind me, smiling.

"You," I said.

"Why so jumpy?" he asked, flashing his wicked smile.

"I'm always jumpy. At least I have been lately with everything going on."

"It's understandable, but still just try to relax. No one can hurt you here."

"Good to know."

"So why have you come? Or does cleaning weapons really sound that interesting for you?"

"I want to know more about you guys. And I don't care what Jax says. I just want to know who I'm staying with. Apart from the whole being the supernatural police."

Rohl smiled. "Okay, then follow me." He walked ahead of me. I started to follow him. I followed him towards the back of the huge room, where the others stood by a table cleaning their weapons. "Hey guys," Rohl said. "We have a little spy."

I smiled shyly. "Hi," I said.

"So," Jules said. "Finally found your way up here. Where all our secrets are."

"Hm?"

"Jules," Jax said.

"Enough, Jax. You don't run the show around here. You're just here temporarily like Addie." Jax groaned.

"What brings you here, Addie?" Genevieve asked.

I turned to Rohl. "Tell them," he said. "It's okay, they won't bite."

I looked at them. "I want to know more about you guys," I started. "Since I'm going to be staying here with all of you, I think I have that right."

"Oh bloody hell, here we go," Jax said. "It's not enough that we save your life and let you stay here, but now you want to know about us too. Wow, this just keeps getting better and better."

"What's the big deal anyway?" I asked.

"What *is* the big deal, Jax?" Jules asked.

"You want to know what the big deal is?" Jax said. "She's human, that's what."

"Are you saying that you're not?"

"No...it's...just, you're not one of us. You can't be trusted. How can we possibly tell you what we are and what we do? You are an outsider to us."

"Really? Is what you are worried about? That I'm going to spill all of your secrets to someone like my friends. My friends probably think I'm dead right now, so it doesn't matter. It's not like there's a lot to tell, right? I mean, I know you guys are Regulators. What more could there be?"

The room got quiet.

"A lot more," Jules said. I didn't say a word.

Jax sighed then looked at me. "So you really want to know about us?" he asked. "Every single little thing?"

"Yes," I said. "I do. Anything at all. Just so I can make sense of this situation I'm in. It doesn't have to be everything, just something. I'm lost here in this world that exists now."

Jax nodded and put his crossbow down. "This is going to be a long story, so you might want to get comfortable," he said. "And don't blame me if everything you were ever taught as a child is thrown out the window."

I nodded, standing where I was

"We are Regulators, you already know that. We come from a place called Arcania. It's a place that is in a realm that lies in between dimensions in our very own universe.

"The Arcania realm is an old realm filled to the brim with

supernatural creatures and beings of all kinds. Even some you may not know of. It's ruled by a person we call The Head of the Realm and the High Council. Years ago the supernaturals of the realm were tired of staying just in the realm. They wanted to live somewhere else.

"Through years and years of begging The Head of the Realm at the time decided that they could go live in other countries. That's when the problem started. The supernaturals started causing chaos almost everywhere they went, pointing that blame on The Head for giving them free rein in the first place. He then decided that the supernaturals needed to be governed in the real world since he had to stay in the realm at all times."

Jax took a break, making sure I was listening.

"So everyone in the realm is some kind of supernatural?" I asked.

"Nope," Jax said. "Not all. There are, believe it or not, some supernaturals that birth children who don't get their supernatural trait. That's were us Regulators come in. Since we don't really fit in the realm, The Head then got the idea of using us as the supernaturals' outer realm police.

"He took it to the High Council, they agreed, and here we are today. Being used, trained, and bred to do something that shouldn't have happened in the first place."

"But wait, if it wasn't supposed to be this way, why not make all of the supernaturals go back to the realm?" I asked.

"It's not that simple," Jax said. "Most of them have gotten used to living outside of the realm and don't want to go back."

"And they've bred as well," Genevieve said. "Making more of them who were raised outside the realm. The real world is all they have ever known."

"Plus, this has been going on for centuries now," Dayton said.

"It's not like it just happened yesterday."

"Believe us, it would be more trouble getting them back in the realm than just policing them like we do," Rohl said. "And they have a right to live outside the realm as they please. After the first supernaturals caused havoc in the human world, in order to keep them in line The Head of the Realm signed a bill making it legal for them to leave. Since he signed it officially it can't be taken back. It's an official law now. It can't be changed."

"But with that bill signed they have to obey the rules that followed it," Jules said. "Number one: they must remain hidden from all mankind and blend into society."

"Two: they must report to the realm every few years on their wellbeing or let a Regulator check in on them," Rohl said.

"Three: if they use any kind of magic they must keep it to themselves or don't use it at all unless they return to the realm," Dayton said.

"And Four: they must not, for any reason, cause havoc on humanity," Genevieve said.

"That includes spells of any kind, hurt, pestilence, grief, tragedy, trickery," Dayton said.

"And the most important of all..."

"Death," they all said together.

"They have their rules too?" I asked.

"Yes," Jax said. "They have their rules that they must follow, and we have ours."

"But wait, if they have rules then your job should be easy, right? If they obey them everything is good, right?"

"Once again, it's not that simple, Addie," Genevieve said.

"You're talking about taking beings or creatures who know nothing else but what they do and who they are, and you try to take that away from them. All just so they can live in another place undetected," Rohl said. "It's not as easy for some as you would think."

"Take a werewolf for instance," Jules said. "A werewolf can change whenever they want to, not just during a full moon. Though during a full moon they have little to no control over it. They feel the lunar energy radiating off the moon. They can't help it, they've got to turn. If they lose control and someone sees, it can ruin everything that Regulators and the Arcania realm have worked centuries to protect."

I looked at him, not really getting it.

"Humans finding out that the supernatural exists," Rohl finished for me.

"Our job is not just to keep the supernaturals in line," Jax said.

"It's to keep the human world separate from the supernatural one," Rohl finished. "It's a tougher job than you think."

"Then again, it's their fault for wanting to live outside the realm," Dayton said. She had a point, but I understood why they would want to live and see the world, so to speak.

"Are you starting to get it now?" Jax asked.

"Yeah," I said. "I think so."

"There's a lot to know about what we do," Jules said. "A lot, but the longer you stay here the more you figure it out."

"How long will that be exactly?"

"However long it takes," Jax grunted.

Jules rolled his eyes. "Like I said before, Jax, this isn't your domain, so don't act like you make all the rules here."

"Whatever," Jax said.

"Which brings me to my next question, are all of you from the realm?" I asked. "I mean, I know you are, you kind of just told me, but you two have accents so I…"

"Yes we are from the Arcania realm, Addie," Rohl said, smiling. "That we are from indeed."

"Rohl and I are just from a different part of it, if you want to put it like that," Jax said.

"What part?" I asked. "Sorry, I'm asking a lot of questions, it's just…I want to know."

"It's kind of hard to explain if you have never lived there. Have you ever heard the saying 'the world is a melting pot'?"

"Yes, we learn that in school. America is one actually."

"Well the same goes for the realm. There are people of all races and cultures there, some with accents, some not. Both of our family backgrounds are English, mine also has French as well and Jewish."

"Our ancestors originated in England but moved to the realm to further their powers," Jax started. "Some of them were born without the supernatural gene, so they became Regulators, and years later, here we are today."

"So your families aren't supernatural then? I mean you guys all didn't come from werewolves or vampires or witches. You guys were born without any of that in you?"

"Correct," Jax said. "A lot of the families that have Regulators nowadays came from Regulators a long time ago. Once many children were born without any connection to the supernatural, when they grew up and had kids they passed that trait down to their own, and then it continued."

"So now almost all Regulators born come from natural-born Regulators," Rohl said."

I nodded.

"Rohl and I normally stay at the Safe Haven in England, where we are over the various supernaturals there," Jax said. "But we were called to help the Regs here to catch one that had escaped from a prison over there."

"Why you two?"

"Because we are the best," Rohl said, smiling. "Or so they say."

"Rohl also has family ties here as well," Jax said. "His father at one time lived and worked here when Regs where in short supply."

"Okay, now it's making sense," I said. "But how did you get here?"

"Portal," Rohl said. "The realm is full of them. You just find one or open one, think of where you want to go, and then step through it."

"Though some portals can be set to go a certain place," Jules said.

"But that's another story," Jax said. I looked at him. "You got what you want about us. You'll have to wait to hear the rest. That's enough for today, or for now at least."

I nodded, still wanting to learn more but not believing everything I just heard. I suddenly realized that this whole supernatural thing was bigger than I thought it was. How did I ever end up in a mess like this?

CHAPTER THIRTEEN
SUPERNATURAL 101

As the Regs cleaned their weapons I browsed the endless supply of books on the various shelves. I ran my fingers over the endless rows of books, trying to find something to read. *I bet all they have here are books about the supernatural,* I thought. *What else would they have?* I walked down a little farther and found something that caught my attention.

A huge worn book with a dark-green leather cover trimmed in gold was sitting on a wooden podium with a light shining right on it.

I walked over to it. Stroking it with my fingers, I tried to read the front cover, but it was in another language. I tried very hard, but there was no way I could pronounce it.

"Ah," someone said from behind me. I turned to see Jules walking towards me with the others right behind him. "I see you've found our most prized possession. Our very own *Pecus et Creatura.*"

"Your what?" I asked.

"It's a book," Genevieve said. "A bestiary."

"Again what?"

"It's a book of beasts, beings, and creatures," Jax said. "Bestiaries contain collections of all things supernatural from every culture and country ever known."

"This is just one of a few we have," Jules said. "Every Safe Haven is required to have at least one, and it's normally this one. This particular bestiary goes back centuries. It's the oldest one out there."

"In that case, everything I would want to ever know about

anything supernatural is right here in this book?" I asked.

"Yep, everything and more," Jules said. "Go ahead, open it."

"Jules," Jax said.

"Shut it, Jax. She already knows that things go bump in the night when she's asleep. Now she can find out what they are."

Well now, I don't know if I want to open it after that statement, I thought. But part of me was curious. I wanted to know what is really out there. I put my fingers on the side of the book and lifted its cover. I was expecting a lot of dust, but there was hardly any. I guess they used it a lot. I flipped through the parchment pages, looking at all of the different things in it.

Color pictures showed what the creature or being would look like, along with a brief history, strengths, and weakness. Every page I read went into so much detail, sometimes in too much detail. Suddenly I got an idea. I flipped through the book, quickly trying to find what I was looking for.

After what seemed like forever, I gave up.

"What where you looking for, Addie?" Genevieve asked.

"I was looking to see what those things were that attacked us last night," I said. "I couldn't find anything. Well, at least nothing that would match what they were exactly."

"Yeah, we gotta look that up as well," Jules said. "Guess we'll be doing that today as well."

"You didn't find anything?" Rohl asked.

"Yeah, because she knows what to look for," Jax said.

I glared at him. "Seriously? Do you really think it takes 'special training' to read a damn book?" I asked.

"Apparently it does, or you would have found it in there. If you can't find it in there then it's not meant to be found."

"Let me look again." I started flipping through the book again. At least it was alphabetized. Once again creatures and beings matched some qualities that the things had but not all. Disappointed, I looked up at the Regs. "Well, I guess it doesn't exist then if it's not in here after all," I said, sighing.

"No, it has to be," Jules said.

"You heard Jax," I told him. "If it's not in here then it's not real or whatever."

"No, that book is ancient. It has to be in there."

"Jules is right," Genevieve said. "It has to be."

"Unless," Dayton said.

"Unless what?" Jules asked.

"It's another chimera."

"A what? Do you really think it could be?" Genevieve asked. "Yes, it all makes sense now, kind of. What else could it be?"

"Well, then this is a new one," Rohl said. "Better, stronger, faster. They are getting almost impossible to beat."

"That makes three kinds now," Jax said. "Boy, he's really getting bold."

"He can get bold and imaginative at times," Dayton said. "But it will come back to bite him in the ass pretty quick."

"Not if he's smart and cunning," Jax said. "And we all know he is."

"Excuse me!" I called out.

They all looked at me.

"What the hell is a freaking chimera?" I asked.

Jax sighed and hung his head then turned to me. "A chimera is a beast in Greek mythology with the body of a goat, the head of a lion, and a snake for a tail. In interpretation, it represents three completely different sets of DNA or parts that can come together and share one, creating a whole."

"That sounds completely insane. There is no such thing..." I started to say, then I remembered where I was and what I had seen. It could be a possibility. They were dealing with the supernatural here. Anything could go.

I shut my mouth just as Jules walked over to the book and started flipping through the pages. He stopped at a particular page in the Cs and pointed to a picture. I stared when sure enough I saw in the picture a beast standing on a cliff side with the body of a goat, the head and paws of a lion, and a snake for a tail. Creating one messed-up creature.

I looked back up at all of the Regs. "This is it?" I said. "This is a chimera."

"Yep, in the flesh," Jules said. "Well on the page, really." He chuckled and smiled. I gave a small smile back.

"But this doesn't look anything like the things that came after us," I said.

"The chimera isn't just a beast itself," Jax said. "It's also a term in both science and the supernatural. In science there are real animals out there that are considered chimeras. They look like one animal but have the characteristics of two more."

"I've heard of that, but I didn't know there was a term for it. Either that, or I wasn't paying attention."

There was a short pause.

"Wait, so those things were chimeras?" I asked.

"Something on the lines of it, yes," Jules said. I was glad he answered and not Jax. "Like Jax said before, there are chimeras in the animal world and in the supernatural world. The ones in the supernatural world are usually made, though. I've never seen a natural chimera. Now that is something that doesn't exist."

"The guy that we are after makes these chimeras," Dayton said.

"Or so we think," Jax said. "We don't know for sure."

"Oh we do know for sure. I've proved that over and over again, you just don't want to listen."

"How have you proved it?" I asked, not really wanting to know.

"Got a sample of one a few months ago. Ran it under a microscope, did a few tests on it. The DNA came back as a werewolf, loco, and rougarou combined."

"A what? A what? And a what?" I asked.

Dayton rolled her eyes at me. "Whatever," she said. "That part is not important. The bottom line is I proved those things were mixed, but this one..." she gestured to Jax, "...didn't want to believe me. Three sets of different DNA sharing one body, a chimera. I rest my case." I half expected her to take a bow.

"It's not that I didn't want to believe you," Jax said. "It's just...no one has ever tried to make monsters into more monsters. It's not right. It screws up the whole supernatural balance."

"Well you should know that we live in a world that is unbalanced anyway. And that sometimes there are some people out there that just want to break the rules," Dayton said, folding her arms. She glanced at me then looked back towards him.

Okay, what was up with that? I thought. Something told me that Jules and Dayton really didn't get along well with Jax. Guess that made three of us.

"Also," Dayton said, looking back towards me, "my family, the Devereaux's, are inventers. They were some of the first Regulators. We kind of have a knack for inventing and trying new things. With that said, I knew that the creature, the first chimera we ran into months ago, was not a normal creature. It was something more... monstrous."

I gulped, scared now.

"Don't worry, Addie," Rohl said. "We will protect you. We won't let any of those things get to you."

"Do you think there are still more to come?" I asked.

"Oh yeah," Jules said. "If you are wanted by him, then he'll do whatever it takes to get to you."

"Who is this he you keep speaking of? I want to know."

"That's another story," Jax said. "You know everything you need to right now and then some. Lesson over with. Go bother someone else." He started to walk off.

I shrugged then noticed an area farther to the right of where we were standing with cabinets, stands, charts, and a table. "What's that over there?" I asked.

"Ugh," Jax sighed.

"Don't worry, I think I can take it from here," Jules said to Jax.

"This is our Rockology area," Jules said as we made our way over to the area. "Gaspar has one too. Actually he has his own study area like we Regs do."

"Really?" I asked. "He's a Reg too I'm assuming?"

"Yes, but he's retired in a way. He still helps us if we need him, like our mentor."

"If we can't find or do something, we go to him for help," Genevieve said. "He does a lot for us."

"Yes, he does. Anyway, like I was saying, this is our Rockology area. We have a series of crystals, rocks, precious stones, and agates here. We use them to boost our strength, energy, and healing."

"Seriously?" I asked. "Rocks for healing?"

"Yep, they heal, make you stronger, faster, less fatigued."

"Haven't you ever heard of medicine and steroids?" I asked.

"Can't use them," Rohl said. "Our bodies don't react the way normal people would to modern things like that."

"Because you're from the realm."

"Exactly."

"How would you even use a stone for healing? Wave it over yourself? Hold onto it? Crush it up and eat it?"

Rohl laughed. "No," he said. "We don't do that."

"We do this," Jules said, facing me, holding a red stone in his hand. He placed the stone on his arm and said something I couldn't make out. He removed his hand, and I watched in amazement as the stone dissolved into his skin right before my eyes.

"Oh my gosh," I almost screamed. "How...how did you do that?"

"With a little bit of practice and magic," he said. "The stones are made to disappear into our skin."

"But what about a reaction like...I don't know. That can't be good making it dissolve into your skin like that."

"It's fine, Addie, we do this all the time. That's what we Regs do, what we are trained for, what we are built for. How do you think the beings in the realm have survived all these years in it? By using stones, crystals, and more."

"That's impossible."

"Haven't you figured it out yet that almost nothing is impossible," Rohl said, "in our world?"

"Nope, I guess not. I guess I'm still looking for something to be normal."

"Well, then you are going to be looking for a long time." He smiled at me. I had to look away from him. I was starting to drown again.

I noticed a few charts placed on the wall. "What are the charts for?" I asked.

"Listing all of the stones, crystals, agates, and other magic rocks out there," Jules said. "We gotta know what we are working with."

"And what they are used for," Genevieve said. "You can't just mix and match some of them. There are rules for using them."

"Like what?"

"Take agates for instance," Jules said. "Both are good in combat and for healing, but they are very strong. So strong that you don't want to mix it with other stones that can do the exact same thing. It would be too overbearing."

"Not to mention you could kill yourself," Rohl said.

"Death by an overdose on rocks. Never thought I'd hear that in my life."

"It's possible," Jules said. "Trust me."

"Some rocks we use just for fighting, and some we use just for healing," Genevieve said. "We use agates for both of those things, but when it comes to healing it has to be a life or death situation, since they are so strong."

Rohl looked at me. "Is all of this making any sense?" he asked.

I thought for a moment. "You know what, it kind of is." And it did in some weird kind of way. Just like in medicine. You didn't want to use Tylenol when you've had a tooth pulled or a broken bone. You wanted something stronger so you could heal faster.

"But that's not all they are used for," Genevieve said.

"Really?" I asked. "What else are they used for?"

"Just about anything, really," Genevieve said.

"Protection, balance, remembrance, enhanced sight, wisdom," Jules said. "You name it, there's one for it."

"And you guys use all of them?"

"Yep, we sure do," Genevieve said. "We also wear necklaces that keep us connected to the realm that are made of stone too."

"What necklaces?"

Genevieve touched a small chain around her neck and showed me a flat purplish-blue cut stone that sparkled without sunlight.

Dayton reached under her high collared blouse and pulled out an octahedron-cut stone of the same color. All of the boys then revealed black leather bracelets with the same stone cut into different shapes as well, all with the same glittering effect.

"Whoa. What are they?" I asked.

They are realm stones cut from a portal and made for Regulators only," Genevieve said.

"They keep our connection to the realm even when we are not in it," Jules added. "When we wear them they make us feel safe."

"They also help us go to and from the realm," Dayton said, placing her necklace back under her blouse. "There are many ways we can enter the realm, but wearing a piece of a portal makes it easier to go back and forth."

"How does that work?" I asked.

Dayton bit her bottom lip. "It's a bit complicated to understand. Maybe you can learn another time."

I wasn't going to hold my breath on that.

"I'm sure you'll learn in time," Genevieve said, smiling.

"What do you do if you needed a stone for something but didn't know what you needed to look for?" I asked, dropping the portal subject.

"Then we'd look it up," Genevieve said. "As Regs we must learn what each and every stone and crystal means, even if it takes us a while."

"And there are some things that we are still learning, I might add," Jules said. "We don't know everything. That's why we have plenty of books to look through."

"I'm sure that would be hard to do. I mean, you guys have like no reading material at all in here," I tried to joke. Genevieve, Jules, and Rohl laughed. Dayton and Jax did not.

"She's a comedian too," Jax said. "How wonderful."

"Oh shut up, Jax," Rohl said. "Bloody hell, mate, just have some fun for a change."

"I'll have fun when we go back home and this stupid mess has been cleaned up." Jax slammed his fist on a table. I heard the wood crack a bit.

"What mess?" I asked. "The one this guy started?"

"That's enough questions for today," Jax said coldly. "You've gotten what you came here for and then some. If you learn any more, we'll have to take you to the bloody realm."

"Now let's not go that far, Jax," Dayton said. "She wouldn't last one day in the realm."

"Oh and why not?" I challenged.

"Because people like you can't live in the realm. It's another world. A place that is not supposed to exist. Its atmosphere..."

"Please, I don't need a lecture on the realm. If you say I can't go then I won't. I have no business there anyway."

"Good girl," Dayton said.

Whatever, I thought. *Like I wanted to go to their stupid little realm anyway.* Still it would have been cool to have an adventure like I'd always wanted, but at what cost? My life maybe? No way. I just needed to stay here for a little while until things get under control, and everything would go back to normal.

"So why Louisiana?" I asked. "Why did the supernaturals decide to come here?"

"New Orleans serves as an almost beacon for the supernatural," Genevieve said. "That's why it's a popular place for them to come and live and thrive."

"Another question, why do you guys dress weird?"

"It's not weird where we come from, if you are wondering,"

Genevieve said. "But there is a very good reason why we dress so vintage."

"The first Regulators didn't have a lot of clothing options when they first came about," Jules said. "So they found whatever they could and made a series of costumes that could be both comfortable and that would protect them from many of the supernaturals they would face."

"And ever since then it's just became the style, but now they call it something."

"Is it called something?" I asked.

"It's just standard Regulator gear, but here in your world it has a name," Genevieve said.

"I've heard a lot about it from the English side as well, who normally stick with the Gothic rock style, but this one has become pretty popular in pop culture in recent years," Rohl said.

"Steampunk," Genevieve said excitedly.

"Steampunk?" I questioned.

"Yes, steampunk. Finally, after all these years, people are starting to take notice of our fashion sense."

"No matter how strange it is," I said.

"It's not just the fashion," Dayton said. "It's the technology and weapons as well. The First Regulators didn't have a lot of that either, so they make did with what they had. That's why many of our weapons are made so we can pay tribute to our ancient ancestors."

I nodded, understanding the whole vintage, new age look they were all trying to pull off. And as I started looking at it more, it really didn't look too bad.

No one spoke for a while.

"Well, I hate to keep this quietness any more...quiet," Rohl said, "but we really do need to get these weapons cleaned, Addie."

"Yeah," Jules said. "If not, Gaspar will give us another lecture on weapon hygiene."

"And no one wants another one of those," Genevieve said. "Just so you know."

"Okay, I got the message," I said, my tone light. "I'll get out of your hair."

"About time," Jax grunted.

I rolled my eyes and was headed for the other side of the room when Butch and Gaspar came in. Butch was walking very fast-paced towards us with an angry look on his face while Gaspar was running behind him talking. I couldn't make out what he was saying, but it sounded like Gaspar was trying to reason with Butch for some reason.

"I can't believe you've even allowed this," Butch said as he came towards us. "Of all things..."

"It's not like I had a choice," Gaspar said. "What was I supposed to do?"

"You know damn well what you were supposed to do, all of you." He stopped when he got to us then looked at me and pointed. "You," he said. "I know exactly who you are."

CHAPTER FOURTEEN
SECRETS REVEALED

"What!" I asked, looking at Butch.

"You heard me, girl," he said in an angry voice. "I know who you are, where you are from. I know it all."

I looked around the room at everyone, confused. "No," I said very assertively. "No you don't. You don't know who I am."

"Oh yes I do."

"Like I told you before. You don't know me, I don't know you. You never knew me, and you never will. I'll be outta here."

"If it was up to me you would have never even stepped foot in this facility ever. Not even for one second. I would have thrown you out and let the demons have you."

"Whoa, hey now, that's a little harsh," Jules said. "Plus it's not up to you."

"It's up to Gaspar," Genevieve said, walking towards me. She stood to my side and so did Jules. I looked back and forth between all of them. I saw that even Dayton and Jax came to stand around me. I turned around to see Rohl standing behind me very close. I saw something shining in his left hand. I looked closer and saw a small knife. The ceiling windows were letting the sun shine on it.

What are they doing? Are they protecting me?

"What's going on?" I asked. "Please, someone tell me."

Butch grunted. "Like you don't know," he said.

"No I don't. I don't know. Let me get this in your twisted mind. I don't know anything about what you think I should know about.

I was thrown into this unwilling, and I'm just doing my best to survive it."

Butch looked at Gaspar. "You didn't tell her?" he asked.

I looked to Gaspar. "Tell me what?" I asked.

Gaspar looked at me then looked down to the floor, sighing. "I...I," he stammered. "Can't. I can't tell her, no, I just can't. She doesn't need to know."

"Need to know what?"

"You ask too many questions, Addie," Jax said. "Just leave it alone. Trust me. What they know you don't want to know."

"Yeah and why not?" Tears now threatened to spill over my eyes.

"For your own good," Genevieve said.

Butch let out a huff and started pacing. "I can't believe this," he said. "I can't believe you are protecting her after everything that happened."

"That was a long time ago, Butch," Gaspar said. "A very long time ago. She was young and innocent in all of it, still is. She had nothing to do with it. There is nothing more to be angry about."

"Angry about? Angry about?! People died, Gaspar, good people. Don't you remember? Brothers, sisters, moms, dads. Hardworking people. And you're going to let her stay here and act like there's nothing wrong."

"Because there isn't, not anymore. What's done is done, and it cannot be undone. She is not a part of this. It was not her fault."

"I don't care. She was a part of it regardless of whether it was her fault or not. She had a part in it."

"You're letting your judgment get the best of you, Butch, trying to blame things on people who should not be blamed. Trying to fill a void that you cannot close."

"And you wonder why."

I listened as the two men talked, lost and confused. What happened a long time ago? How was I involved? Did a lot of people die like Butch said they did? Oh no, did I kill somebody?

"If I could just ask a simple question?" I said.

"No," Butch said. "No, you don't get to ask anything, do you hear me. Anything!" I jumped back and ran right into Rohl, who put his hand on my arm. I felt safe just standing next to him. I could tell the others were getting ready to do something. Their body language was tense. Fear and panic crept into my system. I cowered back into Rohl.

"Gaspar, can't you see that by letting her in here you risk hurting yourselves," Butch said.

"I'm sorry, but I don't see it that way," Gaspar said.

"You old fool. She'll be the death of you, the death of you all. Do you understand?"

"Yes I do, and therefore I don't care. And neither should you."

Butch turned to look at me with pure rage in his eyes. "Well I for one refuse to do as you say," Butch said. "I've spent twelve long years rebuilding my life, and I'm not going to have it fall apart all because of this stupid little girl."

"You don't have a choice," Gaspar boomed. "Either stay here or rot in a cell in the realm. I'm sure your old friends in the Iron Bars prison would love to see you again."

That shut Butch up. He looked at me with dark eyes then left the room. The others relaxed, but I was far from that. "Gaspar," I said. "What the hell is going on?"

Gaspar wiped his forehead with a handkerchief he got out of his pocket then looked at me. "Addie, my dear," he said, his voice soft. "I think it's time we talked."

I followed Gaspar to another part of the castle along with the Regulators. This part was farther back and more to the middle of the castle. I tried to keep what Gaspar wanted to talk about out of my head as we made our way down a long hallway. I started looking at the different things on the walls. What hung from posts looked like flags with different creatures on them.

A few I recognized as a griffin, Pegasus, chimera, and ogre. The others I didn't.

What could Gaspar possibly want to talk to me about? I wondered. What Butch said didn't make any sense. In his mind it did, but how could I possibly be a part of it? That would mean being a part of this world. This supernatural world that was not even supposed to exist. My head hurt just thinking about it.

After walking down the long hallway, Gaspar led us to a door. He pulled a big brass key out of his pocket and opened it. He walked in the dark room. I turned around to look at the Regs. "It's okay," Jules said. "He's not going to hurt you."

"Where is he leading me?" I asked.

"To his studies," Genevieve said. "We have many here, all filled with different archives."

"The one we were in is the main one," Jules said. "He probably needs to explain something to you, and he might feel a bit comfortable doing it in his study."

I nodded, still not sure.

I walked into the room.

A few small candles were mounted on the walls and provided a little light, but I still couldn't see much. I heard Gaspar snap his fingers, and in seconds the room lit up a bit more, revealing cabinets with glass jars filled with various things, an experimental area, a Rockology area similar to the one in the big study, a desk, and a huge table right in the middle of it.

"Whoa," I said. It wasn't as big as the main study, but it had just as many things in it.

Gaspar walked over to one of the glass cabinets then looked at me. "Please have a seat," he said. "And get comfortable. We have a lot to talk about." I sat down at the long wooden table. Gaspar walked towards the end of the table and put his hands on it. He looked like he was in pain. Beads of sweat were starting to form on the sides of his head.

"I assume that they have told you a lot of things," he said, looking behind me towards the Regs. I looked back at them. They were all standing along the back wall looking like they were in a police lineup.

"Yes they have, but it's not their fault," I said, turning to Gaspar. "Please don't blame or punish them. I was the one asking questions. Questions that I probably shouldn't have asked." I didn't want Gaspar putting the blame on them like he did last night when they came home late. It wasn't fair. Granted, he didn't look like the type to be completely harsh on them for anything, but I still didn't want him to blame them because of me.

"Well I'm sure you have some questions about what just happened back there with Butch."

I nodded.

"Then I shall start with the truth."

"Gaspar..." I heard Jax start.

"It's okay, Jax," Gaspar said, holding up his hand to cut him off. "It's all right, she needs to know for her own good." Gaspar swallowed then straightened his body. He looked right at me. "You are not a normal girl, Addie," he said. "You are far from normal."

I sucked in a breath. "What does that mean?" I asked.

"It means what you think it means. You are not normal, in a state of being human, that is."

I tried to read between the lines of what he was staying. Finally, I got it. "I'm supernatural?" I asked.

"In a sense," Gaspar said. "Then again, in not such a sense." He was so confusing me. "You are not of this world, Addie," Gaspar said, finally telling me. I guess he could sense my confusion. "You are from a different world set in the many dimensions our great universe has."

"I'm from the Arcania realm?" I said in a question-like form.

"Yes you are. You are from the Arcania realm. A wonderful place, I hope you get to see it one day."

"Wait, if I'm from the realm then what am I? I mean, I have to be something if only supernaturals are from the realm, right, then what am I?"

"There are not just supernaturals in the realm."

I thought for a moment. "The Regulators. I'm a Regulator?!"

"Partly one," Gaspar said. "But the trait is in you. It's the reason why you can see us. It's the reason why you can see this place through the magic and the masquerade."

"See you?"

"When we Regs are out on a job we sometimes use special crystals or stones, even gems, to help us blend in with everyday life here in New Orleans. I know for a fact that you can see past that."

That explains a lot, I thought. "But I can't see everything." I pouted. "I can't see everything that has to deal with your world. I think my mind may have tried without me knowing, but it would just end up in a big headache and my friends thinking I'm crazy. I know I can see this castle, but can't everyone see it?"

"I'm sure that the Regs have explained magic to you." He glanced behind me.

"Yes, the rooms, the stones, how everything in this world is a lie, but I just don't understand how a whole building or castle can be hidden right in the middle of a busy city. Is magic really that powerful?"

"I wouldn't underestimate it if I were you."

A chill ran down my spine.

This is ridiculous, I thought. *I came here for safety, and now I find out that I'm from the freaking Arcania realm. This is just beyond crazy.* Considering the fact that I hit crazy a millennium ago. I could feel panic rising in my body, followed by fear, and pain, and anger because that didn't explain why Butch acted like he wanted to attack me earlier.

"What else is there?" I asked Gaspar. "There has to be something else. Butch wouldn't blow up at me if being a Regulator was it."

Gaspar looked up towards the ceiling.

"Gaspar, come on," I said, my voice rising. "There has to be more to who I am than that. What was he talking about how I'm at fault and that a lot of people died? What happened? Did I do something?" I was standing now, trying to get him to talk. He looked at me with sad eyes.

"I'll get to that later," he said. "Right now there is more for you to learn."

Frustrated, I leaned back in the chair. "Okay." I folded my arms and crossed my legs. "Then talk, please."

Gaspar took in a breath then looked at me. "It all starts with your father, John François," Gaspar said.

I froze. "My father?"

Gaspar nodded. "A long time ago, your father was a top notch Regulator. One of the best that I had ever seen. I was his mentor when he was younger, and his friend."

"What about my mother?" I asked.

"Your mother, Clara Clemet, was a part of a special organization in the realm known as the Women of the Wise. They hold information about the realm dating far back to when the realm was discovered. They know its secrets, weaknesses, and everything about it. They studied it as well. We Regs turn to them for help when we need it."

"They were like Regulators?" I asked.

"Nope, not even close," Gaspar said. "They are scholars, philosophers, experts in magic and knowledge. They never once step foot into a battle or hunt down a supernatural. Not even now."

"Wait, they are still around?"

"Yes they are indeed. Without them the Regs would be almost nothing. They were the ones that gave the Regs the idea of using stones and crystals to help us fight and heal. They give us a lot when we need it and ask for nothing in return."

"Yes, they are practically saints," Dayton said.

Gaspar and I turned around.

"Sorry," Dayton said, not meaning it. "Didn't know it wasn't an open discussion." *Just shut your damn mouth,* I wanted to say to her. *This is about me, not you.*

I turned back to Gaspar.

"The Women of the Wise," I said. "Do they have any special powers or anything?"

"Yes they do," Gaspar said. "They have the ability to see things others can't. They have the power to see things for what they truly are and look past the magic. Their minds are more powerful than that of a Regulator's. We can see things as well, but it was the Women of the Wise who taught us first."

"What about magic? Can they use it?"

"Anyone can use magic if they put their mind to it. Although it would help if they were a witch, warlock, fairy, or any other magical being. The Women of the Wise are very powerful, don't get me wrong, but they do have their limitations to what they can and can't do."

"They...are human then. Just like you guys."

"Yes, just like us, but they can also use magic just like us. We are similar in a way. The only difference is that they didn't want to be a Reg."

"I'm sorry, what does all of this have to do with me? Not that I don't want to know about my mom and dad, it's just, Butch looked like he was getting ready to kill me back there."

"In time you will know."

"No, I want to know now! Quit stalling, Gaspar. I want to know now! I need to know, please." I hoped he could hear the desperation in my voice.

Gaspar started to shake, but not because he was mad.

"Just tell her, Gaspar," I heard Jules say. "She's going to find out anyway if Butch keeps acting like that around here."

Gaspar looked at them. "Fine," he said. "I will, I just don't know where to start."

"How about you start with the fact that her father was trying to destroy the realm," Jax said. "That should get the story started."

I almost fell out my seat. "What?" I asked.

"It's not true, it's not true," Gaspar wailed. "It was a misunderstanding. That's all."

"So his followers say," Jax said.

"You're not helping anything, Jax," Jules said. "So for once in your life shut the hell up."

"You're not my boss. I don't have to listen to you," Jax bit back. Soon the boys were about to go at it.

"All right, all right, that's enough," Gaspar said. "It's hard enough to tell Addie this without you guys adding your own opinions, so just shut it for now." The boys calmed down. I started to shake. Did my father really try to destroy the realm?

"Gaspar," I said, holding back tears. "Did my father really try to destroy the realm?"

"No, no, sweetie, of course not. This is what happened." He held a finger up to me then walked over to a table and got a remote control. "Sorry," he said. "I think it would be easier to explain it this way." He pressed a button, and the table in front of me turned into a huge map. One that I did not recognize.

"Whoa," I said. "What is this?"

"This is a map of the realm," Gaspar said. "The story goes a lot better with his visual aid." Gaspar walked up to the table. "You see, the realm is divided into different parts: Alinjaer, Sathmore, Chiikatorra, Outlansigh, Eitenhabe, and Sombara. They are also known as the Northern, Southern, Eastern, Western, Center, and the Dark realms. Each one has their own amulet containing power from them. When used together they can create immense power that can be good or bad."

I listened as the story went on.

"Your father got a hold of these amulets and tried to use them himself, but not for evil," Gaspar said. "He was trying to change the realm. He didn't like the way it was run, from the Regulators, to the Women of the Wise, to just everything. He was going to change it. He was going to balance it, using the amulets to do so."

"What happened?"

"Well, he didn't succeed. When word got around to the High Council of what he was trying to accomplish, a task force was sent out to destroy him. He sought me out to help. I did everything I could to keep him and Clara safe, and he repaid the favor. By this time the two had married and were expecting you. More and more Regulators were sent after your father and mother regardless of what the circumstances were. Your mother, being of the Wise could possibly make the amulets work, but there was no guarantee."

"Why not?"

"These amulets are very powerful. They don't require simple magic to use. It takes a lot of power and a lot of skill to work them to bring out their full power."

"So even with my mother's experience, no matter what that was, it was a possibility that they wouldn't work?"

"Exactly, but your father didn't want to give up. Later on, a vampire king by the name of Orfeous found out what your father was doing and tried to get the amulets for himself. He chased your father for years trying to get them. Created such a fuss that he became the most wanted vampire in both the realm and the real world.

"After you were born, John almost gave up until he went into hiding with your mother and you. But that did not last long. Orfeous' men eventually caught up to him, and he was killed along with your mother. He confided in me just a week before he was killed that he had hidden the amulets in various places where no one would ever find them. To this day no one has."

"So what's the big deal?" I asked. "They are safe, aren't they?"

"Well, it's a good thing and then it's a bad thing. Yes, they are safe, but then again, they are..."

"They are lost to the realm," Jax said. "Amulets that are centuries upon centuries old are lost forever because of your dad."

"Hey, I don't think that's a fair judgment, Jax," I said. "My parents died fighting for something that they believed in. They wanted to change the realm, that doesn't sound so bad."

"They weren't trying to change it, they were trying to destroy it. Don't let what this sorry excuse for a Regulator has to say about it. He was friends with your dad, of course he's going to take his side."

"Don't you dare talk like that! You weren't around, so you can't make any judgments on it."

"You weren't either."

"Enough, both of you," Gaspar said. "There is no need to fight about this." I stared Jax down as he took his place back along the wall. An overwhelming feeling came over me, and I started to feel dizzy. I didn't even realize I had stood up until I looked down at the floor. My parents, two people I never knew, wanted to change the place where they lived for the better, only to be thought of as traitors.

On top of that, they died for nothing, leaving me behind. Now people hated me because of them. I couldn't believe it. I felt sorry for them now more than ever, and for my poor aunt and uncle for trying to keep me safe from it all. Tears filled my eyes, but I held them back. "Well, I see what my aunt and uncle wanted to keep me away from."

"What's that?" Jules asked.

"The truth," I said, looking at him.

"That your parents were nothing but low-life blokes trying to destroy the realm and everything in it," Jax said. "Yeah, I wonder why they would try and keep that from you."

I could feel the heat rising inside of me. I could feel my face flush. I'd had enough of him and his bad attitude.

"You listen to me, Jax whatever the hell your last name is," I said. "My aunt and uncle gave up a lot to make sure that I was safe from all of this, and all I ever did was hurt them. I got bad grades, had a bad attitude like you, and put them through hell, and for what? So they could get killed trying to protect me. Do you know what that even feels like to have that on your conscience?" I took in a breath as a few tears fell from my eyes.

"And I am going to have to live with that for the rest of my life," I said in almost a whisper. "They deserved better than that. They were the only family I had left. My only aunt and uncle."

"Actually," Gaspar said. "They were not your real aunt and uncle."

I turned to look at him. "What?" I asked.

"They were not your real aunt and uncle, Addie. In fact, your mother was an only child and your father had one sister, but she didn't speak much with him after the confusion with the amulets."

I could feel hot tears strolling down my face. My aunt and uncle. Two people who raised me since I was a young child were actually not really related to me in any way. Pain, hurt, betrayal, all washed over me at once. I could feel the room spinning. I pressed my hand to my forehead, trying to calm myself.

The room started to get darker. Then soon everything went black.

CHAPTER FIFTEEN
TREASURE IN A BOX

"Addie, Addie," I heard someone call. I couldn't see anything. All I could see was a swirl of purple, dark blue, light blue, and sparkles. I stared into this massive thing like it was going out of style. It slowly swirled around and around. Tantalizing me, hypnotizing me. "Addie, Addie," I heard the voice say again.

I felt someone grab my arm. "There you are, sweetie," a woman said as she wrapped me in her arms. I could smell the sweet aroma of roses and mint. "Honey, you scared me."

"I'm sorry, Mommy," I said.

"It's okay, just don't go running off like that. This place is big. I don't want you to get lost."

"Okay."

"Come, your father and I have a meeting. Please stay close to me." I shook my head then walked with her down a long white hallway trimmed in gold with marble flooring. I gazed at the high ceilings, wanting to somehow fly up there and touch them. I held on to the woman's hand as she led me to a beautiful golden castle door. "Now," she said, "here we are."

She opened it and a huge bright light came out.

"Addie, Addie," I heard Genevieve call.

I opened my eyes and looked up to see the faces of Gaspar,

Rohl, Genevieve, Jules, Dayton, and Jax all staring down at me. I felt the cool floor on the tips of my fingers and a sharp pain in my head. I touched my hand to my temples and started to rub them. Did I just faint for real?

"Addie, are you okay?" I heard Genevieve say again.

She offered me her hand, and I took it. Jules and Rohl helped me up too. "Addie," I heard Genevieve about to start again.

"Don't," I said harshly. "I'm fine." I glared at her a bit. She shut her mouth then cowered back. "What do you mean my aunt and uncle weren't my aunt and uncle?" I asked Gaspar.

He gritted his teeth then looked at me. "I think you know the answer to that question, Addie," he simply put.

"That's...that's impossible. How could they not be related to me, they freaking raised me."

"They were told to," Gaspar said. "As part of orders from your mother and father."

"To protect you," Jules said.

"From what?" I asked.

"From all of this." Jules gestured to the surrounding room. "What else?"

"Okay, so they were told by my parents to protect me from what's really out here in New Orleans?"

"Yes, that about sums it up," Jules said, smiling.

I shook my head. "It certainly does not. That does not sum any of it up."

"How come it doesn't?" Jax asked. "They were given orders to protect you at any cost from this world that we live in. They accepted, did what they were told, and died doing it. That's what they were supposed to do. You should be grateful."

I balled my hands into fists. "Don't you dare think for one

second that I am not grateful for what they did," I said, tears filling my eyes. "Deep down I was always grateful, I just never showed it." Now I was really starting to feel horrible about this whole damn situation. As messed up as it was, I still couldn't get over the overwhelming feeling that there was still something more.

"If my aunt and uncle," I started, "weren't really my aunt and uncle, then who were they?"

The room got really eerie quiet.

"That's enough for today," Gaspar said. "I think you need to go rest and take all of this in."

"But..."

"Addie, listen to Gaspar," Jax said. "Enough is enough."

"A while ago you were saying that he was a sorry excuse for a Regulator. Now you're agreeing with him?"

"This time he is right.

"Oh come on," I said, having had enough of this. "Really? You guys are going to tell me all of this and then just try and quit on me now? My world and my life have already been destroyed. Might as well take a knife to what's left."

"All right," Gaspar said. "You're right, you need to know." He took in a breath. "Your aunt and uncle were really two very trusted Regs that your father grew up with and thought of as a brother and sister. When the issue with the amulets was going on, both your mother and your father were worried about your wellbeing. You were the only link to their bloodline, so they wanted to keep you as safe as possible.

"Your parents went to Wanda and Jeff asking them to protect you, and if anything was to happen to them they would keep you and raise you. Not telling you what really goes on in the world. They wanted you to grow up as a happy child. Far away from the hell we live in now.

"Because they weren't the only ones keeping tabs on you," Gaspar said. "I was too."

"Wait, you..."

"I knew who you were the minute you stepped through those castle doors, Addie." He turned to the Regs. "We all did."

"Wait so," I glanced around the room at everyone. "You all..."

"We all knew," Genevieve said. She sounded like she was sad. "We all knew who you were. We had orders as well to protect you at any cost."

"By who?"

"By me," Gaspar said. "And the High Council. They told us that Orfeous' forces were getting stronger and that it was only a matter of time before they found you. Wanda and Jeff were getting worried too. With all of the crime escalating in the city, they knew something was up."

I couldn't believe it. They knew who I was, and they acted like they didn't just to protect me more. Confusion washed over me, and I was starting to feel dizzy again. I couldn't stay here any longer. How could I trust these people? People that I didn't even know well. People that would rather keep me in the dark than tell me or warn me that my life was danger.

I couldn't take it anymore.

"I...I..." I said. Tears filled my eyes. Everyone was staring at me. "I gotta go." I started out of the room.

"Addie, wait," I heard Gaspar call. "I still think there are some things that we need to talk about..."

"I've heard enough for today," I almost screamed. "Please, I just need to rest."

"Addie, please," Genevieve said. "If you just let us all explain..."

"There is nothing to be explained. I'm living with a bunch of people who would rather keep the truth from me to protect me than to tell me what's really going on. That proves to me that I can't trust either one of you."

"That's not how it is," Jules said. "Honestly."

"Well honesty is out of the picture. But you guys don't care, right? I mean, you had 'orders' from the High Council to protect me, right? I'm just another case to you guys, that's all."

"It's not like that," Gaspar said. "Please, just let me explain."

"I told you I've heard enough. I don't want to hear anymore. I'm going to my room, you guys go clean your stupid wicked weapons or whatever. Get ready for the next case to come. I'll get out of your way." I walked out of the room. I made my way through the castle and found my room with really no trouble at all.

I walked in, slammed the door, and jumped into bed.

Every emotion, every tear, every bit of pain, sorrow, hurt came back as soon as it had faded. I thought of my aunt and uncle. How they tried to protect me, and all I did was cause trouble for them. I thought of Ava and how if I knew something was going on in this town I could have saved her. I didn't have any proof that she was killed by supernaturals, but I still had that feeling now more than ever.

I thought about my parents. I didn't know them, but I felt sorry for them, doing everything they could possibly think of to protect me and have it all go down in vain. It was too much. I let the tears fall. I screamed, cried, punched my pillows. I had never felt so much all at once, it was just too much. I sat in my room and cried for hours. No one came to check on me, and part of me didn't care.

They had more important things to worry about than me.

Night started to fall. I could see it out of my window. At six I heard something at my door. I looked to see that a full plate of food had been slid under it. I got off of my bed and walked over to it. A note had been placed on the plate.

I figured you'd get hungry, so I brought you something. I'm so sorry this happened to you. We are here for you, just know that.

—Mildred

Yeah, because you were told to, I thought. I was sure she was in on it too.

I didn't really have an appetite, but I took the plate anyway. I sat down at my desk and picked at the green beans, mashed potatoes, and roast beef aimlessly. I tried to eat a little bit, but I could only eat so much. My stomach was still full of emotions. I ate what I could then pushed the rest aside.

I glanced at the walls in my room.

I could feel them staring at me. Closing in like they were going to crush me. Suddenly I felt claustrophobic. I felt trapped. Disoriented. I had to get out of the room. I ran to the door, opened it, then ran down the hallway. I stopped once I got to the main entrance. I sat down on a chiffon couch to catch my breath.

Getting out of the room wasn't enough.

I needed to get out of the castle.

There was no way that I could. From what I learned from Jax, only crystals could open and possibly unlock the front doors. And I knew just where to get one. I walked to the main study and went over by the Rockology section. The moonlight coming in from the windows provided just enough light so I could see.

I searched the area, trying to find that same crystal that Jax had used. Finally, I found it sitting on a pedestal like it was the most beautiful thing in the world. I took it then started back downstairs. I walked up to the huge wooden door, holding the finger-shaped crystal in my hand. *There is no way this thing can open a big door like this,* I thought. *There is just no way.*

I waved the crystal over the door and nothing happened.

I knew it.

Upon looking at the door I realized there were symbols on it. Getting an idea, I held the crystal back up to the door and traced the symbols in the air with it. The symbols on the door started to glow then I could hear the door unlocking. It opened and I smiled. *Wow. Magic really does work.* I put the crystal in my pocket then headed out of the door.

I walked through the arbor towards the wrought iron fence then once again used the crystal to trace the symbols on the gate. I then stepped onto the sidewalk. The French Quarter was pitch black except for a few streetlights and other signs glowing bright. I felt lost standing there on the sidewalk. I couldn't even tell where this place was in the French Quarter.

I looked down the sidewalk and realized that we had to be on the outskirts of the Quarter. By the looks of it, not very far from the old Mint. With that in mind, I started walking down the sidewalk, mapping the way in my head from where we all were last night on Danneel Street to pass the old Mint.

After finding out the street I was on was Barracks Street, I made my way down another street called Decatur and eventually found my way on Canal Street. Relief filled me when I realized I could find my way home. Though I wouldn't be going back to much of a home, it beat staying in that castle.

As I started down Canal after taking just a few steps, I decided to hail a cab. When one stopped I opened the door and got in.

"Where to?" the driver asked.

"The Garden District," I said. "Please."

"Pretty late to be out, kid, don't you think?"

"Maybe, what's it to you?"

"Just an observation."

"Well I didn't ask for your observation, did I?" I snapped. I wasn't in the mood for anything, especially nosey-ass cab drivers. The guy shut up and kept driving. Thirty minutes later, I was in front of my house. "Thanks," I said, getting out of the cab.

"Wait kid," the driver said. "Aren't you forgetting something?" I looked at him. He held out his hand.

Oh crap. Money, the one very important thing I left the house without.

"Okay, hang on a second," I said. "I'll go get some from the house."

"Yeah right, I've heard that one before," he said.

"I'm serious. I'll go get your money." I walked in the house and froze. Flashbacks of what happened poured into my mind like a waterfall. I tried to fight back every single one of them. I heard the cab horn honk, bringing me back to reality.

I found my aunt's purse and pulled a few bucks out of her wallet. I found her driver's license inside it, along with a few credit cards. I looked at her picture, tears filling my eyes. *All of this time,* I thought. *All this time she never told me the truth.* She had the chance but she never took it, and now look what happened.

I put the wallet back in the purse then walked back outside to the cab, but it wasn't there. I looked up and down the street and still no sign of it. Brushing it off, I walked back in the house. Out of all of the places I could have gone I wanted to go somewhere that felt familiar. Yes, things happened here, but it was still my home no matter what.

It was better than an enchanted castle full of strangers.

I walked into the kitchen, running my fingers along the granite countertop. I walked upstairs, running my hand on the white walls. I stopped at my room then continued down the hall. I walked into my aunt and uncle...Wanda and Jeff's room. I walked in slowly. *Maybe there is something here that they had from my parents,* I wondered. *Since they all knew each other so well, maybe they have some things of theirs.*

Something to give me an idea of what they were like.

I started rummaging through the room, not coming up with too much. I looked in every nook and cranny I could find in the room, and I was coming up short. *This is ridiculous,* I thought. *I have no idea what I am even looking for.* But something told me that I did. I would know what I needed when I found it.

I knelt down and started to look under the bed. I pulled out a few boxes, a guitar case, hats, old books, still nothing. Then I found something that caught my attention. A small white jewelry box, about the size of my palm sat in the center. I reached out and took it. I held it in my hands. It felt light and was trimmed in a fancy gold pattern. I gently opened the box and gasped at its contents.

Inside was an egg-shaped gold amulet with the gold twisted to resemble branches. As I examined it I realized there was something inside it. I could see a white stone through the twists of the branches. The stone itself was egged-shaped as well. It hung from a big gold circle that was running through a bail at the top. I gently coaxed it out of the box. A long twisted gold chain came out along with it.

I stared at the amulet. It was so pretty, so captivating. I'd never seen anything like it. What were they doing with something like this? It looked so expensive. I never once saw Jeff buy Wanda any jewelry. It's not like he had to, I guess, they were guardians after all. They had one job to do, protect me at any cost.

I put the necklace back in the box and held on to it. Something told me I needed it.

I got up with a heavy feeling. Memories of my life here flooded me. I remembered my aunt giving me a bath after my friends and I spent an afternoon in the park playing in the mud. She laughed when I came through the front door covered head to toe in mud and leaves. She laughed as she bathed me.

I remember watching my uncle fix my bike outside in the driveway. I remember watching, getting all excited to ride it again. I remembered them both teaching me how to ride, how to behave, how to eat, how to drive. They taught me a lot of things. Things I never even really thought of until just now.

Thunder crashed outside, and I remembered coming in here one night when a bad thunderstorm had hit and I was scared. They let me in their bed, and I slept all through the night knowing I was safe with them. They always kept me safe no matter what. I didn't care if they were just guardians, they were family to me, and I let them down.

An overwhelming feeling hit me, and I sank to the floor, crying yet again. I shook and sobbed, but no one was there to comfort me this time. After a few minutes, I gathered myself together. I wiped the tears from my eyes then started to rise. Out in the hall I heard a thump. I froze. Panic and fear rose inside of me.

I stood my ground.

I heard another thump.

I started to shake.

Another thump.

I really started to feel in danger.

I braced myself for whatever would show itself at the door at any moment. Thunder and lightning crashed outside as the thumps got louder and louder. I could just vaguely make out a shadow of what looked like something human. I shucked in a breath as whatever it was showed itself.

As the lighting flashed I saw the lone figure of the cab driver.

My panic faded, replaced by rage. "There you are," I said. "What the hell? I went give you your money and you weren't there. You couldn't wait five damn minutes."

He didn't answer.

"I told you I would have it. I wasn't lying."

He still didn't say anything. Something wasn't right. I stepped closer to him and realized that he wasn't even looking at me. "Hey." I snapped my fingers. "Are you okay?" He looked at me then stopped. He was pale, very pale. "What's wrong with you?" I asked.

He didn't answer. Instead he fell over flat on the floor. Then that's when I saw it. Blood covered his back, neck, head, and legs. The skin on his back had been completely ripped off, exposing skin, muscle, and bone. Part of the back of his head was missing too. I could see parts of his brain covered in blood. I couldn't believe he made it up the second floor like this.

My hands flew to my mouth as I tried to cover a scream.

Then I heard something else. An inhuman growl. I looked into the hallway, and in the darkness I saw a monstrous face and two glowing red eyes.

CHAPTER SIXTEEN
THE HUNT

I stared at the creature in front of me, a shiver running down my spine. I slowly tried to move my hands away from my mouth. Part of me knew that was a bad idea, for fear that I might scream and set the thing into attack mode. It stood in the doorframe just a mere ten, maybe fifteen, feet away from me. Every time the lightning flashed I could see its features.

I had never seen anything so grotesque in my life. It was crouched low to the ground, its body resembled that of a gargoyle. Huge fangs poked out from the creature's ugly bat-like face. I could see wings pinned flat against the back. Claws the size of crayons dug deep into the carpet. I heard another growl. The growl sounded so inhuman that it made my skin crawl. I could practically feel the dark energy around me.

Drool started to drip from the creature's abhorrent mouth. A sickening feeling filled my stomach, partly because of the drool and also because I was here in this house all alone. I glanced around the creature, trying to see if I could run past it very quickly, but even with it being so low to the ground it was still very big and took up a lot of free space in the doorway.

Why doesn't it just attack me already? I wondered. *I know that's what it wants to do, not that I'm rushing it.*

I took a small step back, and it growled again. I stopped when it did. I took another step back, this time it growled and came forward. I was starting to notice a pattern every time I moved. It's like it couldn't see me unless I moved. That's it, it sensed movement, so all I had to do was stay still, and it couldn't see me. But I couldn't just stand here forever or until someone came looking for me.

I needed to get out of here and fast.

Without even thinking, I took a step forward. The creature jumped at me, and I jumped back a step. "Let me through," I demanded, not knowing where this would lead. It made some sort of growling, laughing noise that only made my stomach go weak. "Leave me alone. I have no business with you."

It started to growl, only this time it was saying something. I listened closer.

"Need it," it hissed. "Need it."

"Need what?" I asked.

"The box."

Confused, I looked down at the box and stared at it. The white box I had found earlier was still in my hand. The box. Why did it need the box? It wasn't after me, yet I knew it would take me out just to get to it. I couldn't let that happen. There was something about this box...something that I needed from it. I couldn't let anyone get to it. Not even this big ugly-ass thing.

I looked up at the creature. "If you want it," I said. "Then you're going to have to go through me to get it."

It hissed. "Sure will," it said. "With pleasure."

It started for me.

I let it come for me then moved out of the way at the last minute. It ran into the bed and got tangled up in the throw blanket that was on it. I started to head for the door. I was just about there when all of a sudden I could feel a hand on my ankle. The thing grabbed me and pulled me. I fell to ground, the box flying out of my hand.

The creature then got on top of me, hissing and growling at the top of its lungs. It started to lash out at me. I could feel claws rip my shirt and sink into my arm. I screamed and started to try and fight back. It was no use, it was too big and too powerful. *This is it,* I thought. *It's going to kill me.*

I turned my face to the side as it lashed out at me again. I saw the box just a few feet away. I needed to get it, but couldn't let this thing have it. I wracked my brain, trying to think of something on me that I could use to fight back.

The crystal!

Reaching in my pocket I pulled out the crystal. With all of my strength I plunged the crystal in the creature's chest. It let out a piercing screech. Veins of light started to spread across its body. I used that to my advantage and pushed it off of me. I got up, grabbed the box, and ran out of the room just as a piercing white light came from it.

It shook the whole house, and I fell just as my foot hit the bottom of the stairs. I looked up at the top of the staircase, hoping and praying that I wouldn't see the creature. After a few minutes of waiting, I was sure that I had killed it. I got up with shaky legs and ran out of the house. Rain pelted me as soon as I ran outside.

Oh hell, I thought. *Where do I go from here?*

I couldn't go back to the Safe Haven, I couldn't go to Maggie's house or Max's or even Ava's. I was really on my own now.

Shaking from head to toe, I caught my breath and tried to take control of my racing brain. Suddenly I heard a loud crash. I turned around to see a winged figure on the roof of my house. It looked like the same one that I just killed only bigger. It perched itself so perfectly on the edge of the roof, looking at me. Like the other it let out a loud piercing sound, and I screamed.

I started running down the street.

I could hear flapping wings so clearly even through the rainfall. I looked back to see where it was. I could see it flying just over the rooftops. I ran as fast as I could down Seventh Street then turned and started down Sixth Street. I turned around once again to see where the creature was, but I didn't see it.

I turned back around and almost ran smack into it.

I screamed and it let out another roar. I started to run. I could feel claws rip my shirt and skin. I whined then kept running. I needed to find a place where I could hide. I couldn't hide behind a house, I would risk putting others in danger. I decided to go to the only place I could think of to hide. Audubon Park.

I made my way down Sixth Street. I saw a few taxis pass, wanting to take one, but I knew it was out of the question. I'd have to explain why I was so cut and bloody, and I didn't want to have to go into that. Finally, I had made it to the entrance to the park.

I walked into the park, which was dead silent, eerie dead silent. I walked through the park with the creeping feeling that someone was watching me. I heard the sound of wings flapping and hid behind a huge oak tree.

I saw the creature flying in the sky, no doubt looking for me.

When it flew off I came out from under the tree. I sucked up enough bravery to go further into the park. Besides the street lamps and the full moon, I could hardly see anything in front of me. I walked ever so carefully, trying to figure out what I should do next. I stuck my hand in my jeans pocket and felt the box in it.

Relief filled me as my adrenaline was starting to wear off.

I spooked as the wind blew the huge oak trees. I heard bugs, dogs, lake water flowing, all giving me the creepy vibes. And the rain coming down wasn't helping. *This is ridiculous,* I thought. *I'm sixteen and still afraid of what goes bump in the night.* Of course after

I just found out that everything does go bump in the night, maybe it's not such a silly thing to be scared of.

After a while of walking, I saw a huge archway with animal statues next to it. The zoo. That would be a great place to hide. I ran over to the entrance gate. "Damn, it's locked," I said, shaking the fence. I heard a screech then looked up into the sky. The creature was coming back. Without hesitation I grabbed the fence and started climbing it.

I landed on the other side.

I started running into the zoo. Not a sound came from any of the animals as I passed. It was just as quiet as the park. I passed by the monkeys and didn't see a single one. I walked towards the lions next. I didn't see them either. Or the tigers, or the bears, or the mountain goats, or any of the animals.

What is going on? I thought.

A sinister feeling started to overcome me. They all had to be here. Something couldn't have just wiped them all out. Could it?

Suddenly, I heard a screech, but it didn't come from the sky. This sounded like an animal. I ran back the way I came and saw the monkeys in their trees screaming their heads off. I'd heard them before, but this sound was different. They were screeching, hollering, jumping up and down, like something was after them.

One monkey jumped from the tree to the bars of the cage right in front of me. Looking straight at me, it screeched and I winced, stepping back a bit. Next I heard the lions roaring, the goats bellowing, the birds screeching, elephants bellowing. Soon the whole zoo was alive. Panic started to fill me. They couldn't be doing this because of me, right? No, I didn't do anything to them.

They didn't sound right, which scared me. They sounded like a warning.

They were trying to warn me or each other or whatever. Something was here right now. I started to look around, but I didn't see anything. Almost all the lights were out, and my eyes were having a hard time adjusting to the dark. I walked further into the zoo with the animals still screeching. I couldn't take it anymore. Whatever was here right now, they could see it and I couldn't, which made me panic more.

I covered my ears with my hands, trying to drown out the sounds. "Enough!" I screamed. "Stop! Please just stop!" They continued on. *I've got to get out of here*, I thought. I ran, trying to find my way back to the entrance.

As I ran I heard something. I stopped and listened. It sounded like someone was walking behind me. The animals around me got louder and louder. I stopped in my tracks and slowly started to turn around. A pale guy with red eyes stood merely twenty feet from me. A growl came from his throat. I jumped back a few steps. He came forward and flashed white teeth with sharp fangs.

Vampire! I screamed then started to run.

Tears blurred my vision as I ran for the nearest exit, which I could not find. I ran around the zoo trying to find some way out. I even tried to find a map, but I couldn't even manage to do that. I turned one corner and found two more vampires, both hissed as I approached. "Ahhh," I said, turning around the other way.

As I ran, a few more jumped out at me. Then more and more. Soon there were at least twenty vamps after me. Exhausted, I stopped for just a few seconds to catch my breath. I could hear them behind me. I started running again, only to be stopped by more vampires. I tried to run another direction, but it was no use. More vampires had come, blocking my every exit.

They had me surrounded.

Vampires of almost every race stood around me in a circle. Some male, some female.

Some of them were smiling and laughed mercilessly as I cowered before them. Fear, pure fear, surged through me like my own blood. One, a black guy, lunged at me. I yelled and fell back, landing on my butt and hands. They all laughed. I guess this was how vampires treat their prey. They taunt and play with it like a cat does with a mouse, then when the prey has had enough they attack.

I just wondered how forty-something vampires were going to all...drain my blood.

I stayed on the ground, afraid to move. Then another one, with big muscles in a sleeveless shirt, walked up to me. He knelt down in front of me. He grabbed my shirt and sniffed me. "Is it her?" a young guy in the crowd asked.

"Oh yeah," the big vamp in front of me said. "It's her all right."

I started to shake.

"Say your prayers, girlie," the big vamp said. "You're going to need them where you're going." They all laughed. Suddenly the vamp who spoke earlier jumped. I looked up and noticed an arrow in his chest. He didn't fall, but he looked dazed nonetheless. The vamp in front of me growled, looking around.

More arrows came flying, hitting the vampires but not killing them, just stunning them. I looked around to see where they were coming from then I heard his voice. "Let her go." I turned around and saw Rohl standing on the roof of an educational center. Jax was standing by the center along with Genevieve. I didn't see Dayton or Jules.

"Regulators," the big vamp said. "I should have known you guys would show up soon."

"Then if you knew that, why did you corner her?" Jax asked, crossbow raised.

"We have our orders, just like you have yours." He let me go as he stood up.

"Well I like our orders better," Rohl said. "We get to kill, and you go down."

The vamp hissed. "You wouldn't dare come after us. There's nearly forty of us and only three of you."

"Five of us," I heard Dayton say.

Some of the vampires moved out of the way, and I could see her and Jules standing ready to fight. The big vamp laughed. "That's still not that much compared to us."

I turned back to look at Rohl. He smiled that wicked smile. "We'll see."

"Attack," Jax yelled. Jules, Dayton, and Genevieve all started for the vampires. Rohl flipped off the building, landing on his feet so gracefully I couldn't take my eyes off of him. He ran over to me and gently grabbed my arm.

"Are you okay?" he asked.

"Kind of," I said. "Not really. How did you know where to find me?"

"Dayton slipped a tracker on you when you weren't looking."

"What? When did she do that?"

"Who knows, she's really good at that." He pulled me to my feet then stood in front of me. Vampires came at each and every one of them. Jax and Jules would shoot them then Dayton and Genevieve would cut their heads off. Rohl killed the ones that came at us, but I could tell he wasn't very happy about standing in one place. "If you want to go help them," I said, "then go."

"Are you sure?" he asked.

"I'm sure. Go help them please."

He nodded then ran towards the nearest vamp. Dodging him

then cutting off his head. I stood and watched as the fight went on. Jules would shoot the vamps then the rest would behead them. Whatever was on the end of his arrowheads must have been something to slow them down. At one point Jules was in the center of the action, too busy to notice the vampire sneaking up behind him.

"Jules, behind you!" I screamed.

He shot an arrow then turned around. The vamp came to him, and he jumped three feet in the air then did a flip. He landed on his feet behind the vamp, and before the vamp even realized what happened, he cut his head off. Close to the zoo café, Dayton battled three vamps at once. As skinny as she was, she could fight, but soon they got the best of her.

One pushed her. She stumbled and fell against the wall of the café, knocking her weapon to the ground. The vamps smiled. I put my hands over my mouth to keep from screaming. Dayton looked around and picked up a nearby mop and started using it as a staff. She swung it back and forth, keeping the vampires back. Then when they weren't looking Jules came and cut all three of their heads off with a huge sword.

Across the area I heard Genevieve scream for Jax.

I looked and saw five vamps all trying to pin him to the ground. They just about had him too. I saw Rohl take two vamps down not very far from me. "Rohl!" I called. "Jax!" Rohl looked up at me as he pulled his sword out of a vamp. He then looked towards Jax. "Help him," I said. But Rohl didn't move. "Help him please," I begged.

Rohl shook his head.

Why won't he help him? I wondered. *Doesn't he care if he gets killed?*

A howl made me jump. I could hear something huge climbing the building I was standing in front of. A few seconds later, a huge creature had jumped from the building and was attacking the vampires that were on Jax. I could practically hear the creature's teeth sink into the flesh of the vampire. It shook the vamp like a ragdoll then dropped it once it was dead. It turned around to look at me, and I realized it was a big wolf.

I gasped at the pure size of the thing. It had to be as big as a draft horse, maybe even bigger. It growled at me with red eyes sticking out like suns against its dark brown coat. Rohl whistled, and it looked at him. Rohl shook his head, and the wolf nodded. Then it turned back to the other vamps. Two more wolves came running from out of nowhere, one tan, one gray.

They joined the battle and more wolves came.

I stopped counting after six wolves had shown up. There were just too many. They fought the vampire clan with the Regulators until there were no more. I went to walk over to Rohl when something grabbed me. I turned and saw that a vampire had gotten me. I screamed and tried to fight him off.

A huge brown wolf came out of nowhere and grabbed the vampire. It pulled the vamp off of me and started to behead it. I cringed at the sight but was happy that the wolf killed it. When the wolf was done it looked at me. I took a few steps back, not knowing if it would attack me. But it didn't, instead it just looked at me with huge kind brown eyes.

Where have I seen those eyes before?

My thought was interrupted by the sound of a whimper. I turned to see that the gray wolf's paw was injured. "Are you okay?" I asked, knowing that was a stupid question.

I started to walk over to the wolf, but Rohl stopped me. "Don't," he said. "She'll be fine. Werewolves can heal on their own, haven't you ever seen the movies?"

I ignored him. I didn't care. She was hurt, and I wanted to help.

The gray wolf looked up at me, and I could see the kindness in her eyes like she was thanking me for wanting to help. "You're welcome," I said. She bowed her head.

A black wolf suddenly crossed my path growling at me. I jumped back. "It's okay, Ulrich," Jules said. "She didn't mean anything by it."

Ulrich looked back at me. He sighed then made a low howling noise. Some wolves started to come to him, others didn't. The big brown wolf from earlier also made the same sort of low howl. The rest of the wolves came to it, then they all left going their separate ways, disappearing into the night.

I turned to the Regs. "Werewolves and vampires," I said. "Seriously?"

"Hey, don't sound so surprised," Genevieve said. "We told you that all the supernatural things that you thought weren't real, are, and you just got a big taste of it."

"Yep, what's more of a welcoming to the supernatural world than a big fight between the oldest enemies of all time?" Jules said, smiling.

I, however, wasn't finding it very amusing.

"Look, Addie, we need to go," Rohl said. "Before more come."

"I'm not leaving,"

"Don't be stupid," Jax said. "Let's go."

"No, I'm not going anywhere."

"Addie."

"No, Jax, you don't tell me what to do. None of you do. I couldn't stand being in that castle. Not one more second. I'm probably better off on my own anyway. That's how you guys want it, I know."

"Listen here, you little brat," Jax said, coming up to me. "Yes, we were told to protect you. Yes, we knew who you were when we met you, but that doesn't mean you go running off thinking you can survive on your own when you have things like that after you." He pointed to a decapitated vampire.

I cringed at the sight.

"They want you for what your parents did," Jax said. "They are hunting you, and we are only ones who can protect you, 'cause believe me it's going to get worse."

I didn't know what to say. Tears filled my eyes, but I held them back.

"He's right," Genevieve said. "In a way. Come back to the Safe Haven. Everyone misses you."

"I bet Butch doesn't," I said.

"He's one person."

"And a bit of an ass too," Rohl said.

"We can protect you," Genevieve said. "That's what we were told to do, and we will no matter what."

I thought about it for a little while. "Okay," I said. "Fine, I'll go. I guess I really don't have a choice, right?"

"Not really," Jules said, smiling. I smiled a little too. I would go back only because I didn't know where else to go. I thought of the box and felt for it in my pocket. I started walking with the Regs after Dayton used her device to clean up the scene. I was shaken by everything. Somehow my mind didn't want to process what just happened, but I knew better. Like Jax said, this was the hunt for me.

And they wouldn't stop until I was dead.

CHAPTER SEVENTEEN
VICTIMS

I followed the Regulators towards the Safe Haven. I dreaded with every step that I took what would be waiting for me inside. Probably a distraught and angry Gaspar met with a fuming Butch. I braced myself as I walked in the door. "We're back," Jules called. "Safe and sound once again."

"Ah you all," Mildred said, walking up to us with Gaspar not far behind her. "It's so good to have you all back safe." She hugged all of the Regulators.

I took a step back when she came for me. "I don't think I deserve a hug," I said.

"Oh come now, yes you do. You more than anyone." She wrapped me up in her arms. I hugged her back.

"Everything is going to be okay, Addie," Mildred whispered to me. "It's all going to be all right."

I hugged her tighter, tears spilling over my eyes.

"There she is," I heard a gruff voice say.

"Now, now Butch, we talked about this," Mildred said, putting herself in front of me. "There has been no harm done. Addie just got a little freaked, that's all."

"Spare me, old woman," Butch shouted. "I don't need to hear it. She has put us all in danger by leaving. Something could be on its way here right now because of her sneaking out."

"Actually we took care of what was after her, sir," Jules said.

"What?" Gaspar said. "Who came after you?"

"More like what," I said, "before what Jules is talking about."

Gaspar and Butch looked to Jules to hear more. "Vampires," he said.

"Vampires," Gaspar gasped.

"Yes, vampires," Jax said. "A whole clan of them, but we took care of it and as usual cleaned up after. I'll have my report in the morning." Gaspar nodded, then it happened. Within seconds Butch had pushed Mildred out of the way and had grabbed me. He pushed me up hard against the wall. I could feel his tight grip on my arms from my skin to my bones.

"Don't you see what you have done, girl?" he asked. "Vampires? A whole coven of vampires was after you...don't you see what's happened here?"

"No...no," I sobbed. "I mean I can't..."

"You can't because you don't want to believe the truth. You believe what he says." He pointed to Gaspar. "When I was the one who served with your father, I knew the kind of man he was!" Butch's grip tightened on me, and I started to shake. I cried out, wanting it to stop.

"Butch, please, you are hurting her!" Gaspar yelled.

"You should have gotten rid of her while you could have, Gaspar," Butch said in a sinister voice. "I should do it and save the vamps some trouble."

"Okay now, that's enough," Rohl said. "Butch, let her go..."

"You don't tell me what to do, boy."

"You've been drinking. I can smell it on your breath."

"Let her go now, Butch," Jules said. "She has nothing to do with you."

"Butch, please," Mildred pleaded as Genevieve and Dayton helped her off of the floor. "Let the poor girl go." I could see the rage in Butch's eyes and knew that he wasn't going to let me go anytime soon. I could also smell alcohol on his breath.

I saw Rohl pull something out of his back pocket. It shined in the dim light. "Really, boy?" Butch asked. "You're going to fight me?"

"Only if I have to," Rohl said, his face going dark. "Now let her go." After an almost deadly stare down, Butch released his grip on me. I fell to the floor with shaky knees. "That's just like your father," Butch said to Rohl. "Taking up for the other party, only to have it become your downfall in the end." He walked off.

Genevieve and Dayton helped me up.

"Are you okay?" Genevieve asked.

"Yeah," I lied. "I'll be fine. I'm just going to go up to my room and pretend that this whole thing never happened." I started up the stairs. "I'm really sorry for running away," I said, turning around to look at all of them. "That was really dumb and a stupid move on my part. I won't do it again, I promise."

"It's all right, Addie," Gaspar said. "It's understandable."

"I don't want to be ungrateful to any one of you. I'm just trying to get used to all of this. So forgive me if I come over that way, it's not my fault. I'm just trying to do the best I can with what has happened." I gave a small smile then walked in my room.

I walked through the castle the next day trying to avoid everyone at any cost. Which was pretty easy. I had eaten breakfast with them then proceeded to my exploration, which almost never seemed to end. There was always something to find here no matter what. It was enough to keep me busy and away from them. I wasn't ignoring everyone on purpose, I just needed some time to process everything.

I hadn't seen any sign of the Regs, Butch, or Gaspar all day, and that was a good thing. It meant I was doing great at avoiding them, but I was also getting worried. I turned down one of the corridors I was in and headed towards the big study. I walked in and saw the Regs towards the back going through a huge book. Upon looking closer, I realized it was the bestiary.

I started walking a little closer.

They all looked like they were in a huge discussion. Jax and Jules were sitting down at the big round table talking—arguing really—Dayton was sitting next to Jules taking what looked like notes, Genevieve sat next to Jax with her back towards me, and Rohl was standing with his hands placed on the table, the bestiary in front of him.

I watched them for the longest time, not realizing I was staring.

"Hey, Addie," someone called.

I broke my trance and looked up. Jules had spoken to me. "Oh hey," I said, caught off guard. "Sorry, I forgot I was standing here."

"No problem." He smiled, flashing his perfectly white teeth that would make any Crest spokesperson jealous.

"What are you guys doing?" I asked, knowing I shouldn't.

"Researching chimeras. We need to brush up on our knowledge of them," Genevieve said. "So we can figure out how to kill them."

"We also need to track down Orfeous and his men," Jax said. "A few of those vampires got away last night, and I know damn well they'll be reporting back to him soon."

Terror rose within me. "Do you think they'll come here?" I asked.

"No they won't," Jules said. "This place is warded and very hard to find."

"Plus Orfeous' vampires don't come to the French Quarter," Genevieve said. "They prefer darker places."

"Oh I see." I started to feel a little shaky. Flashbacks of last night played in my head, and I shuddered. I didn't realize how close I came to losing my life. I caught Rohl's eye for a minute. He was staring intensely at me. I could feel my knees buckling underneath me. "Well I guess I'll let you guys get back to it then," I said, breaking the awkwardness.

"Okay," they all said then went back to working.

I left the study and almost ran into Gaspar. "Oh hello, Addie," he said. "Are you feeling okay today?"

"Yes, actually I am just tired still, but I can't seem to sleep anymore."

"I know where you are coming from. A person can only get so much sleep until they've had enough."

I nodded.

"I'm glad I ran into you. I wanted to ask you about what happened last night."

I froze. "What for?" I asked.

"Well I've already gotten the Regs' side of the story, and I'm afraid I need yours. Dayton said she noticed some claw marks on you that are not from the vampires but from something else. Did anything else happen before you went into the zoo?"

My heart caught in my throat. I couldn't tell him about the amulet I found or the gargoyle-looking thing or the taxi driver. That would mean reliving it, and I did not want to do that. Still, Gaspar ran this place. He was over the Regulators and me, so I guess he needed to know. "Yes," I said after a few seconds. "Something did happen before the vampires."

"Come on," he said. "Let's go to my study."

We walked to his study, where I sat down in the same chair at the same big table with the map of the realm on it. Gaspar fixed us both some tea and then grabbed a parchment notebook and a quill. "So, what else happened last night that you can remember? Now I just want you to know that this is not me trying to make you relive what happened. I just need this for my reports for the High Council."

"I understand," I said, sipping my tea.

"Good then. All right, so what happened after you left the Safe Haven? Or really how did you leave the Safe Haven?"

I took in a deep breath. "I used one of the crystals Jax used to open the front door. I saw him use one and figured it was easy, and it actually was."

Gaspar wrote that down.

"Okay, what happened next?"

"I tried to figure out where I was. Once I did I walked through the French Quarter and eventually took a cab back to my house."

"Why did you go back there?"

"I needed to get away from here after what you had all told me, I..." I took in breath. "I couldn't take it. I needed to go back to someplace familiar to collect my thoughts."

"That's quite all right and is understandable. I'm not here to judge you, Addie, I promise that." I smiled and he did too. "After you went back home, what happened then?"

"I went inside to get some money for the cab I took, but it was gone. I didn't think anything of it at the time, then I walked back inside. I went through the house remembering all the good times I had there with my..." I cleared my throat, "with Jeff and Wanda. I started going through a few of their things, trying to find anything they had that might have belonged to my parents at one point."

"Did you find anything?"

I swallowed. I didn't know if I should tell him about the amulet or not. What if it was one from the realm? No, it couldn't be, my father hid them all. I decided not to tell him about it, that it could wait for another time. Right now it was safe in my room, hidden where no one can find it. "No," I finally said. "No, I didn't find a single thing."

"If I may add this, your parents did leave whatever belongings they had to you."

"Wait, really? Where?"

"In the Arcania bank. There are family vaults there dating back centuries, but you have to be of a certain age to obtain them."

"I understand."

"Your parents left practically everything they owned to them, hoping they would give it to you one day."

"Can you find out how old I have to be to get it?"

"I sure will."

I nodded, tears filled my eyes.

"Now then, what else?"

"After that, I heard something. I waited a few seconds, then the taxi driver showed up. I tried to talk to him, but he wouldn't talk. He just kept staggering towards me. He then fell to the ground, and I saw that the skin of his back had been ripped to shreds. The back of his head was missing, and he was covered in blood."

Gaspar quickly wrote everything down.

"Then I heard a growl," I said, wiping tears away. "And this big ugly gargoyle-looking creature was standing in the hallway. It came after me, and I fought it and finally killed it."

"Using what?"

"The crystal I had from when I opened the front door. I took it out and plunged it into the thing's heart, and it burst into flames, I guess. I saw a white light when I ran away, so I guess that was it."

"Did you say it looked like a gargoyle?"

"Yes, why?"

"Nothing, it's just...well, the gargoyles here in New Orleans are used for protection. They never attack anybody."

"They can come to life?"

"Yes they can, but it takes very powerful magic to make them turn against the very people they are meant to protect."

"What are you going to do?"

"I'm going to look into it. This is not supposed to be happening."

"That's not all that happened."

Gaspar looked at me. "What else happened?" he asked, almost on the edge of his seat.

"It talked to me," I said, shaking.

"What did it say?"

"That it was just after me, that's all. Could it be working for Orfeous?"

"I doubt it, but you never know. Orfeous has a way of getting people and beings on his side. That's how he was able to go against your father so well. This needs to be looked into as soon as possible."

I nodded.

"Thank you for your time, Addie, I know this can't be easy for you, but we'll get things straightened out here soon."

I nodded once again.

"Gaspar, if I could have a word with you please," I heard a woman say. I turned around to see Officer Demouchet standing in the doorway.

"Officer Demouchet?" I said.

"Addie," she said. "What are you doing here? I thought you were..."

"Dead perhaps," I finished for her.

"Yes, yes I did. I was called about a home invasion a few weeks ago. I went to the address, saw it was your house, and there was no sign of you."

I stood up and looked at her.

"I've been here," I said. "Being protected by them, the Regulators."

"So you..." She looked at Gaspar. "She..."

"Yes, Rae," Gaspar said. "She knows the truth now about everything. Her parents, the supernatural, everything."

She looked at me. Next thing I knew she was hugging me. "I'm just so glad you are safe," she said. "I figured that the Regs got to the house in time, but when I didn't see you, I thought the worst. But you're here now, safe."

I hugged her back, thinking for one second that she was my aunt and that this was all just a dream.

She pulled away from me. "Anyway," she said, wiping tears away, "I have the full house report you wanted, Gaspar."

"Perfect, just lay it on my desk. I'll look at it later," he said smiling. Officer Demouchet did what she was told then walked out of the room.

"What? Why? How?" I started to say.

"Ah," Gaspar said before I even had time to react. "It's not my place to speak on her behalf. If you want to know, why don't you go ask her yourself?"

I looked down the hall then back at him. "Okay, I will." I walked out of the room.

I saw Officer Demouchet walk down the hall and into a room. I followed her and stopped when I got to the door. It was a small office like the one at the station. I gently knocked on the door, and Officer Demouchet turned around. "Addie," she said. "Yes, I figured you would follow me. I'm sure you've got some questions."

"Yes I do," I said, walking toward her. "A lot. If you don't mind me asking them"

She smiled. "Of course not. I'm ready to answer them, whatever they may be." I walked towards her as she sat in her chair. I could tell she was getting herself ready, but before I could ask anything, a picture on the edge of her desk caught my attention. It was a young boy around eight or nine smiling with reddish hair and big brown eyes.

"Who's this?" I asked.

She looked at the picture. "My son Reese," she said. "He was nine in that picture. So full of life and energy. He was a good kid."

"Where is he now?"

She looked down then looked back up at me. "Buried in St. Roch Cemetery."

"I'm so sorry...I didn't know." My face started to feel hot with embarrassment.

"It's all right," she said, her voice cracking a bit. "He's been gone a long time now. In fact he's the reason why my husband and I got into this."

"How? What happened?"

Officer Demouchet looked down at the floor.

"I'm sorry. You don't have to tell me if you don't want to," I said, realizing I was being insensitive. "It's none of my business."

"It's all right. I don't mind. There are not many people I can talk to about what happened, and talking helps."

I nodded, understanding.

She took in a breath. "It happened eight years ago on a hot summer night. My husband and I were sleeping in our room, and Reese was in his. Around midnight or so I heard Reese calling out for me. I woke up and smelled smoke. I woke my husband up, and we both raced to his room. It had been scorched so bad everything was just cold black, but Reese wasn't there.

"We heard him call out from downstairs, so we ran. There next to the front door was my little boy on the floor, gasping for breath with a swarm that looked like fire around him. It was dragging him out of the door. I grabbed his hand and tried to pull him back, but it was no use. The swarm was too strong.

"Eventually it won, and it pulled my baby boy out of the door without a single sound. My husband and I ran outside looking for it, but we never could find it or Reese. We searched for hours, weeks, months, even years, and still never found out what happened. We tried everything, but nothing helped."

She took in another breath. I knew this had to be hard for her even after so many years. "Finally, I decided to turn to a psychic to see if she could pick up on Reese's energy. She tried and tried but nothing worked. That's when an older man reached out to me and said that he could help."

"Gaspar," I said.

"Yes. He told me about the supernatural, about the ones here in New Orleans, and most importantly the Regulators. After that, things started to make sense."

"You never found Reese though, did you?"

"Nope, not yet. We didn't even find a body. A few of his clothes and toys are buried in a casket. I still have hope that one day he will come back. I just have to keep praying." I felt for her. Tears started to come to my eyes, but I blinked them away. She wiped away a few tears of her own. I prepared myself for the question I needed to ask next.

"Officer Demouchet," I said.

"Please, Addie," she said. "Call me Rae."

"Rae then. That night on Bourbon Street, do you think that Ava was killed by something supernatural?"

She looked at the floor then at me. "I don't think. I know."

My knees felt like they were going to give out. I knew that she was killed by something supernatural. I just didn't want to believe it. I still didn't, even though I just heard the words clear as day. Tears came back into my eyes again and threatened to stream down.

"I knew it the minute I saw you on Bourbon that night," Rae said. "I knew what happened to Ava was a result of the supernatural. The Regs and Gaspar told me about you and the people that are after you. When I asked you questions I couldn't believe you didn't know anything, and they told me to keep it that way."

"To protect me," I said.

"Yes, exactly."

I couldn't believe poor sweet Ava had to get caught up in the middle of all of this. They were after me but got her, that's not fair. None of this was.

"It's not right, is it?" Rae asked. "That's what you're thinking right now. I can tell."

"Yeah," I said. "That's exactly what I'm thinking."

"It might not look like it, but things will get better. I promise."

I nodded, not believing, but I still did.

"Well I've got some work to do," Rae said. "Both supernatural and police."

"Okay," I said. "I'll leave you to it then."

"Thanks, and hey if you ever need anyone to talk to, my door is always open."

"Thanks."

"No problem."

I walked out of the room. Tears stung the back of my eyes.

Finally, I knew the truth. Ava was killed because of something supernatural. Because of this stupid messed-up world, she and Rae, even Reese, had to suffer because of it. Me too, and it seemed like it would never end. We are all just victims.

I gathered myself together then headed back towards Gaspar's study. I peeked in and saw him at his desk writing. I'd been meaning to ask him about what he said about me being able to see the supernatural. That part I still didn't get, how could I "see" it? What's there to see? If I could see it, then what was it supposed to look like?

I gently knocked on the door.

"Hello, Addie," Gaspar said, looking up from his desk. "Did you talk to Rae?

"Yes I did," I said.

His face went somber all of a sudden. "I'm sure she told you about her son, right?"

"Yes she did. It's so sad. I feel so sorry for her."

"As do I, but we are helping her, I promise you that."

"I don't doubt that, not for a second."

"Great that's good to hear."

"Gaspar, I wanted to ask you something."

"Yes, my dear, what is it?"

"Do you remember telling me about how I can see the supernatural?"

"Yes I do, what about it?"

"Well I just wanted to know how am I exactly supposed to see it? I mean, I get it. I can see this castle, but what else did you mean by that?"

"I meant that you can see things normal humans wouldn't be able to see. For instance a person might see a normal, average-looking guy walking down Poydris Street and not think anything about how he looks, acts, or dresses. But you on the other hand can see past the magic he presents to make himself look like an normal person."

"So deep down he might be a vampire, but I and only I would know that just by looking at him?"

"Yes. Many supernaturals use magic to cover up what they really look like. Also if there is a supernatural nearby, you can sense their energy they produce."

"Can the others do that?"

"Yes, but it takes years of practice for them to get it just right. There are certain signs they have to look out for and feelings to focus on."

"Like what?"

"I'll explain that in due time."

I nodded. I looked at the floor, but I could feel Gaspar's eyes on me. "Is there something wrong, Addie?" he asked.

I looked at him. "Why?" I said. "Why now can I suddenly see everything?"

"Who knows. Maybe it's because you are getting older, there's more supernaturals in New Orleans now than there was, or maybe it was just a matter of time before your background caught up to you."

"Before, I think I would possibly see something, but it's like my mind couldn't process what I was seeing. After, I couldn't see it. I would get really sick."

"The reason you couldn't see it was because there was something making you not see it. That something was blocking it from your mind. Your eyes would see, but your mind wouldn't process it."

"What could possibly do that?"

Gaspar pulled out a small bottle of pills. "Do these look familiar?"

he asked, pulling out a small white pill.

"Hey, those are the vitamins that my aunt, I mean Wanda, used to give me."

"They are not vitamins."

"What are they then?"

"They are a mixture of herbs and magic plants created to block the mind from the supernatural."

"That's not possible."

"Addie, I think you'll find that a lot of things that are not possible are possible in this world now that you know everything." Gaspar put the pill back in the bottle. "We have a word we like to use in the supernatural world to describe people who have been told of the supernatural," he said. "We say they have been awakened. And I think you have. You still have a long way to go, but you'll get there. I know you will."

I didn't react.

"You have a lot to learn, and I'm sure you will," Gaspar said. "Now if you will excuse me, I need to get back to my report."

"Yes, sir," I said.

I turned to leave when I caught a glimpse of what Gaspar was working on. At the top of the page written in perfect calligraphy was my name and facts about me. Not one thing about my account with the gargoyle had even been mentioned. I looked at Gaspar, but he didn't notice. I started to wonder what he was really working on.

CHAPTER EIGHTEEN
REASONS AND RULES

With a flaming face I walked out of Gaspar's study. What was he doing with those notes on me? Why was he taking them? Were they for his report? Or something else? If it was, then what? Questions cluttered my brain, making my head hurt.

"You look deep in thought about something," I heard someone say.

I looked up and saw Rohl standing just a few feet from me. I jumped when I saw him. "Damn it," I said. "You scared the hell out of me."

"I do that a lot, don't I?" He smiled and I melted.

"What are you doing here?" I asked, my voice a little tense.

"I came to talk to Gaspar. What are you doing here?"

"I just finished talking to him about what happened last night so he can do his report."

"If that's the case, then why do you look pissed off?"

"Because I think he is doing more than just his reports for the High Council."

"What makes you say that?"

"I kind of saw the paper he was writing. It had notes about me like my hair color, things I've been doing since I got here, personal things, but nothing about the attacks last night. I think he's up to something, something bad."

Rohl smiled, slightly shaking his head. "Boy, he never changes," he said.

I stared at him. "What?" I asked.

"Gaspar doesn't just work on what we Regs report to him about our missions. He also studies things, all things, and he writes them down. Looks like his new interest is you."

"Well what's so freaking special about me?"

"That you are part Regulator and part Women of the Wise. That's enough for him. He probably wants to know how you work, what powers you could have."

"He did tell me that I can see things that others can't. Like you guys do."

"That's true. Since you are part Regulator and Wise, your powers, whatever they may be, could even be stronger than ours."

"What powers? That's another thing I don't understand, what powers could I have?"

"It just depends. Regs have heightened senses that normal humans don't. We are also faster, stronger, better than them in any way."

"That's why you're considered supernatural?"

"Yes it is. Some Regs have powers or abilities from whatever their family had, depending on their heritage of course."

"Makes sense."

Rohl nodded. "That's why Gaspar is studying you. He wants to know what makes you *you*. He's not trying to do any harm, I promise."

I relaxed a bit, but one thing was bothering me. "Regulators and Women of the Wise can't have children together," I said. It came out more like a statement than a question.

"Exactly," Rohl said. "They never had, so that's why Gaspar is interested in you right now."

"No, I mean why can't they have children together?"

"It is forbidden. It's one of the High Council's rules, and it needs to be followed by everyone."

"Apparently my parents didn't get the message."

"I'm sure they did, they probably just didn't care, as some of us tend to do with their rules." Rohl paused. "When it comes to us Regs and the Women of the Wise, the realm is very strict on what we can and can't do."

"I see." A sadness came over me.

"What's wrong," Rohl asked.

"Nothing. No, something. I just...I can't believe that I'm still a part of something like this. You would think that by now I would be used to it."

"Addie, it's only been a few days since you found out. It's going to take some time to get used to things."

"Gaspar said that there is still a lot for me to know. I do want to know everything. I just don't know where to start."

Rohl suddenly looked sharply at me. "I know a place where you can start," he said. "And it's right here in this castle."

"Where?" I said.

"I'll show you, come on, let's go." He grabbed my hand and started heading down a hallway. He led me through a few hallways and a flight of stairs. Soon we were at a farther part of the castle staring at a huge door similar to the main door, just not as big. Rohl pulled out a blue crystal like the one Jax had and started waving it over the symbols on the door.

Each one lit up blue then the door opened.

The door revealed a dimly lit room filled with books, desks, a sitting area, drawing boards, a small lab, and a fireplace. A musty smell hit me as soon as I stepped into the room. Dust covered most of everything. By the looks of it, it hadn't been used in a while, or ever. "What is this place?" I asked. "Another study?"

"In a way," Rohl answered, stepping more into the room. "This was where the Women of the Wise used to stay when they did their studies. It was only ever used by them."

"Wow, really?"

"Yep. Back then some of them would stay in the various Safe Havens all around the world."

"How many Safe Havens are there?"

"As many as there are countries. Each state in America has one, so there's fifty right there. Some countries, depending on how big that country is, have multiple spread across it."

"All accommodated by Regulators."

"Exactly." He smiled as he paced the back row of books, looking at me.

"Why don't the Women of the Wise stay here anymore?" I asked.

"It's because of their supervisor, their higher-up. She said that they were not treated well when they stayed here. I don't know how, but I try not to ask."

"I see. Do they have their own place to stay then?"

"Yes they do, it's in the realm. It's like our Safe Haven here, just not as dark and dreary. It's actually quite nice."

I looked all around the room once again. A lingering thought soon hit me. "Why did you bring me here?"

Rohl's face went soft. "You wanted to know more about your past, so I figured this would help. Anything that the Women of the Wise knew and used is right here in this room. They worked at these desks, they read these books, they sat by the fireplace. Your mother might have been here at one point."

"Seriously?"

"I am. Anyway, it is a good place to start."

I started to look around the room. Joy filled me at the thought that my mother could have at one time used this room for her studies. I started to take a few steps when I noticed something in the middle of the room. A huge book like the bestiary sat perfectly on an ivory pedestal right in front of the desks.

The book had white leather with a pattern on it trimmed in gold. Something in an unknown language was written on the front. I walked over to the book and placed my hand on the cover. "What is this?" I asked. "Another bestiary?"

"Yeah, it's like one," Rohl said, coming up behind me. "It's the book the Women of the Wise use for their studies. It has everything in it from spells, to potions, to beings of all kinds."

"Why can't you guys just use this for everything?"

"Well we could, but the only problem is..." I blocked him out and opened the book. A language I had never seen was written on each and every page. "It's written in code," Rohl finished. "Not one of us, not even Gaspar, can read it. It's for the Women of the Wise and them only."

"I see," I said, flipping through the book.

On one page I saw symbols, patterns, pictures of bottles of potions. Just random things.

The text resembled Greek and Arabic writing mixed with something else. I highly doubted it was any such language, though. The book's pages were worn and faded with age. I saw a few pictures of creatures, some I knew, others I didn't. I wanted to take the book up to my room and spend the rest of the day looking at it.

As I continued reading, another thought popped into my head. "Why couldn't the Women of the Wise have children with Regulators?" I asked, looking up at Rohl. "Wouldn't that be like the ultimate fighter, having the knowledge of the Wise with the skills and strength of the Regulators?"

"Hm?" Rohl said, tilting his head towards me. "I've never thought of it like that before. But no, there is a reason, a very good reason why the two never reproduce with each other."

"What is it?"

"The Women of the Wise have always been a very powerful group of women. Therefore their founder believed that in order for them to stay that way they must remain pure."

"Pure?"

"Pure."

I couldn't understand what he was talking about or what he meant until finally it hit me. "Virgins," I said.

"Yes, virgins. Their leader thought that if they stay that way forever their powers would be stronger. They can't get married or have any kind of sexual relationship with anyone. That's also why their colors are white and gold. The white symbolizes their purity while the gold symbolizes the greatness of their powers and knowledge."

"But don't you think that's wrong? Taking someone's right to marry or the right to be with someone intimately?"

"Like I said, we all have ours rules and we must abide by them. It's not right for me to question it. Though I do sometimes, in secret."

"It didn't stop my parents."

"No it didn't, and I know they were happy together right up until the very end." I smiled, feeling a sense of pride for my parents, whom I barely knew, for taking actions for something they felt was wrong. I went back to the book, flipping through the pages while Rohl stood next to me. One page stuck out to me. It was not filled with pictures or what looked to be directions. The code was angle-spaced and took up the whole page.

It looked like a spell. I touched the page and ran my fingers over it. Suddenly the room and everything in it turned black.

A little girl with blonde hair skips down a long white hallway trimmed in gold, singing to herself. As she skips, she notices an open door at the end of the hallway. She sprints over to it and places a hand on the door. She looks around to make sure no one is watching then slips inside. The door has led her to a dimly lit room.

In the center of the room is a book on a pedestal open to a particular page.

The little girl walks over to the book and places her little fingers on it. Suddenly the door opens behind her, and a shrill voice rings out. "What are you doing in here?" a woman asks. "You're not supposed to be alone. Get back here this instant!"

The little girl, unfazed by the woman's harshness, walks over to her and heads out the door. She looks back at the book one more time before disappearing down the hall.

I took a breath then collapsed to the floor.

"Addie," I heard Rohl say.

I sat up, putting my hand to my aching head. I felt hands grabbing me, trying to pull me up. "I'm fine, I'm fine," I said to Rohl and Gaspar. "It's not like this is my first rodeo."

"What happened?" Gaspar said. "What were you doing?"

"I was looking at the Women of the Wise book. I touched it and I just blacked out."

"Addie, you didn't just black out," Rohl said.

"I didn't?"

"No your...your eyes glazed over."

"What do you mean by 'glazed over'?"

"After you touched the book you looked up, then this yellow film went over your eyes. That's why I went to get Gaspar. I didn't know what was happening."

That freaked me out. What the hell? What did that mean? "Okay, so I blacked out and a film covered my eyes," I said. "I bet that happens, like, all of the time in the supernatural world."

"Actually it doesn't," Gaspar said.

"Oh well, lucky me." I walked to the other side of the room.

"It has happened, but usually there is a reason," Gaspar said. "The reason being when a person is trying to remember something. Something that is important."

I thought back to what I had seen. It seemed like I had seen it before or something like it. Yes, right after Gaspar told me about my parents. I fainted and I saw the same little blonde girl with a woman who also had blonde hair. Could the little girl be me? And could the blonde woman be my mother?

"I've done that before," I said. "After you told me about my parents."

"I remember," Gaspar said. "Did you see anything then?"

"Yes I did. I saw a little girl with blonde hair walking down a white hall trimmed in gold. A woman soon appeared, also with blonde hair. She took the little girl's hand, and they walked into a room together. After that, I came back into the real world."

"What did you see this time?"

"The same little girl, same walls, and then this book in a room I don't think the girl was supposed to go in. When she tried to look at the book, a harsh woman came in and took her away from it." I took a breath. "Gaspar, could that little girl be me?"

"It is possible," he said, a look of ponder on his face. "Those pills you took, they must have not just been able to block your mind from the supernatural. They must have been suppressing your memories as well."

"I didn't know that was possible," Rohl said.

"It is if you use the right spells, magic, and herbs, which the Women of the Wise have access to."

"That's where the pills came from?" I asked.

"Indeed. Now that you haven't been taking them your mind is trying to remember everything that was blocked."

"Do you think this will be happening more often?"

"Oh yes, very well, yes. This is just the beginning, I'm afraid, but we are here to help you no matter what."

I nodded then bit my lip. I bet Gaspar was dying to write this down. "You can write this down if you need to, Gaspar," I said, trying to smile.

"What?" he asked, appalled.

"I saw your notes on me a while ago. I got mad and Rohl explained that you are just studying me because I'm like rare or the missing link or whatever. And I'm sure you are dying to write this down."

I could tell Gaspar was at a loss for words. "Well with your permission I would love to do that," he said. "And I'm sorry for the notes."

"It's okay, and you can keep taking notes. I want to know more about myself too. Before long, I might even be doing a study on myself." Both he and Rohl laughed. "Well I think I'm going to go lie down," I said. "My head hurts from all of that."

"Please do," Gaspar said. "And if anything else happens or if you need anything, just call one of us."

"I will." I walked out of the room feeling relieved and relaxed that I seemed to be finally settling in with everyone. The only thing I couldn't shake was the look of pure horror on Gaspar's face when he was telling me that I would be remembering things now. Was he really that worried, or was there possibly something I wasn't supposed to remember?

I had taken a quick nap then headed downstairs a few hours after lunch. I felt better, but I also felt a little weak. Gaspar said this was only the beginning of what I would be going through now that my mind was trying to remember things. I still didn't know what. I guess my childhood, but what teenager remembers their childhood anyway?

I started down the hallway towards the mezzanine in the front entrance. As I walked through the hallway towards the stairs, my head started to hurt again and my vision blurred.

I saw a big field that was slightly hilly, with tall grass and a few trees here and there. It was late evening and shadows were beginning to form. Two small kids were playing in the field, a little girl and boy. The girl had blonde hair, and the little boy had dark hair that was parted on the side and some hung down in his face.

The two ran around in circles, laughing and playing. Just being normal little kids.

The memory faded, and I came back to reality. I took a few breaths, trying to recall what I just saw. I put my hand on the wall, trying to steady myself. The little girl I recognized, it was me, but the boy I didn't know. After I gathered myself together, I walked down the stairs. Rohl, Jax, Genevieve, and Dayton were all standing in the huge foyer next to the entrance talking.

Rohl looked like he was somewhere else.

I thought back to the little boy and realized his smile resembled Rohl's. But that couldn't be. That would mean that I knew Rohl when I was younger, if my memory was really coming back. As I thought back to the boy I remembered he had dark hair that was parted, brown eyes, and he was dressed in all black like Rohl did now. I replayed the image in my head, looking at Rohl as I did so.

No there is no way, I thought. *Could I have known Rohl in my past life?*

The doors of the Safe Haven burst open, and a severely beat up Jules staggered through, spilling blood everywhere. "Jules," Genevieve called. "What happened?"

Jules grunted as he came closer to us, holding his left side. "Remember those vampires from last night?" he said. Everyone nodded. "Well the ones that got away caught up to me. Tried to get me to reveal where we have Addie hidden. I told them that I wouldn't give up her location for nothing, even my own life. And well, they believed me." He winced.

Jax and Rohl quickly ran over to him and helped him stand up.

"Look at these claw marks," Dayton said, walking up to him, gently pulling back his ripped shirt revealing deep claw marks. They even went through the thick leather cassock he was wearing. "These look like the ones I saw on Addie yesterday. Vamps didn't do just this to you, something else did."

"The claws are not from a werewolf," Rohl said. "They wouldn't attack one of us."

"And it's not from anything else here in New Orleans either," Jax put it. "What was it?"

Jules smiled a bit, but it faded. "You're not going to believe me if I tell you."

Dayton looked at him. "Tell us," she said.

"Okay, it was...a gargoyle."

I put my hand over my mouth.

"What?" Dayton asked.

"No way," Genevieve said.

"Are you sure it was a gargoyle?" Rohl asked.

"Very sure," Jules said. Jax and Rohl helped him sit down on a chiffon chair in a nearby corner. "At first I didn't know what it was until it came into the light. I didn't think they, the vamps, were going to attack me at first, then they did. I think it was more of a training rather than a killing."

"Why do you say that?" Jax asked.

"Because the vamps I saw looked like they had just been turned. They were nervous and scared of their own shadow. But three I recognized from last night. They were leading them, telling them what to do."

"Where does the gargoyle come in?" Dayton asked, kneeling down by him.

"A few more vamps showed, with it tethered to some kind of leash. There was another one that looked like it was mixed with something. As soon as I was able to get my blade and take it down it, it went down. The other one not so much."

"So they were controlling it?" Jax asked.

"Looked like it. It roughed me up more than the vamps did, then they just left me for dead. I got one of my jaspers out and used it to give me enough strength to get me home and figured Gaspar would do the rest."

"We need to get him up now," Dayton said.

Just as she was about to get up, Jules started to heave.

"Jules, are you okay?" Rohl asked.

He kept on doing it, gasping for breath at the same time.

"Jules, what's wrong!" Dayton screamed. Jules fell to his knees, having trouble breathing. Jax ripped what was left of the cassock off of Jules. The skin around the claw marks was starting to turn a grayish color, and a faint smoke was coming off of them.

"He's been poisoned," Jax said. "Get Gaspar now!"

Dayton and Genevieve ran to get Gaspar while I watched in horror as Jules twitched around on the floor gasping for air.

CHAPTER NINETEEN
FAMILY MATTERS

An hour later, Jules was lying on a bed in the hospital wing of the Safe Haven, all bandaged up and sleeping. After Jax and Rohl brought him in, Gaspar started mixing up some herbs to give him. He placed a few stones on his wounds along with the herbs. The stones sunk into his body as soon as they hit his skin. The bleeding had stopped, but he was still in bad shape.

I was standing by his bed along with everyone else, shaking.

"He'll be all right," Gaspar said smiling to everyone, checking him one last time. "Just let him rest, and he'll be good as new in no time."

"He said he was attacked by a gargoyle," Jax said. "Is that even possible?"

"That's the conclusion I'm coming to, unfortunately."

"What do you mean by 'unfortunately'?" Dayton asked in a harsh voice.

"I mean, I've gotten a report on a gargoyle attack already. I have no idea what's going on, but I am going to get to the bottom of it."

"Who else got attacked by a gargoyle?" Genevieve asked.

I spoke up, "Me." My voice sounded so small and weak. "I was the other night. Not just one, two in fact. I killed one, but the other flew off."

"It could be the one that attacked Jules," Rohl said. "It's not like they are coming to life all of a sudden."

"Looks like they are now," Jax said.

"All of you, please go now, let Jules rest. I'll report to you if anything has changed," Gaspar said. All of us except Jax left the hospital ward.

"Is Jules going to be okay?" I asked.

"He's going to be fine," Genevieve said. "I've seen him pull through worse."

"He's strong," Rohl said. "He can take it."

"Gaspar is just worried about this vampire business. And now that the gargoyles are getting involved, it's getting way too out of hand."

"But we are here, that's what we have been trained to do. To keep these things under wraps and keep people safe."

"I just don't want anyone else to get hurt. I know I still barely know you guys, but I..."

"Stop it," Dayton said, standing in front of us.

I stopped in my tracks. "What?" I asked.

Dayton turned around. "Just shut up. Stop acting like you care about Jules, stop acting like you care about any of us. I know you don't."

"I never said that."

"You said that you didn't want to be here."

"Yeah, that's completely different than saying I don't like anybody, and I never said that."

"You might as well have."

"What's this about, Dayton?" Rohl asked.

"I'm saying maybe Butch was right. Maybe the minute we were told who she was we should have just left her alone or at least not have taken an agreement to protect her. She obviously doesn't care. She ran away once. Maybe next time we should just let her go."

"Now hold up, we were given orders to protect her no matter

what, and we need to abide by that. If we break it you know what will happen."

"I'd rather take the punishment."

"Dayton."

"No think about it, Gen. Look what's happened. There are vamps after her, Jules was almost killed, and there are apparently now gargoyles running around. And all of this is happening because of her." Anger was starting to rise in me. If Dayton didn't shut up soon she was going to regret ever saying anything.

"Your point?" Rohl challenged.

"My point, we do all of this for her, and does she care? No, she doesn't. She would rather run away and get her ass killed than appreciate anything that we are doing for her." She turned to me. "Jax was right, you are a little brat."

I clenched my fist, trying to not make a fool of myself.

"That was one time, Dayton," I said. "I'm not going to run away again. I see it's not worth it and that I'm safe here. You can't blame me for that one time when I wasn't thinking straight."

"A person should be responsible for whatever actions they take no matter what."

"You're just saying all of this because Jules is in there." Rohl pointed to the hospital ward.

"No, I'm saying this because it needs to be said."

"And what's that going to accomplish, Day? Nothing," Genevieve said.

Dayton got quiet for a minute. "You know what is the stupid part about this?" she said. "Jules put a tracker on one of those vamps from the other night hoping that it would lead him where they are hiding. He wanted to take them out before they could possibly report to Orfeous. He was trying to help you."

I just looked at her. I couldn't find anything to say.

"I guess this is how it's going to be from now on. Us busting our asses trying to protect you from the big bad world out there."

"And how is that any different from what we do now?" Genevieve snapped.

"Because we were not just trying to protect one person." Dayton took one last look at me then turned around and disappeared down the hall.

"She didn't mean that," Genevieve said. "She's just upset because of Jules, but he'll be fine. I know he will."

"No, I think she meant it," I said. "Every word."

"Don't let what she said get to you," Rohl said. "Dayton can be a little over dramatic sometimes."

"Yeah and headstrong."

"She made some good points, though. Like I said, I just don't belong here." I looked at both of them then walked to my room and stayed there for the rest of the day.

Night was starting to fall. I was in my room looking at the pendant I found at my house. I changed my bed to a four-poster bed with mint green covers and canopy to match. I sat cross-legged on the bed, holding the pendant up high. It sparkled in the light. The more I looked at it the more I thought that I had seen it before, just where?

I heard a knock at my door.

I put the pendant in the box and hid it under my bed. "Come in," I said. Rohl opened the door and stepped into my room, and my stomach did a flip when I saw him. "Hey," he said.

"Hey," I said as casually as I could despite my racing heart.

"Are you okay?" he asked, walking towards me.

I took in a breath. "Yeah," I gasped. "I'm fine, why do you ask?"

"Dayton kind of riled you up, so I just wanted to make sure that you were okay."

Why do you care? a voice asked inside my head.

"I'm good, really I am. I was a little shook up by her words, but I'm better now."

Rohl took a step forward and leaned against the post. He looked at me then spoke. "You're lying," he said in a low voice.

"Come again?" I said, gawking at him.

"I can tell that you are lying."

"I'm not lying,"

"Yes you are."

"How do you know that?"

"I can tell by your body language. You're tense, your eyes aren't focused, you're timid, and your voice went up a few octaves."

"Big deal...so I'm lying. I do that a lot." I shrugged then looked at the covers.

"What are you really feeling?"

I thought for a while. When it was right I spoke. "Mad, sad, hurt, anger...everything. She had no right to say those things. I care that Jules is hurt. Hurt because of me, because he was trying to protect me."

"He was just doing his job, Addie, what we all do."

"Well Dayton is acting like it's my fault, like I'm the one who attacked and clawed him to death."

"Dayton takes things very seriously. She can also overreact as well."

"And she doesn't like me, her and Jax both. I'm surprised he's not with her on this."

"He knows that Jules was doing what he was trained to do, what we were all trained to do."

"What, do the job or die trying? Something like that?"

"In a way, actually, yes. It goes something like that."

"Is that why you didn't help Jax the other day? Because if he was killed then you could write it off as died in battle? Because that was wrong."

"I didn't intervene because I knew the wolves were coming. I knew they would help him. That and Jax is at his best when he's in a life and death situation."

"Oh."

"We are straying away from the point here."

"The point being I'm fine, okay, really. No tricks, no lies, I'm fine. I just want to sit here and relax and hope that Jules will get better."

"He will, he'll be fine, don't worry."

I let out a breath.

Rohl got silent all of a sudden. "Addie, I don't want you to think that we are protecting you because we have to," he said in a soothing voice. "We are protecting you because we want to."

"Dayton said you had orders to protect me," I said in a mocking tone. "Orders that you can't break or suffer the consequences."

"It's because we wanted to, not because we fear the punishments. When Gaspar and a few members of the High Council told us what needed to be done, we all agreed because we wanted to."

"Did you guys have a choice, or was Dayton just overreacting again?"

"Yes we did. We could have left it up to some other Regs, but we all agreed. Dayton is overreacting. She's just trying to intimidate you. This was an agreement on our own merits, so stop acting like we were forced to, because we weren't."

"What, the High Council just came to you all and said 'protect her' and that was it?"

"No, this is what happened. The High Council has at least two hundred members on it. The Regulators make up the most of it. Those few Regulators got together and chose us to protect you when Orfeous escaped his prison in England."

"Why was he there?"

"Being kept away from the world. That and he was born there. After he broke out of a maximum supernatural prison in England, the Regs there knew where he was heading. Here in the states to Louisiana for you. They assigned many Regs to capture him and Jax and I to help assist protecting you, which we accepted gratefully."

"Not Jax I bet."

"He has his reasons for accepting, he'll just have to tell them to you in time when he's ready."

"Why would the Council want to protect me from Orfeous? I thought they would hate me because of my parents."

"They can't punish a person if they've done no wrong. That's like locking up a murderer's son when he hasn't spilled a drop of blood. It's wrong. They also have a rule about protecting those who are innocent. You are, despite what your parents may or may not have done. You didn't do a thing wrong, yet there is someone after you. By their laws they must protect you or have someone else do it."

"I bet Butch doesn't give a damn about that."

"He's just one person. Besides, the part of the Council that wanted us to protect you was on your parents' side a long time ago. They didn't want to see them pay for something that could help the realm. The other part of the Council didn't agree, so there was some conflict. It was settled, but by that time your parents had already been killed."

I didn't know what to say.

"There are some good people on the Council," Rohl said. "And there are some bad. Just like every Council."

"How does the High Council work?"

"First of all, there are three Councils. The Head's Council, who only report to the Head and him only. The High Council, they are in charge of the Regs, and The Bureau of Enlightenment. They are over the Women of the Wise, they also make up a small part of the High Council."

"Are they separate from the High Council or on their own?"

"Not really, though we define them as separate, but others don't. They've been trying to gain an official unity from the High Council for years now.

"Anyway, The Head's Council is just strictly there to help the Head make laws and enforce them. To tell you the truth, they really don't do a lot. From what I've seen, it's the High Council that does all the hard work."

"Was anybody from the Bureau of Enlightenment on my parents' side as well?"

"I think a few, but not many."

I frowned.

Rohl looked down. "My father was on your parents' side as well," he said. "That's how I know all of this, in case you are wondering."

"You don't talk about your parents much. What were they like?"

"I don't know if that's a subject you would be interested in."

"Hey, you know my parents' story, now I want to know yours, and I won't stop aggravating you until you tell me." I was just about to start singing a really stupid song at the top of my lungs when Rohl started to speak.

"Okay, I'll tell you. It's not much, but here it goes. My mom was a bitter, old self-loathing drunk who didn't give a damn about me or my dad after my brother died. He was her pride and joy so I've been told. And my dad long after that disappeared, and I haven't heard from him since and probably never will."

I looked at Rohl really closely. I could see a bit of pain on his face, but I doubted he would show any more than that. I wanted to cry for some reason. I wanted to hold him and tell him I was sorry for him. I wanted to wrap him up in my arms and tell him everything was going to be okay. But I restrained myself from doing that. "Oh," was all I could say. "I'm so sorry."

"Don't be," he said. "I'm not looking for sympathy. It is what it is."

"Don't you miss them?"

"Not really. I've been on my own since I was at least fifteen. I can take care of myself. I got to admit I do owe at least that much to my dad. He did teach me how to survive on my own and not always depend on others and to fight."

"What was his name?"

"Roland Sivan. My mom named me after him, except..."

"Except your name is spelled with an H in it so that way you would at least be different from him in some way." I covered my mouth after that came out. "What?" I said. "How did I know that?"

"You've probably overheard Jules talking about it," Rohl said like nothing happened. "He picks on me all of the time because of it."

"Maybe." I knew I had never heard anyone since I had been here talk about Rohl and his name before.

"She wanted me to be different than him," Rohl spoke. I turned back to him. "My mom. She wanted both my brother and I to be different from our father, but we weren't. She wanted to raise us outside of the realm as far away from the supernatural as possible. Being a Reg got to her after a few years and made her go into a depression. That's why she drank. After she saw my brother get killed, she got worse and never recovered."

"I'm sorry."

"Once again don't be, she wasn't a good mother anyway. She was always yelling, complaining, smoking, whatever. My early childhood was rough. When my dad stepped in, that's when things got better. He taught me to fight, hunt, anything I wanted to know against her wishes. He made sure my brother and I would become great Regulators, and I think it has paid off."

"I'll say. The way you attacked those vampires the first night you saved me, you moved like nothing I've ever seen before."

Rohl smiled. "I guess it has paid off then."

I smiled too. It felt good knowing that we were connecting like this. "Before he disappeared, he was on your parents' side, and so am I. I just want you to know that," he said after a few minutes.

"Good to know. Why did you tell me all of that?"

"I don't want you to live here thinking we have to protect you because we were forced to. I want you to live here in peace and feel safe. You've been through enough already."

I felt a warmth that I hadn't felt in a while come over me. "Thanks," I said. "That's good to know."

"We really are all here for you, Addie, not because we have to but because we want to."

"I think I understand now."

"Good, I'm glad." He looked out the window. "Well I guess I'll let you get some sleep." He started to walk away.

"Rohl," I said.

He stopped at the door. "Yes." He turned to look at me. I wanted to tell him about the vision I had of the two kids, then I decided not to. "I was just wondering is it possible for me to maybe get out of here one day? Just to get a change of scenery."

"We'll have to check with Gaspar on that, but it might not be a problem. As long as one of us goes with you and you don't try to run away."

"Believe me, I've learned my lesson. If I run away, things come after me." I smiled a bit.

Rohl smiled back. "I'll see what I can do. Goodnight."

"Goodnight." He left the room.

At two o'clock in the morning, I lay awake in bed, tossing and turning. I kept dreaming of a little boy in the middle of some wooded area, pale-faced and scared to death as black shadows swarmed around him. He cried for help, but no one came. I could feel his pain, his sorrow, his fear, everything. I finally just decided to wake up. I was then afraid to go back to sleep, because every time I closed my eyes I saw his little face.

I got out of bed and opened my door.

The candlelit hallway was dead silent. All of the doors were shut, and I could practically hear everyone sleeping. I walked towards an end table at the very end of the hallway and took out a candle and candlestick holder. I lit the candle with another then started walking around the castle. I felt like a ghost haunting a place they once used to live in. I felt empty and drained, all because of that stupid dream.

Or was it a dream?

Gaspar said my memories were going to start coming back, but that couldn't have been a memory. I didn't even recognize the little boy. He didn't look like the one from yesterday, the one that resembled Rohl. So who was he? I walked through the castle, trying to ease my mind. I found a door on the bottom floor of the castle that I had never seen before. From where it was placed, it looked like it went down.

No way, a dungeon! I thought. *Awesome.*

I opened the door into a stone hallway. I could just make out a light at the end of it. I started to walk down it. Excitement, thrill, and fear of the unknown filled my body as I walked. My feet were starting to get cold from the stone floor. I followed the light to a huge room with a fireplace and what looked to be a blacksmith shop.

The room was barely lit, just like the rest of the castle. Metal, tools, and weapons were all hanging up on the walls or on rickety old wooden shelves. A huge stonework table was in the middle of the room littered with metal scraps, worn tools, and bits of weapon parts. The room itself looked to be completely made of stone. It also smelled like ash, wet stone, rusted metal, and dirt.

I jumped when I heard someone clear their throat.

A man who had to be around thirty-five, wearing an old flannel shirt, blue jeans, and a work apron, was walking over to the fireplace with some wood. He threw the logs on the fire then backed up as it roared to life. He said something that I couldn't make out then walked over to the worktable. He started hammering something and didn't even realize I was there.

I hid behind the archway that led into the room and watched him work for a while. He assembled what he was working on so quickly it was unbelievable. At the same time I wondered who he was. I hadn't heard anyone mention they had a blacksmith in the dungeon. If he was in here, then I wondered what else was hiding in this castle.

Suddenly he stopped hammering something and looked towards

me. "Well," he said. "Are you just going to stand there all night in the cold, or are you going to come out?"

Hotness filled my body. *Oh no,* I thought. *He knows I'm here. Now I have to show myself. No I don't. I could just run away. For all I know he could be something that's after me. Then why is he in the castle? Hidden maybe for a reason.* I shook my head to stop the thoughts.

I stepped from behind the archway and placed my feet at the very edge of the step that led down into the room. The man looked at me, face expressionless, hammer still in hand. He put it down then wiped his hands with a cloth. He looked me up and down.

"Well look at you," he said, smiling a bit. "I never thought I would see the day. You've gotten so big. It's good to see you again, Adalyn François."

CHAPTER TWENTY
HEROES

I stared at the man in disbelief. "What?" I asked horrified. "How do you know my name?"

"Oh I'm so sorry," he said, shaking his head. "I forgot you don't remember me. You were *so* young, it's no wonder you can't. My name is Nils. I knew your parents."

Nils. The name didn't sound familiar, then again it did. It seemed like I'd heard it mentioned before. I just didn't recognize him at all. He knew my parents, so another ally or enemy? "You knew my parents?" I questioned cautiously.

"Yes I did," Nils said. A somber look fell upon his fair-skinned face. "They were good people. It's a shame what happened to them."

"You were a follower of theirs, I suppose, or you supported them, am I right?"

"I did to the very end. Still do if that's possible."

I didn't know what to say at that point. I wanted to ask him what he was doing in the dungeon, but I didn't want to get into anything personal. Still he was a follower of my parents. He believed in what they were trying to accomplish, I needed to know more. "Why are you down here in the dungeon and not with everyone else?" I tried to ask as carefully as I could.

Nils smiled then looked at me. "I don't really think of this as a dungeon. More of a dreary basement, more or less."

It's got a creepy feel, creepy lighting, and it's in the lowest part of the castle, I thought. *Call it what you want, it's a dungeon. All that's missing is the torture devices.*

"I see," was all I could say.

Nils chuckled. "So tell me, what are you doing up so late?"

"Couldn't sleep."

"Bad dreams."

"Yeah, how did you know?"

"Lucky guess. That, and there is something about this castle that seems to give people nightmares. I've seen it a lot, more so with the younger Regs that come through here for training."

"Great. I'm living in a haunted castle."

"A well-protected haunted castle," Nils joked then smiled. I smiled back and was starting to feel more at ease. He wasn't dangerous, but there was something off about him that I just couldn't quite put my finger on.

"What are you doing up so late?" I asked.

"Fixing things, my specialty."

"Is that all you do?"

"No, I help keep the castle clean like Mildred. I make weapons for the Regulators mainly. It's not a lot, but it keeps me busy." As Nils talked he worked on what looked like a huge sword. I could only imagine who was going to get it.

"Are you a Reg?"

"Oh no, far from it, I'm afraid."

"So you just make weapons then and clean?"

"Pretty much. Like I said, it's not a lot, but it is something to do. I've always been good with my hands, so I ended up here thanks to your father and Gaspar actually."

"I'm guessing you knew my parents well then."

"Very." Nils paused for a moment. "If it wasn't for their kindness, I wouldn't be here right now."

"How did they help you?" I stopped. "Sorry, I just have a lot of questions. You're like one of the few people I've encountered that hasn't tried to kill me."

"It's all right, it's understandable. You're confused, and you want answers. I know you didn't get a chance to grow up with your parents. I'm happy to tell you anything about them."

"Start with you, please. How did they save you?"

Nils gave a wary smile then looked down at his worktable. "It's very hard to explain," he said with a pained expression on his face.

"Whatever it is, I won't judge," I reassured him. "Nothing is really out of the ordinary as far as I'm concerned anymore."

"Okay then." He smiled. "I'm...not what you think. I'm different from you, the Regs, and others."

"Do you have a special gift?"

"It's far from a gift, more like a curse really. Because of it the High Council wanted to kill me a long time ago when they found out I was living in society. They put the order in for my arrest and death until your father, mother, and Gaspar stepped in. They all got together and went up against the Council to remove the punishment that was in store for me."

"Wow, they must have really cared a lot about what they were doing."

"Very, so much that they died for it. The bad thing is I can never repay them for it."

"I'm sure that you just living is repayment enough for them. I know it would be enough for me."

Nils looked at me. "You look just like your mother Clara," he said. "But I know you've got the spirit and spunk of your father."

"Yeah, that spunk that has gotten me into more trouble in one summer than in my whole life."

"I heard about your friend. I am so sorry."

"Thanks, I just wish knowing what I do now...I just wish I could go back and redo it so that way...she wouldn't have gotten killed."

"I understand the feeling, believe me, I do." I could still feel something off about Nils. It wasn't anything bad, it was just staring at me right in the face and yet I couldn't figure out what it was. It was driving me insane.

"I know there is something about you," I blurted out without thinking. "I just can't figure out what."

"That's another thing your mother could do. See things other people couldn't, even some Regs couldn't compete with the skills she had."

"Gaspar told me that things would start to come clearer to me since nothing is blocking my mind anymore."

"Looks like they are starting to."

"I'm still having a bit of trouble. So what are you? Since we are talking here." I stopped. "That came out a little too harsh."

"It's okay, Addie. I told you I would tell you anything." I nodded, but I didn't want him to get mad if I overstepped a line. "Let's try something, if you don't mind."

"Sure, what?"

"Try and read my energy. I'm sure that Gaspar has told you about reading energies."

"In a way, yes. I'm still learning a lot."

"People, no matter who they are or what they are, all have energies they give off. Some different from others, especially if they are a supernatural. If they are, then you can tell what just by studying them and reading their energy."

"That must be what I feel coming off of you."

"Look at me, really look at me, and try to read my energy." I looked hard at Nils and did what he told me to do. In my mind I compared the other things I had felt when the gargoyles, vampires, and werewolves were around me, but nothing matched what I was feeling. His energy was weird. It was dark and sinister, with kindness and compassion mixed in, even I guess it would be called humanness.

What the hell was he?

Finally, I gave up and just said something. “Vampire mix?” I asked.

Nils chuckled. “Nope,” he said. “Kind of close, though. Demon.”

“Demon!” I backed up a few steps.

“Part demon actually. A Nephilim to be specific.”

“What’s that?”

“It’s a being who is part angel or demon and human. They are in the Bible. They are also very rare.”

“And apparently they are hated by the Council.”

“Pretty much. Supernatural beings and humans are never supposed to reproduce. It’s strictly forbidden.”

“There are a lot of thing it seems that are forbidden when it comes to the Council.”

“Indeed there are.”

“But if you’re half demon, then how come I’m not getting an evil feeling from you? I would think of all creatures a demon would give off a darker vibe.”

“It’s because my humanness if covering it up. Just because I’m part demon doesn’t mean I am evil either. Just wanted to clear that up.”

“I believe you. I don’t know you that well, but I don’t think you would hurt anybody unless you have to.”

“I wish the Council would see it that way. That is why I’m here serving them so I wouldn't be killed, but I had to do something. I couldn't just live my life in peace. Working here isn't bad, though."

"I'm starting to see that."

"Good, I'm glad."

"How are you part demon by the way? You don't have to answer that. I'm just being curious again."

"It's fine. My mother was a human, but my father was a human possessed by a demon. When a demon possesses someone, that demon's spirit pushes the human spirit down, overpowering it. If a person is dead and the demon enters them, it's easier because the human's life is gone. All the demon has to do is enter the body and take over. Then the person is a full demon."

I was shocked. I didn't know what to say.

"That was the case with my father. His vessel was dead, so he took it over. By the time my poor mother found out what he really was, it was too late. She was pregnant with me and had no way out, and you can't exactly kill a demon spawn."

"Did she survive giving birth to you?"

"Yes, just barely. She raised me until I was old enough to take care of myself then she left. I have been on my own ever since."

Sounds like Rohl a bit, I thought.

"Once I understood what I was, I hid until the Council found out. I had met your father years before that, though, when he and some Regs were battling some demons. I helped them fight the demons using the few powers that I possess, and we became good friends. I met your mother later. I never saw a couple more right for each other than them."

Tears filled my eyes at the thought of two young people loving each other despite the whole world being against them. I'd like to see Nicholas Sparks write something like that.

I wiped the tears away and yawned.

"Getting tired?" Nils asked.

"Just a bit," I said. "Not that you're putting me to sleep, it's just getting late."

"Yeah it is. You might want to go get some sleep. I'm sure you have a lot to do."

"Yeah, sitting around here doing nothing all day."

"It's better than being chased by vampires." I looked at him. "I heard about that too." He smiled.

I smiled back. "Thank you for telling me all of this. I really appreciate it."

"It's no trouble, and thank you for not running screaming when I told you I'm part demon."

"I'm sure I'll be running into scarier things in the near future."

"You might."

"And thanks for helping me figure a few things out, it's helped a lot."

"No problem, kid." I nodded then started to walk off. "I am your godfather after all."

I stopped then turned around. "What did you just say?"

Nils looked at me. "I'm your godfather."

"Wha...what? How? What?"

"Yes, it's true. I am your godfather."

"Wait, if you are my godfather, then why didn't you take me in after they died?"

"At the time the Council..."

"They interfered."

"Yes, they did, but only to protect you. The same with Wanda and Jeff. They all decided that it would be best for you to live with them and not me. They figured that you would be safer with them, but legally I am your godfather. The Council just overruled it."

"I understand." And I couldn't believe that I actually did.

Nils looked down at the floor then back up at me. "I'm glad that you are safe, Addie," he said, voice cracking. "More than glad. If something had happened to you, then I don't know what I'd do."

"Well I'm fine for now, so don't worry. I've got people wanting to protect me and me wanting to protect myself and what my parents stood for."

"That's good to hear."

I yawned again.

"Go back to sleep. You need it."

"Okay, I will, night." I started to walk towards the steps. I turned around and ran to Nils. I wrapped my arms around him, hugging him with all of my might. He didn't hesitate in hugging me back. I felt his warmth and felt safe, at peace. I held onto that feeling for a while. When I let go, tears were in his eyes.

"Thanks," I said once again.

"No problem." He petted my head.

Feeling extremely tired I walked out of the dungeon and towards my room. I got into bed with heavy eyes. I thought about what Nils said over and over again, feeling more proud of my parents than ever before. They weren't criminals like Jax painted them to be. They were regular people, as far as being regular went in the realm, who wanted a change in their world. They helped people, they saved people. What's wrong with that?

My parents lived like heroes and died like heroes. Now I wanted so badly to find out more about them and open up the rest of my past as well.

When I finally drifted off to sleep, I dreamt of heroes instead of a crying boy.

A week later, I still couldn't get what Nils had told me about my parents out of my head. I decided to start searching for more information about them. I started with the old Women of the Wise study that Rohl took me to. I looked through mountains and mountains of books but couldn't find anything about my mother. I then went looking in the big study. I went up the spiral staircase leading to the second level, once again feeling overwhelmed by the number of books.

From the top I could see the whole study. I was also a lot closer to the skeletons that were hanging down from the ceiling.

I saw the Regs sitting at the same table with books and papers all in front of them. *I can't believe the High Council expects people no older than me to deal with beings as dangerous as Orfeous*, I thought. *That's just cruel.*

I understood why they did it, then again I didn't. How could someone have so much power over you to choose the way you live for you?

Quit thinking that, Addie! I scolded myself in my head. *You're not here to justify how the Regs work. Stop worrying about it.*

I cleared my head then started searching again.

Granted, I didn't know what the hell I was looking for. Just something that might talk about my parents. If they were a big deal in the Arcanian realm history, then there had to be something about them. After searching shelf after shelf, I finally found a book that could help me. It was about the size of an average school textbook, as thick as one too, with the title *The History of Arcania* on its faded purple cover.

I took the book over to a table by a bay window and sat down.

I started flipping through the pages, trying to find something about them. I saw the longer version of the story Jax told me about how the Regulators became to be. What he told me was indeed true, but he left out the part about how the Regs back then killed any supernatural thing that lived outside the realm, regardless if they did anything wrong or not. It reduced the population until a kindred soul decided that it wrong to do that.

I read the whole book pretty much and found nothing about my parents. So much for being a book on the history of the realm. I closed the book then looked outside of the windows. I could see the French Quarter. I pictured myself walking down the street, going to Café Demount with my friends, hanging out and having a good time. Now I was stuck here being protected from an evil vampire.

I wanted to go outside. I wanted to feel the warmth on my skin, smell food being cooked from the restaurants, and not get attacked by freaking everything in the world.

Soon, soon, soon enough this would all be over with. The Regs would catch Orfeous, and I could go back to my normal life. As normal as it would be after knowing all of this.

I pressed my fingers to my forehead, sighing. I needed something else, something more. I saw Gaspar walk over to the Regs and give them something. They talked for a while, and then it hit me. Gaspar! He was in charge of this place, so if anyone would know anything, it would have to come from him. I remembered seeing some kind of file cabinet in his study. Maybe he had records of past Regulators. That could lead to my dad.

I stood up, put the book back on the shelf, and slowly made my way down the stairs. I was out the double doors in seconds. They didn't even notice I was there. I made my way to Gaspar's study. I turned the doorknob and it opened.

I walked into the study then walked over to the vintage filing cabinet. Every drawer had a letter on it, so I started with the F's. I opened the drawer and took out a faded folder. Sure enough I was right. The cabinet did contain the files of some Regulators. Whether they stayed here or not was another thing. Still it was something. I put the file back then started going through all of the F's.

I found every other last name F from Fabiano, Fares, Fanetta, Fayina, Flario, Frey, but no François. I sighed then closed the drawer. I found another set of files and started looking through them but came up empty. I searched all though Gaspar's study, coming up empty every time. If he knew my parents so well, then he should have something on them, right? Guess not. I sat on the floor almost in tears that I came up empty handed.

I looked towards the filing cabinet, a curiosity hitting me.

I opened the S drawer up and started looking through the files. When I found the one that said *Sivan, Rohland* I took it out. I opened the parchment file and started looking through it. On one page listed Rohl's height, weight, current age, eye and hair color, just his overall features. On another page listed what he was good at as a Regulator. It had things like stealth, combat, swordsmanship, keen eyesight, agility, even detective skills.

I started to wonder if all of their files were like that.

I put Rohl's back then started looking in the R's for Genevieve's next. Gen's was about the same as Rohl except it listed *sex appeal* as a quality. That didn't surprise me, Gen was beautiful, something I wanted to be. I then looked through the D's for Devereaux and the B's for Baptiste for Dayton and Jules. They were still pretty much the same except for the weapons, and Dayton had inventor listed as one of her qualities. All of their ages were about the same as well. Between two and three years older than me.

The only one I couldn't find was Jax, and I looked all through the W's.

I put the files back then closed the drawers.

"Looking for something?" someone said.

I screamed then turned around to see Gaspar and Rohl standing behind me. "I...uh..." I stuttered. "I was...um...I..."

"Snooping," Rohl said, smiling. Gaspar smiled as well, and I couldn't tell if I was in trouble or not.

"I was not snooping," I said. "I was..." I sighed. "Okay you caught me. Yes I was snooping, but for a very good reason."

"I'm sure it was," Gaspar said. "I highly doubt you would go through my things without a purpose."

I stood up from the floor and decided to come clean. "I met Nils down in the dungeon last night. He told me a bit about my parents, and I just wanted to see if I could find out more about them."

"I see," Gaspar said. "Did he...um...tell you anything else?"

"Nothing much, only that he is my godfather."

Gaspar's face fell.

"When were you going to tell me?"

"I don't know. I didn't think it was important just yet."

"Important? It's so important. Never mind, that's not the point right now. The point is he told me about how my parents saved him because the Council wanted to kill him. I've heard stories about them, and I just want to know more."

"I understand, but unfortunately I don't have any records of them anymore. The Council destroyed them after your parents died."

"They did?"

"Yes, they pretty much erased anything that had to do with them."

"What about the Women of the Wise?" Rohl said. "They keep records like crazy. They almost never get rid of anything. Even if it's a hundred years old."

"That's true, but they hardly let anyone look at their archives. They are very private about that, especially when it comes to past members."

"I'm guessing it's a long shot then," I said.

"No, I wouldn't say that, I...it's very hard to explain. I could ask their Head Madame Pythia, but I doubt she will let us come if that is our only reason for visiting."

"Can you at least try? Please, Gaspar. It's all I've got. I'm very curious now, I need to know." I took a breath. "I just need something, anything besides their names and stories. I want more if that's possible. Also I've been remembering a few things as well. Actually I don't know if they are memories or cruel nightmares."

"Have you now. Like what?"

"Just things, horrible things. Things that I can't decipher if they are real or not. I know my memory is coming back, but is there a way to speed up the process a little? I feel like there is something important that I have to remember, and I need to remember it soon."

Gaspar looked at Rohl then back at me. "There is one thing," Gaspar said. "But we'd have to go to the realm."

"What is it?"

"It's in the Women of the Wise's castle. There is a process they do to help people remember certain things. That's the only thing I can think of that will help you."

"But it's dangerous," Rohl warned. "Some people see things that they never wanted to see and end up losing their minds because of it."

"Oh Rohl, that's just an old wives' tale. But he is right. The process can be a bit harsh, but the Women know what they are doing."

"They can help me remember?"

"They can and possibly."

I didn't know what to say. Part of me wanted to go to the realm, to the Women of the Wise and get my memory and past back, then another part wanted to stay behind for fear of what I might find. Still I might never get this chance again. Jax's story could be right and my parents could have been doing things for their own benefit, or they could have been trying to save their home. Needless to say I needed to find the truth and now.

"Let's go to the realm," I said.

CHAPTER TWENTY-ONE
THE REALM

I followed Gaspar and Rohl back to the main study. Everyone was still there at the table looking through books. "Change of plans," Gaspar said to them. "We are heading to the realm."

"What?" Jax asked. "Why?"

"Addie wants to learn more about her family. I figure the best place for her to learn that is within the realm."

"No way. She is not going to the realm, Gaspar, are you crazy? Have you completely lost your mind?" Jax said.

"She can't go to the realm," Dayton spoke up. "She just can't."

"Why can't I?" I almost shouted. "What is so bad and dangerous about the realm? After all, you are all from there, so why can't I go?"

"Because you're a target."

"I'm a what?"

"A target. Orfeous has vampires and other creatures in the realm looking for you in case you decided to go there. And he figured you would go there eventually."

"How do you know that?"

"From some other Regs," Jax said. "They contacted us a few days ago and told us what was going on in the realm."

"Wonderful, that's great. Now the realm isn't safe either."

"Don't worry, Addie," Gaspar said. "We are still going to get you to the realm. We're just going to have to find a safer way."

"I guess this is going to keep happening from now on," Dayton said.

"What?" I asked.

"You getting your way and screw the rest of us." Dayton smirked and I glared at her, balling my hands into fists.

"Dayton, that's enough," Gaspar said. "If Addie wants to try and find some information about her parents, then we must help her do so. It's her right after all, isn't it?"

Dayton rolled her eyes then crossed her arms.

I rolled my eyes too. I knew she didn't like me, but she didn't have to show it so damn much. "Can we still get to the realm?" I asked when no one said anything.

"Yes we can," Gaspar said. "And we will, just you wait and see. But first, who were these Regs? And are they sure of what they reported to you?"

"They are some Regs from England and Australia," Jax said. "One group was being led by a friend of Rohl's and mine. His name is Sebastian. He was the one who gave us the information, and I know he can be trusted. His regiment were in the realm at the time on a mission, and they ran into a few half-bred creatures that were looking for Addie.

"The other group contacted us as well, saying the same thing."

"Where in the realm were they at the time?"

"Somewhere along the east just past Chiikatorra, from what Sebastian told us. According to the Aussies they are everywhere now, especially by the portal hot spots."

"If we can't take a portal, then how are we going to get there?" Genevieve asked.

"Fireplace and floo powder I guess then?" I said. They all looked at me. "What? It's from a book series, never mind, can we still get to the realm?

"We can still get there by portal, just a very special portal. I'm sure you're all familiar with it."

The Regs looked back and forth at each other.

"No, not the first portal," Jules said.

"Yes indeed the first portal."

"You can't be serious, Gaspar? The first portal? That thing is hardly ever used," Genevieve said.

"What is the first portal?" I asked.

"The first portal is exactly what it is called. It was the first portal ever made and therefore is the strongest of them all. It can take you anywhere you want to go."

"Well isn't that what portals are supposed to do anyway?"

"Yes and no. Most portals are only set up to go one place and one place only, but the first portal can take you anywhere you want. You just have to think about where you want to go," Jules said.

Jax walked over to a column and unhinged a piece of white rope from a notch. When he did a huge map of the realm was revealed from a beam attached to the castle ceiling. The map was as big as a movie screen. "Show all portal hotspots," Jax said. Suddenly the map started to light up with purple circles in different places.

"Sebastian said that all of Orfeous' scouts were placed where all of the portal hotspots are. There are hundreds throughout the realm, all leading to a different part of it. The first portal leads to one place and one place only."

"A clearing behind Arcania Town in Eitenhabe," Jules said. "It's a blind spot in the realm. Almost no magic exists there, the same goes for the town as well."

"It's the safest place in the realm. I can guarantee that," Gaspar said. "Orfeous has no way of getting there. The only way to get to that spot is by this portal."

"Then that settles it. We take the last portal to the blind spot and go from there, right?"

"We still need to be careful, though, Addie. Orfeous may not be able to enter the blind spot, but he can sure get around it."

"We'll have to be ready in case we run into any of his scouts," Jax said. "Everyone pack as many weapons as you can, no matter how big or small, or what they are used for. They could come in handy."

The Regs sprinted over to their weapons area and started pulling out a few things. "This isn't enough," Jules said. "We are going to need more."

"Let's go to the weapons room then," Dayton said. "There's a whole shitload of things I want to try in there."

I followed them out of the study and into a huge room filled to the brim with every weapon imaginable. Quivers with arrows hung from hooks with the bow hanging just beneath it. Long swords, short swords, daggers, knives, maces, spears, throwing stars, and even slingshots were displayed just about anywhere in the room.

Shelves stocked with blades, arrowheads, spikes, ball-looking things, and various other weapon accessories stood on the back wall towards the entrance. Towards the back were other weapons I'd never even seen before. They looked medieval. Talk about a sportsman's paradise. "Okay, now this has got to be the best room I've seen so far," I said.

"Don't say that. You haven't even seen the whole castle yet," Jules said.

Jax walked over to one of the walls and got the biggest sword he could find. "I'd go bigger with the swords, Rohl," he said, wiping the sword off. "Those katanas aren't going to be enough."

"They'll be fine," Rohl said, taking one of the big curved swords out of its holster. "I've always used them, and they have never failed me."

"But we are going up against Orfeous' men," Genevieve said.

"You might need something even stronger than those swords."

"Here," Jules said, picking up an even bigger sword than Rohl's from the rack on the wall. "Take this odachi. If you can't take something down with this, then it can't be taken down."

Rohl took the odachi with a somber look on his face. "Fine," he said. He put his swords up then holstered the odachi, which to me just looked like a bigger version of his swords.

After all of the Regulators were ready, we met up with Gaspar in the entrance hall. I glanced out one of the castle windows and was shocked. Night had already fallen. "It's nighttime already?" I asked.

"Sure is," Rohl said. "Time flies when you're snooping around, doesn't it?" He smirked.

"All right, is everyone ready?" Gaspar asked. We all nodded. "Good, then follow me." We went through an archway leading into a hallway. Gaspar led us through a few more hallways towards a pair of big doors similar to the entrance ones.

He waved a crystal over the doors and they began to open.

They opened onto a stone deck, which led into a garden area. I gasped at the sight. It looked like something straight out of a movie. "Right this way, Addie," Gaspar said. I jumped and started following them through the luscious garden. The Regs' boots clicked on the cobblestone path as we walked past a sparkling pond with ducks, fish, and a small waterfall. Plants and trees of all kinds were growing everywhere, giving the place a sort of jungle feel.

Farther on the right I could see a gazebo with what looked like a small training area next to it. And smack in the middle of it all was a big tree with a hole in its trunk. Gaspar stopped at the base of the tree. "We are here," was all he said.

"Here where?" I asked.

"At the first portal,"

"You're kidding," I almost laughed. "The first portal is a tree?"

"It's not the tree per se," Genevieve said. I looked towards her.

"It's inside the tree," Jules said. "Embedded in the trunk so it can be safe. This tree is from the realm, so it has an attachment to it already. When the portal was created it was stored in the trunk but not just anyone can access it."

I could see stripes of purple, blue, indigo, and light pink throughout the tree. It seemed to be almost glowing.

"How do you guys access it?"

"With this." Gaspar pulled something over his head and stuck his hand out, which held a beautiful purplish star-cut amulet. "This is the key to the portal." Gaspar walked up to the tree and placed the amulet on the trunk. I could see all of the tree's energy balled up where the amulet was. In seconds a hole big enough to fit a human appeared with swirling colors.

"Whoa!" was all I could say.

Gaspar looked at the portal then turned to us. "Who wants to go first?" he asked.

Jules stepped up. "Figures," Dayton said. Jules smiled then disappeared into the portal. Genevieve went next, her ruffled Victorian-style dress just made it in. Dayton stepped through, then Jax, then Gaspar. All that was left was Rohl and me.

"Are you coming?" Rohl asked, stepping towards the portal. The moonlight bounced off his face, making him look more mysterious.

"Is it safe?" I asked.

"Very."

I backed up, still unsure. "It's not so bad. Come on." He held his hand out to me. *Why does he have to look so handsome right now?* I thought. *And why the hell did I just think that?*

I took Rohl's hand, and he pulled me to him. "Now I must warn you, going through a portal the first time can be a bit...difficult," Rohl whispered close to my ear.

"Difficult how?" I asked.

"You're traveling through a doorway into another world that is not even supposed to exist. It can get weird. Just stay close to me and you'll be fine."

I stepped closer to him and wrapped my hands around his arm.

"You will feel a tingling sensation, it's normal. You may feel dizzy, nauseous, a headache, things like that as well."

Damn. That sounded like the side effects to a medicine.

"Okay," I said, nodding. Rohl started walking towards the portal. I could feel the force of it pulling us in closer. I could also hear the loud whooshing sound it made ringing high in my ears.

"We're about to enter it," Rohl yelled over the noise. "Just hang on, Addie." I held on tight to Rohl as we stepped into the portal.

We zipped and zagged in different directions. My internal organs felt like they were about to come out of my mouth. My skin felt like a thousand and one needles were poking it. I felt dizzy, nauseous, and uncomfortable. I just wanted it to be over with. Finally, the feelings left when we touched ground.

I stumbled when we did, almost pulling Rohl down with me. But something was wrong. Why was everything dark?

"Addie, open your eyes," I heard Rohl say.

I did what he said. A vast slightly hilly land was before my eyes with very few trees. Tall grass stood up everywhere, and the high sun was making it look so beautiful. *This looks familiar,* I thought, then pushed it away. "So this is the blind spot," I said. "How big is it?"

"A few miles," Jules said. "Trust me though, it feels smaller than that."

"And looks it," Dayton added.

"We need to get to the Women of the Wise as soon as possible," Gaspar said. "Go, it's not that far from here."

"We need to go through the town, right Gaspar?" Dayton asked.

"Yes correct. Let's go." We all started walking.

After barely an hour of walking, we came to an area full of green grass, trees, with a mountainous area in the background. "Wait, this place looks different," I said.

"That's because this is what the realm is supposed to look like," Gaspar said. "Full of rich color, not like the blind spot."

"That's why it's called the blind spot," Rohl said. "For some reason the magic in the realm doesn't reach it. That's why it's not as colorful, but there is enough magic to hold a portal."

I looked around. The realm resembled the garden at the Safe Haven a bit, with just more space and trees. We made our way onto a dirt path. I could hear a stream nearby, and before long, Jules was in it drinking some water. "Really?" Dayton asked him.

"What, I was thirsty," Jules said. I laughed.

After another half-hour of walking, we made it to a big gate and fence. Through it I could see a small town full of people. "What's this?" I asked.

"This is Arcania Town, part of Arcania City," Jules said. "It's where Genevieve, Dayton, and I are from."

"This is part of a city?"

"The city is bigger," Dayton said. "This is just a small country part of it."

"The Women of the Wise are located just past the town," Gaspar said. "Let's keep walking. It's not much further from here."

I started following them again. Finally, after two hours, I saw a castle just a little smaller than the Safe Haven in the background on top of a hill. It was white and trimmed in gold, the Women of the Wise colors. There was a certain hue around it that I could just see. I didn't know if the others could. It looked very elegant, very regal. "Wow," I said. "That castle is beautiful."

"Welcome to Las Kala," Jules said. "Home of the Women of the Wise."

Gaspar walked ahead of us. "Let's go," he said. "I sent a message to them saying we were coming."

"They're expecting us?" Dayton said. "Wow, talking about the royal treatment." Gaspar looked at her.

"Keep your mouth shut," I heard Genevieve whisper to her. Dayton nodded. I followed everyone down a cobblestone path to a big gold iron-made front gate attached to a rock fence nearly ten feet tall. Next to the gate were two very tall lavender trees. We stood there for a few minutes until the gate opened. Gaspar gestured for all of us to enter.

As they walked down the path towards a big water fountain my head started to hurt.

In a flash I was seeing the same entrance but from a different angle. Like I was kneeling down. Suddenly the feeling left and everything went back to normal. "Addie, are you okay?" Jules asked from the glass steps.

I shook my head. "I'm fine I think. I just had a flashback or something."

Gaspar and Jax looked at each other.

"This way, Addie," Gaspar said. I followed them up the steps to some golden doors with leafy deigns on them. Gaspar knocked. A young woman in her twenties with long brown hair and bright eyes answered. "Hi, my name is Storey," she said. "May I help you?"

"My name is Gaspar Forester. I'm here to see Pythia."

"Right this way please, she's expecting you." Storey opened

the door a bit wider and we walked into the castle. "Oh my gosh," Storey suddenly said. "Pardon me being so formal, but aren't you Adalyn François? John and Clara François' daughter?"

I looked at her, not knowing what to say. Her green eyes were bright and shining. I glanced at Gaspar to see if it was okay to tell her. "It's okay," he said.

I then looked back at Storey. "Yes I am. I'm their daughter."

"Oh, that is just like so amazing," she said, practically jumping out of her skin. "I've read and heard the story of your parents so many times."

I nodded, still at a loss for words. "Yeah," I said, voice cracking.

"I heard about what happened to your guardians. I'm so sorry. I met Jeff and Wanda a few years ago. They were very nice people."

"The best." I've realized now.

"Anyway you can all follow me." Storey led us past a huge glass staircase towards another door. The doors led to a white hallway trimmed in gold.

"I've seen this before." I said out loud.

Everyone turned to look at me. "You have?" Gaspar asked.

"Yes, I have. In a vision not very long ago."

"I'm sure we can help you remember," Storey said. "From what I've heard, your mom was a great visionary"

"A visionary?"

"Someone who has a connection to their inner mind and the world around them. They can also have premonitions of the past, present, and future. Not many of the Women of the Wise have a great power like that. It's kind of rare."

"Are you one of them?"

"Not yet, though I hope to be someday. I'm a...guess you can say an intern. I'm studying with them until I can fully start my training.

Then once I train, Madame Pythia decides if I have what it takes to be a Wise."

"You have to go through training just to become a Woman of the Wise?"

"Indeed. It's a lot, but it's worth it in the end." Storey smiled so big it was hard to feel for her. She was giving up her whole life just to be one of them, yet she still believed there's a good side to it. She reminded me of Ava. So much life and energy that I could practically feel it. I felt at peace just standing next to her.

"Given your mom's background," Storey said as we walked on. "Would you consider training to become a Wise as well?"

"No way," I said a little too loudly. "And give up my whole life, my rights. No thank you."

"Doesn't surprise me. That's the kind of reaction I'd expect from an offspring of John François," a cold voice said.

I jumped then looked up towards the glass staircase. A tall woman stood in a long grayish silk dress staring down at all of us. Her gray and white hair was pulled back in a tight bun, her narrow eyes gazed upon me and sent shivers down my spine. Her whole being scared the hell out of me. I hated to admit it, but she made my aunt look like Mary Poppins.

She stood stiffly at the top of the staircase, hands neatly folded in front of her. She had to be at least in her sixties, maybe even older.

"Ah, Madame Pythia," Gaspar said. "How lovely it is to see you again."

"As it is you, Gaspar," Madame Pythia said, not showing any emotion. "And what have we brought in today?"

Well that's rude, I thought. *Talking about me like I'm a thing, yet acting like she's all high class.*

"This is Addie," Gaspar said, placing his hands gently on my shoulders. “She’s the one I sent the letter to you about.”

“Yes, I remember. Normally I wouldn’t bother with such a matter, but since it’s you, Gaspar, I made an exception.”

“And I do appreciate it, Madame, I do.”

Madame Pythia started to walk down the stairs. She stopped when she got to me. I could feel her eyes practically boring into me as she looked me up and down. “You’ve got your mother’s hair and eyes,” she said. “But I bet you’re more like your father. Stubborn, hot-tempered, rule breaker, am I right?”

I glared at her. She had no right to assume I was all of that because of my dad, even if it was true. “Maybe,” I said. “What’s it to you?”

“Addie,” Genevieve warned.

“What? She can’t assume I’m a certain way just because of who my parents were. That’s unfair.”

“She can, she’s the head of this castle,” Jax said.

“Still doesn’t give her the right...”

“That attitude, just like your father. Never blamed himself for his actions, always assumed it was others.”

“Look, lady...”

“Madame Pythia! You shall call me that and none other. You will also learn to hold your tongue or lose it. You will learn to speak when spoken to or else. Maybe staying here wouldn’t be such a bad idea after all.”

“That won’t be necessary, Madame Pythia,” Gaspar said in a shaky voice. “Addie is fine with us until she can find somewhere else. Please now, what must we do in order to help her remember what she wants to know?”

I kept my mouth shut and let Gaspar do the talking. If I was going to get anywhere today, then I needed to keep my mouth shut. I hated it, but I didn't have a choice. Madame Pythia looked at all of us, I guess considering if she wanted to be of help now since my outburst.

"All right," she said. "She can be helped despite being rude. We'll have to do the awakening process tomorrow night. There will be a full moon. It's better for the process to be successful."

"Thank you so much, Madame Pythia," Gaspar said, clasping his hands together. "Thank you."

"You all will stay here tonight. Storey, please escort them to the extra sleeping quarters."

"Yes, Madame. Okay everyone, you can follow me." We followed Storey up the stairs. I could feel Madame Pythia's eyes on my back as we walked. Storey led us halfway to the other side of the castle. Everyone took a room but me.

"Hold on," Storey said as I was about to ask her where my room was. "I have a special one for you." She led me down a hallway to some decorated doors. She took out a big gold key and opened one of the doors. A big room with a white four-poster bed and huge glass windows was before my eyes. The walls were the same as the castle's. Over in the right-hand corner stood a white and gold bureau.

In the corner across the room was a vanity with a huge round mirror and in the other corner was a desk and bookshelf.

"Wow," I said. "This is beautiful."

"It was your mom's room," Storey said. "I thought that you might like to stay in it."

"No one is using it?"

"Nope. No one really wants to after...what happened." Of course. No one wanted to use the room of an enemy. Storey closed the door behind her. "For what it's worth, I didn't think they did anything wrong. They were just two people who wanted to be together. No one should have tried to change that."

"Then why are you working for the same people that didn't want them together?" My voice sounded a little harsh but it's how I felt.

Storey however didn't waver at my tone. "Because I want to make a difference. The Women of the Wise aren't just a group of women with nothing to do, they help people. That's what I want to do in life."

"I see."

"Hearing the stories about your mother inspired me to be a Wise. So I can help people."

"Well I've heard different stories about both of my parents, I don't know which ones to believe, so I'm here now. To find the truth."

"You'll find it here, I'm sure." Storey turned to leave. "No matter what you find, Addie, I hope it helps you in the long run."

"So do I."

Storey smiled then left the room.

For what it's worth, I hoped whatever I find would help me, for my past and future's sake.

CHAPTER TWENTY-TWO
THE AWAKENING

Sleep had finally overcome me and I was able to get some rest, only to be woken up by the sound of a loud ringing noise. "Breakfast is now being served. Please come to the dining hall," a voice over an intercom said.

"Ugh," I groaned. "Really? It's not even eight o'clock yet."

I got out of the super comfortable bed then changed into my clothes from yesterday. Storey was kind enough to let me borrow one of her nightgowns. After I changed, I folded it as neatly as I could and placed it on the bed. I'll give it back to her later. I opened the door and walked down the spacious white and gold hallway.

I tried to remember where Storey had led me. Once I retraced my steps I was able to find the glass staircase. I was just about to put my foot on the first step when I heard a familiar accent. I turned to see Rohl walking with the rest of the Regs and Gaspar. "Hey guys," I said a little too cheerily.

"Morning," Jules said. "How was your night? Did you sleep okay?"

"I did actually. I stayed in my mom's old room."

"I figured Storey would put you there," Gaspar said.

"So where to from here?"

"The dining hall. It's this way," Genevieve said. I followed them down a huge hallway into a room practically covered from top to floor in windows. Light poured in, giving the room a homey feel. Tables were placed just about everywhere, and many of them were full.

"Lets get a table," Gaspar said.

He led us to a far corner close to some windows. I sat with them, not taking my eyes off the outside world that surrounded the castle. Outside I saw some women standing in a circle with their arms up in the air looking towards the sun. They wore off-white gowns with a robe over it and seemed to be in some kind of trance.

"Um..." I said, pointing to the women. "What are they doing?"

"Morning rituals," Rohl said. "Every morning they all take turns in groups and go outside to bask in the sun, praising it for bringing light and warmth."

"It's also a meditation ritual," Dayton said. "Some believe that standing in the sun helps a person concentrate better. The warmth from it helps sooth your body so your mind can work, at least that's what they think."

"Plus it's good for your skin," Genevieve said. "A nice tan can help anybody any day." Not that she had a problem with that.

I watched them for a little while. They stopped their ritual then what looked to be the leader spoke to them. She looked to be in her early fifties with short brown and grayish hair. After she was done, the women bowed to her then started to walk off. Minutes later, they were in the dining hall. The woman who was leading the ritual came last. She looked around the room then spotted me.

Her eyes lit up and she almost squealed.

"It cannot be," I heard her say.

She ran over towards me, almost throwing her arms around me. "Are you...Adalyn? Clara's...daughter?" she stammered.

Shock filled me by the way this woman was acting. She was practically on her knees looking up at me. Her doe eyes resembled Storey's from yesterday, and I couldn't help but answer her. The only thing was I didn't know if I would regret it or not. "Yes. I am."

The woman shuddered then hugged me.

"I knew that had to be you," she said with tears in her eyes. "When I saw you I knew you had to be Clara's daughter. You look so much like her."

So I've heard, I thought.

"I'm sorry," the woman said after she let me go. She wiped her eyes then looked at me. "I shouldn't be acting like this. It's just I never thought I would ever see you again. I'm Sibyl. I was your mother's mentor years ago."

I stared at her. My brain was having trouble forming words. "What was she like?" I finally asked

"Oh she was wonderful. She hardly needed me for anything. She was a natural talent. I just wish you would have gotten to know her."

Tears filled my eyes.

"When I found out that Clara was pregnant..." she started. "I couldn't believe it. Then you were born, and things seemed right. I held you one time, but that was it. I never knew what happened to you after your parents were killed. I thought that you had died with them. I'm so glad you didn't." She started crying then hugged me.

I hugged her back, trying not to cry myself.

Heels clicked hard on the marble floor as someone approached us.

"All right, that's quite enough, Sibyl," Madame Pythia said, walking over to us. "You're causing a scene."

I looked up to see everyone in the dining hall staring at us. Some whispered, some ignored, but I could sense the tension in the air. Madame Pythia put a hand on Sibyl's shoulder. "I think you've made your point," she said in a cold voice. "Now go."

"Yes, Madame," Sibyl said, getting up. "It was so good to meet you, Addie. I hope we see each other again."

I nodded, lost for words.

After Sibyl left the room, I started to feel panicky. Everyone was still looking at me. I felt dread, I felt hate, I felt confusion, anger, sadness, pity, shame. Then I realized I wasn't feeling them myself. Everyone else in the room was. I was picking up on their emotions. I couldn't take their eyes off of me or make them put their feelings away. I had lost control of the situation and started to shake.

"Addie, are you okay?" Rohl asked.

"I...I..." I stammered. "I need to get out of here."

I ran out of the double doors and into the hallway. I didn't know where I was running to, but I ran somewhere in the castle far away from them. I stopped when I was in a small hallway and tried to catch my breath. That was horrible. I hoped I would never ever do that again. I heard someone call my name and looked up to see Rohl coming towards me.

"Are you all right?" he asked.

"No," I blurted out. "And I don't know if I ever will be after that now."

"What happened?"

I took in a few shaky breaths relaying what just happened. "I'm still not really sure, but I think I was picking up on their emotions. They felt them, then I started to as well."

"It's not uncommon. Women of the Wise can do that, but it takes years of training to master it. Your sensitivity is coming through. "

Oh great, another power, I thought. "Can we just do this awakening thing so we can get out of here and go home? These people obviously don't want me here."

"We are. Madame Pythia told Gaspar right after you left that they can do it tonight around midnight. The moon will be at its peak, and it's a full one."

"After that then can we leave?" I sounded so pathetic and weak.

"Yes. Just a few more hours to go. Just hang in there." He gave me a sympathetic look then lightly patted my shoulder.

I could hardly wait.

When night had fallen, Storey came and got me from my room along with the Regs and Gaspar. She started leading us down a dark hallway farther into the castle. "Where are we going?" I asked.

"To the spare room," Storey said. "It's where the Women of the Wise conduct all of their experiments and other things."

I nodded.

The hallway was starting to get darker. "Don't be scared," Rohl whispered to me.

I scoffed. "Me scared? Yeah right." I heard a noise then jumped, bumping into him.

He caught me and said, "Told you not to be scared." I gently pushed him back then kept walking but stayed close to him in case anything decided to jump out.

Storey finally led us through some doors into a big round room with no windows in it. The only light came from the dim candles. There stood Madame Pythia, Sibyl, and two other women I had never seen before. "Welcome," Madame Pythia said. "Everything has been set up. We are just waiting for the moon to rise higher."

"Very well," Gaspar said.

Madame Pythia turned to face my direction. "Miss François, these are Magda and Tonette. They will be performing the awakening process along with Sibyl and I."

I faced the two women. Both were dressed in white gowns with robes over them. Magda was tall, almost six feet at least, with thick dark curly hair and skin to match. She had to be in her forties. Tonette was a little lighter skinned with light brown hair braided from the sides of her face down her back. She looked to be in her late twenties. I nodded to both of them, not really sure of what else to do. "Thank you for helping me. I am grateful," I said, trying to be as formal as I could.

"It's our pleasure," Tonette spoke.

"We need to get Addie ready for the process," Magda said, showing no emotion.

"Okay, what do I need to do?"

"Let us do our job, and do not question anything," Madame Pythia said. I got the hint and walked over to them. Sibyl walked over to a case and pulled out a beautiful tiara that looked like it had been cut from silver and shaped into branches and leaves. In between them were white round stones. All I could do was stare at it.

"It's beautiful," I gasped.

"It's the rare Moonstone Diadem of the Women of the Wise," Sibyl said. "Our founder Ramona, who was the first Wise, made it herself. She made three items all with Moonstones. They are sacred to us."

"Moonstone is a rare stone that helps with remembrance and guidance," Madame Pythia said. She started to walk in the center of the room. "This here is called the Circle of Remembrance," she said, pointing to an imaginary circle above her head. As I focused my eyes I started to see a bit of the shining circle, but that was it.

"The Circle is made of different crystals and stones that help aid a person in remembering, guidance, and protection. The process of remembering something, especially if their memories have been tampered with, can be a very difficult and painful process." She paused then walked up to me. "I know your guardian Wanda gave you special pills to help you not see the supernatural."

"You do?"

"Who do you think was the one who suggested it in the first place?" She tilted her head ever so slightly like she was proud of what she had done. I felt my anger rising. She had no right to interfere with my life like that. It didn't do any good, though. I'd be watching out for her from now on.

"The Moonstone Diadem also helps with this process. Power is restored as the moon shines down upon it. Since it will be on your head the moonstone will help aid your self-conscious and unlock what is trapped inside it. The other stones in the circle help as well. They will guide you safely through the process as it proceeds."

What?

"You'll see what I mean in a minute," Madame Pythia said, annoyed with me.

Sibyl put the diadem on my head. Upon doing so I noticed a necklace strikingly similar to the one that I found in my house. I looked at Magda and Tonette and noticed they had the same necklace. I silently wondered why. After Sibyl put the necklace around me, she guided me towards the center of the room under the Circle of Remembrance.

"Wait just a few minutes while we prepare," Tonette said.

I nodded and stood still. Trying to calm myself down. Rohl then walked up to me. "Don't worry," he said. "It's not so bad."

"You've done this before?"

"Yes I have, a long time ago when I was fifteen."

"Did it work?"

"Oh yes it worked and it's painless, I promise, so you have nothing to worry about." I breathed a sigh of relief. "Just keep your head on straight. You are in fact going into your own mind, your own self-conscious, so it can be a very...unusual place."

"How so?"

"You'll see what I mean." With a smile he left the center of the room.

My nerves started back up again. "Don't worry, Addie," I heard Sibyl say from behind me. "It will all be over soon."

She then faced me. "When the moon powers the diadem, the diadem will power the stones in the circle. When that happens a veil will appear. You must look into the veil. It acts as a portal into your self-conscious."

"Can't I just walk through it?"

"No. The veil is a different kind of portal. It's for your mind and spirit, not for your body. Physically entering it could kill you. Also, exiting the veil before the process is over can lead to death as well."

I gulped, freaking out.

Sibyl hugged me. "Good luck. I know you will be fine though," she said then left me alone.

A few minutes later, I heard a creak almost like something being torn apart. I saw that the women were turning a crank that was opening a small section of the roof. About as big as the Circle. There in the night shown a perfectly round full moon. I looked at it then closed my eyes. I could feel the diadem vibrating on top of my head. I then saw a gold circle start to form above my head.

Individual lights from the other crystals started to appear all around me. After a few minutes, a white misty light rained down from crystals, forming a perfect circle around me. *This must be the veil,* I thought. My body started to quiver, but I wasn't in pain. I didn't feel anything. No emotion, not a single thing.

"Now Addie, just focus on the veil of light," I heard Sibyl say.

"Just relax. Let it take you to the edges of your mind."

I focused my attention on the bright veil that was starting to get very misty. I started to panic when I couldn't see Rohl and the others anymore. "Don't panic, Addie," I heard Sibyl call out. "Relax or it won't work. Calm your mind and body. The stones will do the rest."

I relaxed my body and calmed my mind. I still didn't see how a bunch of stones were going to help my self-conscious remember anything, but it's all I have to figure out my past.

I stared into the veil, waiting for something to happen. Suddenly I felt my body go limp, and I felt like I was floating.

Darkness surrounded me. I couldn't feel anything around me. I felt weightless. I felt no pain, hurt, sadness, or anything. It felt strange, like I was nothingness inside of nothingness, I just couldn't see it. Then I opened my eyes. Whiteness was now around me. No color at all, though it had a slight glitter to it. I looked around trying to find a way out. *Am I in my mind?* I wondered. *If so, then why is my body here?*

I looked at my hands and noticed they were a bit transparent.

I must be in my mind.

I didn't know where else I'd be.

"Okay, so what am I supposed to be looking for?" I asked out loud. The whiteness then disappeared, and I was standing in a room of a small house with white walls and a dark wooden floor. I saw a little girl about four years old sitting at a small round breakfast table by some bay windows drawing. A woman was sitting at the table next to her, speaking to her softly.

The woman had long blonde hair and was very beautiful. I recognized her...but no, it couldn't be. "Mom," I said. She watched the child (me) continue to draw whatever the picture was. A tall man soon walked in. He kissed the woman and petted the child's head. He had short dark hair, slightly tan skin, and was dressed in all black. "Dad," I said.

They must not be able to hear me.

My mom and dad talked to each other, but I couldn't hear them. Four-year-old me turned her head to them, and suddenly I could hear every word. "They're still looking for us, Clara," my dad said.

"I figured," my mom said. "They won't stop until they find us."

"They won't. We really need to start working on how to make the amulets work."

"I've tried every spell and ritual I know, John. I don't know what else to try. It's starting to get to me."

"We'll figure it out, we always do." My mom smiled at him then kissed him. "I just want to safeguard her future," my dad said, looking at four-year-old me.

My mom glanced at me then looked back up at him. "John, we've done everything we can to make sure that if something does happen to us that she will be taken care of."

"But I wonder is it enough? Look how many people have died because of us, have risked their lives for our cause. Sometimes I wonder if what we are doing is right."

"Don't talk like that, of course it is. We have invested years into this since we have found out about the amulets. I don't know about you, but I'm not stopping, not when we and the rest of the realm have risked so much."

"You're right, we can't back out now. But they'll be coming for us any day now. I know it."

"Then we'll have to move again. Singapore is nice this time of year I heard."

My dad smiled. "Let's get through England first, then we'll talk." My mom stood up, hugged, and kissed him. I smiled.

The door was busted open just then, and a huge man walked in. He hissed at my dad, who stood in front of my mom protectively. "Give them to me," the man hissed as saliva dripped from his red mouth, making his pale skin look paler.

"Who are you?" my dad yelled, pulling a huge blade from a holster on his leg.

"Give me what I came for."

"It's not yours to take."

"Yours either."

"Someone had to, might as well have been me, but I don't have them, not anymore. Now please leave my family in peace"

"I can't do that, and you know the reason why."

"Leave," my dad shouted.

"I won't until I get what I want. Give them to me, or I will kill your family."

My mom pulled me closer to her and wrapped me up in her arms. "Please," she said. "Just leave. We don't have what you are looking for, we haven't for a while."

"Liars!" The man slammed his fists down on an end table, breaking it into pieces.

"She speaks the truth," my dad said. "We don't have what Orfeous is after."

"Don't try to play games with me. You know what you have stolen. Now we want it back, it's ours."

"I'm telling you I don't have it. I never did."

"Please, can't you just leave us?" my mom cried, pulling me even closer to her. "We speak the truth. I'm sure he will understand."

"He understands nothing when people steal from him. Give it to me, give it to me now!" He punched the wall, cracking a huge hole in the plaster.

"Okay, okay, I'll get it for you." My dad opened a drawer and started to pull something out. Within a flash he threw something on the tall man that made him scream. A faint smoke came off of him, and burns started to form on his pale skin.

My dad looked at my mom.

"More will be coming," he said. "Take her upstairs." My mom looked at him. She nodded then made her way around the other man, holding me tightly in her arms.

Two more men came through the door just as she was going upstairs. I followed her. She put four-year-old me in the hallway closet. "Stay here," she said. "And keep quiet. I've got to go help Daddy." She kissed my forehead then went downstairs.

I tried to go down the stairs, but something was preventing me to do so.

So I stayed on the second floor. That didn't prevent me, though, from hearing what was going on downstairs. At that point I didn't know what to do. I walked over to the closet and tried to grab the doorknob, but my hand slipped right over it. *I wonder,* I thought. I walked right into the door and into the closet.

I saw my four-year-old self sitting in the far corner with her knees drawn to her little chest and her eyes wide with fear. I wanted to do something, but there was nothing I could do. She couldn't even see me. When the downstairs got quiet, I froze. My four-year-old self noticed the silence as well and got up. She headed for the door.

"Don't do it," I said.

She reached for the doorknob and opened it. She crept out of the closet, looking around. I followed her. She headed for the stairs. "Kid...me...don't do it," I whispered, knowing she couldn't hear me. She started down the stairs. Blood covered almost every inch of the front entrance leading to the kitchen. Four bodies were lying on the floor, one of them belonging to my dad.

Tears filled my eyes as I gazed upon him. Just like my uncle, his throat had been ripped open and his chest had been clawed up. Four-year-old me didn't shed a tear. I guess she was in shock or really didn't realize what had happened. I heard a noise and looked up, so did the four-year-old me. Something was coming from the kitchen. I waited then jumped when I saw it was my mom.

She too had claw marks on her body. Blood poured from her stomach and mouth. She collapsed to the floor, beckoning four-year-old me to her. "Addie," she said through coughs. "Sweet Addie. Be a good girl for Mommy okay."

"Why do I need to be good, Mommy?"

"Because sweetie...I'm not going to make it. I'm sorry. Mommy loves you so much." She glanced at her husband's body. "Your daddy does too." She kissed her on the forehead then wiped away the blood. The rest of her body fell to the floor right next to my dad. Her hand fell on his, and it looked like they were holding hands. I cried, but my four-year-old self just stared.

She knelt down by the bodies and placed her little hand on her (our) mother's body. I could hear her sniffling. I on the other hand was a complete wreck. I heard a noise and jumped. *Now what?* I thought. Another man with a misshapen face came towards four-year-old me. He hissed, and she screamed.

She started to run but tripped.

He came for her and then...something sharp was plunged into

his chest. He fell to the floor, and a man around six feet or taller was standing there. He wiped the blood off of his curved sword then looked at her. “It’s okay, Addie,” he said in an English accent. “I’m here to save you.” She cowered back, shaking from head to toe.

“It’s okay, I’m a friend of your parents. We’ve met before. You portably don’t remember.” She just stared at him. He knelt down. “It’s okay, I’m not going to hurt you.” He held out his hand, and she took it. He then picked her up and brought her outside where some Regs were standing. I followed them. “I got her,” the man said to the Regs. “She seems okay.”

“John and Clara?” a woman Reg asked.

The man holding me shook his head. “These were Orfeous’ strongest men yet. They didn’t stand a chance.” The woman hung her head, cursed under her breath, biting her lip.

“He’s getting the hang of it,” a man Reg said. “We need to stop him.”

“We will, but right now Addie is our main priority. I’ll take her to the Women of the Wise.” The man got on a huge black horse. “Don’t worry, Addie,” he said. “Everything will be all right.” He clicked to the horse and took off.

The sea of whiteness came back and I jumped.

“What?” I said. “Wait, that’s not what I came to see. I didn’t want to see my parents die. I want answers as to who they were, who I am. That’s not what I wanted. There has to be something more, please!” I screamed into the nothingness.

Flashes of light started to appear everywhere. I tried to hide, but there was nothing to hide behind. One flash almost hit me. I dodged it. It exploded, and in its place was an image. It looked like a movie screen. I looked at it more closely and saw two little kids, a boy and a girl running around a huge fountain.

The little girl was me, the little boy I didn't recognize. A man and a woman were walking down some steps leading towards the children. I looked more closely and realized it was Madame Pythia and the man who saved me. "You know it's for the best, Roland," Madame Pythia said. The boy and I still kept running around the fountain, paying no attention to the adults.

Wait...Roland?

"There has to be another way," Roland said. "Any other."

"It is what it is. We will take good care of her, I promise."

"You better, because if anything happens to her..."

"What could possibly happen to her?"

Roland stopped talking. "Come, son, we need to go." The little boy ran to him, and I caught a glimpse of his face. Rohl. It was Rohl at age eight.

"Come now, Addie," Madame Pythia said, extending her hand out to me. "We need to go."

My four-year-old self hesitantly went with her as Rohl and his dad watched.

That faded, then a new image appeared. I was a bit bigger, I had to be at least six years old. I was sitting in a small dark room. A table full of what looked like surgical equipment was placed ever so neatly on a steel tray. I was looking at it shaking. Madame Pythia walked in with two women behind her. "Please," I heard Sibyl say behind her. "You don't have to do this. There are other ways."

"I'm afraid there aren't," Madame Pythia said, turning to Sibyl.

She closed the door behind her.

That image faded and others came. My head was starting to

hurt as my past opened up in front of me. There were images of me screaming, crying, hurt, and I had no idea why. I put my hands over my head, feeling like that would stop the process.

"Keep calm." Rohl's voice popped into my head. "Keep your head." I did that, taking in a few breaths.

I need to get out of here, I thought. There had to be a way out of my self-conscious. There had to be.

I searched until I found a bright golden light. I started following it. Sibyl told me if I came out of the process early I would die. Well I'd seen all I wanted to see so in my mind. The process was over. Not knowing whether it's a good move or not, I walked towards the light. It started to get bigger and bigger and bigger.

I stood at its edges debating whether or not to go in it.

I turned around one last time to my past and knew I couldn't take much more of it. Taking a chance, I stepped through the light and hoped that it would lead me out of my mind.

CHAPTER TWENTY-THREE
ORFEOUS

I felt my spirit go back into my body.

I opened my eyes to see that the veil was gone and I was no longer inside my head. I collapsed to the floor feeling the cold stone underneath. "Addie," I hear many say.

I propped myself up, looking around. "I'm back..." I stuttered, which made it sound more like a question.

"You're back," Sibyl said, standing in front of me, "and okay."

I saw the diadem at her feet. It must have fallen off of my head when I fell. "Is it broken?" I asked.

Sibyl picked it up. "No, it's all right. Ramona made it so it would last a long time."

"Keep that thing away from me then." I started to try and get up, but I was too woozy.

"What did you see?" Gaspar asked me.

"Enough. Enough to know the truth." I looked at Rohl, who was standing a few feet from me. When I looked at him, my childhood came back to me.

I knew him when I was younger. It was his dad who saved me when my parents were killed. I lived in the realm for at least two years while people decided what to do with me. Rohl and his dad would come and visit me. For some reason Roland Sivan didn't trust Pythia, I couldn't imagine why. I grew up with him. He was like a brother to me. No wonder being around him made me feel safe, because he kept it that way.

More and more memories started to come back to me. Things that had been buried for years.

The memory of my parents being killed. I remembered being there, holding my mother's hand, hearing her words, and watching her die right in front of me. I then remembered before school ended when Maggie and I where on Canal Street I was trying to remember something. That's what I was trying to remember. The only question that remained was who was that boy staring at me?

Wanda and Jeff also didn't come for me until later, why I didn't know. I didn't meet Ava, Max, and Maggie until I was at least seven, but I had memoires, false memories of being friends with them since I was five. My whole childhood had been a lie. The question was how many more was I going to have face so I could get to the truth?

Apparently more. Something told me that Madame Pythia was up to something. The memory I saw of me sitting in a room on a chair with surgical equipment next to me on a table proved that. Sibyl was pleading with Madame Pythia not to do something, but Madame Pythia shut the door on her. Madame Pythia let an accomplice of hers fill a syringe with some kind of liquid. The woman started to walk towards me, and Madame Pythia smiled.

Wanda then burst in with Gaspar, startling me and the others.

I don't really know what happened after that, but Wanda and Gaspar saved me from whatever Madame Pythia wanted to do to me. *Was she going to experiment on me?* I wondered. It wouldn't surprise me. Gaspar wanted to study me. Why wouldn't the Women of the Wise want to as well? I couldn't believe that Rohl and I were basically like brother and sister at one point. Wanda and Jeff didn't start taking care of me until I was at least seven. And when I met my friends was all a lie.

How they altered the memories of my friends, I had no idea. Everything else was just...I didn't even know.

I wanted to ask Madame Pythia about what she was going to do to me that day, but I decided to hold my tongue. It wouldn't be a good idea for me to say anything while I was here. She would probably make a big deal about it, then the fault would come to Gaspar and the Regs, and I didn't want that. They seemed like the only ones I could trust here.

"Addie, what did you see?" Gen asked.

"Everything," I said. "I know everything." I looked at Madame Pythia to let her know I was aware of what she was trying to do. She picked up her head a bit, a faint smile appearing just out of sight, but I saw it.

I shook my head a few times. It was killing me. "I'm sorry," I said, pressing my fingers to my aching temples. "It's all just too much. I need to go somewhere."

"We have a lovely hot springs just out in the garden," Sibyl said. "It's a great place to relax."

"Careful of the enfields, though," Magda said. "They can be a bit harsh with newcomers."

"Enfield...what? Never mind, no, I just need to get out of here." I started to walk off.

"Wait Addie, don't get so upset to the point where you run off... again," Jules said.

"I'm not running off, but I just can't stay in this room anymore. I need to go."

"Addie wait, stay, let's talk about this," Gaspar pleaded.

"I can't. I just can't."

"I'm sure you could if you just sat down and tried..."

"I can't, don't you see!? I just can't. I can't talk about anything because there is nothing to talk about. Not when your whole life has been one complete lie." I didn't mean to scream, but I did anyway. They just weren't getting it. There's nothing to talk about. It's straight and simple. They were all looking at me as if I said something I shouldn't.

"Please," I said, almost whispering. "Just leave me alone."

I headed out of the door. "I told you," I heard Madame Pythia say, not even waiting for me to be out earshot. "Stubborn, hardheaded, and vain. Just like her father."

Tears sprung to my eyes, and I ran for my room.

The next night I stood on the balcony of the castle overlooking the garden. I thought about what I had just recently found out and shook with anger every time. Every time I would think of my friends, the memory of me five years old playing in the sandbox would play in my mind. Then there was the real memory of me actually meeting them at school in second grade.

I didn't know how two memories of meeting the same friends could both be in my mind and my mind think they were both right, but there it was. I still didn't understand how a person's memory could be tampered with by just a few pills. There's a lot I didn't understand. I didn't understand how in just one summer I went from being a normal teenager to everyone wanting me dead or worse.

I wanted my life back, I wanted Ava back, my aunt and uncle—no matter who they really were. I wanted this to be over. I didn't want the supernatural to be real. I wanted to just go back or go someplace where I wouldn't have to put up with anything. So I could pretend that none of this ever happened, even if it meant taking back the truth of what really happened to my parents.

Was there some place like that here?

I wasn't cut out for this stuff. I couldn't live in the supernatural world. I didn't belong here, and I never would.

I saw something fly up just out the corner of my eye. I jumped then looked around. I didn't see anything, but I knew something was here. I went downstairs, avoiding everyone, and went outside. I started towards the garden. A cool breeze blew, and I wrapped my arms around myself. I opened the wrought iron gate then went inside. The garden was similar to the one at the Safe Haven, just not as big.

I felt something fly just over me and looked up. I still couldn't see anything, even with the many lights in the garden.

Then right in the center of the garden, drinking out of a fountain, I saw them. About six strange-looking creatures with bodies and back legs like foxes and front legs and wings like eagles were crowded around the fountain. They didn't even look up when they saw me. I started to go towards them. A stick cracked under my feet, and they jumped.

Then they started to growl.

Oh no, I thought. *Now they are going to attack me.*

I felt hot breath on the swell of my back. I turned around to see one of the creatures behind me. I jumped, and the thing looked at me. It didn't attack or swipe at me with its paw. Nothing. "What are you?" I asked. Then I remembered one of the Women saying something about a thing called an enfield. "That must be what you are." The enfield nodded.

It was about the size of a Great Dane.

The enfield made a huff noise then nudged me. I knelt down in front of it and petted its head. I realized there was a collar hanging from its neck with a gold plate on it. The plate said Roxy. "So your name is Roxy," I said. Roxy nodded. The other enfields stopped their snarling finally. They seemed to be calm creatures. "You all must protect the garden then," I said. Roxy looked at me as if she knew what I was saying.

"I bet you feel safe here, secure, like nothing can hurt you, huh? I wish I felt like that. I wish I had a place to call home, but I don't. Not anymore."

Roxy still kept staring at me with big brown fox eyes.

"Wow, I am going crazy. I am talking to a fox, bird thing like it's normal. This place has really gone to my head." Roxy put her paw on my hand. I felt her warmth, her understanding, and her kindness just by her touching me. I looked at her. "Thank you," I said, looking at her in the eyes. She bowed her head then nudged me.

Bang.

Roxy and I both jumped. I looked to see where the sound was coming from, but I couldn't see anything. I heard it again. This time the ground felt like it shook. All of the enfields started to look around. I kept hearing it. I was driving myself crazy with looking around, so were the enfields. Suddenly Roxy started to growl, then they all were. I looked straight ahead where they were looking but couldn't see anything, still something was there.

I could feel an energy from a being. It felt sort of human, I just couldn't make out what it could be. It seems so familiar yet I couldn't quite place my finger on it. I could feel it creeping up on us. Then the enfields stopped growling. I couldn't feel what was in front of us anymore. I kept my guard up, looking all around. Roxy was too. She stayed very close to me.

Something jumped out from the bushes. I jumped back and

realized it was a guy. "I found yooou," he said. I yelled then took a few steps back. The enfields were suddenly on him. They clawed, bit, and finally killed him. I took off running with Roxy not far behind me. I made it to the entrance of the castle by the fountain.

I heard that banging again and looked up.

Someone was in the sky hitting something against the air. As he did so a blue wave appeared and pulsated over the castle and its grounds. Still the man kept hitting and hitting the air. It's almost like there was an invisible dome around it. Finally, the man broke in and headed for me. I dodged him as best as I could as Roxy ran off. "Oh thanks," I said to myself.

The man came back again, this time wielding a huge mace.

I took a few steps back and was about to fall into the fountain. I told the man to come after me, then as he started running at the last second, I moved. He plugged into the fountain. I laughed, but my victory was short lived.

Another guy caught me, this one was just a bit bigger than the other. "Laugh while you can, girlie," he said. "You won't be laughing long." He had me by the shirt, and I did the only thing I could do in that situation. Aim for below.

I kicked him as hard as I could, and he fell.

I took a rock and smacked it over his head. If I killed him I was glad. I sunk to the ground exhausted. I heard a noise and looked up. All of the Regs stood on the glass steps, each with an enfield by their side. Roxy just so happened to be by Rohl. She went and got them for me. More men came, and the Regs and the enfields fought.

I fought with them as best as I could.

There were just too many.

"Addie, get inside!" Jules screamed. "Now!" I started to run for the stairs.

“Not so fast,” someone said. I turned to see a man heading for me. I ran anyway. I felt something sharp enter my leg. I fell to the ground, pulling a dart out of my calf. A burning sensation soon hit me. It felt like I was being stung by a million bees.

I screamed, but no one came.

As I tried to move, the pain got worse. Then I came to the harsh conclusion that it was paralyzing me. I got about halfway up the steps when I finally just couldn’t take it anymore. I stopped fighting and gave in to the pain. “Finally we got her,” someone said. “He’s going to be so happy.” I could feel myself being lifted. Then I was swung over someone’s shoulder.

The man carried me away, and all I could see were the Regulators and the enfields losing their battle.

What must have been hours later, I woke up tied to a post in a huge room. The walls were made of wood, and so was the floor. Huge windows were covered up with wooden panels so I couldn’t see outside. The place looked old and a little run down. *What is this? Where am I?* I asked myself. I could vaguely smell water, fumes from boats, and river water.

Wait...river water? Boat fumes? I must have been back in New Orleans. It sure smelled like it. I had to be. Relief filled me followed by dread. I was still tied up for who knows what reason.

I heard a door open, and two guys came up some stairs. “Well look who’s finally awake,” one of them said. He was a tall guy with cropped reddish-brown hair.

The other one was a bit shorter and plump with curly brown hair and a beard. Both looked to be in their thirties. I stood up as straight as I could, trying to show no fear. It wasn't really working.

Both of them walked slowly towards me. "Boss wants us to keep you company before he gets here," the tall one said. "He better get here soon, or there won't be any more of you left for him."

I shook.

"Eric, no we can't," the round one said. "We have our orders. No one is to touch her unless he says so."

"Then he better get here soon, because I'm thirsty." He flashed huge white fangs at me.

I shuttered. *Vampire,* I thought.

Hours passed. It was now dusk, and still no sign of their boss. Finally, I heard a car pull up. "That's him," the round one said. "I'll go get him. You stay with the girl."

Eric looked at me. "With pleasure." He licked his lips. I tried not to throw up.

"Never mind. You go get him, and I'll stay with the girl."

"But..."

"Go Eric, now, or he'll get mad."

Eric sighed then walked down the stairs. The short one walked over to me. "You better be good for him," he said, "or it will cost you."

As I looked at him I suddenly realized who he was. "Mr. Dex? His expression changed. He looked down at the floor. "So you remember,"

"Yes I do. How can this be? You were dead."

"Did you ever see a body?"

"No just a body bag."

"There you have it then."

"But why? Why are you working for...whoever?"

"That's none of your business." I heard the door open. "He's coming."

I shifted where I stood, terrified at what was behind that door. It opened revealing four vampires. One was Eric, two I had never seen before, and the other was the half-Asian kid from the police station. He looked at me, and I tried to look away.

They all stood by the door in some kind of formation like they were waiting for someone. Then the tallest vampire I had ever seen appeared. He was dressed from head to toe in black and red. His cape touched the bottom of the floor in a huge wave. His long black hair was slicked back and tied together to keep it in place.

"Addie," he said in a low creepy voice. "We finally meet."

I started to shake from my head to my feet.

"I'm sure you know who I am, and if you don't, well, you will soon."

I swallowed. "You're...Orfeous."

"So they have told you." A smirk played across his pale face. "I'm sure you've heard all kinds of things about me, just like I've heard all kinds of things about you."

"Like what?"

"Just that you are under the protection of the lovely Regulators. The so-called protectors of the realm, is that not true?"

"I'll never tell."

"Ha, foolish girl, I already know. The thing is, I just don't know where they are hiding."

"And that's my secret to keep."

"I'm sure I can get it out of you in some way." I swallowed when one of the vampires flashed a knife. Orfeous took it from him then walked up to me. I tensed as his face came within inches from mine. "Don't worry," he whispered. "I'll be gentle." I felt the cool blade on the side of my neck close to my jugular vein.

I felt it cut deep, and I winced.

Orfeous pulled the blade back then sniffed the air. "Ah," he said.

"Fresh blood. It smells delicious."

"Then why don't you just kill me then and get it over with if you think it's that good?" I asked.

"Oh how I would so love to, dear, but I can't, not yet. I need you." He started to walk off. "I need you to tell me where the realm amulets are. The very ones your father stole right out from under everyone's noses."

"What makes you think I know where they are?"

"You are John and Clara's child, are you not?"

"Yes, but that doesn't mean that I know where the amulets are."

"It is to my understanding that you experienced the awakening process from the Women of the Wise, correct?"

"I did, what's that got to do with any of this?"

Orfeous started to laugh. "Oh Addie, you've been kept in the dark far too long. Maybe it's time I did a little awakening of my own."

He paced the room. "You see, the Regulators, the Women of the Wise, the High Council, basically all of the realm want the same thing. The amulets. All of us have our own way of getting them. But the Regs are trickier than me, or so they think. They were willing to let you pursue a dangerous process just to see if it would give them what they want, now isn't that something?"

"Wait, so you are saying that the Regs and Gaspar wanted me to do the process hoping that it would help lead them to the amulets without me knowing?"

"That's exactly what I am saying." Orfeous smiled.

"Why? Why would they do that? Why couldn't they just ask me?"

"Because they knew you could back out. They needed you to fully agree so that way it didn't seem like they were pushing you or causing any trouble."

"They were trying to be the nice guys," the half-Asian guy said, smirking.

"He's right," Orfeous said. "They *were* trying to be the nice guys."

Like you're not? I wanted to ask. I felt betrayed. They not only lied to me, they made me feel like they were actually caring, but all they wanted was for me to tell them where the amulets were, if I could even tell them that. They used me. Pain and hurt washed over me. I started to cry a bit.

"Oh now, don't cry." Orfeous wiped a tear from my eye. His cold finger made me shiver. "It's just what they do. You can't trust a Regulator, that's what I always say."

"Like I can trust you?"

"I'd be better than them. I can assure you that."

"What do you want from me? Besides the location of the amulets, which I have no idea about, as I have told you."

"That is all right because I can help you. We'll be a team, and no one will be able to stop us. My forces are getting stronger, we'll be unstoppable." Orfeous started ranting like a villain in a Spider-Man movie. I ignored him and noticed the wooden ceiling moving a bit. A feeling came over me that I would be okay soon, but I had to keep Orfeous talking.

"Mr. Dex said that you promised him something," I said. "What is it that you promised him?"

"Ha," the Asian guy said. "Like he'd tell you."

"That's enough, Kiaan," Orfeous said. He looked at me. "I have plans. Big plans for both the realm and the real world. I just need those amulets to put that plan into action."

I glanced back up at the ceiling, and the movement continued. "About these plans, do they involve pain?"

"Yes."

"Destruction?"

"Oh yes."

"Chaos?"

"All of that and more. No one, not the realm or the people here in the real world won't know what hit them until it's happened."

This guy is crazy, I thought. Every time he talked about his plans his eyes turned a crimson red. Like Captain Hook's from Peter Pan every time he killed someone. "I want in."

"You do? Oh, are you serious?"

"I am. You're right. I can't trust the Regs. They'd probably turn on me in a second if it means getting what they want."

"Did you hear that, boys? Addie wants to join us. Now this is getting good."

Come on, come on, make your move already, I thought. *I know you guys are here, that's all of you on the roof. I'm not stupid, just make a move.*

One of the vampires noticed the roof moving. "Wait," he said. They all looked up. "Something isn't right here." He started to walk around, looking up at the roof as he did so. After a few minutes of suspense, the vampire hissed. "They're here," he said. "And she brought them."

All of them looked at me.

"No wait, I didn't. I promise," I said, remembering Mr. Dex's words. "They must have been following me here. It's not my fault."

"And I bet telling you that she'd join us was just an act so they could attack," Eric said, walking over to me. As I pleaded with him he grabbed my arm. "She doesn't mean a damn word she says. Not a single word."

"She has lied to you, father," Kiaan said. "What shall we do with her?"

Father?

"Leave her," Orfeous boomed. "Only I decide what to do with her." He walked over, pushing Eric out of the way, and grabbed me. "You're going to regret lying to me." He pulled out a knife and pressed it to my throat. I heard screaming and saw one of the vampires get their head cut off. When he fell Jules was standing behind him with a bloody knife.

About time, I thought.

One by one Jax, Rohl, Genevieve, and Dayton all appeared wearing their unusual clothing. "What are you all standing around for," Orfeous said. "Get them!" the vampires attacked, and so did the Regs. Orfeous let me go then grabbed my chin. "This isn't over," he said. "I will be back for you, and I will take what's mine." He stabbed me in the shoulder, and I screamed.

He took off along with Kiaan. As he left, more vampires came.

Rohl cut me loose, and I fell into his arms.

"It's okay, Addie," he said, petting my head. "We are here now."

"Took you long enough," I tried to joke, but I ended up whimpering instead.

He laughed then let me go. "Stay in the back. When I give the word make a run for it."

I nodded, holding my shoulder. The wound wasn't deep, but it sure hurt. Rohl jumped into the melee, fighting with all of his might.

I did what he said and stayed towards the back.

The Regs took down each vampire they came in contact with. I couldn't help but watch. "Addie, go!" Rohl called. I saw an opening in the melee and ran for the door. I opened it then started down the stairs. Halfway down I felt someone grab my ankle, and I fell the rest of the way on the cold floor.

A vamp popped up from under the staircase and was

coming for me.

I found a piece of piping and started to fight him off with it. He dodged every move I made. I couldn't win. Finally, Jules came and cut his head off. All of the Regs came down from the stairs with blood all over them.

"Are you guys okay?" I asked.

"Yeah, we are fine," Jules said, trying to catch his breath.

"We need to go," Genevieve said. "More will be coming. I'm sure of it."

"Let's go," Jax said.

We started out of the warehouse.

Once we got outside the cool night air hit me. We were definitely in New Orleans and what looked to be the warehouse district close to the river. I could see the Mississippi River, which meant I wasn't that far from home.

"I don't see any way around," Genevieve said.

"Then let's go," Jax said. He started to walk off.

I heard something fall behind me. I turned around to see three vampires standing just at the entrance to the warehouse. We all turned to go another way, and three more showed up. Then more and more. Soon we were all surrounded. I stayed close to Rohl as he pulled out his swords. Once again a fight broke out, and I was left in the middle.

"Addie!" I heard Dayton call.

I looked towards her. She pulled off her necklace and threw it on the ground. The octahedron amulet opened up, and a giant portal was before me. I looked at Dayton. "You have to go. You have to get out of here," she yelled over the chaos.

"I can't. What about you guys?"

"We'll be all right. But you have to go. You have to get to safety.

Go through the portal. It will take you to the Safe Haven. Get Gaspar and get help, go."

"But..."

"Go now!" I could see the panic in her eyes. There was no way they would all be able to survive an attack this big. They barely survived the last one. I nodded, knowing there was nothing I could do but stay safe. I faced the portal, thinking about my friends and how they would act in a situation like this.

I jumped through the portal, flying once again.

CHAPTER TWENTY-FOUR
HIDDEN SECRETS

I landed in the streets somewhere far away from the Safe Haven. I picked myself up from the ground and looked around. I didn't recognize a single thing, and the dark was not helping. *Why didn't I go to the Safe Haven?* I wondered. *That portal was supposed to take me there.* I didn't worry about it any longer and started walking around.

The street, whichever one I was on, had a nice shine to it from a recent rain. Lights from nearby houses shone on the pavement, helping me not walk in the water. Misty rain started to fall on my face as the wind blew. I got halfway down the street and realized I was on Eighth Street in the Garden District. *Home,* I thought.

I resisted the urge to go back to my house, afraid of what could be there. I stopped at a light pole to catch my breath and reflect on what just happened. I just encountered Orfeous. The man responsible for my parents' deaths, the man who wants me dead more than anything, the man who has some kind of plan for the realm and my world.

Thinking about that made me wonder about the Regs and how they were in the Warehouse District right now fighting for their lives. Fighting to protect me. Guilt filled me because I couldn't do anything about it, followed by helplessness and fear. Tears came to my eyes as I let out my emotions. Hopefully I would be better if I did.

Later, I gathered myself together and tried to find my way to the Safe Haven.

It was so far away. How was I supposed to get there without running into anything that wanted to kill me? As of now I realized it was almost impossible.

I just had to stay low and not draw any attention to myself.

As a force of habit I went down Seventh Street to my house, but I didn't go in. Just passing by it made me feel sad, angry, and hurt. So much had happened, it felt like a lifetime now. I started to walk down the street towards Ava's house. I saw her family sitting in the living room. They were looking at a picture frame on the coffee table. I figured it was Ava's since they were all crying.

My heart went out to them. "I'm sorry," I whispered in the night. I wiped my eyes then started walking again.

I walked out of the Garden District then started on the path back to the Safe Haven. On St. Charles Avenue I heard a noise and ran for cover. I didn't see anything but decided to go to a place I knew was safe. School. I crossed over to St. Joseph Street then made my way onto the campus. Lights from the school sign were lit up along with the street lamps, so I could see if something was coming.

Right here. It all happened right here.

When Mr. Dex was killed it seemed like everything went to hell after that. One event triggered another, then another. Like a domino effect.

I went around the back towards the basketball court. There I could hide in the athletic center and wait until morning then make my way back to the castle. On my way there I saw two figures sitting on the wooden bleachers just off of the court. I froze. *No, no, please no,* I thought. *Please don't be vampires. I have no safe place left that's close.*

As I got closer to the figures I realized it was a boy and a girl around my age. As I got even closer I saw that it was Maggie and Max.

"Maggie, Max!" I called.

They both looked my way. "Addie!" they both said. They jumped off of the bleachers and ran towards me. Maggie wrapped me up in a big hug followed by Max.

"I can't believe you are still alive," Maggie said with tears in her eyes. Tears came to my eyes as well. "I thought you were dead. We saw the news that your aunt and uncle..."

"Yeah, well I got away. I still don't know how, but I did it."

"Where have you been this whole time?" Max asked, wiping tears away from his eyes.

I couldn't tell them I'd been at the Safe Haven. A magical fortress built to keep the evil things that lived in New Orleans out. They'd think I was crazy. "I've been staying somewhere," I said, not sounding truthful enough.

"Where?" Maggie asked. "Do you have other family here?"

"No...I..." I couldn't tell them, then again I didn't want to keep them in the dark. They were my friends, the only ones I could really trust. They needed to know everything no matter what. "Okay, I'll tell you. But both of you have got to promise me that you won't say anything to anyone or think that I am crazy, because I promise you it is the truth."

"We won't," Maggie said. "You are our friend. We'll believe you."

We'll see about that.

"Okay, well here it goes." I told them everything from my aunt and uncle to the Regulators, my parents, everything. I didn't leave out a single detail. Both of them just stared at me as I talked. Not saying a word or reacting in any way, and I was glad. I told them about my recent encounter with Orfeous and that now I was on the run from him.

"I left the Regs to deal with his forces, and I didn't look back," I wailed as tears came to my eyes. "I left them to fight them off while I ran. How selfish can I be?"

"You had to," Max said. "Or else this Orfeous guy could have gotten to you and killed you."

I looked at him. "You don't believe me, do you?"

"Yes we do, Addie," Maggie said. "We believe you."

"Why should you?! It sounds completely ridiculous! I mean, vampires and gargoyles and God knows what else is after me. There are people dressed in weird Victorian-style clothing walking around protecting other people and me. I live in a castle that should be in the next Stephen King novel. How does all of this sound sane to both of you?"

"Because it just does. We know you would have no reason to lie to us, Addie. Especially not something involving your life being in danger." Maggie put her hand on my arm. "Plus," she started. "There is something that we need to tell you as well."

I looked at her. "What is it?"

Maggie glanced at Max, who shrugged.

"We have to tell her, Mags," he said.

Tell me what?

Maggie looked back at me. I could see a few tears coming back into her eyes. "Addie, we know about the supernatural in New Orleans."

I froze. "What do you mean you know about the supernatural in New Orleans?"

"I mean...we know what's really in the shadows. We know that the stories we were told as kids are true."

"When you say 'we' you mean..." I pointed back and forth between her and Max.

"Yes," Max said. "I know too."

"H...h...how? Why? It's a secret, or so I thought..."

"It's not a secret when you are one," Maggie said.

I couldn't help but stare at her. "What did you just say?"

She looked down then looked back at me. "I said I'm one of them. I'm a part of the supernatural community here."

I let out a breath. I'd never believed in the supernatural until this summer. Then to find out my best friend was one and had been by my side forever. How could I not have noticed? I blamed Madame Pythia for suggesting I take those pills. Then I blamed Wanda for giving them to me. Maybe she had no choice.

Still it was Madame Pythia's idea in the first place. She caused me to not see what was right in front of me. Now I was the one paying for it.

"What are you?" I asked Maggie as anger rose inside me. "Werewolf? Witch? Vampire? Are you going to turn me over to Orfeous...?"

"No Addie, I'm not," she said gruffly. "There are some good supernaturals here, ones that won't hurt you, that just want to be left alone."

"How am I supposed to believe that? I've been lied to this entire summer, my whole life, in fact."

"Then I guess you're just going to have to trust me. Trust that our friendship is something special to me. Something that I would never betray, being a supernatural or not."

I didn't know what to say or think at that point. I tried so hard to convince myself that what she just said wasn't true, but I knew better.

"By the way," Maggie said, reaching into her one-strap purse and pulling something out. "I'm a fairy." She held the crystal blue wand in front of me. It sparkled in the moonlight.

I gasped when I saw it.

"I was told to be your friend when I was younger," Maggie said as she fiddled with the wand in her hand. "It wasn't until later though that I learned the real reason why I had to be. Why me being friends with you was so important to the realm and the Regulators."

"So being friends with me was just nothing?"

"No, I wanted to be your friend, Addie, my parents just made sure that we stayed friends. I didn't find out until a few years ago the real reason why."

"Let me guess, for my protection."

"Yes."

"Why do people feel the need to protect me and not say anything?"

"Because, Addie, you don't know the dangers out there. You've met Orfeous, right? I can see that you didn't get away unharmed either." She pointed to the wound on my neck. I put my hand over it. "That was him being nice. He can be a whole hell of a lot worse than that when he wants to be."

"I gathered that, thanks. But why not tell me? Why not...Ava?"

"She didn't know. I never got the chance to tell her."

A thought occurred to me then. "You could have saved her that night too."

"No I..."

"Don't even go there. You had your wand that night on Bourbon. I saw it in your jacket I just didn't know what it was at the time. You could have fended off those vampires that killed her."

"You don't understand, my magic is not strong enough. There are certain things that I can and cannot do..."

"I guess saving someone's life is something that you can't do."

"I couldn't, Addie! Not when those vamps were protected against spell work like mine. Whoever put protections on them knew what they were doing."

Our voices rose with every word we said.

Tears were now streaming down my face. "Still you could have done something. Anything to save her. I know she would have done the same thing for you."

Maggie bit her lip. "I tried," she wailed. "But like I told you before my magic wasn't strong enough to stop them. Whoever spelled them had a few years under their belt and knew a lot more than me."

I could see the anger on it, but I acted like I didn't notice. "And you," I said to Max. "How did you find out about all of this?"

Max looked like he was afraid to speak. "I caught Maggie doing a summoning spell outside of school one day," he said. "She saw me and knew she couldn't come up with an explanation, so she just told me."

"I tried to erase his memory, but it didn't work, not that I'm not happy it didn't. That can be kind of tricky."

"So both of you knew, and you didn't tell me?"

"Max knew about me and the other supernaturals, but he didn't know about the Regulators or anything else. I couldn't tell him all of that. If the High Council finds out that I told a human about the supernatural, I'll be in huge trouble."

"What can they do? Take your powers away?"

"Yes they can and more. You don't understand what you are dealing with here, Addie."

"No, I understand perfectly well that my whole life has been a lie, my best friends lied to me, one of my friends is dead, and there is a crazy lunatic vampire running around with freaking chimeras trying to kill me. So I understand perfectly well that my life is officially over before it's even begun."

I screamed at both of them. "You two have no idea what I've been through in these past two months. You just don't know, and I'm not going to sit here and explain it to you. I'm outta here." I started to walk off. I caught a whiff of something that made me start gagging. It smelled like fermenting fruit. I've smelled this before.

Out of the shadows I saw two pairs of red eyes fixated on the three of us. As they came closer two figures appeared.

One was Kiaan, the other belonged to a beautiful Asian girl around my age dressed in a short black and red Victorian-style skirt with a Victorian-style blouse to match, black tights, and black boots. She smiled as she approached us, her red lips sticking out from her pale skin. I looked back at Maggie and Max, who were just as scared as me.

What do they want?

"Well, well, well," Kiaan said. "Look what we have here, Sister, Addie and her little friends. I guess you don't care who gets hurt, do you now?"

I glared at him.

"Now Brother, don't make her mad," Kiaan's sister said. "I don't like my prey angry right before a feeding, it makes their blood bitter."

"She's not for feasting, Sissy, and you know that."

"But what about her friends? They look so delicious, and I just don't think I'll be able to resist." She sniffed the air then started to cough. "Oh what is that horrible stench?"

Kiaan sniffed the air then started coughing. "I say, it is pretty rancid, but the only thing that I can think of with that particular smell is..."

"A fairy," Maggie said, standing by me, holding her wand.

"Ugh, a fairy. I thought I smelled fairy dust," the girl said.

"Can't we just leave?" Kiaan asked his sister. "We can let the others handle it."

"Others?" I questioned.

Kiaan smiled wickedly, and the same human reptilian-looking creatures that had come after me before started to surround us. Maggie, Max, and I huddled together, trying to stay safe. "I'm afraid that won't work," Kiaan said. "You're a little outnumbered."

I saw a figure on top of the school heading our way.

"I wouldn't be so sure of that," I said.

A beam of light suddenly passed my vision. I turned to look and saw that Maggie was using her wand. She blasted flashes of light at Kiaan and his sister. Both jumped out of the way.

Max pulled a pocketknife out and was holding it out in front of him. "A pocket knife?" I said. "Really?"

"It's all I got, I'm not a Reg after all."

I saw Kiaan's sister come for him. "Max look out!" Max turned, and the girl was right in front of him.

She looked at him straight in the eyes, her black bangs almost touched his nose. She took in a breath. "Damn, you smell so good," she said, running her fingers over his face. "I bet you taste even better." She opened her mouth.

I ran and tackled her like a freaking football player.

We rolled on the ground until she pinned me down. "Wow, you've got some nerve attacking a vampire. You know my dad was just trying to help you, to save you from them."

"I'm sure he was. I'm sure we would have been big buddies after it was all over with."

"You've really pissed him off. He's not going to take that lightly."

"Then tell him to come for me. I'll be waiting." She pushed me down harder, slamming my shoulder into the pavement. I felt and heard something crack, and I screamed. She scratched me with her long fingernails, drawing blood from my arm.

I could feel her pushing the blood out, gathering it up on her fingers like lotion. She sniffed it, getting high from it. "Humans are so fragile," she then said. "So weak. That's why they are so fun to play with."

I struggled under her weight.

"My dad wants me to keep you alive, but I'm afraid I can't do that." She smiled, looking at me with her bright cat eyes. "I'll take the fall for it later."

Holy shit, she's going to kill me for real, I thought.

"I'll make it quick and painless."

Adrenaline built up inside of me at the thought of losing my life. I let it build up, and at the last minute I was able to gather enough strength to push her off. She didn't go far, but she was off of me.

"You bitch," she screamed. "You are going to regret that." She started for me. An arrow flew past me and hit her in the chest.

I turned to see Jax standing behind me with his crossbow aimed at the girl. "Run!" he said to me. I stepped out of the way but kept my eyes on the girl. She pulled the arrow out of her chest and snarled.

"Hello Jax, we meet again," she said.

Jax didn't say anything. He loaded his bow and took aim again. I looked around and watched the Regs battle the reptilian things. They all seemed fine from their last fight. Barely any scratches, but like Rohl said they are trained for this. I tried to stay out of the way. I went over by Dayton, who was holding some of the things off with what looked like a stun gun.

"Why aren't you at the Safe Haven?" she scolded.

"The portal didn't take me there," I said after she hit one of the reptiles.

"It had to take you there. It was designed to do that by me. You did something wrong."

"No I didn't. I told you. I jumped through it, and it brought me to the Garden District. Back home."

"Were you thinking about home when you went through it?"

"I was thinking of my friends, but..."

"That's what did it. Portals can be tricky, even ones that are set to go to a certain place." A reptile ran to us, and she threw a knife at it. The knife went in its head then it fell to the ground. "Next time, don't think of anything when you enter a portal," she said harshly. "Or you just might end up in trouble like now." She walked off.

I rolled my eyes. That was the last thing I needed today.

In the far corner of the court Genevieve was fighting some reptiles while Maggie helped. Jules flipped from the bleachers, sending arrows flying everywhere. Max was hiding, trying to stay out of the way. *Where's Rohl?* I thought. I soon saw him beating down some reptiles. I wanted to do something, anything to help them.

Three of them piled on top of Jax, overtaking him.

"No!" I screamed. I ran over and starting to pull one off of him. The thing turned around and looked at me. It hissed, flashing sharp reptilian teeth. I jumped back, almost falling. I saw something shiny on the ground and picked it up. It was a knife from one of the Regulators. I jumped at the thing, holding the knife out in front of me.

It jumped back, trying to make me fall down.

Finally, I ran towards it, plugging the knife straight into its chest. I could feel a burning sensation as the scales rubbed against my skin. The reptile screeched. I pulled the knife out and started stabbing it again. Finally, it fell to the ground, dead. More started to come to me. I fought them off with the help of Jax, though with a knife I couldn't do much, but like Max said it was something.

I pulled the knife out of one. After I did, I felt like I was being pushed to the ground. I fell on my side then rolled over to see a reptile on top of me. It pinned me down and hissed. The knife had fallen out of my hand, so I couldn't protect myself. "Get...off... of...me," I said to it. I tried to push it off, but this thing was much heavier than Kiaan's sister.

Blood then splattered all over my face.

I closed my eyes then opened them to see that Rohl had stabbed the reptile with his sword. I pushed the dead body off of me then Rohl helped me up. "Are you okay?" he asked. I nodded. Just a few feet from us, Genevieve battled Kiaan, and it looked like neither of them were winning. Gen slung a spear at him, he dodged and smiled. He would swipe at her, but she blocked his attack.

It was a real cat and mouse game.

They did that for a while until Gen was able to stab the spear into Kiaan's stomach. He stopped fighting and Gen smiled. "How does that feel?" she asked in her seductive voice. "A little silver and holy water will slow you down." Kiaan fell to the ground on his knees while the spear stayed in him.

His veins started to turn a bluish-gray color, and he looked like he was in pain.

Suddenly he looked up at Gen and smiled wickedly. His eyes turned a bright red then in a flash he took the spear out of his stomach, and in another he had Genevieve pinned up against the concession stand. My mouth flew open as I watched the scene in front of me.

"You think you're so slick, don't you?" Kiaan said to her in an inhuman voice. "With your tight clothes, sexy charm, and seductive words. Let's see how you'll do begging for your life." He opened his mouth, revealing his sharp fangs. Jules came up from behind him and struck him on the head. Caught off guard, Kiaan loosened his grip on Genevieve. She then grabbed something that was around his neck and kicked him to the ground with her thigh-high black boots.

She then threw something that reflected red in the light on the ground and stepped on it. A thick black liquid came from it. A look of horror flashed in Kiaan's eyes. "Not so powerful without it, aren't you?" Jules taunted.

Kiaan looked up at him. "You'll pay for this," he said darkly. Jax, Dayton, and Rohl fought off all they could. I would see flashes of light coming from random places knowing it was Maggie.

Soon the majority of the reptiles had been killed, the others were retreating.

Kiaan's sister looked at him. "Come on, Brother," she said, placing a hand on his shoulder. "Daddy is calling us back. He says to stop for now, but it is far from over." Kiaan looked at all of us as we made our way to where he was still sitting. He got up finally then turned to join his sister and their forces. They started to leave, but Kiaan's sister stopped then turned around so gracefully that it would have made any ballerina jealous.

"As I said before, this isn't over. We will come back one day. You won't know when or where, but we will be back with stronger forces. You can't protect Addie forever, none of you can."

I spoke up, tired of playing games. "Then come on!" I shouted. "You tell Orfeous that I'll be ready. I'll be waiting for him."

"With pleasure." Her eyes lit up red. With a smile and wave she turned back around and walked off into the night.

I then turned to the Regs, quivering. "Are you guys okay?" I asked.

They all nodded. "We're fine," Genevieve said. "Don't worry about us."

"We're worried about you," Jules said, rubbing his wrist.

I looked down at the ground. "I'll be fine too. I just want to get out of here."

"Do you want to go with them?" Jax asked, pointing behind me. "They were going to ask you, just so you know."

"How did you know they were going to ask me that?"

"I just had a feeling."

I turned to see Maggie helping Max to his feet. He had been hiding and out of harm's way, and I was happy for that. But at the same time I couldn't get past the fact that they lied to me. They kept something from me when they were supposed to be my best friends. Not to mention what they knew could have possibly saved Ava, yet they decided to keep it to themselves to protect me.

How could I ever forgive them or trust them again?

I still in a way didn't want to stay with the Regulators. Part of me did know that I'd be safe, but the other part didn't because I was still learning about them as well. Everything was still so new to me that it made me miss my old life. The longing came back, making me want to run over to Max and Maggie and be friends with them again. Then reality set in and convinced me that now was not the time.

Now I needed to be focused on saving myself.

And that meant living with the Regulators, permanently.

I turned to look back at the Regs. "You can go with them if you want," Jax said, looking sympathetic for once. "I know you want your old life back, Addie, but..."

"I do, but I know it's not possible. Not after all of this. I can't go back now. I need to be somewhere safe, and I can't guarantee that I'll be safe with them."

"So what are you saying?" Rohl asked.

I took in a breath. "I know I never wanted to stay with you all, but now I realized that if I'm going to stay alive I need to stay with you guys. It's the only way I can be safe."

"So you'll stay with us?" Genevieve said. "Forever?"

"Yes. I'll stay with you guys." They all smiled, even Dayton, but she could have just been faking it.

I walked over to Max and Maggie. I needed to tell them. "Hey, are you guys all right?"

Maggie smiled. "Yeah, we are fine," she said, brushing Max off. "A little shaken, but we'll live. How are you?"

"The same, just wanting to get out of here."

"Come back to my place. I'll tell you everything you need to know about..."

"I can't, Mags."

"Why not?"

"You know the reason why."

"Addie, you have to come back. I have to keep you safe. It's my job as your friend."

"The Regs can keep me safe. I'm still learning if I can trust you or not."

Tears came to her eyes. "Addie..."

"I'm sorry, Maggie, it has to be this way. I just don't know how to look at you anymore, either of you. Any of it, it's too much."

"I don't trust them."

"I'm learning to."

"Addie, you can't be serious."

"I am. I have nowhere to go, no other family left, and no one I can trust. Therefore I'm going to stay with the Regulators, end of story." I walked off.

I joined the others. "You ready?" Jax asked.

"Yeah, I am. I'm ready to go...home."

"You sure?" Rohl asked. I nodded. "Then let's go." Dayton cleaned up the mess with her gadget then we headed back towards the Safe Haven with Maggie and Max calling my name.

CHAPTER TWENTY-FIVE
DANGEROUS THOUGHTS

When we got back to the Safe Haven, Gaspar, Mildred, Emil, Rae, and Nils all welcomed us. I hugged all of them, then we all started to talk about what happened. "Later," Gaspar said after a few minutes. "Let's get all of you into the hospital ward. My reports can wait." We all hobbled our way to the hospital ward.

We all took a bed once we got there. Mildred and Gaspar examined each of us. I winced when he touched my left shoulder. "I'm sorry," he said.

"It's all right, I know you didn't mean it," I reassured him.

He grabbed some alcohol and cleaned the wound that Orfeous made. "I see a bit of swelling. I'll X-ray it and see what's going on."

He picked up a device that looked like a handgun but with a screen. "Don't worry, this won't hurt. It's just an X-ray gun. Hold still for just a few seconds." Gaspar pressed a button, and a faint blue light came out. He ran it over my shoulder as I sat still. He stopped then started running his fingers on the small screen.

"I'm afraid it's fractured, my dear. Nothing a few stones won't fix."

"Do you need an agate, Gaspar?" Mildred asked from Jules' bedside.

"Nope, it's just a minor fracture. A few quartz and calcites will do just fine." He walked over to a case and started to pull out a few stones. I watched the other Regs get treated by Mildred. They didn't look too bad after all. I didn't hear them complain about anything broken. Maybe they would be fine.

Gaspar walked back up to me holding a tray with four stones on it; a clear crystal one, a pastel green one, a crystal pink one, and a purple and white one. He sat the tray down on a table next to me then picked up the clear crystal. "This is called crystal quartz. It helps with healing and also aids other stones in healing as well. I'm going to use this stone last after the other ones have entered your body."

I nodded.

"This stone is called chevron amethyst. It will block the pain by soothing your nerves similar to Tylenol's healing properties." He placed the white and purple stone on my shoulder. I watched as it slowly melted into my skin. After a few minutes, the pain was starting to leave my shoulder.

"This next one is called cobaltoan. It will release your emotions then kunzite will help you deal with them. I like to use these two together because after an attack a person's body is feeling a lot of emotions. These two will help you find the balance between them." I nodded as he put a pink jagged cut crystal on my chest close to my heart. "This one might sting a little."

I barely noticed anything.

After Gaspar put the pastel green stone (kunzite) on my arm, he then put the crystal quartz on my shoulder. With all of the stones in me now, I was starting to feel a bit better.

"How do you feel, Addie?" Jules asked.

I turned to look at him, changing positions in my bed. "Better. A lot better. Those stones work better than medicine."

"Told ya," Rohl said.

"So what do we do now? Just sit and relax?"

"Yes," Genevieve said. "Just relax and let the stones do the rest. We should all be fine by tomorrow." I looked at the clock; it was almost tomorrow.

Hours passed, and I was still not asleep. All of the Regs were sleeping soundly in their beds. I wondered if there was a stone for sleeping. I got out of the bed and walked over to a huge window. The city was in darkness except for the lights and the moon.

Daylight would be arriving soon, but I was too awake to do anything about it.

I paced the hospital ward, looking at all of the Regs. They fought well today, but I often wondered how long they could keep this up. I'm sure they had other things to worry about than Orfeous. Like they told me they were just doing their job. Still, I wondered if it ever got tiresome for them. I thought about Orfeous and his plans for this world and the realm. What did he mean by that? If he meant anything by it.

While we sat here in respite he was out there plotting, waiting for the right moment to strike. I shuddered at the thought then pushed it away.

I stopped at Rohl's bed, which was the closest to me. The moon was shining on his face, making his skin look luminescent. I pushed some hair that had fallen onto his face out of the way, and a memory of us suddenly popped into my mind.

I was four, he was at least six, maybe seven. We were in a room of what looked like a cottage. He was sleeping on the couch. I was sneaking up on him like a lioness hunting her prey. I growled at him, and he jumped. I laughed, and he gently threw a fur pillow at me. The memory made me smile. We knew each other, we grew up together. His dad saved me. How could they make me forget all of that?

Why did they make me forget that? If what I saw in those memories were right, Madame Pythia looked like she wanted to experiment on me, so why in turn, make me forget half of my life?

I didn't realize that until just now. I knew I hadn't figured out the whole truth, and one day I would no matter what. I lay back down in the bed and let my mind wander, finally going to sleep.

I walked into Gaspar's study the next day to give him my account of what happened the day before. I was feeling much better. My shoulder wasn't hurting as much, but I was still ordered to take it easy since I was the only one who had gotten hurt the worst. The other Regs were taking it easy as well, even though they didn't suffer as much. I think they were mainly just tired. I knocked on the door of Gaspar's study. He was on the other side with Jules, talking.

"Hello, Addie," he said. "What can I help you with today?"

"Oh nothing, I just came to give you my report on what happened yesterday."

Gaspar's face fell. "I'm so sorry that you had to face off against Orfeous. I can't even imagine what that must have felt like."

"It's okay, I'm fine. I'm just glad I escaped with my life."

"You should have seen her, Gaspar," Jules said. "She had Orfeous believing that for one second she was into whatever he had to say. She kept him going long enough for us to come up with a plan."

"That was always your father's specialty. Manipulation. He could convince a rabbit it was a magician and have it pull itself out of a hat, he was so good."

I laughed.

"Anyway, I would like your report on what happened if it's not too much trouble."

"Sure I can, it's no problem. I want to help in any way to get this guy."

"All right, just let me get my notebook out." He hurried over to his desk.

"One thing I do want to know before we start is did you plan that whole thing, you know, with the awakening and stuff?"

Gaspar stopped in his tracks.

"Orfeous told me that it was all part of an act that you wanted me to go through with the awakening process hoping that it would lead you to the realm amulets."

Jules looked at Gaspar. "Tell her," he said. "She needs to know."

Gaspar looked at me with a pale face. "Yes, I wanted you to go through with the awakening process," he started, failing to meet my eyes. "But I didn't know how to approach you with the suggestion, so I just waited around until a good time came for me to ask you. Then you started remembering things. I knew it was already a matter of time before the effects of those pills wore off and you would be asking questions. So I just let whatever happen, happen. It wasn't planned, yet it was. Things just fell into place as they sometimes can."

"It's okay, I'm not mad. I just wanted to know the truth, since sometimes it's hard to get at in this world."

"Yes it is. You'll learn that as you go." Gaspar grabbed a quill and a notebook, and I began to give him my account on what happened. I wasn't as shook up about giving him my take on what happened. I just wanted them to catch Orfeous and put him back where he belonged, wherever that was. After I told Gaspar everything, I stood up then started to walk out of the room. I turned back around at the last minute.

"Gaspar, what did Orfeous mean when he said he has big plans for the realm and the real world?" I asked.

Gaspar looked down. "I'm afraid I don't know that. Orfeous

had that so-called 'plan' of his even before your parents took the amulets. No one still to this day knows what it is or what it involves or even who it involves. It's a mystery."

"And he wants the amulets for his plan."

"Correct. No one knows why. The only thing that the Regs, the High Council, and the people of the realm know is that those amulets have immense power. In the wrongs hands they could do a lot of damage. We mustn't let Orfeous for whatever reason, no matter the circumstances, get his hands on even one of them."

"Many believed it was also a myth to cause terror and chaos," Jules added. "They believed he was bluffing at the time."

"He didn't seem like he was bluffing last night," I said. "I want to help."

"What?"

"I want to help find Orfeous. I want to help find the amulets so the realm can stay safe, to finish what my parents started to..." I trailed off, tears filling my eyes. "To make sure that they didn't die for nothing."

Gaspar hung his head. "I understand completely, Addie, but our orders were given to protect you, not let you finish what your parents started."

"You don't understand..."

"I do, I completely do. But what if something happens to you? What would *we* do? People are counting on us to keep you safe while Orfeous is out there. I can't let you join them in the fight."

I lowered my head. I understood what he meant, but it didn't mean that I was okay with it. "Okay, I get it," I said, holding back my disappointment. "It's too dangerous and I'm not trained, is that it?"

"That's part of it. But Addie, this world...that we live in...this very, very different world is..." He struggled for the right words. "It's a very cruel, unnerving, unforgiving world. I know that you are now indeed a part of it, but there are still some things I don't think you are ready to be a part of yet. Like hunting Orfeous and finding the amulets. That is all just too much right now."

I nodded. "Isn't there anything I can do while I'm staying here? Anything at all?"

"Just relax and enjoy staying here. We are all here to help you in any way. That's all you can do."

"Can I make a few suggestions since I'm staying here? It's nothing major."

"Of course, what is it?"

"In the future if anything, anything at all involves me, please let me know what it's about. No matter what it is or how bad it is, I want to be informed, especially if my life is in danger."

"I don't know if we can do that, Addie..."

"Please, Gaspar. I'm tired of being left in the dark. I've awakened to things, some I'm still figuring out, but I need to know that you guys will let me know anything that could help me. I don't want to be an outcast."

Jules looked at Gaspar. "She has a point," he said. "We can't just keep the truth from her anymore to protect her. I think she has grown out of that now. She's not a little kid anymore."

"Yes, but I made a promise to her parents..."

"And I along with my team made a commitment to protect Addie. By keeping her in the dark she has no idea what's going on or who is going to come after her. By letting her know, she knows what's coming and can be prepared for it."

Gaspar looked at him then at me. He hung his head and sighed. "All right," he said finally. "I guess you do have a point, Jules. We were all trying so hard to protect her by keeping things from her, when all along maybe we should have all just told her the truth."

Gaspar straightened. "From now on we will tell you everything that is going on, no matter how bad it is. But if I decide that it's not safe for you to know, then it's not safe and you shouldn't know it. Is that all right?"

I sighed. I was still going to be left in the dark anyway and not get the whole truth once again. That's okay, I'd figure things out myself. "Okay. Yes that is fine. I'm just sick and tired of being in the dark."

"Then we will shed some light on it, but only what I say you should know. To make things clear I will not keep the whole truth from you. There are still some things that are meant to be left in the dark for a reason."

"I understand."

He turned to Jules. "You tell the other Regs that whatever they want to tell Addie they must first run it past me first, that goes for you as well."

"Yes, sir."

I noticed something shiny and red on Gaspar's desk. "What's this?" I asked, pointing. I looked at it closer and realized it was the thing that Genevieve had stepped on last night that she took from Kiaan.

"It's a claw flask from Kiaan," Gaspar said. "I was analyzing it."

"What for?"

Gaspar didn't say anything.

"Come on, you just agreed that you'd tell me anything I need to know if it's important. This doesn't seem too bad, right?"

He smiled. "Old habits die hard, I'm afraid." He gestured to the claw. "This is a claw flask passed down through Orfeous' family. There are in fact a few of these so-called precious relics in his family. This one, however, can carry liquid inside."

"What kind of liquid?"

"Demon blood," Jules said.

"Demon blood! Why would Kiaan be carrying demon blood around? How can a demon even have blood?"

"They only have blood when they fully possess a human. As in the human's spirit must be completely gone in order for the demon to take over. In turn, the human's blood becomes part of the demon's."

"Kiaan drinks the demon blood," Jules said.

"What?"

"Yes, Kiaan and his sister both drink demon blood," Gaspar said. "They are known as demon vampires. They drink the blood of a demon therefore inheriting the demon's powers. The blood strengthens their powers to the point where they are almost unstoppable."

"The problem is they gotta keep drinking the blood, or the powers will wear off," Jules said. "That's why their eyes glow bright red. It's because of the blood."

"Before summer started, someone kept following me that had bright red eyes. I think it was Kiaan."

"There are other vampires that drink demon blood too. It could have been him, though."

"How many vampires drink demon blood?"

"Too many to count. It's hard to get a hold of, but once a vampire does they run the demon dry until there is no more."

"On the bright side it makes our job easier because there is one less demon to kill or expel," Jules said smiling. I chucked. He could always find the right time to say something.

"Last night when Jax saw Kiaan's sister she acted like she knew him. Who is she?"

"Selena," Gaspar said. "Named after the Greek mythology goddess Selene, who is goddess of the moon and vampires. Of course Orfeous changed it so that way it wouldn't offend the real Selene."

"Her and Jax have a history," Jules said.

"What kind of history?"

"You'll have to ask him that. It's not my place to say."

"Watch out for Kiaan and Selena," Gaspar said. "They are two demon vampires you do not want to mess with, and I have a feeling that the attack yesterday is only the beginning."

"Selena did mention something about this only being the beginning."

"I'm afraid it is, my dear. Be ready and be prepared. This is not going to be easy."

I nodded, showing strength though deep down inside I was shaking.

CHAPTER TWENTY-SIX
THINGS TO COME

Days later, the Regs were back in action, searching the streets for Orfeous as I roamed about the Safe Haven trying to find something to do. I found another sitting area just above Nils' place that seemed to be forgotten about. I liked the room; the only thing I didn't like was the creepy feel it gave me because of the Gothic style. The room was almost in complete darkness except for the candles and two huge stained glass windows.

Vintage furniture sat perfectly placed around the fireplace, looking like a room straight out of magazine. I walked over to the dusty couch and sat on it.

I let out a sigh, thinking what the hell I was supposed to do next. Orfeous would be coming after me. I didn't know when, I didn't know where, but after hearing all the stories about him, I was even more grateful now that I escaped him since many others had not. I felt weakened and drained. What's next for me? What was I going do now? School would be starting back in less than three weeks.

How was I supposed to go back there and pretend that everything was normal?

Was it even possible to do that knowing what I knew now? I was going to be questioning everything from now on, trying to protect myself. It's the only way. If I saw Max and Maggie, I wouldn't speak to them. As far as I was concerned, they didn't mean a thing to me anymore. I could feel someone's presence as I sat there, lost in thought.

I turned around to see Rohl standing behind me.

"Ahhh," I screamed. "What did I tell you about doing that?"

"Sorry," he said laughing. "I don't mean to do it, it just happens."

"Why do you have to be so sneaky?"

"I'm a Reg, it's what I was trained to do. Maybe you shouldn't be so fearful." A memory flashed into my head. We were running around the couch in the same cottage living room, playing. I chased Rohl around and around until he wasn't in front of me anymore. Little did I know that he was on top of the couch hiding behind some pillows.

I walked all throughout the living room, trying to find him then suddenly he jumped in front of me, scaring me to death. I yelled at him, and he apologized for scaring me, telling me I shouldn't be so fearful and to be strong. The memory stopped, and I saw that Rohl was staring at me.

"Are you okay?" he asked.

"Yeah, I'm fine. I just remembered something from my past."

"Oh I see."

"How long does this last? I mean, I thought I had awakened already."

"You have. The awakening process opens your mind up if it has been blocked. The memories were always there. The process stops that. Now all of your memories will come back, but they don't all come at once."

"How many people get their minds blocked?"

"You'd be surprised. The awakening process was invented when Orfeous became public enemy number one of the realm. He would use very powerful magic or even trick a witch into blocking his follower's minds so if they were caught they wouldn't give him up."

"Smart move."

"Yes, but when you are dealing with the power of the Women of the Wise, who have been around for a few hundred years, you're fighting a losing battle."

"A few hundred years? Then how old is Orfeous?"

"Close to six hundred years give or take a few."

"Six hundred years? I know vampires can live a long time, but that's long."

"They can live a while, but that doesn't mean they can live forever. Just like humans, the older they get their bodies begin to age. With age comes slowness, aches, pains, and just feeling rundown."

I laughed. "Vampires can get old?"

"Yes they can. That's why Orfeous has so many people working for him. He's out of shape, but don't let that fool you. He has demon blood to back him up and torture techniques. One sip of that demon blood, though, and he's like a new vampire. That's why he wants his kids to drink it, so they can be even more powerful than they already are."

"That's insane."

"You're not dealing with anything sane anymore, Addie, remember that."

"I don't have to be reminded, I know."

Rohl tilted his head towards me. "Do you really want to stay here? And be honest."

I sighed. "Do you want the truth?"

"I'd rather you not lie to me, so yes I do."

"The truth is I'll stay anywhere that is safe from the outside world. Now that I know what's really out there, I don't have a choice. I have to stay here. I'm not saying I do, and I'm not saying I don't. I'm just saying that I'd rather be here safe and with you."

Rohl smiled.

"And the other Regs," I blabbed, my face flushing.

"I understand." He smiled, and I felt something inside me stir.

Tell him, tell him, a voice in my head said. *Tell him you knew him. Tell him everything you saw.* I looked at the floor, drew in a breath, then looked back up at him. "Rohl...I...we knew each other when we were younger. I saw the memory when I went inside my self-conscious."

Rohl didn't say anything.

"Your dad Roland Sivan rescued me after my parents had been killed. He took me in for a while until Madame Pythia stepped in. We grew up together, we were friends."

Rohl smiled then looked at me. "I know," he said in a small voice.

"You know!?"

"I do, all of it."

"How? Why?"

"Because I was there."

"Oh wait yeah." I blushed.

"My dad was there in England when your parents were killed. He found out from one of Orfeous' men that someone had been sent for your parents. He went to your house and saved you, and you did stay with us for a while until Madame Pythia came to get you."

I stared at him.

"Besides, I knew you would remember me soon," he said shrugging.

"How?"

He reached in his back pocket and pulled out a folded piece of paper. He unfolded and showed it to me. It was the sketch I did of him a few months ago.

"Where did you get that?!"

"After Orfeous had kidnapped you, we all came back here to find something of yours to track you with. When I was searching your room I found this."

"I drew that before I even met you. I still can't believe I drew it."

"Your memories of me were probably coming back at the time."

"That's not all I remember from my childhood spent with you."

"What else do you remember?"

A little boy popped into my head. It was the dream I had of him surrounded by black waves, but it wasn't just a dream. It was a memory. Since the awakening it had been weighing on my mind. "Do you remember when you saved me from those vampires in the French Quarter?"

"I do. I didn't think I was going to be able to beat them all myself, what about it?"

"You said something to me when I asked you were. You said 'your savior.'"

"Again what about it?"

I got up and walked across the room, trying not to meet his gaze. I could feel his eyes on my back. Slowly I turned to him. "A long time ago when your father was around, he wasn't just a Reg, he was the leader of his own regiment, am I right?"

"Yes, he was indeed. He was a very good commander too, until he disappeared."

"One time we followed him when a woman said her son had been taken by demons. Your father found him in the woods surrounded by them. Needless to say he killed the demons, saved the boy, and was a hero."

"And what does this have to do with what I said to you that night?"

I bit my lip. "I think you know, you're just not saying it." He didn't say anything. "People called your father their savior. Little kids would also say that because they couldn't say Sivan."

Rohl smiled. "I was hoping that if I said that then it would trigger your memories of me and everything else about this world."

"You told me you went through the awakening too, why did you do it?"

"The same reason you did. To get my memories back, to get my life back. After you were taken away, my father had my memory of you blocked so as I got older I wouldn't go looking for you. As I matured I started to remember you. Finally and against his will I went to the Women of the Wise and asked them to perform the process on me. They did, and I remembered you."

"I bet they didn't do it for free, now did they?"

"Nope. After the process was over and my memories were coming back, they told me I had to find you and bring you to them. I told Gaspar about it, who warned your guardians, and you were left in peace to grow up happy. That was a few years ago."

"I just don't understand why Madame Pythia wanted me so badly. Why did she not want me to remember anything of this world? And have me not grow up in it?"

"I don't know. She has her way about things."

"I don't trust her."

"You're not the only one."

"I still have so many questions. So many things I can't figure out, and I don't know how to."

"Don't. Leave that to us. Jules told us about the deal you made with Gaspar, that you are allowed to know things but only if he agrees."

"Do you agree with it?"

"I do. There are still things that you need to know and things you should never know. That's just how it's going to be."

"At least I won't be completely left in the dark, if Gaspar keeps his word, that is."

"He will, and you know that. You can trust us, Addie."

"I know I can, it's just...I'm stubborn, okay."

"That you are." Rohl started to walk off. "Just let us worry about everything else, Addie," he said, turning back to me. "You just worry about being a normal teenager. Leave the rest to us."

"I'll try," I said, kind of meaning it. "I will."

Rohl smiled then left.

I reflected on what I had been through this summer. Like Gaspar said this wasn't over. More things would be after me soon, but I had the Regs protecting me. It's a dangerous world out there, and the terror had only just begun. Things would get worse, and I needed to prepare myself for that. No matter what anyone said, I would fight my way through this. I didn't have a choice anymore.

I walked out of the Gothic sitting area and then headed to my room. The box containing the amulet was sitting on my dresser, staring at me. All of the women at Las Kala were wearing one exactly like it, so this necklace had to have been my mother's at one point. I touched the box, wondering what this necklace was used for. It had to be for something besides just a pretty accessory.

I decided to take it to Gaspar. He would know, and hopefully he would tell me the truth, which I was now entitled to. I took the box then went to his study. He was there all right, trying to put Kiaan's claw flask back together.

"Hi, Gaspar," I said, standing at the door. "May I ask you something?"

"Hello, Addie." He looked up from his desk. "Yes you may. What is your question?"

I hesitantly opened the box and showed him the necklace. "I found this the last time I went into my house when the gargoyle attacked me. It was under Jeff and Wanda's bed. I think the gargoyle wanted it."

Gaspar dropped the pliers he was holding. "Oh my," he said, his eyes widening. "Oh my indeed."

"I saw that Sibyl, Madame Pythia, and the other Wise members were wearing necklaces just like this one, so I was wondering if it represents something."

"Not in so many words. The necklace is made of an extremely rare almost impossible to find stone called Puratite. It is encased in gold to protect its power."

"All Women of the Wise have one?"

"Yes, though Madame Pythia's is just a bit bigger than the others since she's the Head."

"What do they do?"

"They help the Women's powers and also keep them in good health. There are a few things they can do, though the full power of these amulets will never be known."

"How come?"

"Because no one has the power to fully activate them. The only one that did so was Ramona, and she took that secret to her grave."

"Oh."

"I'm surprised you found that. I don't remember Madame Pythia letting Wanda take that."

"Maybe she didn't. Is that possible?"

"It is. Wanda never wanted to follow the rules. She was just like your father, but she always made sure that she did what was best for people. Both her and John had that in common."

Gaspar looked at the box in my hand. "Maybe I should take

that back to the Women of the Wise. I'm sure they would love to have it back."

My face fell. "I'm sorry, Gaspar, but do you mind if I keep it? It's the only thing I have of my mother after all."

Gaspar smiled. "Of course. I won't tell if you won't."

"Oh believe me, I won't." I smiled then left his study.

In my room I placed the box on my dresser. I needed to think of a good hiding place. It's not that I didn't trust Gaspar, but I thought at times he'd rather do the right thing and spare people's feelings. I looked around the room. "I wonder..." I said out loud. "If I can imagine this room into anything I want, I wonder if I can imagine something I want."

I closed my eyes and thought of a small, concealable safe right in one of my walls.

I opened my eyes and saw a picture hanging on the far side of my room that I had never seen before. I walked over to the picture and tried to take it off the wall. It wouldn't move. I saw hinges on the side and then opened it like a door. There in the wall was safe. "Sweet," I said. I came up with a code then put the box inside it. The amulet would be safe as long as no one moved the picture. Like they could.

Night fell, and I went to sleep and I dreamed. I dreamed about fighting Regs, lost friends, pain, suffering, Orfeous, the amulets. I didn't know why I was dreaming it. Maybe it was just a nightmare, or a premonition of things to come.

EPILOGUE

In a dark chamber room, a man sat at a station experimenting with different devices and objects. Beakers of all sizes sat on Bunsen burners, some were smoking, others were turning into various colors. The man sat at his station taking apart a dead animal. He opened the poor thing up, taking out the blood through a series of tubs. He picked the animal clean, saving the meat for himself. Then he pulled out a few bones, pushing them to the side.

Blood ran down the side of his hand. He began to lick it, a smile appearing across his face. The chamber door opened, and two men appeared. "You wanted to see us, sir?" one asked.

The man turned around. "As a matter of fact, I did." He smiled. "It's happened."

"What's happened?" the other asked.

The man stood up, smiling like a maniac. "She has awakened."

"Who has awakened?"

"You know damn well who. The girl, the one we need. Addie François."

"Oh yeah, now I remember. You said you need her for something."

"Yes, as does everyone else, so we need to be careful who we run into and keep our contacts with. No one must know of this. Do not tell a single soul."

"You can count on us, boss, we won't let you down."

"You better not. You know what will happen to you if you don't." The man picked up a knife and started running his fingers across it.

The two men cowered in fear. "Don't worry, boss, we won't let you down."

"See to it that you don't. I have a list of things I need; go and get them for me and be quick about it." He handed them a list written in perfect calligraphy.

"Will do, boss, let's go." The two scampered up the stairs then went out of the door. The man sat down and touched a case on his station, smiling to himself. He glanced outside the chamber's window at the moon high in the sky. He smiled once again.

"It won't be long, Addie François. Once you get a good taste of this world, you will be drawn right into it. Then you'll be begging me to help get you out. It's just only a matter of time."

ABOUT THE AUTHOR

Annie Schnellenberger started writing poems at a young age, which eventually progressed into a love for writing all genres. She draws inspiration from everyday life, movies, TV shows, anime, music, and manga, which she is a huge fan of. When she is not working, Annie spends her time reading or working on different writing projects. She currently resides in Amite, Louisiana, with her cat, dog, and two horses.

The first book in the Chronicles of Arcania series, *The Awakening*, is Annie's literary debut.